I0561227

JUST CAUSE UNIVERSE
COMPENDIUM
THE COLLECTED STORIES 2001-2020

IAN THOMAS HEALY

Local Hero Press Edition

Just Cause Universe Compendium
Published by Local Hero Press, LLC
http://localheropress.com

1st Printing
Local Hero Press: trade paperback, November 15, 2020
Printed in the United States of America

All rights reserved worldwide.
Copyright ©2020 Ian Thomas Healy

ISBN-13: 9781971445199

Cover art by Nathaniel Dickson
Book design by Local Hero Press, LLC

This is a work of fiction. Names, characters, places, and incidents are either the product of the author's imagination or used fictitiously. Any resemblance to actual events, locales, or persons, living or dead, is entirely coincidental.

This book's contents and its characters are the sole property of its author. No part of this publication may be reproduced, stored in or introduced into a retrieval system, or transmitted in any form or by any means (electronic, mechanical, photocopying, recording, or otherwise) without written, express permission from the authors. To do so without permission is punishable by law. Please purchase only authorized electronic editions, and do not participate in or encourage electronic piracy of copyrighted materials. Your support of the authors' rights is appreciated.

All stories have appeared in previous publications:

"The Freakshow" from *Just Cause: Revised and Expanded Edition* Copyright 2012 Ian Thomas Healy
"The Scent of Rose Petals" from *A Thousand Faces, the Quarterly Journal of Superhuman Fiction: Issue #10* Copyright 2009 Ian Thomas Healy
"Chinatown Ghost" from *The Good Fight 5: The Golden Age* Copyright 2019 Ian Thomas Healy
"Arrowheads" from *Just Cause: Revised and Expanded Edition* Copyright 2012 Ian Thomas Healy
"Blacklisted" from *JCU Omnibus Vol. 2* Copyright 2015 Ian Thomas Healy
"Winternight" from *JCU Omnibus Vol. 2* Copyright 2015 Ian Thomas Healy

"Summer of Love" from *JCU Omnibus Vol. 2* Copyright 2015 Ian Thomas Healy

"Pride" from *JCU Omnibus Vol. 1* Copyright 2014 Ian Thomas Healy

"The Steel Soldier's Gambit" Copyright 2011 Ian Thomas Healy

"Components" from *The Good Fight 2: Villains* Copyright 2015 Ian Thomas Healy

"Dust to Dust" from *Just Cause: Revised and Expanded Edition* Copyright 2012 Ian Thomas Healy

"Falling" from *JCU Omnibus Vol. 1* Copyright 2014 Ian Thomas Healy

"Gideon's Horn" from *JCU Omnibus Vol. 1* Copyright 2014 Ian Thomas Healy

"Bulletproof" Copyright 2011 Ian Thomas Healy

"Young Guns" Copyright 2011 Ian Thomas Healy

"Tuesday Night at Powerman's" Copyright 2011 Ian Thomas Healy

"Teeth of the Night" from *The Bulletproof Badge* Copyright 2012 Ian Thomas Healy

"Domestic Disturbance" from *The Bulletproof Badge* Copyright 2012 Ian Thomas Healy

"Silent Alarm" from *The Bulletproof Badge* Copyright 2012 Ian Thomas Healy

"Archenemy" from *The Good Fight* Copyright 2014 Ian Thomas Healy

"Graceful Blur" Copyright 2011 Ian Thomas Healy

"Sun-Kissed" from *The Good Fight 3: Sidekicks* Copyright 2017 Ian Thomas Healy

Books by Local Hero Press

The *Just Cause Universe*

Just Cause

The Archmage

Day of the Destroyer

Deep Six

Jackrabbit

Champion

Castles

The Lion and the Five Deadly Serpents

Tusks

The Neighborhood Watch

Jackrabbit: Big In Japan

Arena

Hero Academy

The Path

Cinco de Mayo

Search and Rescue

Rooftops

Plague

Soldiers of Fortune

Just Cause Universe Compendium

Destroyer of Earth

Flint and Steel

The Club

Jackrabbit: Rinse and Repeat

Posse

Extinction Event

Rain Must Fall

Pariah of Verigo

Pariah's Moon

Pariah's War

Three Flavors of Tacos

The Guitarist

Making the Cut

The Scene Stealers

Collections

Airship Lies

High Contrast

The Good Fight

The Good Fight 3: Sidekicks

The Good Fight 4: Homefront

The Good Fight 5: The Golden Age

Muddy Creek Tales

Caped

Other Novels

Assassin

Blood on the Ice

Funeral Games

Hope and Undead Elvis

Horde

The Murder Squad (2026)

Roast Wyvern (and Other Recipes)

Starf*cker

Strings

The Oilman's Daughter

Troubleshooters

Nonfiction

Action! Writing Better Action Using Cinematic Techniques

Author Notes

Twenty years is a long damn time.

In twenty years, you can watch your children grow from babies to adults. You can watch economies rise and fall—multiple times! Some of us put on weight over twenty years. And lose it. And gain it back again. Our hair that used to be dark goes gray, or maybe falls out (I've been fortunate not to experience that last). The world constantly transforms around us, and what is happening now would be unrecognizable twenty years ago, and vice-versa.

The Just Cause Universe has existed in my mind since the '90s, when it was a role-playing-game setting I created for superhero gaming with a group that is still going on today, albeit with a new generation of players joining the old guard. That setting was where some of the most important characters in the JCU first appeared. I didn't start writing actual stories about them until much later, in 2001 when I wrote the story *Bulletproof.* Over the next twenty years, I wrote a bunch more short stories and a whole pile of novels set in the same universe of superheroes. I don't know if I'll write many more short stories—I much prefer the longer form of novels. The stories that are completed do a pretty good job of filling in the cracks and coloring around the edges of the novels, and I've included some of them as bonus features in books. Others have appeared in collections and anthologies, but this is the first time I've collected all of them in one place.

If you're already obsessed with the JCU, it's likely you've read most if not all of these books. If, however, you're new to the series, or still discovering it, there will be some pleasant surprises here for you.

* * *

As always, I have a list of people without whom this book would never have come to pass. Over the years, I've had dozens of beta readers and I'm afraid of accidentally leaving someone by listing who I can remember. Let it suffice to say that if you helped me with any of the stories in this book, I am grateful for your help. Without you, these stories wouldn't be as good as they are.

I do want to give a shout-out to my cover artist Nathaniel, who produced a shining interpretation of Mustang Sally on short notice.

I'm especially grateful to my family for giving me time and space to write when we're all crammed into the same tiny house to avoid catching the plague. And last, thank you to all my fans around the world who inspire me to tell new stories. Stay safe!

-Ian Thomas Healy
October, 2020

THE FREAKSHOW

I remember clearly looking down the great hall and thinking to myself what a waste of Aryan blood; one hundred men—one hundred of the best soldiers in the Reich who had volunteered to die for the Fatherland. Each was strapped to a gurney, elevated forty-five degrees. At the end of the hall was Messer's Device. It crouched like some great, hulking beast, barely containing the energies within its carefully-crafted skin.

Messer gave his usual speech—that the men had been selected for their bravery and their loyalty to Germany for a special treatment that would make them into the supermen they were destined to become. His speech was always the same. I had heard it so many times I could have repeated it word for word; so many times he had sent a group of good soldiers like these to their death.

God in Heaven, how could we have known this time he would have been right?

-Dr. Felix Dietrich, 1942

February, 1942
Aufstein, Germany

The way the castle lights dimmed and flickered worried Jim Scott. The American soldier watched the two-hundred-year-old castle through his field glasses, as he sprawled across a high rock ledge that overlooked the castle. Scott could have been a poster child for the Aryan ideal, had he not been a loyal son of America—

1

six foot four, built like a farmhand, with a strong jaw and a shock of dirty blond hair that had grown out considerably since the arrival of his team in Germany. Officially, their team's code name was *Project Circus*, but everybody from General Eisenhower on down just called them *The Freakshow*.

"Goddamn Krauts don't know a goddamn thing about wiring," grumbled Johnny Stills next to him. He fumbled for his canteen, which Scott knew was full of cheap Swiss vodka. Stills was small, almost rat-like in his appearance and intensity. He was dark-eyed and furtive in his movements.

A few battery-powered lights flickered to life below. "Now's our chance," said Scott. "While they're restoring power."

Stills nodded, wiping his mouth with the back of a grimy hand. "Move out," he whisper-shouted behind him. Two more dogfaces emerged from the low evergreens. William Hester and Ray Downs. Hester was twenty-four, making him the oldest of the group, and wore glasses, earning him the nickname *Professor*. Downs was the youngest, barely eighteen. His overlarge ears made him seem even younger. If it hadn't been for his parahuman ability, Scott would have refused to take him on a mission. It was like having your younger brother along on a date. The four men had infiltrated Germany nearly three weeks earlier with help from the French Resistance and had been making their careful way to Aufstein, where Allied Command said the Nazis were working on some secret weapon.

"Did you guys hear that?" Downs tapped his ear as he attached a rope around a sturdy rock outcropping.

"What do *you* think, moron?" Stills sneered at him, making no effort to connect his own rope.

"Stow that noise, Corporal," said Scott. "We're going to have a hard enough time of this without you announcing our presence to the entire Third Reich. What'd you hear, Sounder?"

Downs shrugged. "Dunno, Sergeant. Sounded like they turned on a big dynamo."

"Couldn't have been," said Hester. "A dynamo makes power, not drains it. Why'd they lose their lights?"

Stills muttered something under his breath that sounded something like "whyncha go ask 'em, shithead?"

Scott ignored his headstrong second-in-command. In spite of Stills' abrasive personality, he was a brilliant tactician and made excellent use of his particular skills. "You guys ready for descent?"

Hester and Downs answered in the affirmative. Downs even sounded eager. They hadn't seen any real action since France, and that seemed like an eternity ago, and more than once, Downs had complained about all the damn sneaking around. "It ain't fair. I want to kill me some krauts," he'd say, fingering his knife.

Scott turned to Stills. "Corporal, secure our landing site. And do it *quietly*."

Stills drew his bowie knife and saluted. "Yes sir," he said, and vanished off the rock with a soft puff of inrushing air.

Stills was what Allied Command called an *exceptional talent*. They all were. Scott had been the first, found by a displaced French researcher named Georges Devereaux. Scott was strong enough to toss a jeep across a parking lot and tough enough to take a fifty-caliber bullet in the chest without even blinking, much less bleeding. He could also fly for almost a mile at a time, something that was more than a leap but less than actual flight. Devereaux had found Scott, thanks to his odd ability to see parahuman abilities in others, and brought him to see some men in the Army. They liked what they saw and immediately enrolled him in Basic. Then they went back to Devereaux and asked if he could find a few more like Scott, whom they code-named *Strongman.*

John Henry Stills was next. He was a teleport, able to move anywhere he could see without traversing the space between points. He simply vanished from one spot and instantly reappeared in his destination. He was a master knife-wielder, having been working in his father's slaughterhouse. Scott had seen him slice a kraut to bloody ribbons in seconds, flashing all around him faster than could be seen. The army code-named him *Flicker*, which he hated. But they let him get away with his antics because he was a parahuman, and there were only four in all the American forces, plus the wild card of Georges Devereaux.

William Hester could imbue objects he could hold in his hand with kinetic energy and then release them with enough force to rupture tank armor. In spite of his tremendous combat ability, Hester was mostly an intellectual. The soft-spoken, bespectacled man was more likely to be found with his nose buried in a book during down time, instead of chasing women or gambling like normal soldiers. On paper, he was called *Meteor*, but to everyone else he was just *Professor.*

Raymond Downs had lied about his age to get into the army. He wanted desperately to be a soldier and to fight the Axis, joining when he was only fifteen. Four months later his mother had come to pick him up from Fort Bening just before he was scheduled to ship out. Downs had nearly died from the sheer embarrassment of it. Two months later he was back when his family doctor couldn't explain why Downs could hear things that were too quiet, too far, and too high-pitched for anyone else. The Army doctors determined his abilities far surpassed normal, and he received a special dispensation to join and a codename, *Sounder.*

When the Army brass had showed their abilities to Albert Einstein, he said, "that's exceptional." The Army being what it was, the four men were referred to as "exceptional talents" from then on. They had been trained for every possible situation the G-men could devise. Eventually Roosevelt had ordered them deployed and they parachuted into France with a few thousand other dogfaces.

They'd had some success aiding the French Resistance by using their special abilities to complete missions that would have otherwise required ten times as many men. Their standard mode of operation was for Sounder to provide the intelligence via sound cues, then Flicker would secure the site, and finally Strongman and Meteor would go to work. Emplaced machinegun nests were no challenge to the four of them, and they could take out a convoy in a matter of seconds. This particular mission was going to require some different tactics. Their objective was gathering information about the project the Nazis had set up in Aufstein Castle.

Scott hadn't been told, officially, what Army Intelligence thought was going on in the castle. Unofficially, he'd been told that the krauts were trying to make their own *exceptional talents*. Allied Command was very interested in their experiments. Project Circus was to gather as much information about the process as they could, and then permanently disrupt operations. Scott was all in favor of the mission. The idea of an army filled with soldiers like himself marching across the face of Europe gave him nightmares.

He checked his watch. Two minutes had passed since Stills had vanished and he hadn't reappeared. If the area hadn't been secured, he would have popped back to report. He nodded at Hester and Downs, who began quietly rappelling down the rock face. Scott watched their progress, checking the castle for any sign they'd been seen. The castle was still mostly dark. Whatever the krauts had set off was drawing plenty of power. Hester and Downs got down to the ground and took up covering positions with their rifles. There was no sign of Stills, but Scott knew he'd be around somewhere. He took one last glance at the castle, then stepped off the side of the rock, letting himself fall.

Flying took a certain amount of suspension of disbelief. Scott always visualized himself parachuting when he fell. He'd actually been tested from heights of over two hundred feet and always landed safely. Well, not *always*. He could still twist an ankle or something else painful and inconveniencing. At least he didn't have to worry about being shot on the way down, as had happened to so many of the other soldiers. He always tried imagining he was an airplane when he launched himself into the air. After about a mile, his brain couldn't seem to handle the impossibility of his motion, and he fell, which was just as unnerving as flying. The doctors thought that they could hypnotize him so he'd be able to fly for longer periods of time, but Scott wasn't about to let them do that.

He reached the ground and unlimbered his own rifle. He heard a soft popping sound and a sudden breeze on his cheek announced Stills had teleported back to them. The smaller man's knife was bloodstained and his grin was shocking and bright in the dark.

"Two sentries in this section," he said. "Both accounted for." He wiped his knife on an evergreen and tucked it back in his sheath.

By now, Scott was familiar with Stills' bloodthirsty tendencies, and tried not to let it bother him. "How many other sentries on patrol?"

"I counted six. Three pairs of two."

"Sounder?"

The youngest soldier closed his eyes, concentrating on the sounds nobody else could hear. "Confirmed," he said in a moment. He chuckled quietly. "Two of 'em are drunk."

"Okay, here's the plan . . ." Scott began, but before he could continue a loud explosion ripped upward from the middle of the castle, sending cobbles and tiles flying.

"Shit," whispered Stills. "Think that's good for us or bad for us?"

An alarm began to wail, sounding very much like the air raid sirens in London. The four men instinctively looked to the skies, half afraid they would see a flight of B-17s on approach.

"Hey, look!" Hester pointed toward the castle. People were fleeing from the main entrance. Some of them were clearly soldiers, but others were in civilian garb or wearing white lab coats. They fought with each other as they grabbed motorcycles, trucks, or whatever vehicles were available. Engines sputtered to life and headlights illuminated the large cloud of dust that was raised from the explosion.

Within moments, the surge of people leaving the castle subsided. "Krauts might have done our job for us." Scott motioned to the others. "Let's move in. Stay sharp."

A ruddy glow in the smoke over the castle roof was a mute testament to a fire still burning inside. The Americans approached cautiously, rifles at the ready. The darkness seemed thick and oppressive as they reached the road, a muddy mess from the quick evacuation of the German vehicles.

The main gate into the castle hung open.

Advancing in pairs, they leapfrogged each other all the way to the castle wall. The stone was conducting a slight amount of heat. Scott figured that the interior must be like a blast furnace if the walls were already warm.

"Sounder, you hear anything inside?"

The young man removed his helmet, clapped a hand over one ear, and pressed the other against the wall, eyes shut, listening intently. "Big fire, glass breaking from the heat, something making a shrieking sound, maybe a steam valve? Shit, *footsteps!*" He pushed himself back from the wall and fumbled for his helmet.

Stills drew his knife. Scott pulled his pistol from his holster; it would be more useful in close quarters than his M-1. They waited on either side of the doorway. A figure staggered out. Stills' knife descended sharply and stopped short when Scott blocked his strike with the barrel of his pistol.

"What the hell, Sergeant?" Stills looked shocked.

"Look at him, Stills. He's no threat."

It was true. The man was badly burned. His clothes were mostly burned away except for the metal parts, which had cooked into the ruin of his skin. He tripped and fell, landing face down in the mud.

Scott had seen men burned by flamethrowers before, but this was worse than anything he'd ever witnessed. Bile rose in the back of his throat. Behind him, Downs vomited against the side of the castle. The man's limbs trembled as if he was cold, but it was surely from the massive nerve damage he'd sustained. Choking back the bad taste in his mouth, Scott reached out a boot and flipped the man over. Carbonized flesh flaked off him in layers. The man's face was gone, charred bone peeking through the cooked muscle. Incredibly, he was still breathing and *whispering* something through his burned lips and tongue.

"Hester," ordered Scott through clenched teeth. Hester was the only one who spoke German. The Professor spat to one side and kneeled down next to the man, disgust leaching from his pores.

"He keeps saying *übermensch*, over and over," said Hester after a moment, getting back to his feet.

"What's that mean?" Downs wiped his mouth. His face had gone as pale as the moon.

"Super man," Hester answered. Mercifully, the man stopped moving as his injuries overcame him.

Scott felt all the strength drain out of his legs. "Holy Christ. What if they did it?"

Stills' lip curled in disdain. He was undoubtedly still upset about Scott stopping him, since he believed the only good kraut was a dead kraut, no matter the circumstances. "Did what?"

"Made someone like us," said Hester.

"Bullshit! How could you make a parahuman?" Stills shoved his knife back into its sheath.

"Nobody knows how we got our powers," said Scott. "I didn't really know about mine until I hit eighteen. You found out about yours by accident, Stills, and Downs didn't get his until after Basic Training. The Nazis have scientists; maybe they figured something out."

The four men were silent for a moment as each considered the possibility of a Nazi parahuman.

"Okay, let's move in," said Scott finally.

"What, in there?" Stills was adamant. "No way."

"That's an order, Corporal. Salvage any documents you can find."

Rifles drawn, they moved into the castle.

The entryway was filled with smoke. A smoldering Nazi flag hung in the middle of the hall. Somewhere ahead, they could all hear the sounds of a fire.

"How come it ain't burning out here?" Downs asked.

"Stone don't burn, kid," said Stills.

They passed through another doorway into a courtyard. There was the remains of a building in the middle of the courtyard where the explosion must have occurred. Some of the cobblestones around the ruin glowed white hot. The force of the explosion seemed to have blown out most of the fire, leaving behind only the charred inflammables in its wake.

"It does if it gets hot enough." Hester coughed through the acrid fumes in the air. "I never heard of anything making this kind of heat except a volcano."

Shattered Klieg lights and warped scaffolding surrounded the courtyard. Scott looked around intently. Up on the castle wall was a steel and glass booth that was in just the spot he would have picked for an observation gallery. The glass was melted and blackened.

"Stills, can you get up there to check that out?"

"Affirmative." Stills winked out of the courtyard and appeared up on the wall. Rifle out, he kicked open the door and peered inside. In a moment, he called out from the doorway. "Sergeant, you better get up here!"

Scott took as deep a breath as he could in the smoky air and concentrated. His feet left the ground and he flew up to the top of the wall. A reek of charred flesh emerged from the booth. Scott swallowed hard, then stepped into the enclosure.

Everything in the room from window height and up had been charred black. Ash eddied in the air currents. Two people had been seated in chairs, presumably to watch the events unfolding in the courtyard below. Their legs and lower bodies were relatively unharmed, but from the waist up, they were essentially unrecognizable lumps of charcoal.

"What is this?" Scott asked, disturbed at the strangeness the scene entailed.

"Some kinda observation tower. I figure there might be some notes or something here, but I didn't want to touch nothin' without your approval first." Stills glanced at the two smoking corpses. "Shitty way to go. Must have been one hell of a burst to cook 'em like that!"

Scott clicked on his electric torch and began searching for anything he could take with him back to Allied Command. A shelf of notebooks might have been promising, but they had been turned into lattices of ash that disintegrated when he touched them. He began rooting through drawers in a low file cabinet. Nothing. No notes, no binders, nothing to show but death.

"Sergeant!" Downs' voice was urgent from down in the courtyard.

Scott leaned out of the observation booth door. "What, Sounder?"

"Heartbeat, sir, and it isn't one of ours."

A sudden rush of air and ash behind Scott informed him that Stills had just teleported out. Sure enough, he appeared an instant later next to Downs, already drawing his knife.

Scott vaulted the edge of the wall and dropped the twenty feet to the courtyard. For a trained paratrooper, even one who could fly, it was like any other landing. Hester had his pistol out and was slowly circling, like a hawk preparing to strike. His left hand clutched a fist-sized chunk of rock that vibrated with barelycontained kinetic energy.

"Where is it, Ray?" Scott grasped his own pistol at the ready.

Downs turned around slowly, using his ears like a radar set. "Through there." He pointed to the stone building in the center of the courtyard. It was long, stretching nearly two-thirds of the length of the courtyard itself. A large portion of the roof had been immolated in the explosion. "Sounds like he's inside a metal box by the echo of it."

"Maybe he can tell us what happened," said Hester in a hoarse, choking voice.

"Move in," said Scott. "And watch yourselves. It's still damn hot in here."

The four men advanced to the building. The entry doors had been blown off their hinges and lay smoldering on the courtyard cobbles. Two by two, they entered the building.

Inside was a long, low-ceilinged hall. Strange metal implements lined each wall at regular intervals, twisted into unrecognizable shapes by the heat. Small metal boxes were bolted down by each sculpture. Scott approached one cautiously and flipped open the catch with the tip of his rifle. Inside it was a smoke-stained German army uniform. He looked back down the hall, trying to picture it before the accident.

"Beds. These were beds." Hester stepped up next to him. "That's why the footlockers are here."

"That doesn't make sense. Was it a hospital?"

Hester looked grim. "Not a chance. This looks like a lab of some sort. These poor guys were subjects." They glanced down and saw charred bone fragments amid the ash remains of flesh and bedding.

"Sarge, in there." Downs motioned to a bank of heavy clothing lockers against one wall. He and Stills stepped up to them. The young man closed his eyes, listening intently next to each door. He stopped at the third locker, opened his eyes, and nodded. Stills took up a position on one side of the door, Downs the other. Scott and Hester raised their weapons, preparing for the worst. Stills nodded and raised his fingers in a silent count. *One . . . two . . . three!*

Downs yanked open the door and a man pitched forward onto the charred floor. He coughed and choked, rolling onto his side. A rope of mucus and blood trailed from his mouth. His skin had an odd, waxy sheen to it. With horror, Scott realized his eyes had been burned out; their remains leaked down his cheeks.

In his hands, he was clutching a notebook.

"This him?" Scott asked. Downs nodded, eyes wide. "Professor, check him out and confiscate that book. Downs, Stills, check the rest of the lockers, including the footlockers."

Hester dropped to his knees and started to pull the notebook away from the man. The man started and closed a desperate hand around Hester's wrist, babbling something in German. Hester kept his cool and asked the man a question. The man stuttered as if he was drugged.

"Give him some morhpine," said Scott. "Maybe it'll help us get some answers from him."

As the drug kicked in, the man became somewhat more lucid. He spoke rapid-fire German, as if he was trying to get all of his thoughts out before he perished from whatever it was that was eating him up inside. Hester took frantic notes in the man's notebook. Most of the man's speech was so jumbled and incoherent that he couldn't make heads or tails of it.

Stills and Downs returned from their search to report. "One hundred footlockers. One was empty, and there was no sign of a body beside it." Stills glanced around the room.

The man on the floor began to laugh. Not just *laughing*, thought Scott with horror, but *cackling* like an insane witch in a motion picture. His whooping laugh degenerated into a thick, bubbly cough that spurted bloody mucus from his mouth and nostrils. Hester recoiled from the grotesque droplets.

"Yah . . . yah . . . one lived!" The man spoke in heavily-accented English.

"You speak English?" Scott stepped forward.

"Ya . . . a little." The man's laughter fell into a hacking cough.

"What do you mean, *one lived*?" Stills eyes narrowed.

"The experiment . . . it was . . . success! Thousands die so that one may live. *Heil Hitler!* We have created . . . your superman!"

"What the hell does he mean by that?" Downs shouted.

"I think that's obvious, kid," said Hester.

"*No!* He's . . . he's sick or something. Look at him. He doesn't know what he's saying." Downs' face grew dark beneath the soot stains.

"At ease, *Private*," growled Scott.

"We're supposed to be the only ones. They told us we were the only ones!" Downs raised his rifle as if it were a club.

"Stills," said Scott. The teleport popped from his spot to reappear directly behind Downs. He yanked the rifle from the boy's hands. When Downs spun around in fury, Stills cuffed him hard across the face, sending him sprawling. "Stills, stand down," Scott bawled in his best drill-sergeant's voice.

Downs didn't rise from where he had landed in a heap. His voice was racked by sobs. "We're supposed to be the only ones," he repeated as he gasped for air.

Scott stalked over to the boy. "We don't have time for this. *On your feet, soldier! Atten-SHUN!*"

Months of conditioned reflexes kicked in and Downs jumped up, ramrod straight, tears tracking clean streaks down his sooty face. "Sorry, sir." He gulped and wiped his nose, and then paused, listening. "Does anyone else hear that?"

The other three soldiers looked around warily, weapons raised. "Hear what?" Scott snapped at him.

"That sort of humming, whistling sound. Kind of like before a steam valve busts."

Another cackling laugh emerged from the forgotten man on the floor. His flesh seemed to be moving from waxy to almost liquid, like it wasn't sticking to his bones anymore. "Ya . . . Messer's Device . . . it will pulse again . . . all will perish."

Hester started as if he'd been goosed. "Device?"

"What's *pulse*?" Downs looked frightened.

"It's bad, whatever it is." said Scott. "Stills, take that journal. If anything happens, you get clear with it."

"But Sergeant—"

"That's an order, Corporal. Move out, boys, asses and elbows!"

The four men ran for it, back down the hall and through the entryway. They cleared the castle wall and were pelting across the mud for the evergreen forest across the road when a light as bright as day erupted from the castle behind them.

Scott had a sensation of being as transparent as glass, followed by a twisting, wrenching pain. His mind whirled madly as it tried to reconcile the fact that he had just been teleported. Acute vertigo hit him like a right hook and he fell hard onto a rocky surface, retching from the dizziness and the awful sensation.

That's when he heard the screaming. He tried to focus his spinning eyes. A fiery orange and red blur resolved itself into the largest explosion he had ever seen. The castle had been flung apart by the force of it, and the evergreens had been knocked flat, burning so fast they exploded as the water within their trunks flashed into steam. He realized he was up on the high mountain that overlooked the castle, or what was left of it. He shivered violently, although from the cold or the altitude or the sudden shift in location he couldn't tell.

The screaming continued and Scott saw Stills writhing on the ground in agony. His left arm was missing halfway through his bicep, as neat as if someone had lopped it off with a band saw. Blood poured out of the stump.

Scott forced himself up to his knees, fumbling for his pack and for the morphine. The world spun around him as he found the emergency kit. He flopped down next to Stills, whose screams had softened to animalistic moans. He ripped off the sleeve of his fatigues and fashioned a tourniquet around Stills' arm. Even in the darkness, with the angry glow of the fire below, the man had gone deathly pale.

Stills had lost so much blood; Scott was afraid that the morphine would kill him, but he wasn't a medic and wouldn't trust himself to alter a dose. In a few minutes the narcotic took hold of Stills and his whimpering subsided.

Scott hunkered down next to him to wait until morning. Neither of them was in any shape to travel, and if Stills was going to die, it would happen in the next few hours. There was no sign of Hester or Downs. Scott was certain they had died down below in front of the castle. The heat from the explosion had been so strong that where there had been mud was now cracked earth with a glossy sheen over it. The forest had been leveled, and what hadn't been blown to splinters was burning away.

He had a fair idea of what happened. When the device pulsed, it had blown up, like an overheated boiler. In the fraction of a second after the burst, Stills had reached out to Scott, who happened to be right next to him, and teleported them both up the mountainside.

Stills was able to move more mass sthan himself, since he could teleport with a full pack, but he'd never attempted to move another whole person. His body must have rebelled at the attempt and left part of itself behind. Scott felt fortunate to be all in one piece and to not have any parts of the local landscape impaled through him. Teleporting to an unseen location was one of Stills' great fears; he was afraid of materializing in the same space occupied by another object. Army doctors had no idea what would happen if he did.

Scott knew that no matter what else happened, he had to get that notebook back to the Allies. He had to tell them what they'd learned at Aufstein, that the Nazis were trying to create their own parahumans.

And he had to tell them that they'd succeeded.

THE SCENT OF ROSE PETALS

February, 1946
New York City, New York

I am an old man. But once, I was much younger, and held the heart of a goddess.

I'm sure many men throughout the ages have doubtless thought of their women as goddesses, but to this day I still believe mine really was.

She called herself Lady Athena. She was one of the first heroes, part of the fledgling American Justice team that so enchanted the nation after World War II. Most of them were veterans of the war, but not her. Her background was as mysterious as her powers. How well I remember the newsreel footage of her and her companions as they flew unaided above the streets of New York to demonstrate their abilities for an adoring populace.

I was just a guard at the First Federal Bank and Trust over on Bleecker Street back then. It was my first job since I'd left home. Too young to serve in the army before the war ended, I'd found myself in competition against thousands of veterans for positions. Fortunately for me, not many wanted to be bank guards. It wasn't a very prestigious or glamorous occupation, but I earned enough to rent the room in a house run by a woman named Mrs. Tidwell, and provided for the occasional movie or trip out to Coney Island to watch the submarine races. It was a simple life and it suited me well after a childhood in rural Pennsylvania amid the Amish and Mennonites.

I nearly lost my life the day I met Lady Athena, and all because our bank manager, Mr. Maxwell G. Jackson the Third—he insisted on including his lineage every chance he got—had this newfangled idea about leaving bank guards unarmed to seem more friendly to bank customers. It was no wonder he couldn't keep men on his payroll. All the uniform did was make us easily-identifiable targets. Bank robberies were no more common back then than they are today, but that day was the exception I will never forget.

There were six of them. They acted like many veterans I'd seen: cool under pressure but on a hair trigger, ready to unleash violence without any provocation. They wore maintenance coveralls and knit caps against the cold of the Fall, and ran inside the bank brandishing service pistols. One had a submachine gun that he must have brought back from the front lines. I had no idea what to do. My training had consisted mainly of a tour of the bank so I'd know where to direct customers. The robbers ordered the patrons and tellers to lie down on the tiled floor. I wavered, uncertain what to do. I knew I had to protect the bank, but I had nothing more than a ring of keys on my belt. I'm not sure what I was thinking when I unclipped them. I was no fighter, no soldier like these men clearly had been.

"Well, look at this," grunted one of the men. "Looks like we got ourselves a hero, boys. What're you going to do, hero? Going to make us stop? Get down on the floor, hero."

"Do something, Stanley," Mr. Jackson hissed at me under his breath. "Or you're fired. You're a guard, for God's sake!"

I didn't know what to do, but I knew I wasn't about to take a bullet for a man who thought so little of me that he wouldn't allow me the necessary tools to perform the job for which he'd hired me.

Helplessly, I sank to the floor. My ears burned with shame and impotence. The robber laughed at me and turned his back just as a gust of freezing wind blew through the lobby and sent deposit slips and receipts flying like snow.

"What the heck?" yelled one of the robbers as a cloaked and helmeted figure drifted in from the street.

She seemed far more imposing than her stature implied. She might have been five and a half feet tall—only an inch shorter than me—but with her velvety maroon cloak billowing around her in wind that seemed to swirl at her whim, she seemed the largest person I'd ever seen. Her bronze helmet with its plume of crimson feathers kept her face shadowed except for her eyes, which flashed bright like sodium arc lights. Curly black hair spilled out from under the helmet to flap in the breeze. Under her cloak she wore a bronze breastplate over a red tunic and skirt, with lace-up sandals. The part of my mind that was only human noticed that she had great legs. She held a spear in one hand and had a small round shield buckled to the other.

I knew Lady Athena only by reputation and from the newsreels I'd seen at Saturday matinees, but here she was right in front of me. She tilted her head down towards me slightly, and I swear she winked at me from under her helmet before she turned her attention to the robbers. Those worthies all stood with their guns dangling loosely from their sides and their mouths hanging open in shock.

"You boys had better give me those before you hurt somebody with them," she said in a soft voice redolent with power. "Give up now and I'll go easy on you."

Two of the robbers shook their heads and slid their guns across the floor. "I didn't sign on for fightin' no superheroes," grumbled one of them as he knelt and put his hands on his head.

Three of the others wavered uncertainly. But the fourth, the fellow with the submachine gun, wasn't having any of it. "You picked the wrong day to come to this bank, little lady," he hollered, and raised his weapon.

"So did you," she whispered.

The robber unloaded his clip at her. The terrific racket made all of us clap our hands over our ears. She casually raised her shield, as if she had all the time in the world, and deflected every single bullet. I saw the sparks on her shield from each impact. Somehow, she directed every slug up to a point in the ceiling over the robber. His eyes grew wide as she stood before him, unharmed, and pointed over his head. Like a fool, he tilted his head back to look. A piece of masonry cracked loose and fell right onto his upturned face.

The other three robbers surrendered without a fight.

Later, I watched as the police bundled the six robbers—one nursing a broken nose and wounded ego—into the paddy wagon. Mr. Jackson fawned over Lady Athena and tried to get her to come back to the bank again for a photo opportunity. She politely turned aside his attentions and suggested he might want to review his security procedures and arm his guards. Then she smiled at me and turned to go. I knew in that moment I had to speak to her, to make her more real in my mind somehow. I slipped my hat off my head, held it in my hands before me, and twirled it nervously.

"Ma'am . . ." I felt my tongue swell in my mouth from nerves.

"Yes? Are you all right?" she asked in her soft contralto. Her eyes no longer glowed with that unnatural light and instead sparkled with amusement.

"Yes," I replied. "I . . . I wanted to know if you're okay. That guy shot at you." The words came in a rush, and I winced at how much I sounded like a moonstruck teenager.

"I'm fine, Stan," she said. "Thank you for your concern, though."

"How do you know my name?"

"I overheard your bank manager use it," she replied. "He's not a bad man, your boss. Give him a chance."

"Thanks." I wondered where I'd find the spine to say what I really felt. She brushed past me. In her wake, I could smell the scent of fresh-cut roses. "Uh . . . Lady Athena?"

She paused, turned slightly, and looked back at me. "Yes?"

"Would you . . . do you . . . like movies?" I felt like a kamikaze pilot who'd committed to his final, fatal approach into a ship, unable to change his mind.

She smiled. "Yes I do, Stan."

And just like that, the pilot found a control surface that let him pull out of his crash dive. "Maybe would you like to go to a matinée? This weekend? W-with me?"

"I would enjoy that." She went on to say she'd meet me outside a theater on the West Side. Then she left the bank. I watched as her cape swirled around her ankles and she flew straight up into the air, which left more than a few jaws hanging loosely in surprise from those on the ground.

Mr. Jackson was saying something to me, but all I could hear was the sound of her voice replaying in my mind.

* * *

Saturday found me seated on a bench outside the theater, dressed warmly against the first freeze of the season. I had my hat pulled down over my ears and the collar of my overcoat turned up. I'd been so nervous all morning I'd had to change my shirt twice because it would get soaked under the arms. I had debated myself around and around whether to buy her flowers or anything, but in the end I'd talked myself out of it. Flowers would seem too forward, I figured, especially since she didn't really know me and I knew nothing about her except what I'd seen in the papers.

"Hello, Stan. I hope I'm not late," came a friendly voice. I stood by reflex and turned to see her standing there.

She hadn't worn her costume. Somehow I knew she wouldn't, but I hadn't ever pictured what she might look like out of it. She was likewise bundled against the cold, in a scarlet wool coat with a white scarf wrapped around her neck. She wore a matching white hat, one of those French ones that always looked lopsided to me. Unlike most women, she wore her dark hair down, with only a few pins in strategic locations. Without her helmet, she looked beautiful. Her skin was tanned and exotic, her eyes large and dark, teeth white, lips ruby red. In spite of the cold weather, she had a fresh rose pinned to the lapel of her coat. I had never considered myself to be especially good-looking, but here she was, this smooth-skinned angel, smiling radiantly and honestly at me . . . at me! . . . warming me like a bonfire.

"N-no," I stuttered.

She placed a friendly hand on my arm. "Stan, relax. I don't bite. Being a superhero is just what I do. I'm just like any other girl."

"Not like any other girl," I countered. "What should I call you? Lady Athena?"

"Athena is fine." She shivered. "Let's go inside. What's playing?"

I had already bought our tickets, so we went inside. The young fellow in his sparkling usher's uniform tore them and handed back the stubs as he cheerfully wished us to enjoy the show. During the twenty minutes before the lights darkened, Athena and I talked. She didn't tell me too much about herself, and apologized for it. "I still have an identity to maintain," she explained. She did tell me that she'd lived in New York all her life, but her family had emigrated from Greece. She loved flowers and grew them when she wasn't doing her work with American Justice. She asked me about myself, my job, my family, where I grew up. And she seemed so honestly interested that I grew very comfortable speaking to this beautiful woman.

There was a newsreel with some headlines about Korea, then a Bugs Bunny cartoon that made us both laugh. The movie was a musical with Gene Kelly with a lot of singing and dancing and I'll admit I thought it was kind of boring. Athena seemed to really like it, though, and once clutched my hand during one of the big dance numbers, her eyes shining as she watched people cavorting across the screen. She didn't let go right away, so neither did I.

By the time the matinée let out for the day, a light snow was falling. It spiraled down on the capricious currents between the buildings. Athena flung her arms out, spun around like one of the dancers in the movie, and laughed at the weather like a child. "I love the snow," she confided to me. "It always feels so magical."

I shivered. "It always makes me feel cold," I said. "There's a diner over there. How about a cup of coffee and a slice of pie?"

She grinned, her cheeks red from the wind. "Sure. I love pie."

I smiled back with a confidence I didn't know I had. "Everybody loves pie."

* * *

Our first date turned into a second. Then a third. Suddenly, without even planning it, I'd acquired a girl, and Athena had acquired me as well. She had that disarming honesty about her feelings which made it easy to swallow the fact that she was a superhero and I was, in her words, "refreshingly mundane." We went to more movies, and to the theater. We went to a fight and saw Rocky Marciano knock out Joe Louis. When summer came, we went to baseball games.

Many of our dates ended with us sneaking back into Mrs. Tidwell's house or, less frequently, in one of the finer hotels downtown when I could afford it. Athena was wealthy but didn't embarrass me by offering to pay for many things.

The overnight stays in the hotels were always memorable. We'd share champagne and strawberries, and later make love on the softest beds ever. I never told her I had only ever been with one other woman, and she never asked. She seemed experienced, and taught me a great many things about both of us. Sometimes, when we finished, we'd lie naked beside one another, the scent of rose petals filling the room, as the smoke from our cigarettes curled up to mingle overhead much like we had previously.

"Stanley." She rolled up onto one elbow and looked down at me one summer afternoon. Her black curls, damp with sweat, hung around her face like the ribbons on gift wrapping. She only called me Stanley when she wanted to discuss serious topics. I forced myself to look away from her flawless skin, bosoms curving forward to perfectly-formed nipples like candy kisses. "I think it's time I brought you home."

"Home? You mean to where you live?" Even after months of dating, I still had no idea where Athena lived or worked. She had perfectly valid reasons for not telling me. If I knew that much about her, I was a liability that an enemy could exploit. There weren't many super-villains back in those days, but the few who plagued American Justice wouldn't hesitate to use me as leverage against her, and she didn't want to risk me. It took me some time to come to grips with that secrecy, but she was so honest about everything else with me that I had no real reason to complain.

"Not so much where I live," she replied. "My flat isn't anything special. I'll take you there sometime. But I want you to meet my family, and they to meet you."

I wondered if she'd been reading my mind. I didn't know if she counted that among her myriad powers and abilities. Unlike the rest of the American Justice heroes, her powers weren't clearly defined. As near as I or anyone else could tell, she could do just about anything she thought to try. I'd seen her fly, listen to a conversation across a park, or locate one of my missing cuff links by the way sound echoed off it. The fact was I'd been going down to Schlener's on 28th Street pretty often and looking really hard at this one ring, trying to decide if I dared buy it for her. I'd even thought about bringing her home to Pennsylvania to meet my parents and sister.

"Sure, I'd be honored to meet them," I said. "When?"

She rolled out of bed, comfortable with her nakedness. She steadfastly refused to cover herself with a blanket or sheet. "Now. Today."

I stabbed out my cigarette in the bedside ashtray. "Today's good." I thought again of that ring in Schlener's. "I'll just go hop in the shower so I'll make a good impression." I tried to maintain the same casualness and lack of modesty she so naturally exhibited and strolled into the bathroom. A few minutes later, she knocked on the door.

"You are so wonderful, Stan," she said as she slipped into the shower with me. "I was so lucky to meet you that day in the bank."

"Not as lucky as I was," I countered. She laughed and threw her arms around me. We made love again under the spray, and shouted with laughter when it would suddenly get ice cold from someone turning on a tap elsewhere in the hotel.

* * *

Athena's "family" turned out to be the rest of American Justice. They waited for the two of us in their penthouse suite in one of the prestigious downtown office buildings. I had never met any of them before in person, and never even seen any of them except in the papers before that day.

I think I'd have rather met her parents. I imagined they were wealthy, beautiful people to have raised such a lovely, cultured person as Athena. The American

Justice heroes were much scarier to me. Here was Dr. Danger, the world's greatest archer, who sat with Colt, the woman who could outrun an express train. Flashpoint, the Negro war veteran, glared at me with open distrust and hatred. Kid Crash, the all-American teen-ager with the freckles and the ability to blow up things he touched, looked lost amid the adults. The White Knight seemed mundane without the glowing suit of armor he normally wore in public. Only John Q. Public, the man of a thousand faces, seemed genuinely pleased to meet me. He shook my hand and introduced himself, wearing the square-jawed face most people expected to see on him.

Wherever Lady Athena went among her companions, she was like a cool breeze on a summer's day. She spoke in low, soothing tones to introduce me, and their prejudices melted away. Dr. Danger and Colt insisted I call them by their given names of Adrian and Judy. Athena whispered to me they were secret lovers. I looked at the two of them and wondered how anybody couldn't see their attraction to one another. Kid Crash wanted to talk baseball with me. Even Flashpoint, the angriest man I have ever met in my life, softened up enough to crack a genuine smile.

Being around people of such power and reputation was heady and exciting, like hanging around with university professors or Hollywood actors or sportsmen. We ate hors d'oeuvres and drank cocktails (except Kid Crash, who was only allowed ginger ale). We talked about politics and crime and the state of the world and I felt like I had been accepted. Athena hung on my arm much of the afternoon, comfortable to display her affection for me to her compatriots and fellow men-at-arms.

It must have been hours later when our discussion about dinner was interrupted by a pair of New York City policemen, sent by the mayor to request American Justice's help with what they called "a situation."

Athena spoke with them briefly to get the details, and then asked the rest of the team to suit up. She kissed me softly, and said I could wait in their headquarters while they dealt with the incident.

The White Knight wrapped himself in a suit of armor made from glowing light. Despite the heat of the evening, Flashpoint shrugged into an overcoat and fedora and strapped spring-loaded holsters over his wrists for his matched pistols. Colt put on her own red fighting togs that showed off her shapely legs while her lover Dr. Danger slung his bow and quiver of custom arrows across his back and tied a scarf with eye holes over his face. John Q. Public always wore an off-the-rack suit so he could disappear into a crowd at a moment's notice. Athena slipped her helmet into place. Her cloak fluttered around her in the breeze from the open terrace.

The others headed for the express elevator to the ground floor. Athena hung back briefly to deliver me a passionate kiss. I knew at that moment I'd head to Schlener's the next day, to buy that ring I'd been thinking about so much. I was certain I wanted to spend the rest of my life with this woman, this heroic goddess who had stolen my heart.

* * *

I switched on the radio and sat quietly on the edge of a chair and listened as a reporter described the events unfolding downtown.

"-Dies and gentlemen, it's some kind of giant . . . mechanical monster, stalking down Forty-Seventh Street! The sheer size of it . . . it must be at least thirty feet tall!"

In the background, I could hear rumbling sounds of destruction, punctuated by the whine of electric motors, the hiss of steam, and a ponderous rhythmic thumping that had to be footsteps.

"It looks like a dinosaur, with steel pincers for arms. Oh my . . . it's stopping in front of a building and —

Ladies and gentlemen, it has just picked up an automobile and thrown it like an empty can. Diamond merchants are frantically gathering up their stock and fleeing for their lives."

I realized with a start that this monstrosity was attacking the diamond district. It was a single block where merchants traded the precious stones, dealing in amounts of money so large I couldn't even begin to imagine.

"I see something in the sky. It's Lady Athena, flying this way. That means the rest of American Justice can't be far behind. Yes, there is Colt, running up Fifth Avenue, followed by a car driven by Dr. Danger and escorted by motorcycle policemen!"

Even though I knew what to expect, to hear about the people I'd just met going into action excited me and made my heart pound. And underneath that excitement, I discovered fear as well; fear that something might happen to one of them.

I hadn't had to deal with that fear much since I began to date Athena, simply because there hadn't been much need for American Justice in their capacity as superheroes. They'd made a few public appearances and halted a few mundane crimes, but nothing that couldn't have been handled by regular police. This time was different, though, and I found myself afraid for her.

The radio newsman went on to describe a fast-paced, confused battle, punctuated by loud crashes and bursts of static. American Justice divided itself into two groups; some attacked the infernal machine and the rest moved civilians to safety.

Athena, Kid Crash, and Dr. Danger battled the monstrosity, each in their own way. Dr. Danger shot forked arrows at it to slice through its hydraulic lines and wiring. Kid Crash used his explosive powers to shatter the thing's armor. Athena dug her spear into the machinery, which ruined motors and stripped gears.

Between the three of them, they made short work of the giant mechanical creature.

While they fought, Flashpoint, Colt, the White Knight, and John Q. Public helped get the civilians to safety. Every few sentences, the reporter managed to slip one in about the other heroes bravely saving innocent lives.

"But wait, what's this?" cried the reporter. "A man is running across the street, holding a case. Another man is chasing him . . . It's John Q. Public, calling for him to stop, thief! He must have stolen somebody's diamonds! The man stops and turns . . . Is he surrendering? No, he's got a gun! Watch out, John Q.!"

A gunshot sounded clearly from the radio speaker.

* * *

It was stiflingly hot the day we buried John Q. Public. He'd sold his life for the sum of eight thousand dollars' worth of diamonds. He wasn't the first member of American Justice to have lost his life in the line of duty, but it had been two years since Apollo and Flicker bought it, and only Flashpoint and Colt had been on the team that long.

The Tyrant had been behind the monster machine attack. A brilliant scientist and criminal mastermind, he'd built it solely as a diversion. While it raged through the Diamond District, attracting police and American Justice, he and his cronies had quietly gassed a wing in the art museum, leaving two hundred patrons suffering the aftereffects of the induced unconsciousness. Then they had carefully removed several paintings worth a combined total of two million dollars.

There had been a great hue and cry, and people were calling for American Justice to disband in the wake of such an embarrassment. Speculation ran rampant that American Justice had somehow been involved in the heist. The FBI announced an investigation of the team. A seemingly never-ending flow of faceless men in dark suits and hats asked pointed questions of anyone connected to the team.

Athena did her best to shield me from such attention, but short of locking me inside the team's headquarters, it was a practical impossibility. Even I was eventually cornered in a room at the bank by three G-Men and questioned mercilessly for almost three hours about American Justice. My boss, Mr. Jackson, had been looking at me funny ever since and I was afraid I was going to lose my job.

But all that seemed far away as the casket containing the mortal remains of a man known only as John Q. Public were lowered into a hillside grave. Besides American Justice, there were maybe another fifteen graveside mourners. I assumed they were Public's family or friends. None of them spoke to us.

The pastor finished speaking his words. We each tossed a rose upon the casket and said goodbye in our own ways. Then the group broke up. Public's other mourners hurried away as if they were afraid to be seen in the tarnished company of American Justice. The other heroes had worn dark suits, as had I, but Athena had dressed in her costume. She'd chosen to replace her helmet and red cloak with a hooded cloak of black velvet.

"Walk with me, Stan," said Athena quietly.

Despite the heat, it was a beautiful morning. Birds sang in the trees, bees zipped between the gravestones and looked for flowers. The peace of the hero's final repose made me think about my own mortality, and that I'd sure like to be buried in a place just like this.

We walked across the carefully-mowed grass, around trees and gravestones, and eventually wound up atop a small hill where a slight breeze moved Athena's cloak around her ankles.

Not a word had passed between us since she bade me join her, but now Athena turned to face me, and the sight of tears in her eyes frightened me. I never thought

I'd see such a human response from the woman I thought of as a goddess. I held out my arms. She slipped into them and buried her face against my shoulder. I wasn't sure what else to do, so I just held her, and we stood that way for a long time.

"I'm sorry," I said as she finally stood back and wiped a last errant tear from one eye. "I never had a chance to really meet him, but he seemed a decent fellow."

"Oh, he was," replied Athena. "You'd have gotten along famously. That's just how he was. He could make friends with anybody." I offered her my handkerchief but she declined and drew herself up a little straighter. "We need to talk, Stanley."

Something in the tone of her voice scared me. "About what?" I asked guardedly.

"About us. You and I," she replied.

My heart hammered in my chest so hard I'm sure she could hear it.

She turned away from me for a moment, took a breath as if she was going to speak, but then faced me once more. "Stan, I love you."

Suddenly it felt like I was being lifted into the air by a thousand balloons. I smiled back at her, and felt in my pocket for the little velvet-wrapped box that held the ring I'd purchased two days ago. "I love you too, Athena."

"And that's why it's so hard for me to say we can't see each other any more."

As quickly as my spirits had lifted, the balloons all popped and hurled me back to the hard earth. The box fell from my nerveless fingers to nestle back in my pocket. "W-what?"

Her face drew into a frown. "Bad times are coming, Stan. A storm is growing on the horizon. It's going to swallow up American Justice and anyone associated with us."

"I don't care," I said, and meant it. "Athena . . . you're the greatest thing that's ever happened to me. I don't want that to end. Especially not like this."

"Oh, Stan," she said. "I can't let you be pulled into this. You're a wonderful person and I care about you so much. But this . . . this can't work between us. I don't ever want you to be waiting for me to come back from a mission and then I don't. You deserve better than that."

"I don't care," I repeated doggedly. "I love you now. I want to stay with you for the rest of forever."

She sighed, looking at her hands. "I always wondered why these powers came to me," she said. "And at times I have cursed them, wishing I could be done with them. This is one of those times." She raised her head. "But I can't be done with them, Stan. They're part of me, and I have to use them to do what I can to help people. It's the only way I can sleep at night." Her eyes dipped down to my pocket just for a fraction of a second, but in that moment I realized she knew about the ring. "And I had to tell you this before things go any further. I wish it could be different, but it can't."

I wanted to be angry. I wanted to scream and shout and break things, but instead I just bowed my head. "I understand," I said. And in a way, I did understand perfectly why she'd come to this decision.

"I'll never forget you, Stan. You made me feel so special."

"You are special," I said. "You're a superhero."

She shook her head. "That's just my job. You made me feel good about everything not part of my job. Thank you, Stan. I'll always love you."

She turned away. Tears tracked down her cheeks once more. The scent of rose petals filled my head as wind swirled around her cloak to fill it. She flew away from me one last time, a departing vision in crimson and black. "I'll always love you too, Athena," I whispered as she left me forever.

I am an old man. But once, I was much younger, and held the heart of a goddess.

CHINATOWN GHOST

November, 1948
New York City, NY

A lesser man might have stayed indoors on a night with a frigid wind carrying stinging sleet. Or perhaps a smarter man might have, Adrian thought. He crouched on the fire escape of a tenement, cold wetness seeping through his headscarf, and watched the street through Army surplus binoculars. He might not be a lesser man, but he was willing to entertain the idea that he was being stupid in his heroism.

He hadn't intended originally to become a costumed hero, like the members of the team known as American Justice. They had returned to America as war heroes, first for their efforts in Germany and the in Pacific. Adrian was rich, fit, and bored. He had a gift for archery, and had lobbied for its inclusion in the canceled '44 and then the '48 Summer Olympics in London. Despite his efforts, the Committee had passed with the excuse that it was too soon after the War to introduce an event that hadn't been included for a quarter of a century. Disappointed, Adrian had thrown himself into his training with no clear idea what to do with it.

In '46, American Justice had debuted in New York, and everything changed. The veteran heroes wore costumes, hid their faces behind masks, and fought crime with fantastic abilities far beyond those of normal men. They were called parahumans, and they rooted out criminals wherever they could be found.

Adrian read everything he could about the team. One wall of his basement workshop was plastered with articles and magazine covers. He imagined what it would be like, fighting crime as a masked hero. Then it occurred to him there was no reason he couldn't do exactly that. He had the resources in a sizable inheritance from his parents who died in a boating accident shortly after his nineteenth birthday. He had the skill with a bow to perform shots that rivaled the legend of Robin Hood. Someone who had trained with him at the club said he was like a surgeon with a broadhead. From there had been a short stretch to call himself Dr. Danger and start patrolling the streets and rooftops of Manhattan. Perhaps it was a young, rich man's fantasy, but he knew he had made a difference. He had saved lives.

He was crouching on a fire escape in the sleet that evening with intent to save more lives.

Someone had been grabbing prostitutes off the streets. Four had disappeared in the past week and a half, approximately the same time the weather had turned and fewer people had been out at night. The police weren't keen to follow up on the disappearances of women of ill repute, and American Justice was busy doing its own thing. That left Manhattan's masked archer to pick up the slack. A friend of the fourth missing woman had spotted him in an alley and called to him for help. When he arrived, she poured out her tale of terror amid a flood of tears and exhortations for him to find her friend. Word spread throughout the community of streetwalkers that they were being hunted, and barely any women at all were trying to work in the chilly, wet weather. Those who were clustered together, careful not to be caught anywhere alone and careful about which johns they went with and which they sent packing.

Adrian had gone to his usual haunts, information sources he'd developed over the past half a year. Pawnshops. Seedy bars that catered to a lower-class clientele. A massage parlor in Queens. A bookie in the Bowery.

Nothing.

Nobody had heard anything about prostitutes being kidnapped. No bodies had turned up, which suggested the women might still be alive, which in turn suggested that someone had a reason for keeping them alive. Whatever the reason, Adrian was certain it was a situation they would gladly abandon given the chance. It galled him that he couldn't find even a hint of what might have happened. It was like they had disappeared off the face of the world.

That was why he monitored the lone streetwalker as she stood under the awning of a closed watch-repair shop. She was near enough to a streetlight that a passing driver might see her and take a fancy, but far enough away not to be obvious about it. For three nights, he'd been staking her out, well aware of the irony of his own spying behavior. As easily as Adrian found her, the kidnappers might do so as well. He hoped no harm would come to her, but if it did, he would be ready with his tools of the trade.

In the summer, when he'd begun his adventuring, he'd picked a swashbuckling-style outfit because he thought it gave him a suitably dashing look to match his *nom de guerre.* He wore pirate boots with the tops folded down, tight-fitting trousers, a loose blouse with his quiver strapped over it, and a scarf tied over the top half of his head and face, leaving only his eyes visible. Now that the weather had turned, he'd added a greatcoat and an old-fashioned tricorne hat. It wasn't the warmest outfit he could have worn, but it made what he felt was a reasonable accommodation to comfort while retaining his overall swashbuckling look. Icy water trickled off the brim of his hat and still found its way inside the turned-up collar of the coat. He wished he could pop into an all-night diner for a cup of soup or hot coffee.

He wondered who would break first, him or the streetwalker below. She had her arms wrapped around herself with a coat that looked uncomfortably thin for the weather. Go home, he silently implored her. Safer for you there. She reached into her purse and pulled something out—perhaps a couple of coins—then glanced in the direction of the pay phone on the corner. It looked like she was about to give up for the night and call for a ride.

At that moment, a nondescript sedan pulled up to the curb alongside her, engine rumbling and wipers slapping away accumulated sleet. The streetwalker went into business mode, bending over to speak to the driver and opening her coat a little to show off her cleavage. The sedan's rear doors opened and two men emerged, wearing long dark coats and hats pulled low. Adrian's pulse quickened and it took everything he had not to leap to the screaming woman's defense as they shoved her into the back seat.

Adrian stuck an arrow between his teeth and went over the side of the fire escape, sliding down a cord he'd tied earlier for just such a quick descent. He landed in a puddle in the alley below, splattering slush everywhere as he whipped his bow off his back. He nocked the arrow, drew, and fired it at the departing car's taillights. The arrow was one of his own design. A spring rode right behind the arrowhead. Behind it was a small battery-operated transmitter that would operate for half an hour before it ran out of power. It was an ungainly arrow, prone sometimes to flying off course or other times the transmitter would shatter on impact despite the shock absorber. This time, he saw the arrow punch into the car's sheet metal, just above the bumper. The car neither slowed nor stopped, suggesting the driver must have thought the bang of impact was either a backfire or a pothole. It turned a corner and disappeared.

Adrian sprinted through the sleet for his own car, a new Mercury with the latest factory options and a few he'd added himself. He dug in his pocket, found the key, and slipped inside behind the wheel. He started the engine and opened the glove box. Instead of gloves or documents, he had installed an armature with his transmitter tracker. Wires ran from it back into the glove box. He switched it on and waited impatiently for the device to warm up. Adrian shivered in the ice cold air from the vents, realizing how wet he'd gotten crouching on the fire escape. He needed a better cold-weather outfit—something insulated and waterproof.

His tracker featured a ring of eight lights corresponding to the cardinal directions. Two glowed to life, pointing in the approximate direction of the transmitter. It wasn't a perfect system, but it was the best he could manage with his basic understanding of electronics. He pulled away from the curb, the wipers adding rhythm to the basso rumble and treble hiss of tires on wet pavement. He hoped his makeshift transmitter wouldn't fail due to the weather and drove faster than was probably prudent given the conditions. In a few minutes, he spotted the taillights of his prey. Instead of trusting the tracker, stayed a block back and crept along so as not to raise suspicions. Between the weather and the late hour, the streets were mostly empty, making his pursuit easier.

Adrian kept the target car in view and occasionally switched off his headlights to make it appear as if he had disappeared. The target car rolled into Chinatown and Adrian grimaced. No wonder there hadn't been any sign of the women who'd disappeared. Chinatown was a black hole, full of gangs and secrets and lies, and very, very few women. American immigration laws for Chinese were highly restrictive, and almost all of those who did manage to make their way through Ellis Island or other centers were male. Adrian frowned as he considered the likely fate for women being kidnapped off the streets and brought into Chinatown. Sex slavery was something *nice* people didn't talk about, but *nice* people didn't normally deal with the kind of criminal scum that Adrian fought on a daily basis.

Despite the lateness of the hour, the street still glowed with neon and flickering lanterns in windows. Adrian knew his car would be even easier to see and pulled over to park behind a delivery sedan with flowing, hand-lettered pinyin characters on its rear doors. He sat there with the car idling, watching as the other car went three blocks farther, then made a left turn. He advanced slowly, nosing the car out into the intersection before making the same turn. The other car had vanished, and Adrian kept one eye on his tracker and the other on the road as he cruised up the street. When the lights changed, he made a note of the building in question. It was a nondescript tenement amid all the other closely packed buildings. He continued onward for another block, turned left again, and parked the car.

Keeping his hat pulled low over his headscarf and coat collar turned up, he slipped into a narrow alley nearby. It was too tight for a car, almost too tight for two men to have passed each other without turning sideways. He slung his quiver, quickly assembled his bow, and strung it. Ready for action, he moved through the walkway toward the building where the target car had disappeared. Overflowing trash cans competed for space with stacks of wooden crates and boxes, making it difficult to pass through the alley without knocking something over. Adrian briefly considered climbing up to the rooftops, but this part of town offered no convenient fire escapes.

The path between the buildings was dark and narrow and wound around like a river meandering through a box canyon. Adrian found the building where the transmitter had led him. What he'd thought was a tenement was an old carriage house instead. He listened at a door leading into the alley but heard nothing except splattering sleet splattering down. He tested the handle to see if it might be unlocked. As it started to twist, he sensed motion behind him and started to turn.

A hard blow crashed against his skull and he spun into darkness.

* * *

Adrian awakened to throbbing pain in his head. Before he even opened his eyes, he reached up to gingerly feel the hard lump behind his ear. It was tender and his headscarf didn't appear to have dulled the blow in the least. He realized after a moment that he was still wearing the headscarf, although his hat and coat didn't appear to still be on his person. He was lying on a thin mattress set on a floor. The tiny skittering sounds of cockroaches were all too familiar to him from some of the terrible places his crusade had brought him over the past six months. He cracked his eyes open, resisting the temptation to leap to his feet in an unfamiliar location.

A flickering naked bulb overhead cast a dim light through the room. Years of water damage and tobacco smoke stained the ceiling. From his position, Adrian saw a window with the shade drawn and the glow of a red neon light flashing behind it. A lamp sitting on a small table underneath the window was switched off. Beside the table, a shadowy figure sat in a wooden chair with arms crossed and face hidden by the brim of a hat pulled low.

"You're awake," the man said in a heavily accented voice. Adrian pegged him as Chinese, although to be fair it wasn't a wild assumption given his most recent location. "You should not be here, *bairen*."

Careful to keep his hands in plain sight, Adrian gingerly sat up, feeling his head throb with every motion. The mattress, like everything else in the room, was filthy. His skin crawled the way the roaches skittered around the edges of the floor. He saw his coat and hat sitting on another chair in the corner, along with his quiver and his bow. He glanced at the man by the window and back at his equipment, wondering if he could get to it before the man shot him or otherwise attacked. Maybe on his best day he could, but not when he was still woozy from a blow to the head.

"You would not make it," the man said as if reading Adrian's mind.

"Fine," Adrian retorted. "You didn't kill me or unmask me, so you have some other agenda. Why am I here? And where is *here*, anyway?"

"Chinatown, of course," the man said. "You were about to make a big mistake."

"And who are you?" Adrian's tone was challenging, but he didn't feel the bravado he was trying to display. In all the months of his adventuring, this was the first time he'd found himself in this kind of predicament.

"Nobody special."

"I'm not calling you that. What's your name?"

"Jingshen. And you are Dr. Danger. You should not be here."

"You already said that."

Jingshen raised his head enough for Adrian to see the light reflecting off the man's dark eyes. His face was crisscrossed by a network of fine white lines in the man's natural skin tone. They looked like scars, but if they were, Jingshen must have suffered a horrific injury. Adrian had once seen a mobster after he'd been flung through a plate glass window by Strongman of American Justice. That man hadn't had as many cuts as Jingshen must have. "Do you speak Cantonese?"

"No."

"You do not read it, either." Jingshen didn't make it a question.

"No."

"You have no *shungyu*."

"I don't know what that means."

"Reputation. Prestige. You might call it *cachet.*"

"Aren't we a walking thesaurus? Look, I've got a mission to fulfill, and you've delayed me long enough. I'm going to take my bow and walk out of here."

Jingshen stood. He wasn't as tall as Adrian, but his movements had a fluid grace that made Adrian nervous. "No, you are not."

So it would be a fight, then. Adrian had been in any number of scraps since he'd begun his career. Most guys didn't know anything about the rudiments of boxing, which he'd studied and practiced, and tended toward brawling instead. The problem with being trained in a specific style of fighting was that training tended to assume one's opponent followed a similar style. Adrian had learned quickly that although knowing how to fight was all well and good, what really mattered was knowing how to win a fight quickly. That was one reason he liked archery; he could win most fights before he ever had to get up close and personal with someone.

He raised his fists and took a step toward Jingshen. The other man twisted around, springing into the air, and kicked. The next thing Adrian knew he was lying on his back on the floor, gasping for breath. He coughed and rolled over, trying to get back onto his feet.

"Stay down, white man."

"No!" Still fighting to get air, Adrian struggled up and forward, lunging for Jingshen.

Jingshen slapped his charge aside and drove an elbow into the back of Adrian's head. He crashed to the floor again. "Stay. Down."

Adrian groaned and got to his hands and knees. He was close to the chair in which Jingshen had sat. He grabbed it by its legs and swung it around.

Jingshen caught the chair, pulled it from Adrian's hands as easily as if it had been an intentional handoff, and wound up sitting in it facing Adrian. When Adrian tried to follow up with another attack, Jingshen slapped his fist out of the way without even getting up from the chair. Suddenly his fist floated only a half inch from Adrian's nose. "Are you done?"

Adrian leaped back, and the fuzziness in his brain cleared. He realized Jingshen had thoroughly beaten him and probably could have killed him outright at any time. Instead, the Chinese man had held back. He lowered his head and his fists. "Yes, for now."

"Take your bow and go back to your people. Stay out of Chinatown."

Adrian went over to the corner where his gear was stashed. He shrugged his shoulders into the coat and slung the quiver and bow over his shoulder. He didn't even consider trying for a sneak attack after seeing the speed and ruthless efficiency Jingshen had used to defeat him. "Women have been kidnapped. Stolen from the streets. I followed a car here. I'm trying to save them."

"You can't," Jingshen said.

"Do you know where they are?" Adrian rounded upon the smaller man, careful to keep his intensity under control.

Jingshen looked away.

"You do know!" Adrian clenched his fists, aching to beat the information from Jingshen and knowing he couldn't. "Tell me. Tell me where to find them."

"It is not for you to help." Jingshen sounded miserable suddenly, and Adrian wondered what the man was holding back from him.

"Are you in cahoots with them? Are you defending the kidnappers? Because karate wizard or not, I will fight you until you tell me what I want to know."

Jingshen's mouth fell open. "Karate?" He paused, then laughed. "Oh. Oh, no. Not karate. Not this time." He sobered. "You should not have come here. The Tongs would see you cut to pieces."

"Not if I see them first. There's not a gangster alive that can outrun an arrow."

"You would kill them?"

"It's not my first choice. I don't want to start a war. I just want to save those poor prostitutes before they are . . ." Adrian stopped as he considered what the women already did for a living. "Well, it doesn't matter who they are. I'd try to save them regardless. So you need to stand aside and let me do my job. Keep knocking me down and I'll keep getting back up."

Jingshen nodded. "I believe you would. I . . . did not expect you to be an honorable man. There are not many here in this city, in this time."

"Do you know where to find these missing women?"

"Not for certain, but I have an idea."

"Will you tell me?"

"No . . ." Jingshen adjusted his hat to ride lower on his face, obscuring it in shadow. "But I will take you."

* * *

The sleet had turned to snow and it was starting to build up on the street. Patches of white reflected the harsh orange and red neon prevalent in the local signs, none of which Adrian could read. He'd begun to think Jingshen was right about him being in over his head, but that was part and parcel of being a hero.

Jingshen was far more than he seemed, and Adrian was burning with questions that he feared might forever go unanswered. The Chinese man had left his coat behind in favor of a tight black sweater. He had clips attached to the back of his suspenders and had placed a thirty-inch baton wrapped in black electrical tape into each clip. Clearly, the man's training extended beyond mere karate—or whatever it was. Maybe he could teach Adrian a thing or two about infighting. The more he pursued his justice crusade, the more he realized he couldn't always stand off at a distance and shoot arrows.

"Where are we going?" Adrian asked.

"To ask the right person the right questions." Jingshen paused under an awning and removed his hat to shake the water off it. His hair stuck out in all directions. Seeing his face clearly for the first time made Adrian stare. The man was younger than he'd expected, perhaps even younger than Adrian. His eyes, though . . . they had the shadows of a man haunted by the things he'd seen; the sort of things that aged a man far faster than time.

"Okay, I'm following your lead."

The two men crossed the street, passed through a narrow alley, and wound up at a door with pinyin characters scrawled in paint that had run before it dried. A sharp, vinegary smell emerged from building. Jingshen stopped at the door. "Expect to fight lackeys before we reach the man we must speak to. Try not to kill them. Restraint will reflect favorably upon you."

Adrian nodded, feeling his pulse quicken.

Jingshen rapped on the door in a quick, syncopated pattern. A moment later, a small panel in the door slid aside and a rough voice spoke Chinese from a darkened room beyond. Jingshen replied in kind. The man on the other side uttered a curt laugh and slammed the panel shut.

Jingshen moved in a blur and wedged one of his sticks into the panel. The man on the far side made a curious grunt which terminated suddenly as Jingshen shoved the stick into what Adrian imagined was the other man's face. He heard the sound of a body slumping to the floor behind the door.

"How are we supposed to get in now?" he asked.

"They will open the door." Jingshen levered the panel open with his stick and shouted something in Chinese through the hole.

Adrian heard indistinct shouting in response. He drew a ball-tip arrow from his quiver and nocked it to the string. Ball-tips could break bones and knock out opponents without killing them, and he suspected questioning would play an important part in the next phase of his mission. He stepped a few feet back from the door, giving himself enough time to fire an arrow and draw another before someone closed with him. "How many, do you think?"

"Not many. Five or six."

"Five or six," Adrian muttered. "That's *not many*?"

The shouting reached the door and Adrian heard the sound of locks being released. The door was thrown open.

The first man out clutched a decades-old Tommy gun. Before he could pull the trigger, Adrian loosed his arrow, catching the man in the center of his forehead. The blow might have cracked his skull but probably didn't kill him. Nevertheless, he went down as efficiently as if he'd been shot with something lethal.

The next two men fell under a barrage of blows from Jingshen's sticks. They whistled through the air, carving visible trails through the falling snow as they struck wrists, elbows, necks. Their weapons, a pair of broad-bladed knives and a revolver, clattered to the pavement.

Adrian shot another ball-tip beneath Jingshen's raised arms, catching the next man in his sternum. He gasped as the arrow knocked his wind out, then fell in the doorway. Jingshen glanced back at him and nodded. "Only four, it appears. Come, we'll go in and ask our questions."

Adrian kicked aside the fallen weapons so they wouldn't be in easy reach of anyone who awakened prematurely. He retrieved what arrows were still usable. "What is this place?"

"Hip Sing Tong."

"I don't know what that means." Adrian followed Jingshen into the building. The vinegar smell intensified and a cloying smoke drifted through the air.

"Heroin."

Adrian stopped in the middle of the hall. "This is a . . . an opium den?"

Jingshen snorted. "Opium is a drug for old men. Heroin is where young men make their dollars now."

"It's made here?"

"Made, packaged, distributed."

"And you've done nothing to stop it, even though you knew?"

Jingshen turned to face him. "What would you have me do, *bairen*? I am just one man."

"So am I."

"You will not destroy this place."

"Why not?" Adrian challenged. "Will you stop me? It's the right thing to do, and I think you know it. You're not as aloof as you pretend to be."

"Tonight, you are seeking your missing streetwalkers. Hsing Shou will know where they are."

"And he'll just tell us if we ask nicely and don't take a torch to his drugs?"

"Something like that."

A footstep down the hall made both men freeze in the darkness. Adrian's blood pounded in his ears and he reached for an arrow, barely daring to breathe.

Jingshen smashed his open palm into Adrian's chest, knocking him backward as the light and thunder of a machine gun filled the hallway. In the flickering flash from the barrel, Adrian saw Jingshen's body shudder as bullet after bullet smashed into him. "No!" Adrian cried. He yanked an arrow from the quiver, selecting it by the pattern of its fletching without having to look. He dragged the arrowhead against the hallway wall, igniting it like a strike-anywhere match. He raised the flaming arrow to his bow and sent it flying up the hall in barely a second. Instead of blowing out the flames at the tip, the wind of the arrow's passage dragged the fire along the shaft, which was coated with a flammable resin. The firebrand buried itself in the chest of the man with the machine gun. He fell back against the far wall, dropping his gun and staring in mute shock at the flaming arrow sticking out from his ribs.

"Jingshen!" Adrian knelt by the other man.

Jingshen grabbed his arm. "I am . . . fine. Give me a moment." He rolled onto his hands and knees and grunted. With a sound like gravel falling, bullets rained down from the Chinese man's torso to clatter on the floor. He coughed once and spat out a final bloody bullet.

"You . . . you're one of them! A parahuman."

"I don't know what I am." Jingshen stood. "But I do know that I hate being shot. It hurts." He looked up the hall where the gunman had died with the flaming arrow still burning against his chest. "That was unwise."

"I didn't have much time to think about it. For all I knew, you were dead." Adrian glared at Jingshen. "You could have told me you're bulletproof."

Angry voices sounded further down the hall, shouting in Chinese.

Jingshen shouted something back and the voices stopped.

"What did you say?"

"I said we are here to speak to Hsing Shou. If they allow us passage to do that, we will leave when we are finished."

"What if they don't?"

Jingshen nodded toward Adrian's quiver. "Then I hope you have enough arrows."

* * *

In cowboy boots with silver spurs, Hsing Shou looked like he'd stepped out of a dime store Western novel. A pistol rode in a Kansas loop on one hip, angled for a cross-body draw. His leather vest was fringed at the bottom and he peeked out from beneath a dusty bowler hat. He smirked at Jingshen and Adrian as they stood before him. He hadn't required them to surrender their weapons; clearly he felt protected well enough with the dozen men standing behind and to either side of him, armed to the teeth and muttering.

"Jingshen. You bring a foreigner here. Into my house. You kill my men. I am disappointed." Hsing Shou spoke in heavily accented but understandable English. He must have been doing so for Adrian's benefit, to make it clear he had nothing to hide. "I thought we had an understanding, you and I."

Adrian glanced sharply at Jingshen but the man's face was impassive. "We have nothing."

"Foreigner?" Adrian asked. "Last I checked, Chinatown is still in New York."

"You are a foreigner here, *bairen*. As far as you are concerned, you are in China now, and you are trespassing." Hsing Shou laughed. "I could kill you now and that would be the last anyone heard of Dr. Danger."

"I'm looking for some missing women. I tracked the car that took them here to Chinatown," Adrian said. "I'm betting you know where they are."

Jingshen sighed at Adrian's lack of diplomacy.

"We are not permitted to import our women," Hsing Shou said. "Therefore we must use yours."

One of Hsing Shou's men apparently translated what he said and several of them laughed.

"Prostitutes or not, they have dignity. They have the right not to be enslaved. Or raped. Now where are they?" Adrian clenched his fists, aching to put an arrow right into Hsing Shou's smug face.

"What makes you think you have any power here at all, *bairen*? One word from me and my men will kill you where you stand."

"They may kill him, but you cannot kill me," Jingshen said. "Better than you have tried and failed. I will keep coming until you are all dead and then I will find another Hip Sing man to tell me where the women are."

For a minute, nobody said anything. The tension made it feel like the entire room was vibrating. At last, Hsing Shou smiled and lowered his head. "Of course. *Tangrenjie Gui* has found his voice at last. We have always known this day was coming. Very well. Perhaps we can come to an . . . arrangement."

"What arrangement?" Adrian asked, suspicion making his voice hoarse.

"If I tell you where to find your white whores, you will take them and leave Chinatown. I never want you to set foot within its boundaries again, Dr. Danger. If you do so, your life is forfeit. You cannot hide behind *Tangrenjie Gui* forever. You will be hunted down and killed. Chinatown is mine, *bairen*. Those who enter it live or die at my decree." Hsing Shou grinned. "Decide quickly. My dogs are anxious to be let out to play."

Adrian glanced at Jingshen, but his face was an impassive mask beneath the shadow of his hat brim. "Yes, I can live with that."

Hsing Shou motioned to one of his men, who bent down and listened to his boss whisper to him. The man tucked his pistol into his waistband and left out the back of the room. "Very well. I have sent instructions ahead to have the women released and you will be led to a place where you can retrieve them." He spread his hands in mocking generosity. "Go in peace, my friends."

A gaunt man with a thin mustache and a large overcoat stepped forward, a pistol clutched in one eager hand. He spoke in curt Chinese and Jingshen responded with a single syllable.

"We are to follow him," Jingshen said softly.

"They're going to kill us," Adrian muttered.

"They will try."

"I'm not bulletproof."

"Then don't get shot." Jingshen's mouth twitched in a momentary half-smile. Or perhaps it had just been a trick of the light as the men went down the hallway.

* * *

Hsing Shou had left Jingshen his sticks and Adrian his bow and arrows. Adrian wondered if it was to lull them into a false sense of security or to make their approaching deaths seem somehow more honorable. Regardless, he was grateful for the weight of his quiver against his back. He only wished it were heavier with arrows. Hsing Shou seemed like the kind of man who had resources to waste on excess, and that likely extended to the hit squad awaiting them in their eventual destination.

The thin man led them to a doorway into a courtyard that stank of the garbage piled around the edges, highlighted by a growing white blanket of snow. He pointed to a door across from them.

Adrian and Jingshen stepped out into the new fallen snow, making dark tracks as their boots sank into the black mud below. "They must think we are fools to go along with this," Jingshen muttered.

"Wiser men than us would have stayed home tonight, warm and dry."

"And yet here we are, neither warm nor dry."

"Two fools," Adrian agreed. "They'll take us when we reach the middle."

"Dr. Danger!" Hsing Shou's voice echoed across the courtyard from somewhere behind them. "I am almost ashamed to kill a fool such as you. Almost." He laughed and Adrian *moved*.

He spun around in a crouch, already setting a ball-tip arrow to string as an object the size of a baseball arced toward them through the snow. Adrian's vision narrowed to a tunnel, making a straight line between the tip of his arrow and the incoming grenade. He loosed his arrow and it sped straight and true, catching the grenade dead center. The heavy ball-tip deflected the explosive away from its intended course to explode against the wall of Hsing Shou's heroin production facility. Shrapnel peppered him but his coat absorbed the worst of it. Part of the wall behind him collapsed and screams of pain emerged from behind it.

Guns erupted around them and Adrian ran slipping and sliding through the snow to crash into a pile of garbage against a wall. He saw a muzzle flash in a second floor window and a bullet creased his side, stinging like he'd been attacked by a vicious cat. He shot an arrow into that window and a man tumbled out, clutching helplessly at the shaft coming out of his throat.

Jingshen seemed to be everywhere at once. His sticks flashed through the snow and he leaped into the path of oncoming bullets like a tiger charging at a spear to slay the hunter holding it. Adrian rolled aside as bullets from a Tommy gun on full auto chewed into the mud. A frog-crotch arrow lanced out and sliced the support spar of an awning. It collapsed onto the gunmen beneath and they cursed and shouted in Chinese as they tried to extricate themselves. Jingshen was on them in a moment, his sticks whistling and beating a rapid Gene Krupa tattoo on the indistinct shapes beneath the canvas.

Fire burned through Adrian's leg as a bullet lodged in the meaty part of his thigh and he lost his balance. He still shot an arrow through the chest of the man who'd fired at him and pinned him to the wall like a butterfly in a display case. Flames licked at the side of the heroin building. Adrian suspected it might burn up completely before the nearest fire department managed to get through the storm to help.

Jingshen hauled him to his feet. "I told you not to get shot," he chided, pummeling a man who charged at them with a sword.

With no time to reach an arrow, Adrian used his bow like a staff to deflect the blow of another man with a long knife. The blade caught on the wood and stuck for a moment, allowing Adrian to drive a solid right into the man's face, breaking teeth and bone. Behind him, Jingshen fought in a flurry of hand to hand, kicking and swinging his sticks. More men charged in, armed with knives and hatchets. Adrian ducked beneath a hatchet blow and Jingshen's foot lanced over his head, catching the assailant on the side of his jaw and sending him spinning away.

Adrian grabbed an arrow from his quiver and pounded it down into the foot of a knife-wielder, who howled in sudden agony. He grabbed the man and spun him into another hatchet-man and both went down. Jingshen drove his sticks down tip first into the backs of each man's neck with sounds like gunshots.

And just like that, the battle was ended. Adrian and Jingshen stared at each other, sides heaving in exhaustion. Jingshen looked like he'd absorbed an armada's worth of bullets. The bits of lead rained down from him as his body rejected them. "Are you . . . all right?" Adrian gasped, suddenly feeling the pain from his wounds.

"I told you . . . not to . . . get shot." Jingshen sounded amused, finding a spark of joy despite the carnage around them. "Now what?"

One of the men Adrian had shot groaned, the arrow still sticking from a spot just to the left of his aorta. Only by the grace of a half inch was he still alive to feel the pain the arrow had inflicted.

"You missed," Jinshen said.

Adrian snorted. "I'd like to say I winged him on purpose, but that would be a lie. Hey . . ." He addressed the wounded man lying on the snow. "You speak English?"

Jingshen asked him a question in Chinese. The man coughed out a weak response. "He does not speak English. I will translate for you until he dies. He does not have long."

"Ask him where the women are." Adrian fervently hoped they hadn't been in the building behind him, now engulfed in flames. He could hear sirens in the distance as someone must have finally gotten through to a fire brigade.

Jingshen listened to the man's response, interspersed with coughing jags and bloody foam leaking from his mouth. "There," he said at last, pointing across the courtyard. "That is the brothel."

"Is it defended?"

"Not as well as it would have been before this." Jingshen motioned to the courtyard.

"Tell them we're coming in, and we'll destroy anyone who gets in our way." Adrian looked down at the man with the arrow in his chest, realized he'd died, and stood. His fingers ached from the cold, but not so much he couldn't put one of his few remaining arrows to the string.

Jingshen took his sticks in both hands once more and issued his warning as they approached the door at the far end of the courtyard. It opened as they reached it and both men tensed. Instead of the attack they expected, an old man made himself visible in the doorway and then held it open for them. He bowed his head and whispered something in Chinese. "He says nobody inside will harm us. He hopes we will extend the same courtesy," Jingshen said.

"Do you believe him?"

"I do."

They entered the narrow hallway, Jingshen taking the lead and keeping one shoulder to the wall so Adrian had a clear shot past him if needed. A few men stepped to the doorways of the tiny rooms so they could be seen and bowed their heads as the first man had. "Why are they doing this?"

"They do not wish to offend or anger us. They are afraid of us."

"They should be." After the combat in the courtyard, Adrian was finding it difficult to keep his temper up when he was confronted over and over by men not wishing to fight. "Ask them where the women are, and tell them we're taking them and leaving."

"They are in the room at the end of the hall," Jingshen said after a brief conversation with one of the other men. "They are . . . they have been given heroin to make them . . . docile."

One of the men looked up from his position of contrition and said something directly to Adrian in Chinese. His expression was haunted and Adrian couldn't even guess as to what he'd said. "Well?" he asked Jingshen.

"He asks you not to take their livelihood away. He says Hsing Shou will punish them."

There was the anger Adrian had been struggling to maintain. He felt his pulse pounding as the enormity of what he'd been asked struck him full force. These men . . . these inhumane monsters . . . they'd rather see women drugged up and abused until death rather than look for new employment. "Get out," Adrian said in a thick, rage-choked voice.

"What?" Jingshen asked.

"Tell them to get out. All of them. Anyone left inside this building is going to die in it after I get the women out of here."

Jingshen raised his head enough that Adrian could see the faint surprise on his face. He studied Adrian for a moment, perhaps to determine whether he was serious. Then he relayed Adrian's warning to the men in the hall. They all left their rooms and filed out, moving with a nervous haste, as if Adrian's fury pushed them out like rowboats ahead of a wave.

Adrian and Jingshen found six women, five Caucasian and one Chinese, sprawled on cots in a roach-infested room that stank of vomit and feces. All the women were dirty and stank of sweat and abuse except for the one whom Adrian had seen kidnapped. Half were naked or mostly naked while the others wore stained cotton shifts. They had needle marks on their arms and legs, and were so dead to their surroundings that they didn't even react when roaches ran across their bare flesh.

"Help me get them out of here, for God's sake!" Adrian's voice was rough and he had to clench his teeth to keep from breaking down into tears at the sight of such human misery. It was the first time in his experience as a costumed hero where he'd encountered such depravity. He hoped it would be the last time, but feared it would only get worse as he kept up his crusade.

The Chinese woman and one of the Americans were so thin they were looked like bags of loose bones wrapped in sore-covered skin. Adrian and Jingshen each lifted one into their arms and went out the same side door the men had left through. The pain from his wounds made Adrian wince with every step and he wished he had the ability to heal as Jingshen did. "There," Adrian said, nodding at a delivery van with a faded picture of a chicken on the side. "We'll put them all in the back. Make them comfortable, and I'll take them to the hospital."

Jingshen wrenched open the van's rear door with one of his sticks. Chicken droppings stained the van's floorboards, but a tarpaulin was rolled up beside one of the fender wells. They spread it out, covering the worst of the mess. "I will bring out the others," Jingshen said. "Stay here, make sure no harm comes to them. Can you start the motor?"

Adrian nodded. He'd hot-wired cars before. He would have to come back for his own car later . . . assuming it didn't get stolen in the meantime.

It took him a few long minutes to find the right wires beneath the van's cracked dashboard. As Jingshen brought out the last woman, he managed to get the engine to crank over and shudder to life amid a cloud of smoke. Jingshen shut the van's door. Adrian engaged the emergency brake and got out, leaving the engine running. He extended his hand to the Chinese man. "Thank you," he said. "I couldn't have done this without you."

"You are a good man," Jingshen said. "It was my honor to help. Be a better fighter, though. You cannot always shoot arrows."

"Maybe you could teach me some fundamentals."

"Perhaps." Jingshen paused. "Will you stay away from Chinatown?"

"Perhaps," Adrian replied. "Seems like you could do a fine job protecting this area yourself. Maybe I'll only come by if you need help. Somehow, I don't think you'll need much." He paused. "Oh, there is one more thing." He reached into the van and withdrew his bow and a single arrow with a heavy, cylindrical tip.

"What will you do?"

"Shoot an arrow." Adrian aimed the arrow at the door from which they had emerged and let it fly. The arrow, packed from tip to tail with gelignite, pierced the darkness. A moment later, a brilliant, hot explosion rent the air as the explosive erupted. The front half of the building blew apart into flaming splinters.

Jingshen's eyes were as wide as the full moon as he stared at the devastation Adrian had wrought, and then turned his eyes to Adrian.

Adrian gave him a grim smile.

Jingshen smiled back. "Perhaps shooting one arrow is not so bad. Farewell, Dr. Danger."

"Make it Adrian. You ever need me, leave a message at Frank's on Second Avenue. They know how to reach me."

"What does *Adrian* mean?"

"It means *from Adria*. Not very interesting. What does *Jingshen* mean?"

"Spirit. Like one's essence."

"Spirit also means *ghost*. The Chinatown Ghost has a nice, heroic ring to it."

"Perhaps." Jingshen shook Adrian's hand and then faded into the shadows.

Adrian put the van into gear and drove far faster than he should have toward the hospital, precious cargo in the back. He smiled to himself, in spite of his cold, wet clothes. In spite of the aching bullet wound. In spite of the stench the chickens had left behind. He didn't always win when he put on the mask . . . but sometimes he did.

ARROWHEADS

There were so many doors open for me then. I was young, rich, smart, good-looking, and I lived in New York City—the greatest place anyone who was anyone should live. I could have done anything I wanted to.

What I chose to do was put on a mask and fight crime with American Justice.

-Adrian Crowley aka Dr. Danger, *Dangerous: The Autobiography of Dr. Danger,* 1964

August, 1949
New York City, New York

Adrian Crowley crouched in the shadows of the rooftop overlooking the warehouse. He was a tall man, cresting six feet, with an athlete's build honed from thousands of hours on his private archery range. The tool of his trade rested across his back, a curved piece of yew that hung from custom clips on the back of his quiver.

His costume was piratical in nature; flowing white cotton shirt, dark blue pants tucked into folded-down boots, a dark red sash and a matching kerchief tied around his head, incorporating into it a mask that hid his eyes.

He called himself Dr. Danger; he just liked the sound of it.

He fiddled with a small Geiger counter that he'd removed from a pouch on the side of his quiver. Tiny clicks emerged from it at an elevated rate. He frowned behind his mask and adjusted the dials, but it continued to report that radiation levels were significantly higher than they should have been around the warehouse. It looked like the information from his source was correct. He'd checked the warehouse from three different angles and each time the Geiger counter clicked like a tap-dancing flea circus.

The sound of an engine made him shrink back into the shadows. He replaced the counter into his pouch and watched over the edge of the adjacent building. A long, low Hudson slid around the corner, lights off, engine rumbling just above an idle. Two guys got out of the back seat, wearing trench coats and fedoras. Moonlight glinted off the Thompson submachine guns each man held. They looked around, furtive and suspicious, daring anyone to challenge their superior firepower. Then, apparently satisfied, one of them raised an electric torch and flashed it down the alleyway in three quick bursts.

Headlights appeared around the corner and a step-van rolled into the alley, its badly-tuned engine raising a cloud of black smoke. The other man walked past the front of the Hudson to the delivery door of the warehouse and rapped on it with the butt of the gun in a short, syncopated pattern.

In a moment, light streamed into the alley as the door raised against the squeaky protest of poorly lubricated bearings. The Hudson glided into the well-lit interior of the warehouse, followed by the belching van. Adrian watched as the door was lowered, leaving the alley once again bathed in darkness. He hadn't realized until the door opened that the windows of the warehouse had been either covered or painted. *Stupid and careless*, he thought to himself. *Never assume anything.* He'd been playing at superhero for almost a year and still felt like a wet-behind-the-ears novice. It had been a lark, the diversion of a bored rich boy who'd inherited his wealth from war profiteering, who'd been slowly dying of terminal boredom until discovering his uncanny knack for archery.

Who'd decided to become a superhero, like those of American Justice. Unlike them, he didn't have amazing parahuman abilities to bring foes to justice. But they didn't have his archery skills, or his arsenal of special arrows.

With a seasoned eye for gauging distances, he estimated how far away the warehouse was from his vantage point. Alleys in the industrial part of town were deceptively wide; much more so than they looked. To misjudge distance here was to invite a tumble to the pavement or worse. With enough room for the Hudson to have opened both doors and the men to walk past them, he figured it was ten feet across.

Unfortunately the two sentries remained below, slouching in the alley and smoking unfiltered cigarettes. They would have to be dealt with before he could safely leap across the gap, or else they would raise the alarm. He drew one of the ball-tipped arrows, finding it by the shape of the fletching. He machined the special tips on a lathe in his workshop. Instead of a sharp point, this particular type of trick arrow was tipped with a blunt steel bearing the size of a golf ball. They were heavy and ungainly projectiles, and not very accurate over distance. On the other hand, they were useful for knocking opponents down and out, instead of killing them outright.

Adrian had never killed a man, and didn't intend to start. The political climate following World War II had been mostly permissive toward vigilantes, especially with the formation of American Justice by parahuman veterans of the War. South of the old Mason-Dixon line, though, vigilantes were lynching colored folks and burning down churches. Because of that, someone was going to make it illegal sooner or later. Adrian hoped to stave off that time as long as possible, and leaving the bad guys alive and hurt but contrite looked pretty good to the general public.

And a good public image was imperative to a guy who dressed up like a pirate with a bow and lurked around the rooftops of New York City.

He lifted the bow off its clips, its familiar weight comforting in its presence. He measured the distance to the men below at about a two-thirds pull. A ball-tip could knock a man out with a nasty bump on the head, or it could crack his skull. It was a fine line, but he'd spent many hours perfecting his techniques. He took careful aim at the first man's head, using the glowing tip of his cigarette as a reference point.

He released the first arrow. In a blurred economy of motion, he drew a second ball-tip just as the first one struck. As the man dropped like a rag doll, Adrian pulled back on the string a second time. The other sentry was just starting to react to the sudden fall of his partner when he was likewise struck, the impact knocking his hat off into a puddle.

The only sounds from the entire encounter had been the thuds of the ball-tips striking scalps, the crumpling sounds of the men falling, and the clink as the deflected ball-tips bounced to the pavement. Adrian listened intently for a few minutes, making sure that no suspicions had been raised. Eventually, satisfied that he could safely cross the intervening distance to his target warehouse, he took a few running steps and leaped across the alley. Bow in hand, he advanced across the warehouse roof, looking for a way into the building itself. There was a sudden puff of breeze that ruffled the sleeves of his shirt. He stopped, sensing danger.

A long blade slid across his throat.

"Don't move, archer, and lose the bow." Breath redolent with garlic washed past Adrian's face.

"Easy there, chief. You'll get no trouble from me." Adrian relaxed himself, preparing to unleash a flurry of kicks upon his attacker. He dropped the bow carefully, glancing down at the blade across his neck. There was something odd about its shape and position. The arm holding the blade was far too short, and even in the shadows, it was plain that the blade was the length of a sword. With a start, he realized that the man was not holding the blade, but that it replaced his arm altogether.

There was only one man Adrian knew about that had a sword for an arm. "Flicker, I'm one of the *good guys*. We're on the same side."

"Let him go, John," came a voice from somewhere above them. Adrian looked up and saw a man hovering casually in the air, ten feet above them. He knew it was Strongman, of course, but it was still quite a shock to see him flying unsupported. Strongman wore a tight-fitting bronze-colored reflective body suit with red accents, cape, and hood. He'd once explained in an interview that the bright colors made him a better target, and since he was bulletproof, he'd rather that the bad guys shot at him than at his teammates.

The blade was removed from Adrian's throat—not by it being pulled away, but by suddenly vanishing in a puff of air. Flicker reappeared several feet away. He wore a dark body suit, made out of a material that trapped the light. Where Strongman was bright, Flicker was darkness incarnate. Even the blade that extended from the stump of his upper arm was made out of non-reflecting Damascus steel. His face was also masked.

Adrian stooped down to pick up his bow, checking it for damage. He'd built it to be as hardy as possible, because one never knew when a bow would need to be used as a club in close quarters, but it was always good to check.

"You're gonna believe him just like that?" Flicker grumbled behind his mask.

"Perhaps," said Strongman as he dropped to the ground as gently as if he'd been lowered on a crane. "But before you kill him, I'd like to find out more about him." He turned his attention to Adrian. "We've read about you in the papers. It's a pleasure to finally meet you."

"You always make your introductions like this?"

"Please forgive John," said Strongman. "He's never been especially trusting."

Flicker swung his sword blade back and forth. "Yeah, well, he's wearing a mask, isn't he? He's obviously got somethin' to hide!"

"So do we," said Strongman.

"Nobody wants to look at radiation scars, Jim. The pirate over there looks like he hasn't even ever cut himself shaving."

"The mask is to protect my identity." Adrian felt sheepish. He'd thought that his first meeting with American Justice would be more . . . *heroic*. "Unlike the two of you, I have a private life that I'd rather not complicate with my nighttime activities."

"He's got a point there, John," came a new, feminine voice. Adrian looked and saw the other three members of American Justice standing by the edge of the warehouse roof. The three newcomers were veterans of the war, like Flicker and Strongman, but they had fought against the Japanese in the Pacific.

Colt, the woman who had spoken, was pretty behind her short haircut and pilot's goggles. She wore a dark red leather jacket over a stylized ballet leotard and tights. Her heavy black jump boots had thick, knobby soles, and a pair of horseshoes were incongruously slung at her waist. Adrian knew that she could run as fast as a speeding car and her other reactions were similarly accelerated.

Beside Colt was Flashpoint, the colored man. He could generate powerfully bright bursts of light to blind and confuse opponents. He wore goggles like Colt, but his were smoked. His costume was a set of light gray coveralls with numerous pouches affixed to it. A pair of automatic pistols was strapped to his waist in well-oiled leather holsters.

At their feet sat a wolf, tongue lolling out past razor-sharp teeth. The wolf was called Gray, and was a real-life werewolf. Adrian couldn't remember for sure, but he thought that the alter ego of Gray was an Indian from one of the southern reservations.

"All right, we'll concede your identity . . . for now," said Strongman. "What are you doing here tonight, Dr. Danger?"

"Working on a tip," said Adrian. "Someone's buying uranium, and there's a group selling it downstairs in this building."

Colt gasped and glanced toward Strongman. Adrian was sure that either he had shocked her with his revelation, or confirmed a suspicion.

"And you were going to just bust in and start shooting arrows at them?" Flicker sounded disgusted.

"Something like that," said Adrian. "Last I checked, smuggling was still illegal. I don't like the idea of somebody else building an atomic bomb. It's bad enough that the Russians have one now."

"So you've been working the seller's angle?" Strongman asked him.

Adrian nodded. "It's a branch of the Mob. I don't know where they got the uranium . . ."

"Nevada," said Colt.

"We've been working on this case for a few months now," said Strongman. "But from the buyer's angle. We know who's been trying to obtain the ore, and we think we know why. We just found out the transaction is going to happen here, tonight."

"Hell, Jim, why don't you tell him everything?" Flicker scraped the point of the sword across the warehouse roof.

"You know what your problem is, Stills? You don't trust anybody." Flashpoint spoke for the first time, his voice deep and mellow like a French horn.

"That's right, I don't. And it's kept me alive this long!" Flicker teleported suddenly right in front of Flashpoint, who started but refrained from further provocation.

"That's enough, John. If we're going to fight amongst ourselves, we might as well let the Nazis win." Strongman glided in between the two of them, gently pushing Flicker away from the black man.

"Nazis?" Adrian asked. "I thought that show was over a few years ago."

"The buyers are a group of Nazi officers that escaped prosecution and relocated to South America. Specifically, Brazil," said Strongman. "I don't think I have to tell you why they're purchasing uranium."

"To build an atomic bomb," said Adrian, his voice grim. "So they can use it on us."

"Or a reactor," said Flashpoint.

"What's a *reactor?*" The term was unfamiliar to Adrian.

"It's a device that creates power through a controlled atomic reaction. We encountered a prototype in Germany. It's why we wear masks." Strongman's voice took on a note of sadness.

"All right. So we've got the Mob selling uranium to the Nazis. Sounds tailor-made for people like us." Adrian twanged his bowstring for emphasis.

"Us, maybe." Flicker's voice took on a nastier quality than it had before, something Adrian wouldn't have believed possible. "Nobody said nothin' about you."

Strongman sighed. "Well I'm saying it now, or do I have to make it an order, Corporal?"

"Yeah, yeah, I know," grunted the black-garbed man.

"They brought a truck in a few minutes ago," said Adrian. "The whole building's already reading hot on my counter. If they're going to do the deal tonight, it's probably going down soon, if not now. Any idea how the Nazis are going to move out the ore?"

"I'm sure they'll use a boat. They just need time to load it and make their getaway." Colt was quivering like her namesake, anticipating battle.

"All right then, what's the plan and how can I help?" Adrian asked.

"He's the tactician," Strongman pointed to Flashpoint.

"Three-pronged attack," said the colored man. "Strongman goes in through the roof. His objective is to draw fire and cause mayhem. Flicker 'ports in and handles outlying sentries. Colt and Gray work the guys on the floor, herding them away from the ore towards me, where I can incapacitate them. You . . ." He pointed to Adrian. "Hang around in the rafters and take opportunity shots. Make sure nobody gets away with any ore. Our primary objective is to keep the ore from leaving the warehouse, not to pursue the bad guys. Questions?"

Adrian glanced around at the others. They seemed confident in the plan, apparently trusting Flashpoint's ability to formulate strategies.

"Move out," said Strongman. "John, you and Dr. Danger are with me. The rest of you have two minutes to get to your positions, then we enter the building." Colt, Flashpoint, and the wolf slipped away, heading down the fire escape toward the alley below.

"How are you going to go through the roof?" Adrian asked Strongman.

"Just smash through it, I suppose. It can't be that sturdy. It's just a big box. Why?"

Adrian pulled an explosive arrow from his quiver, putting it to the string. "This is loaded with gelignite. The impact on the head will detonate it. It ought to weaken the roof considerably."

"A grenade, huh? Maybe you ain't so bad after all." Flicker's eyes glinted behind his mask. "Where do you buy 'em?"

"Make them myself," said Adrian. "Where do you want it, Strongman?"

The bronze-costumed man flew into the air, drifting toward the center of the warehouse roof. "Think you can hit right here?"

Adrian smiled. "Give me a ten second countdown."

Strongman pulled back his sleeve and checked a slim wristwatch. "Okay. Ten . . . nine . . . eight . . ." Strongman rose higher into the air, inverting himself in preparation for smashing through the warehouse roof.

At four seconds, Adrian released the arrow. It arced up into the night sky. Four seconds later, it dropped and struck the precise spot that Strongman had marked. The explosive charge shook the roof of the building and a burst of flame and smoke rent the sky.

Strongman lunged downward, heedless of the fiery cloud of the explosion, hitting the roof like a missile. The rooftop, overstressed and weakened by the gelignite arrow, split open like an overripe fruit, sending a cloud of dust and debris high into the sky. Flicker chuckled behind his mask. "Nicely done, Doc. That'll get their attention for sure." He teleported to the edge of the gaping hole, looking inside for his first target, then gave a whoop of pure joy and vanished.

Adrian was already running for the edge of the hole as he heard gunfire erupt inside the building. Inside the base of his quiver was a coiled silk rope and a grappling hook. Spying a metal pole protruding from the roof, he looped the hook around it and lowered himself into the hole.

Below him, he saw Colt and Gray running amid a large group of men, all armed, who were trying unsuccessfully to hit any of the heroes. There was no sign of Flicker or Flashpoint, but Strongman had just picked up a shipping crate and was preparing to hurl it at a group of men peppering him with their Tommy guns. Glancing around, Adrian saw a wide horizontal beam that should fit his needs. He kicked his legs, swinging on the rope, hoping that it wouldn't tear on the jagged edges of the ripped roof.

As Strongman threw the heavy shipping crate, sending the men flying, Adrian released the rope and flew across the intervening space to catch himself on the beam. In a moment he had clambered up to straddle it. He unlimbered his bow again, seeing a bright flash like a magnesium flare out of the corner of his vision. Blinking away the spots, he began looking for opportune targets.

The first arrow he fired was a ball-tip at a man carrying one of the ugly-but-efficient German submachine guns. The man was stitching bullets across the floor toward Gray, who was mauling another gunman's hand. The ball-tip smashed into the man's wrist, shattering it and causing him to drop the gun. He let out a yell audible even over the sounds of guns and combat. A second ball-tip silenced him, catching him across the temple.

Colt dashed underneath him, holding her horseshoes like they were boxing gloves. A 60-MPH punch sent a gunman flying in an explosion of tooth fragments. Adrian sent a shower of arrows in her wake, now using pointed arrows to pierce the arms and legs of the gunmen. A new, heavy chatter filled the air as two men raised an air-cooled belt-fed machine gun from the trunk of the Hudson and fired at Strongman. The heavy caliber bullets didn't penetrate his flesh, but their kinetic impacts knocked him into a support beam for the warehouse. Already overstressed by the weakened roof, the beam buckled and Adrian's perch bent almost ninety degrees, dropping him toward the floor.

He knew he was going to land badly. The floor below was covered with splintered shipping crates and debris from Strongman's actions. He tried to twist himself in midair, the way he'd been taught by a French acrobat. A dark red blur smashed into him as he fell, the impact knocking him flying laterally to smash into a stack of cardboard boxes. The empty boxes absorbed much of the force of his landing. He shook his head to clear it as he realized that Colt was lying on top of him. She had deflected his fall into the boxes. She was breathing heavily, her face flushed. Their eyes locked and in that moment, Adrian was hooked.

Her hand, trembling slightly, brushed against his cheek and the edge of his mask, as if she would gently lift it away from his face. Thoughts of preserving his identity were far away in Adrian's mind, and it felt like time itself had ground to a halt.

The feeling only lasted for a fraction of a second, though, because a stream of fifty-caliber bullets tore through the boxes. Adrian jumped one way and Colt the other to get clear. He spotted his bow where it had fallen and dove for it, yanking one of the Japanese frog-crotch arrows from his quiver. The man firing the machine gun by the Hudson had a terrible grin on his face as he swept the barrel this way and that, driving Strongman back into the warehouse walls. In one smooth, sweeping motion, Adrian grasped his bow, drew the arrow back, and let fly.

The forked arrow sliced neatly through the belt feed of the machine gun and in a moment the thunderous fire halted. That gave Gray and Flashpoint an opening. The wolf leaped across the Hudson, his claws scrabbling on the shiny black paint, and came down hard on the man who'd been feeding the chain to the machine gun. The man's scream turned into a gurgle as Gray clamped his jaws down on the man's throat, tearing it out as neatly as a sculptor removing a lump of clay. The man who'd been firing the gun staggered as a dark third eye appeared in the center of his forehead. He crumpled to the floor. Beyond him, Flashpoint lowered one of his smoking pistols and winked at Adrian.

For a brief moment, all gunfire in the warehouse stopped and Adrian thought that perhaps they'd won. Suddenly four figures in gray overcoats and helmets rushed in from the dockside entrance. Almost in unison, they each tossed a handled grenade in a carefully-planned dispersal pattern. Two of them impacted right where Strongman was digging his way out from under a collapsed wall. The resulting explosion demolished the remains of that corner of the warehouse, burying him under several tons of debris.

The four newcomers raised their rifles, advancing into the warehouse, which was starting to burn from the various detonations. A black blur appeared among them, swinging a bloodstained sword. A surprised head parted from its shoulders in a spray of blood. The other three reacted with impressive speed, firing toward the teleport. Adrian thought he saw Flicker stagger even as he teleported away.

Flashpoint popped off three flashes in rapid succession, bringing his pistols to bear on the three remaining overcoats. Gray yelped as a burning crate exploded, scattering fiery splinters across his coat. Even though he had to be seeing nothing but spots from Flashpoint's powers, one of the men snapped his rifle around and fired at the sound of the wolf.

Adrian, realizing at last that this engagement would require him to cross the line he'd set for himself, drew a broad-tipped hunting arrow and put it through the throat of one of the three men. The remaining two fired back, taking cover behind a forklift.

Colt was frantically trying to pull flaming debris away from the pile that had trapped Strongman. Even though he couldn't be hurt by the crushing weight, he could still be burned or suffocated. She was moving faster than she ever had before.

"Danger, help Gray!" Flashpoint called as he crouched behind a packing case and reloaded his pistols.

Adrian looked around and saw the wolf was pulling Flicker across the floor by his good arm, a trail of blood streaks in his wake. He lunged for the wounded man, helping to get him behind some cover just as the two overcoats opened up again.

"Who the hell are those guys?" Adrian shouted over the din.

"SS," coughed Flicker, pulling his mask off. Adrian started with revulsion, realizing why the man wore a mask. His face was terribly scarred, as if he'd been burned. Blood trickled from a corner of his mouth. "Got a . . . real good look . . . at the guy I cut."

"SS?"

"Yeah . . . *Schutzstaffel* . . . I really hate . . . those assholes." Flicker grimaced from the pain of his wounds. He'd been shot in the torso and abdomen. "Can't feel . . . my legs."

Colt appeared beside them, her costume blackened and smoke still rising from it in places. "I can't get him out! I can't even tell if he's alive under there!"

More gunfire came from the SS troopers, providing cover for four other men to grab a pair of heavy strongboxes and head for the dockside entrance. The entire front wall of the warehouse was burning.

"That's the uranium!" Flashpoint shouted.

A voice outside the warehouse urged the men to hurry in German.

"They've got to have a boat," said Adrian. "If they get to it, we'll never stop them. We need a diversion so we can get past those troopers!"

Flicker coughed, spattering blood flecks. "I can . . . still do that . . ."

"No!" cried Colt as the teleport vanished.

He reappeared in midair, several feet over the *Schutzstaffel* who were firing from behind the forklift. He tumbled down on top of them like a giant rag doll, swinging his sword at them as he fell.

Adrian was already up and running, reaching for another hunting tip. Gray was even faster, closing on the men carrying the strongboxes. Behind them, Flashpoint used his powers again to try and blind anyone trying to draw a bead on them.

The two SS troopers made short work of Flicker. They raised their rifles again, preparing to fire at Adrian and Gray. Suddenly Colt whipped past from behind them. As she dashed past Adrian she hung something on the arrow he was about to release.

Arming pins.

The troopers blew up.

A furry gray body staggered away from the explosion to collapse on the warehouse floor. The wolf transformed partway into a man but then froze before completion. A pool of blood spread out beneath him. "Gray!" cried Colt. "I didn't see him there!"

"He's gone," said Adrian. "I'm sorry."

"No time for that now," said Flashpoint. "Get after the uranium. Don't wait for me." Adrian realized that the colored man had been shot and was holding a bloody rag against his leg.

Adrian wanted to say something, but had no idea what. At first, he thought it was his ears ringing from the explosion, but then he was certain that he heard the sound of an engine from the dock. He ran out of the burning warehouse and saw a motorboat pulling away from the dock with six men on board. He ran to the edge of the dock and released his arrow. A man on the boat tumbled into the water and didn't surface again.

Adrian drew back, fired, and sent another Nazi off to sleep with the fishes. Then he lowered his bow before firing any more arrows. "Out of range," he said to Colt as she ran up beside him. Tears ran down her cheeks.

"Only temporarily," said Colt. She pointed to where a small motor launch was moored. In a blur of motion she had the boat untied. Adrian slid into the seat behind the wheel. He thumbed the starter as Colt jumped into the other seat. The engine coughed twice, then rumbled to life. Adrian thrust the throttle all the way forward and locked it into place. The powerful motor roared and the boat's prow lifted out of the water as it accelerated away from the dock.

Even though it was late at night, there were still enough lights along the docks reflecting in the water that Adrian could see the path carved by the other boat. "Where do you think they're going?" He shouted over the din of the boat's engine.

"They've got to have a bigger ship out there somewhere. Something that will get them back to Brazil."

An idea occurred to Adrian. "Take the wheel a moment." Colt slipped in front of him, allowing him to pick up his bow. He reached into his quiver for one of his experimental arrows. He always carried three or four of them, different projects he was developing.

The arrow he drew forth had a pair of strange bulging packages wrapped around the shaft. He dragged the tip of the arrow along the boat's gunwale, igniting the phosphorous powder that in turn touched off the fuse. Before the fuse burned down to the flare, he pulled the bowstring back to his cheek and shot the arrow high into the night sky.

The flare package lit as the arrow ascended, burning magnesium powder to make a bright, white light. So far so good, thought Adrian. As the arrow reached the zenith of its arc, the secondary fuse burned through and the fireproof chute deployed itself. The flare arrow wafted down in the sea breeze, dropping like a star falling in slow motion.

"Nice," said Colt. "What else have you got stashed in that quiver?"

"I wasn't entirely sure that would work," Adrian said. Ahead, he could see the other speedboat heading for a tall, dark pillar.

Colt took one of her hands off the boat's wheel and pushed her pilot's goggles up onto her forehead. She squinted into the distance at the other boat's destination. "What is that?"

"Buoy?"

Colt shook her head. "No light on it."

The other boat slowed and pulled alongside the pillar. The water around it began to bubble and foam as it rose. A narrow, dark hull popped onto the surface, water draining away through dark openings.

A U-boat.

As the men on the other boat began to climb aboard the U-boat's deck, hauling the uranium-filled strongboxes with them, other men flowed out of what Adrian now realized was the conning tower. Some of them assisted the unloading of the boat, while the others unlocked the deck gun and swung it around toward them.

Colt spun the wheel hard and the boat heaved around a tight corner, nearly swamping itself as the gunners opened up. Adrian nearly fell overboard from the maneuver, only just managing to catch a tie bar. Heavy shells blasted fountains of water into the air, barely missing their boat.

"I'm not really equipped to take on a submarine." Adrian struggled back to the front of the boat. "What's the plan?"

"Plan?" Colt flashed him a brilliant smile. "You're the Eagle Scout. I'm just the cabbie." She whipped the boat around in another tight turn to avoid a trail of shell impacts.

"Okay, let me think for a second."

"No pressure, Doc. They're only shooting at us."

Adrian drew another explosive-tipped arrow from the quiver, which was now the lightest it had ever been in a single foray. "Well, I can do something about the shooting, at least. Can you get us to within fifty yards?"

"I better get one hell of a tip for this," said Colt. "Traffic is murder this time of night." She bounced the boat over a slow breaker and pointed the prow directly at the U-boat. The shells from the deck gun impacted closer and closer.

The shot would be impossible to aim using any type of conventional technique. The speed and rocking motion of the boat were too much. Fortunately, Adrian didn't aim so much as he fired instinctively. He always seemed to know exactly the right time, the right direction, and the right amount of pull for a given shot. He knew without conscious thought when to take the shot.

When the moment was right, he fired. The gelignite-filled arrow hit the U-boat's deck right where the deck gun was bolted down. The explosion blew the gun right off into the water, along with the gunners manning it. Nevertheless, in the short time it took for that shot, the other soldiers managed to get the strongboxes inside the vessel.

Adrian was about to say something to Colt but the words stuck in his throat. A Nazi officer was floating in midair, his body limned with a glow of pale energy that was visible even in the light of the flare. He glared at them with the contempt of someone confronting a nest of insects. The feeling of sheer power that came from the man was sobering. Adrian dropped an arrow from nerveless fingers; it splashed into the bilge.

The officer looked down at two wounded men on the deck, his face devoid of emotion. He raised his hands in an obscene parody of Christ. Raw energy flowed from his hands, incinerating the men and blasting seawater into steam. Satisfied that there was nobody left to be questioned by American authorities or superheroes, the officer landed upon the deck of the U-boat and stepped inside the conning tower.

The U-boat began to submerge. Colt throttled down. Adrian lowered his bow. The flare arrow finally hit the water and fizzled out into darkness in a few moments. He dropped into the seat next to her.

"They win this time. We'll have to find out what they're going to do with the uranium and get it back."

Colt nodded. "Jim said that his unit had investigated the creation of a Nazi parahuman back in the war."

"You think that was him?"

"God, I hope so. Otherwise it means there's more than one." Her hands were shaking.

"Are you all right?" Adrian took her hands in his.

She nodded. "Combat shakes. I get them every time." A weak smile crossed her face, now lit only by moonlight. "By the way, I'm Judy."

Adrian returned her smile. "Adrian."

BLACKLISTED

October, 1953
New York City, NY

"Hot chocolate for the lady." Adrian Crowley offered up the china cup to Judy Gordon with a gallant sweep of his arm, crammed full of muscles from many hours spent drawing a bowstring and releasing arrows toward the enemies of Truth, Justice, and the American Way. Known to the rest of the world as Dr. Danger, Adrian tried to cut just as dashing a character in private as he did in public. Instead of his trademark pirate blouse with the headscarf and sea boots, he wore slippers and a shirt without a tie.

Judy was perched on a divan in the penthouse suite that Adrian had converted into the headquarters for American Justice, the World's Greatest Superheroes. She was a veteran of World War II, unlike him, and had fought against the Japs in the Pacific and even faced their own national parahuman, a young man known as *Asahi* in Japanese, which translated to *Rising Sun.* Judy was Colt, and could outrun just about any vehicle on the land and could even catch an airplane as it was taking off. Her appetite had been off recently, and it was worrying Adrian. An untouched plate of crackers and cheese lay in front of her. She accepted the cup from him and took a careful sip.

The rest of the team hadn't arrived yet. Georges Devereaux had called an urgent meeting. The French scientist and philanthropist had been responsible for initially discovering the first American parahumans and had stayed on as the team's manager after the War.

Judy stared unblinking into the fireplace. "Hey love." Adrian slipped onto the divan next to her. "What's the matter? You're very quiet tonight. Is something bothering you?"

She turned to look at him. Her eyes were red and puffy, as if she'd been crying. How had he missed that? "I *am* worried, Adrian. I'm worried about Georges and those stupid hearings and the Russians and everything. I'm worried that this is turning into the kind of world that . . . that you wouldn't want to raise a child in."

"Oh, I wouldn't worry too much about it." Adrian smiled at her. "Everything's going to . . . Judy?" He stopped as tears began to trickle down her cheeks.

She took a deep, quavering breath. "I'm pregnant, Adrian."

His jaw dropped. His brain raced through possible responses as fast as she could run. Most he discarded as inappropriate. A few he passed over as callous. Three would get him tossed off the balcony, and it was a long way down from the forty-third floor. He settled on one that was probably the best choice. "How far along are you?"

"Eight weeks, the doctor thinks."

Adrian considered some options. He took hold of her hand. "I . . . I don't know what to say, exactly. This isn't something I planned for."

She rounded on him, suddenly angry. "Something *you* didn't plan for? What about something *I* didn't plan for?"

"I'm sorry. God, I'm sorry." Adrian looked away from her anger. "Look, this isn't how things were supposed to be. I was going to wait until the spring to ask you."

She sniffled and wouldn't look at him.

"Sweetheart, please." Adrian slid off the divan to kneel on the floor in front of her. "I haven't even bought a ring yet, but I wish I had. Will you marry me?"

She glanced at him. "You're not just saying that because I'm pregnant?"

He smiled. "Of course not. I'm madly in love with you. I have been for years, ever since that first night on the docks."

Judy smiled through her tears. "Yes, how well I remember it. Here we thought we've been so dashing and romantic with our sneaking about and our trysts and now you're going to make an honest woman out of me. Of course I'll marry you, Adrian. I love you very much." They embraced and he brushed away her tears.

"Should we tell the others tonight?"

"No. At least, not until we hear what Georges has to say. I really am worried about those hearings. That Senator is a *monster*."

"I couldn't agree more." The grim voice came from the doorway to the suite. They turned to see Isaiah shrugging out of his camelhair overcoat and slouch hat. The tall black man looked much more imposing in his civilian garb than in his Flashpoint costume. "I believe we're all going to be in considerable trouble by the end of this week."

"Why do you say that?" Adrian took a poker and stoked up the fire a bit.

"Georges will be up in a moment with Peter and Elliott. He'll explain things. Maurice isn't on duty tonight." Maurice was the regular evening doorman for the building. Isaiah's eyes popped like flashbulbs, a tiny sampling of his ability to blind others as Flashpoint. "I had to come in through the kitchen."

Adrian sighed. It was easy to forget Isaiah was black after spending four years working with him. Society didn't let anyone forget, though, and often reared its ugly head in misguided attempts to put the brilliant man in his perceived place. "Someday you won't have to, Isaiah. I know it frosts you."

"It's garbage." Isaiah hung his coat and hat on the rack and stepped over to the fireplace to blow on his hands and rub them in front of the fire.

The balcony doors swung open in a blast of cold air and snow. Winter had come early to New York. Lady Athena strode in, her robes fluttering. She was a small woman but carried a presence of majesty about her that made her seem much larger. Her robes were fine crushed red velvet, worn over a bronze breastplate and Greek-styled helmet. She had marvelous powers of the mind, allowing her to experience the perceptions of others. Athena removed her helmet, setting it on a table, and shook out her thick, black hair. "It's not a night fit for flying. I should have called a cab."

"Why wear the costume at all? Wouldn't an overcoat be warmer?" Adrian handed her a cup of hot chocolate.

"And drier." She took a grateful sip of the hot drink. "But if I'm going to fly, I'll be damned if I'll let somebody recognize me out of costume."

That was fair, thought Adrian. Even Judy resisted using her super-speed when she wasn't *dressed* for it. The door to the suite opened again and Georges walked in, followed by Peter, The White Knight, and Elliot, Kid Crash.

Adrian was struck by how *old* Georges looked. He hobbled like his feet were sore and his white hair that normally made him look dignified instead made him seem decrepit. He had deep black circles of exhaustion beneath his eyes that almost looked like he'd been beaten. The way he was sighing, Adrian wondered if perhaps their benefactor had been.

Peter was a true golden boy, blonde hair, blue eyes, played football for the University of Alabama Crimson Tide, and could wrap hard light around himself like armor. His dislike of Isaiah was due to the latter's skin tone, and an unfortunate source of conflict within the core group of American Justice. He kept his feelings in check most of the time, and he didn't even acknowledge Isaiah's presence as he hung his own coat.

Elliot was just a kid, a greaser with his hair done up in a duckbill and a sprinkle of pimples across his forehead. He looked like trouble in his leather jacket and engineer's boots and dirty jeans, but at least he'd put on a clean t-shirt. He could make things explode apart just by touching them, like he was a walking bomb.

They all exchanged brief pleasantries and drinks were passed around—cognac for Georges, scotch for Peter and Adrian, club soda for Isaiah, who didn't drink, and a Coca Cola for Elliot, who was only seventeen.

"Ladies and gentlemen, we're finished." Georges looked around at his friends, deep sadness in his eyes. "American Justice has been blacklisted."

"How can they do that?" Adrian felt numb with disbelief. "I mean, we're a bunch of patriots for God's sake. Judy and Isaiah are veterans!"

"Yes, but consider the rest of you. You all wear masks. You all conceal your identities." Georges looked at him. "I've worked hard to keep your identities private."

"For good reason." Peter spoke up in his gentle southern twang. "Some of us have families to protect."

"Or reputations." Athena was wealthy, like Adrian, and part of New York's social elite—the daughter of a Greek shipping magnate.

Georges nodded. "I understand that. However, there are more parahumans in the world now than ever before. Steel Wolf in Russia. Eagle Claw in China. Both are communists, of course. Then there is the mystery man you saw four years ago, who I believe may be the same one who the Nazis created in Aufstein. The Senators believe there is an abnormally large number of parahumans concentrated here in America. Specifically in American Justice. They're suspicious that one or more of you may be communist infiltrators."

"That's preposterous!" Judy snorted her disbelief. "I saw American soldiers in the Pacific who were less patriotic than we are."

"Did they make you give up our names?" Athena fixed her gaze upon Georges.

Georges sighed and downed his drink. Peter quickly refilled his glass. "They tried. I pled the Fifth Amendment. They threatened me with everything they could do legally and some things I'm certain were against the law. They called me a Communist and a coward. If I weren't already a citizen I'd be deported. As it is, I've been put on the blacklist. I'll have to leave the country if I'm ever to achieve anything more."

Peter shook his head. "What about the rest of us? You said *American Justice* was blacklisted. The whole team?"

"What's *blacklisted*?" Elliot looked up from watching bits of energy dance around his hand.

Isaiah folded his arms. "Just listen, kid. You're going to learn something about how the real world works."

"They're issuing subpoenas for those of you whose identities aren't known. Anyone who doesn't respond is going to have his file turned over to the FBI. As for Judy and Isaiah, they're going to cancel your pensions and blacklist you as well if you don't immediately retire." Georges turned his head in a slow pivot, regarding each of them in turn. "Senator McCarthy is introducing a bill to create a national registry of parahumans. If you don't register, you become a federal fugitive. If you do, you become a stooge for the government. It will probably pass. He's got a talent for getting things like that accomplished."

There was a long pause as the implications of Georges' statements sunk in to all of them.

Adrian was the first to break the silence. "Well, I guess the question is what do we do now?"

Isaiah stood up. "Not hard for me. There's a man in Chicago, Elijah Mohammad. He's teaching the ways of

Islam. I believe I'll go and look him up. I've spent years teaching lessons to those who needed it." He made a flicker of light appear over one of his hands, like lightning. "It's time I learned something myself."

"I've heard of him." Peter's eyes narrowed. "He's a troublemaker. You'll be in just as much hot water with him than if you stayed here."

Isaiah shrugged into his heavy coat. "Maybe so, but it might as well be trouble for something I can believe in, instead of for an ideal that doesn't exist in America anymore." He turned and walked out of the suite without another word.

"Good riddance. Never liked that nigger anyway." Peter shrugged. "Guess I'll head back home. Don't know that my powers are going to be much good in civilian life, but I aim to make something out of what I have."

Judy leaned back, nibbling on a cracker. "I might as well retire. I've been thinking about settling down with someone and starting a family."

"Well it's about time." Athena chuckled.

"What do you mean?"

The Greek woman laughed. "The way you and Adrian carry on is ridiculous. You may be fast, Judy, but subtlety is a lost art on you." She looked at the others, a determined glint in her eyes. "I'm not quitting. Let them do their worst. I can work in the darkness as easily as the light. These powers are gifts. We should use them, and use them for a just cause."

"*It's better to light a single candle than to curse the darkness.*" Adrian smiled. "I couldn't agree more. Street crime isn't going to go away, and I'm most effective against it anyway. I started out working in the shadows and I can go back to them anytime. I'll keep on, at least, for awhile." He brushed Judy's cheek with the back of his hand. She reached up and took it.

Elliot snorted in disgust at the two lovebirds. "I ain't quittin'. Bein' a superhero's too much fun."

Judy glared at him. "Isn't this a school night? Don't you have homework?"

"Yeah, but Georgie said it was important so I snuck out."

"Well, try not to blow anything up when you sneak back in, Kid Crash." Adrian paused. "And do your homework."

Peter stood up. "I guess this is goodbye, then. No reason for me to stick around what with the snow and all. It's been a pleasure, friends. I hope we'll meet again."

"Stay in touch, Pete," said Athena. "Especially if you ever need us down in Alabama."

"I will. Thanks, y'all." He finished his drink and left the suite.

"And then there were three." Adrian looked at Athena and Elliot.

"There will be others." Georges' voice was filled with surprising conviction. He'd claimed to be able to detect parahuman powers, and from everything Adrian had seen, the man was spot on in his abilities.

"Oh?" Athena's armor clanked as she turned to look at him.

"Doctors Watson and Crick. They've made great strides in understanding DNA and how it affects us."

"What's *DNA*?" Elliot asked.

"I don't know," said Adrian.

"I hope that their work can validate my theory that parahuman powers are tied to the core essence of a person, not thrust upon them through an accident or intentional design."

Judy yawned. "You're getting way over my head now, Georges. You know I get that way when you start to talk science."

"So what do we do now?" Elliot set down his empty Coca Cola bottle and looked over at the bar as if something stronger might be forthcoming.

"We lay low for a month or so." Adrian rubbed his chin. "There's nothing so pressing that we can't take a break. We need to give Georges time to get set up in France and to put his money where it will do the most good."

"Plus we've got a wedding to plan," said Judy.

"Who's getting married?" Elliot winced as Athena reached over and smacked him on the top of his head. "Hey!"

"Honestly, Elliot. How are you even passing the eleventh grade?"

"In the meantime, we'll have to set up a new headquarters. Someplace more secret and more secure. If you are all convinced that we should continue, it's going to be outside the law," said Adrian. "Perhaps Athena's father has a warehouse that he might allow us to use."

Athena nodded. "I can work something out with him. He appreciates the work we do. And as far as roughing it in the shadows, I've got Gypsy blood in me. I can do that as long as it takes."

"A toast, then." Georges raised his glass. The others followed suit. "To Athena's just cause. May it always guide us to do the right things."

The group echoed Georges' sentiment. "To just cause."

WINTERNIGHT

March, 1962
New York City, NY

It was a very small ad, in the *Village Voice*. Pete might not have even noticed it if he hadn't been looking for a job. *Do you have special or unusual talents or abilities? Are you capable of feats impossible by normal standards?* And there was a phone number under it. That was all— two lines amid all the places looking for dishwashers and street sweepers.

What the hell, he thought. Maybe they would know what to do with someone who could do what he did. He dropped a dime into the pay phone and dialed the number.

It picked up on the second ring after a series of clicks that made him wonder if he was connecting to another country. "Are you a parahuman?" The voice had undertones of an accent he couldn't place. He shot nervous glances around at the people hurrying by the phone booth, wondering if someone was spying on him.

Pete hadn't been prepared for that question or the abruptness with which it had been asked. "I, uh, don't know. I think so."

"What can you do?"

"I . . . can make things get colder." The pause that lasted so long he wondered if he'd been hung up on. "Uh, hello?"

The voice rattled off an address, following it with a date and time: ten A.M. the following morning. Then he really did get hung up on, and he never had half a chance to write down the address so he wouldn't forget.

For some reason, though, the street number and name burned into his brain, so that he remembered them as well as he did his own address. Pete debated whether or not to go back home at that point, but remembered that his father had come in last night with a couple of fresh bottles of bourbon, and he was a mean drunk and meaner when he was hung over.

Spring hadn't yet sprung, and it was cold and rainy. The cold didn't bother him at all, especially since his powers had developed, but he didn't care for being wet, so he'd taken his father's anorak when he left the house that morning. He took a bus down to Times Square and sneaked into a XXX movie theater to get some sleep. Sometimes he watched the movies when the girls were pretty, but this one was full of nothing but old, worn-out whores so he settled down in one of the cleaner seats near the back of the theater, ignoring the quiet noises that came from the patrons and letting the bad soundtrack lull him to sleep.

Pete dreamed of a world rimed in frost, where everything had a beautiful soft sheen of ice coating it. He walked through Central Park, and each leaf was perfectly preserved in its frozen prison. It was beautiful. People were solid blocks of ice, caught in the very acts of everyday life. Here was a jogger, columns of ice supporting his feet in the middle of a stride he would never complete. There was an old woman with her hand in a box of popcorn and expectant pigeons waiting by her feet. He'd always hated the birds. Rats with wings, his father called them. He casually kicked at one of them and it shattered into a hundred pieces, shining red and gray in the cold sunlight.

Pete awoke with a start as the film stuck and melted against the bulb. There were groans and catcalls from the scattered moviegoers, and more than a few curses from those who weren't finished with their personal business yet.

His actual abilities were nowhere as powerful in scope and breadth as they were in his dreams. He could chill a soda into a popsicle, even on the hottest day, and could lower the temperature in a closed room by about twenty degrees, which made the muggy New York summers tolerable, but that was about it. He'd never even have suspected he had the powers at all, if he hadn't started dreaming about them and woken up with ice in his sheets several times. A little experimentation proved that he was in fact a parahuman, like the guys in Just Cause and the Atomic Generation.

Pete thought about what to do about it a lot. He could put on a costume and go knock on the door of the Atomic Generation's headquarters, but his power was kind of stupid, and he figured they'd probably just laugh. Just Cause was even worse. They were a bunch of old guys in their thirties and even forties, and as far as he was concerned were in the same category as his father, if in a different class altogether. He briefly entertained the idea of becoming a back-alley vigilante like the one called Boilerplate, but his daydreams of freezing would-be muggers and rapists in their tracks while receiving grateful thanks from beautiful victims could never be more than just fantasies. He couldn't give someone more than a case of frostbite, and it would take a long time. Not a very glamorous ability for a superhero.

So he decided that his powers were nothing more than an interesting sideshow. The three-ring circus of his life continued on, powers or no, and he had to balance living at home with a drunk for a father with trying to find a place that would hire a long-haired kid like him so he could figure out how to get out from under his old man's roof. He checked his watch. It was either very late or very early, depending upon what side of sleep one was on.

He wasn't really sleepy anymore, so he decided it was early and left the theater. He had several hours before his appointment and was nervous and jittery. A cup of coffee at an all-night diner didn't help his nerves or his jitters, but there was something all the same about the tired waitress who still managed to put a bit of bounce in her too-old hips for him that made him feel like maybe it'd be a good day after all.

He spent the next few hours drifting around town, wandering wherever his feet took him. He smoked the last cigarette from the pack of Lucky Strikes he'd pinched from his dad and wished he had some grass. A fat man leaned out of a car window and yelled at him to get a haircut. He showed the man his middle finger and threw a rock at him when he pulled over, presumably to come and kick Pete's ass.

Deciding it would be better to make himself scarce until his appointment, he went underground. He jumped a turnstile and slipped onto the first train that came into the station. He got off at the next stop, not really caring where it was. It turned out he wasn't too far away from the address in question, so he decided to walk the rest of the way.

It was a bland, faceless office building, like half of the city. His grandfather's New York had been a place of beauty, of individuality, of steel and glass. Pete's was plastic and had no soul. He scowled at his reflection in the glass of the door. Just another drifter with no future in a world that didn't care about anything anymore. His t-shirt was dirty and his leather jacket scuffed. His jeans needed patching and his hair hung around his face like the filthy forelimbs of sewer rats. Who in their right mind would hire anyone like him? He made a fist and watched frost spread over it. Maybe that would be enough. He pushed open the door and entered the building.

It seemed to be abandoned. The office he was supposed to find was on the second floor. A single dingy light bulb lit the stairwell and dust hovered in the air, swirling in his wake like cigarette smoke in a crowded bar. Accumulated trash lay in the corners of the stairwell. He found the office and let himself in.

Unlike the rest of the building, this office seemed neat and clean, although unfurnished. A single swivel chair sat in a pool of yellowed light in the room's center. The walls were covered with dark paneling and there was no exterior window.

"Sit down."

Pete jumped, looking around. As his eyes adjusted to the poor light, he saw a loudspeaker on the wall. Next to it was a large, black unit with a round, glassy lens pointed at him. "Am I on TV?"

"Sit down." The voice repeated with more than a hint of unpleasantness.

Pete spun the chair around and sat on it, leaning his elbows on the back the way he wasn't supposed to in school.

The lights went out completely. A sudden feeling of nausea washed over Pete. He felt like he'd just been turned inside out. "What the hell?" The lights came back up just as suddenly, and he was in the same chair but in a different room.

This new room was a different size and shape from the one he'd just been in, containing both a desk and a man sitting behind the it. Pete started to sweat and realized that it felt a lot more like New York in midsummer than in early spring. He saw movement to one side of him and glanced over to see a skeletally-thin black man with his hair done up in funny, spiky braids. He smiled at Pete in an unfriendly way and moved to stand next to the man behind the desk.

The other man was big, and built like a soldier. He looked like pictures Pete had seen of his grandfather when he'd been in World War I, with closely-cut blond hair and blue eyes. He couldn't tell the man's age. He was definitely younger than Pete's father, but his eyes seemed like they belonged on a much older man.

"My name is Heinrich. Welcome to my home, Mr. Foss." His trace of a foreign accent made him sound cultured and exotic.

"Mr. Foss is my father. I'm just Pete. Where am I and how did I get here?"

Heinrich gave him a benevolent smile. "As I said, Peter, you're in my home, which happens to be in a charming little hamlet called Guatemala City. As for how you got here, you're not the only parahuman around here. Hadrian, here, is quite an artist at exoteleportation."

The black man smiled again in a predatory fashion.

"Exo . . . what?"

Heinrich smiled. "Hadrian, the shades, if you would?"

Hadrian smiled and raised a hand. Several shades around the room were drawn, like magic.

Pete saw blue surf and whitewashed buildings outside. "Holy shit!"

"Yes, it's quite beautiful. Tell me about your powers, Peter." Heinrich leaned forward and clasped his hands atop the desk.

"You ain't some kind of cop, are you?" It wasn't against the law to be a parahuman, but there were reasons that American Justice and the Atomic Generation were masked and had secret identities.

"No, Peter, I'm not. Please go on."

"Oh, uh, right. I can make things get colder."

"What kind of things? How much colder? Have you ever empirically tested your abilities?"

"Things I'm touching, I guess. And the air around me. I can make a popsicle out of a can of soda or cool a room when it's hot. I don't get cold when it's cold outside." He shrugged. His powers sounded really stupid when he tried to explain them out loud. "I guess it's not really much at all."

Heinrich stared at him with his too-old eyes, then poured a glass of water from a pitcher on his desk and pushed it across the desk. "Demonstrate, please."

Pete picked it up slowly, casually swirling the water around the edge of the glass. He'd never actually used his powers before where anyone would notice. He took a deep breath and *focused*. The water froze into a solid mass in mid-swirl with a crackling sound, followed by a gunshot as the drinking glass split into two pieces, cutting him. "Shit." A thin runnel of blood streaked across his palm. He bent to pick up the pieces on the floor.

"Leave it." Heinrich's tone commanded unquestioning compliance. "I have servants for that." His tone softened and he smiled. "Well, Peter. An impressive display. I suspect you are quite a bit more powerful than you realize. Hadrian?"

The thin black man nodded. "Definitely, mon." He licked his lips in a most disconcerting way. "Me seen great power there, but is trapped. He afraid what happen if he give himself over to it completely."

"You have nothing to fear any longer, Peter." Heinrich extended a hand. "You are to be congratulated. You are one of the elite supermen destined to rule."

"Rule? Rule what?"

"The world, of course." Heinrich said it as if it were the most natural response.

Pete's mouth dropped open and he couldn't think of anything to say.

"Allow me to explain." Heinrich leaned back in his chair and kicked his heels up onto the desktop. "I am like you, Peter, and like Hadrian. I have powers that over time I have developed to a high level. You will develop yours as well in order to complete your destiny."

"Destiny?" Pete's voice was faint. This had suddenly gotten much more complicated than he was ready to accept.

"My abilities were born of fire, and fire is their very nature. My *Fuhrer* hoped to create his ultimate superman. In this, he succeeded most admirably. However, his success was ultimately his downfall. You see, his pitiful Aryans were still only men who would rule over other men. In the end, he realized that by my creation, he had doomed himself. He tried to have me killed." Heinrich smiled. "He failed. It was the last thing he ever did. I know the truth, Peter, about what I am. About what *you* are. About what *any* parahuman is.

"We are gods that walk among men. Our destiny is to rule this world. Not as Aryans over Jews, or white slavers over Negroes, but as the next step in human evolution. Do you understand?"

It was a lot to take in at once. "I . . . think so. You're saying it doesn't matter what race you are if you have super powers?"

"Exactly!" Heinrich dropped his feet back to the floor and leaned forward. "We are the supermen. We who retain the powers of legend are those who shall lead."

"And it doesn't matter if my powers are weak or stupid?"

"Oh, your powers are neither weak nor stupid, Peter. Hadrian is never wrong in his assessments. Even if they were trivial, the simple fact that they exist at all means you are chosen for greatness over all the mere humans."

"And you want me to join you in . . . in whatever it is you're doing?"

Heinrich's eyes glowed with feverish intensity. "I would have any parahuman join me in my crusade, no matter whom. Come, walk with me." He stood, taking a white panama hat from a rack and opening the door onto a street filled with sweaty, smelly, brown men and women conducting their business transactions in an open-air marketplace. Pete shrugged and followed him out.

"Look at these people, Peter. In time they will worship us as gods, as will all men."

"So you're going to take over the world?" It sounded so corny in his ears he almost couldn't bear to say it.

"Eventually, but I take the long view—much longer than the Inner Circle could. First I must find my army with which to act. There are so few of you, and Hadrian does not work quickly at finding you." They walked to the end of the street and turned left, heading toward a beach with sand bleached white. "Once we are ready, we shall rise up and take control. Mankind will not be able to resist our powers. They will submit or be destroyed."

"They'll try to stop you." As soon as he'd spoken it, Pete wished he hadn't.

Heinrich stopped and placed a heavy hand on his shoulder, turning him. "Who?"

"The superheroes. American Justice. The Atomic Generation. They won't let you get away with your plan." Pete suddenly feared for his life. He didn't know what Heinrich could do with his powers, but he was afraid he was about to find out.

Heinrich laughed. "Of course they'll try. They can't see past the sheep they protect. But even a strong fortress can be destroyed from within. I am grooming them, even as I groom my own recruits. My minions work against them, and other so-called heroes. The heroes train, and grow more powerful in their abilities, so they can fight other parahumans. Eventually their powers will grow, and they will become so far advanced that they will learn that my way is truly the only way for them to find a peaceful, fruitful existence."

The sea breeze rippled through the trees at the edge of the beach. Pete watched as a handful of brown children, nearly naked, ran screaming and laughing through the sand. "What about the ones who don't join you?" He kicked at a small rock.

Heinrich's smile turned wistful. "They shall be destroyed. I cannot divide my attention between ruling and fighting usurpers. We parahumans, and our progeny, will be the great leaders of humanity. Those who blind themselves to the truth doom themselves to destruction."

"So let me get this straight. You want me to join you, to become more powerful, and eventually to be in charge of the whole world?"

"Yes."

"And if I don't, I'll be destroyed?"

"Of course."

Pete actually considered saying no to see what would happen. He thought about his drunkard father and how much he hated him. He thought about all the men in Times Square and how pathetic they really were. Heinrich had a way with words, and Pete could really see how much better he was already. And his plan didn't sound so bad. It would be like being a king or a president, and those guys got all the good stuff. It wasn't like anyone was going to really get hurt or killed or anything. They'd just . . . take over. Pete understood then that this was exactly what he'd been looking for without even realizing it.

He smiled at Heinrich, seeing him as the great leader he was. "Sign me up."

Over the next few weeks Heinrich showed Pete his operation. He was an ex-Nazi SS trooper, and he planned for contingencies that *nobody* would ever think of. Pete asked him about it, and Heinrich laughed, telling him something about the best-laid plans of mice and men. Pete wasn't the only parahuman working with him, either. There were five altogether. They all had neat code names like they did in the Atomic Generation and Just Cause. Pete was Winternight. Hadrian was The Teacher, but nobody ever called him that. Mouse was a Czech immigrant named Marek. The last two were from Los Angeles—Jorge the Jumping Bean and Angelo, who called himself Suncore. Pete eventually found out that Heinrich called himself

Isotope. Hadrian explained to him what an isotope was, but all Pete understood was it had something to do with atomic bombs.

Hadrian was terrifying enough to plague Pete's nightmares. He had powers that came from his mind. He could teleport himself and others. He could move things without touching them. He could also read minds, and *do things* to other people's minds. Pete wasn't too thrilled when Heinrich ordered him to accept some *treatments* from Hadrian. He didn't know what to expect, but figured it would probably hurt. Most of the things they did on Heinrich's orders hurt. He said that overcoming pain was the essence of strength, and that the pain they inflicted upon themselves would make what others would inflict upon them much less severe.

"Sit down, mon." Hadrian licked his dry lips with a gray tongue. Pete did so, nervous about what might be forthcoming. The thin man walked around the chair to stand behind him. Even in the tropical temperature, heat poured off his body with a bright, coppery scent. Pete jumped as too-hot fingers touched his recently-shorn skull. He imagined them sinking through his stubble into his skull like hot pokers. "You got to relax, mon. Me say this be no pain, yah. Could be you like it. What you know 'bout brain? 'Bout architecture?"

The question put Pete off guard, which was probably Hadrian's intent. Get the kid thinking about something else and he won't notice that you're burning holes in his head. "Architecture? You mean like a building?"

"Yah, mon. Mind be like a city, with streets and alleys. Follow?"

"I guess so."

"Good. Now, me say your mind city empty. No people, mon. Nine of ten buildings empty."

"Why?" Once he found a path through Hadrian's difficult accent, Pete realized the man had some interesting things to say.

"Most buildings got no doors. Me say people in your city see buildings but no go inside. What you think in there?"

Pete felt a sudden twinge somewhere behind his eyes and knew Hadrian was *doing something* to his brain. "I don't know."

"Listen to me say. Your powers. Me say they in building you put door. All have this building. Only you build door, mon. Only you have powers. Follow?"

Twinge. "I think so. So what are you doing, building more doors?"

Hadrian chuckled and waves of heat conducted across Pete's head from his fingertips. "No, mon. Door is easy." *Twinge.* "Me build an elevator."

"Huh?"

"Building is open, mon. You in on ground floor. But the buildings tall, mon. Me say you need an elevator." Something that felt like a railroad spike impacting one of Pete's ears made him flinch. Hadrian's fingers tightened around his skull and kept him from moving. "Me say each new floor of your building make you stronger."

"You mean you're making my powers stronger?"

"Yah, mon." Hadrian stopped the first session after half an hour, needing to go and rest himself. Using his own powers made him tired.

As time went by, Pete's powers did improve. Each session gave him a little more to work with, and he began to look forward to Hadrian's treatments eagerly, in spite of the pain. He went from being able to make a popsicle to being able to freeze a cubic mile of jungle. Sure, the ice didn't last long in the equatorial heat, but the look of pride in Heinrich's eyes when Pete did it made him love the German man like a father. Pete could drop the temperature to about ten below zero in an enclosed space. He could even hit moving targets and freeze them to the ground, walls, or in midair.

Suncore and Pete developed a neat tandem attack. Pete would freeze something as solid as he could, then Suncore would hit it with a jet of flame. The sudden temperature shift would cause stuff to shatter. If it didn't, like as not Mouse could break it with his bare hands or Bean could jump onto it, increasing his mass to that of a car.

They trained hard until Pete believed they were the most powerful parahumans in the world. With Hadrian's treatments and Heinrich's constant, commanding presence, they all exhibited levels of power that would even outstrip Just Cause.

When they weren't training, or getting treatments from Hadrian, the team was getting lectures about parahumans from Heinrich. Pete couldn't remember ever paying so much attention in school as he did to Heinrich. "Now remember . . . The other parahumans in this world are *not* your enemies. At least, not yet. Any parahuman may be recruited. Anyone may be turned. They may see you as enemies, but you should see them as potential allies. Kill one of them, and you may eliminate the one who can be the capstone in my great plan. None of them are to be killed without my direct order. The loss of one parahuman may be a greater tragedy than the loss of ten thousand normal humans. We must fight to preserve their existence, even as we battle them so that they will become more powerful."

"But, Heinrich, I don't get it." Suncore who wasn't nearly as bright as his namesake, and privately, Pete called him *Dimbulb*. "Why do we want them to be more powerful at all? Ain't they trying to knock us down? It's easier for us if we can squash them like bugs."

"Yes it is, Angelo, but that doesn't fit in with my plan." Heinrich looked at them all sternly. "The more powerful any parahuman becomes, the more distanced he will become from normal people. He will then look to others of his own kind for acceptance. Those others will be us, and we will welcome him with open arms."

Suncore shrugged, and Pete could tell he just didn't get it.

"Trust me, Angelo. We're going to rule this world, the way we were always meant to."

Suncore grinned. Heinrich played to his base instincts whenever he needed undying loyalty.

"So now what?" Bean asked.

"Go forth into the world," ordered Heinrich. "Test yourselves. Test other parahumans. Report back to me regularly. This world is yours for the taking.

"Take it."

SUMMER OF LOVE

August, 1969
New York City, NY

"It's a concert, mom, not an orgy." Fifteen-year-old Faith Crowley rolled her eyes at her mother's ridiculous stance.

"It's going to be a bunch of hippies smoking weed, taking acid and God-knows-what-other drugs, and listening to that horrid protest music. Absolutely not." Judy Crowley stamped her foot with petulance that belonged more to someone her daughter's age than her own.

"Mom, it's good music. It's about peace and not killing anymore and ending the war." Faith realized she'd said the wrong thing as her mother's face darkened with approaching fury.

Judy's voice was quiet but intense. "Some of us are veterans, young lady, and you wouldn't even have the freedom to spit on our soldiers if it wasn't for us. You might remember that the next time your hippie friends are burning flags and calling our boys things like *baby-killers* and *murderers.*"

Faith's protest lost all momentum. Judy fought valiantly with the rest of the American parahumans in the Pacific against the Japanese in World War II, followed by an eight-year stint as the speedster Colt in American Justice. Faith's father, Adrian Crowley, went on to form the underground superhero group Just Cause back in '54, along with Lady Athena and Kid Crash. He led the group until Faith was nine and he broke his hip in a bad fall. Realizing he was an old man playing a young man's game, he'd retired to write a bestselling book about his experiences. Now he worked with the fledgling Parahuman Rights Association, traveling the country to champion legal protection for parahumans.

The law was clear. Using parahuman abilities had been declared illegal in 1954, and anyone caught doing so would be arrested and charged with a federal crime.

Like her mother, Faith had developed super-speed powers, evident even as a baby. More than once the two of them had torn through town, a laughing, often-naked toddler pursued by her furious mother at two hundred miles per hour. Now fifteen—practically an adult!—Faith spent as much time as she was allowed hanging out at Just Cause's secret headquarters in a Brooklyn warehouse. Her mother knew she went there, but didn't know she'd created her own costume and alter ego of Pony Girl.

Someday soon, Pony Girl would make her debut on the parahuman scene. Until then, Faith kept the costume hidden in an old shoe box at the bottom of her closet. She pulled it out every few days to make sure it was still there and still fit. She hadn't grown much taller over the past year, but filled out in other places that caused the costume to bind and ride up.

Faith wondered how to get through to her mother, but dismissed it as a lost cause after only a second, a typically quick decision for the young speedster. Instead, she substituted volume and cheap insults for logical argument. "You're such a square!" She sped off to her room in a whirlwind of carpet fuzz, pictures rattling on the walls in her wake.

By evening, things calmed down somewhat in the Crowley house as Faith shared a sullen chicken casserole with her mother, who bravely kept trying to open new lines of conversation about anything besides folk music festivals. Finally, Faith retired to her room, flung herself on her bed, and listened to the hippie station on her little transistor radio.

A pebble sailed in through her open window to bounce off her stomach. She slipped to the window and looked down. Her steady, Bobby Thompson, grinned up at her from the darkness along the side of the house.

She kept her voice a spare, breathy whisper. "Hi, Bobby."

"Hi, yourself. Can you come down?"

She nodded and carefully crawled out the window onto the porch roof. Months of practice had taught her which shingles squeaked and which drainpipes were loose. She shimmied down the pipe at the corner of the house, her bare feet finding plenty of purchase on the siding. She turned around to find Bobby only inches from her. She gave him a quick buss across the lips and danced away.

"You know, I could watch you climb up and down that pipe all day." He took her hand and they walked up the street.

"I can't go to the festival. My mom won't let me. She's pretty hacked off at me."

"Well, that's kind of what I wanted to talk to you about." Bobby dug in his pocket and pulled out a small, round piece of metal to show her.

"What's that?"

"The rotor from the distributor on my dad's car."

The term meant nothing to her, and she shrugged.

"It means his new Oldsmobile won't start. He'll have to take the bus to work tomorrow. I can put this back on and we could take it."

"You mean boost his car?"

"You want to go to the concert or not?"

"Of course I want to go, but stealing a car? That's a felony, Bobby."

"We're not really stealing it. It's my dad's car, which practically makes it mine too. Don't sweat it. We'll be gone a few days and then we'll bring it back. Sure, we'll get in trouble, but we'll have seen the show, and that's something we can remember forever."

"I don't know . . ."

Bobby stopped and put his hands on her shoulders, turning her to face him. Moonlight sparkled in his shaggy hair. "They're saying this is going to be the biggest concert ever. Maybe there'll never be anything like it ever again. I want to be there. I want to experience what it feels like to have thousands of people all singing to the same music together. This is the kind of event that can change the whole world, and I want you to be there with me."

When Bobby flashed his earnest, serious side it made Faith weak-kneed. "Okay, Bobby. I'll go."

"Cool. Pack a bag tonight for a week or so. We'll book out of here after my dad leaves for work in the morning. I figure we'll get up there sometime tomorrow and be back on Tuesday. Sound like a plan?"

She nodded and kissed him. A carload of kids hooted and whistled as they drove past, mufflers barely containing the sound of their poorly tuned engine. They ignored the catcalls, having only attention for each other for the brief moments before Faith had to return home and sneak back into her room before her mother noticed she was missing.

After passing through a nervous, sleepless night, Faith threw a few clothes in her school backpack and, after considerable debate with herself, the Pony Girl costume. One never knew, she rationalized, when it might be needed. Realistically, though, she knew her mother would tear her room apart while she was gone and it would be better if the costume wasn't around. Her mom was really going to wig out when it all came to a head.

A car horn honked outside, making her jump. She looked out the window and saw Bobby waving from the driver's seat of a brand new car. He looked nervous and excited. She scrambled out of her room and down the stairs, her backpack bouncing with every step.

"'Bye, Mom." She yanked open the front door.

Her mom called from the laundry room without bothering to come out. "Faith? Where are you going, honey?"

"Out."

"Do you have a dime for the phone?"

"Yeah, Mom."

"Call me if you're going to be late."

Faith bit her tongue to keep from cracking up. She tossed her backpack into the back seat of the car and piled into the front next to Bobby.

He indicated the bucket seats with a shrug. "Sorry about the accommodations, but I didn't pick out the car." He popped the clutch and smoked the tires. The car jolted forward.

"Bobby!"

He grinned. "Just kidding around. I packed some sandwiches, some Cokes, and there's a Thermos of coffee for the drive."

"I don't drink coffee, Bobby."

"I know that, but you also can't drive a stick, and it's a long drive to Bethel."

The Olds had a factory-option eight-track and Bobby brought a short stack of some of their favorites. As they drove, they sang along to Arlo Guthrie, Sly and the Family Stone, The Who, Hendrix, CCR, and of course, Janis Joplin and Joan Baez.

"How long will it take?" Faith sipped on a Coke.

"I'm not sure. It's about a hundred and fifty miles, but I bet the roads will be packed. They're saying there could be a hundred thousand people at the show. Even with six people per car that's, uh—"

"Like seventeen thousand cars." Faith laughed. "You really ought to pay more attention in math class."

"Yeah, and they're all heading up to a tiny little farm in rural New York." Bobby checked the clock on the dash. "We'll stop for lunch, but once we get into the area we might have to walk in. We'll probably get there tonight sometime. Do you have any cash?"

Faith nodded. "Eight bucks. I've been saving it up for awhile."

"Hold onto it. I've got enough to fill the tank a couple of times plus to buy some food when we get there. Son of a bitch!" Bobby honked the horn at a guy in an AMC station wagon who cut them off.

"Don't have a cow, Bobby. Where will we stay when we get there?"

"I thought we'd either sleep in the car if we can park close or else I threw a couple of blankets in the back. We can roll them up and carry them with us." He tried very hard to look straight ahead at the road instead of glancing at her.

Faith took another pull from her Coke. "Bobby, I want to make something perfectly clear. I'm not going to go all the way with you. I'm not ready yet."

"Thought never crossed my mind."

"Liar. You're sweet. You know I'll probably give in sooner or later." She patted his leg and smiled as he blushed to the roots of his hair.

They stopped for lunch at a roadside diner in Newburg. As the waitresses delivered hamburgers and hot dogs to the other patrons, two vanloads of hippies in the parking lot were grilling vegetables on a hibachi in defiance. Their vans were painted with large, friendly flowers in all the colors of the rainbow. One of them strummed a guitar in a tuneless kind of way.

"Hey, friends," called out a man with hair and beard halfway down to his waist. "Don't go in there and eat the flesh of your fellow creatures. Come and break bread with us and we'll sing some songs together."

"That dude's stoned," said Faith.

Bobby nodded. "They probably all are, but the truth is I'd kill for a burger. Buy you a malted?"

"Oh would you, kind sir? I'd be ever so grateful."

While they ate, a New York state trooper pulled into the lot, causing the hippies to melt back into their vans and evaporate. Bobby stood up so quickly that he knocked over his water. The waitress glared at him from behind the counter.

"Sorry." He dug in his pocket and tossed a couple wrinkled singles at her. "Keep the change."

Faith was right on his heels as he rushed out the door of the diner, almost bowling over the trooper.

"Easy there, son." The officer hitched his belt up over a donut-swollen belly. "Wherever you're going, it'll still be there."

"Y-yes sir." Bobby strode to the car with forced calm.

Faith grasped his hand tight to try and keep him from freaking out. "Very slick, Bobby."

"Shut up."

"Hey, don't have a cow. Your dad's not home from work yet. He doesn't know the car's gone."

They climbed into the Olds and Bobby fired up the big block. He goosed the clutch a little on the way out of the lot, and the tires squealed just enough to cause the trooper to look up from his piece of pie and glare out the diner window.

"Bobby . . ."

"Sorry, just nervous. I don't want to get stopped. I, uh, got some stuff from Rich that I don't want to have to explain."

"Oh." Faith's voice became frosty. Rich was one of Bobby's friends—a troublemaker and a dropout. She had a fair idea of what he meant by *the stuff*. She knew Bobby smoked the occasional joint, although he never did around her and never asked her to. She could overlook one small flaw in a boy who was in all other aspects very attractive to her.

By late afternoon they hit the traffic jam on Route 17. Cars, vans, pickup trucks, and buses were backed up for more than ten miles. Many people had already left their cars parked on the shoulder and were hoofing it. Traffic was at a complete standstill. Faith climbed up onto the hood of the Olds and looked up the road, shielding her eyes from the sun.

"It's gridlock all the way up." She slipped back into the seat. "I think everyone else has the right idea." He nodded and pulled the Olds off the road onto the soft shoulder. They rolled up the sandwiches and cokes inside one of the blankets and tucked the other into the top of Faith's backpack.

Bobby locked the car and double-checked all the doors. "I hope nobody hits it or anything. It'll be a lot easier for my dad if the car's undamaged when we bring it back."

"Just remember where you parked."

"Yeah. If there's a problem I can always ask the lot attendant."

They followed the rest of the crowd, walking on through the afternoon into dusk. The air was redolent with the smells of unwashed humanity, marijuana, and incense, making Faith's nose wrinkle. Bobby asked around about where they were supposed to get tickets for the show, but nobody seemed to know. Finally he just shrugged and told Faith they'd wait until someone who knew what was going on told them what to do.

Faith suggested they save a sandwich each for tomorrow, because it didn't look to her like there was much in the way of concessions. A tent city sprang up in the fields and under the trees. A pond nearby was filled with lots of people splashing in the shallows and laughing. Faith blushed as she realized they were naked.

"Where do you want to set up camp?" Bobby looked around at the trampled ground and the free-flowing civilization that had spread across it.

Faith pointed to the stand of trees. "There. At least if it rains we'll have some cover, and we can still see the stage from there."

The stage was enormous, and even it was dwarfed by the scaffolding around it. Stacks of speakers looked like art deco skyscrapers. Bobby took a deep, sighing breath, trying to fill his entire body with the experience. "This is going to be something."

The night was hot and muggy. Sleeping among the trees might have been pleasant, had it not been for the partying campers that never seemed to stop. Acoustic guitars clamored amid folk singers who seemed more interested in fellowship than actually singing anything coherent. Faith tossed and turned in an uncomfortable state between complete wakefulness and entirely asleep. Next to her, Bobby snored like a chainsaw and kept rolling over in his sleep and pressing up against her in a way that made her uncomfortable. More than once she drove an elbow into his ribs to make him turn over. Eventually she drifted off into a fitful sleep, full of horrid dreams of pain and suffering.

A sound of water splashing on the leaves penetrated the fuzz in her head and Faith sat up, wondering if it was raining. A young man was standing near the foot of the blanket, urinating into a bush and whistling cheerfully. He glanced back and saw Faith looking at him.

"Oh, hey . . . sorry, man. Did I wake you? Mother Nature was calling me real bad."

Faith blinked at him and realized it was morning. She didn't have a watch and couldn't tell the time, but by the grayish light it was still pretty early. "No, that's okay." Her mouth felt dry and tacky.

The man's face lit up with a radiant smile that would have looked natural on a movie star. "Cool. They're supposed to be trucking in a whole load of Porto-sans, but I just couldn't wait." He zipped up his jeans and looked out at the stage, some hundred yards distant. "Gonna be a great show, man. Glad you could make it." He started to stroll away, then stopped and dug inside his fringed vest. "Thanks for letting me use your bush, man."

"Sure."

He tossed a baggie toward her. She caught it and looked down at the packet in her hand. It was a mixture of oats, peanuts, and raisins.

"Enjoy the gorp, man, and definitely enjoy the show. It's already a beautiful day." He sauntered away, whistling a Janis Joplin tune.

Bobby stirred next to Faith, muttered something incomprehensible. She nudged him. His eyes opened and he looked around at the unfamiliar surroundings. "Morning."

"Morning yourself. Sleep well?"

He sat up and groaned. "Ugh. I guess sleeping under the stars isn't as romantic as in the movies."

Bobby sniffed at the trail mix the guy had given them. He didn't think it had been laced with anything. "Who'd spike gorp?"

They washed down the mix with the last of their Cokes and settled in to wait for the first show, watching hundreds and soon thousands of people fill up the land.

"You ever hear of somebody named *Winternight*?" Bobby asked Faith.

It might have been the most random thing he'd ever said to her, but what was even more startling was that Faith actually had heard of someone who used that name. "Why?"

Bobby pointed at a small group of people huddled at the edge of the trees, some forty yards away. They were wearing ponchos or long robes, like Hari Krishnas, and big, wide-brimmed hats. "I been listening to those guys talking. One of them called another guy Winternight. Sounds like a superhero name. Weird, huh?"

"You can hear them?" Faith looked over at the distant group. There were six of them, four men and two women.

"Uh, yeah. I've been meaning to tell you, because I think you ought to know. I've got this cool hearing, you know? Like I can hear things at a real long distance." Bobby blushed, embarrassed. "I didn't know how you would feel about it, but if we're going to be together I don't want to have any secrets from you, and this one's kind of a doozy."

"You're a parahuman."

"Yeah, I guess I am. You still love me?"

Faith kissed him deeply on the mouth. "More than ever. I've got something to tell you, too, but first things first. What can you hear from that group?"

Bobby's forehead wrinkled as he squinted in concentration. "There's somebody else named . . . Bean? Sounds Puerto Rican . . . maybe Mexican. They're talking about something political . . . the BRA? Or maybe the PRA? How they'll respond to the attack. They're arguing about legislation or something."

"Bobby, Winternight is from the Malice Group!"

"You mean those guys who tore up Madison Square Gardens a few years ago? I thought they all got arrested or killed or something."

"Unfortunately not. What're they doing here?"

Bobby screwed up his face, listening hard. "Whatever it is, it's going to happen today—soon, like in an hour. They keep saying *attack*."

"You think they're going to attack the fans? Or one of the performers?"

"Dunno. Why would they do that? Maybe we ought to, I don't know, tell somebody."

Faith opened her backpack and began digging inside it. It looked like Pony Girl would to make her debut at the biggest concert in history. "Where do you think the nearest phone is?" She found the box with her costume and pulled it out of the bag.

"Probably back in Bethel," said Bobby. "But it'll take a while to get there, and it'll take hours for anybody to get up here to deal with them. Should we tell the cops?"

Faith snorted and shoved a blanket into Bobby's hands. "Hardly. If you were a cop here at this event, would you believe anything anyone said to you? Hold this for me, and no peeking!"

"I guess you're right. What are you doing?"

"Changing into something a little more useful." She pulled off her blouse. She'd designed her costume with an equal eye for utility and fashion. Her mother would have thought it scandalous for the amount of skin it showed. She pulled on the tight-fitting red t-shirt, cut off at her midriff, with an angular yellow pattern on the lower half. It was complemented by cutoff tights that stretched from her waist to mid-thigh. She laced up the expensive custom boots Lady Athena had helped her acquire. Over the entire ensemble was a dark red fringed leather vest, which she'd added as a sort of tribute to her mother's Colt costume. She slipped a pair of red-tinted sunglasses over her eyes and tightened the strap that kept them on her face even when running full speed.

"Okay, Bobby, you can look now." He dropped the blanket and she twirled around once for him.

His mouth opened to say something but no words came forth.

"How do I look?" She growled, hoping to jolt his brain back into motion.

"You, uh, you look fabulous. Are you—"

"A parahuman? Yeah. I was going to tell you, too. Eventually."

"Are you in Just Cause?"

"Sort of. Call me Pony Girl."

"What . . . what can you do?"

"I can run. And right now I'm going to run for some help. Even if the Malice Group isn't going to do something right now, they're all right here and maybe Just Cause can stop them before they do whatever it is they're planning. Keep an ear on them, Bobby, okay?"

"S-sure."

"You're so sweet. We'll celebrate tonight if everything works out." She kissed him, revved up her internal engine, and then lit out across the hill.

"Far out," someone shouted nearby as Faith sped across the meadow, a red and yellow blur trailing a wake of pollen and cigarette butts.

In just a few minutes she found her way to the general store in Bethel and skidded to a stop. A line of kids stretched out the door and partway down the street. Inside, she could see a harried man at the counter ringing up six-pack of beer after six-pack of beer. His stock levels already looked dangerously low and the festival hadn't even started yet.

She felt herself flush as all the young men in line looked her up and down. Her superpowers kept her body trim and muscular, but her costume showed off a lot of her womanly assets, so to speak, and she suddenly wished there wasn't quite so much to show off.

"Excuse me." She shoved her way past them to enter the store. She felt a hand brush lightly across her ass and spun around so fast that some of the lighter boxes blew off the shelves from the sudden breeze in her wake.

"Whoa!" A bearded man recoiled. "Sorry, it was an accident!"

She raised an angry finger, ready to give him an earful, but then remembered the reason she was here. "Hey Mister, you got a phone here?" She turned to the storekeeper, who had frozen with one hand partway to the register, his jaw hanging loose. "I'm talking to you, handsome."

"Over there." He pointed toward the wall at a pay phone. "Oh God . . . Please . . . please don't kill anybody."

"Don't worry, man, I'm one of the good guys." She gave him a radiant smile and flashed him a peace sign, hoping she could salvage a good reputation after her initial outburst. She stepped up to the phone, then stopped and turned around. "I left my change in my other tights. Anybody got a dime?"

All eleven of the men in the store held out various amounts of change to her. She selected the dime held by the man who might have "accidentally" groped her, and winked at him. She was beginning to realize the power a costume and commensurate super abilities could have on the general populace, and reveled in the attention.

"Thanks, stranger." She popped the dime into the slot and dialed a number she'd committed to memory a long time ago.

"Hello?" A voice crackled across a poor connection.

"Athena? It's F—I mean, it's Pony Girl."

"Who?"

Faith growled in exasperation. "Think about it for a second, Lady A. I hang out in the clubhouse with you all the time."

"Faith? Is that you? Your mother's worried sick about you. Where are you?"

"Listen, Athena. I'm up at the Woodstock festival—"

"I knew it. I told your mother that's where you'd gone, but trying to find you in a crowd of a half million would be ridiculous."

Faith rolled her eyes. She didn't have time for this nonsense. "Athena, please just shut up for a minute. I have something really, really important to tell you. The Malice Group is here."

There was a pause from the other end of the line. "Are you sure, Faith? They've been laying low for several months. This isn't some trick to get out of trouble, is it?"

"God, I wish it was, Athena. I'm sure it's them, or at least some of them. Winternight's here, and so is Bean. There's at least four more of them. They keep talking about attacking something. I don't know why they'd be here unless they're going to attack someone here."

"Jesus," said Athena. "We heard that they got connected with the Weather Underground back at the SDS convention. Faith, you need to get out of there right now. I'll scramble the team and we'll get up there as fast as we can."

"I can't leave. I'm . . . with somebody."

Faith heard Athena talking quickly to someone else on her side of the connection. "All right, Faith. Promise me you'll stay out of trouble. No superheroics, no costumes, no using your powers."

Faith glanced down at her outfit. "Uh, okay."

"You said you saw six of them? That's almost the whole group. We'll have to take the chopper. Radio said the roads are jam-packed for miles around there. I'll see if I can get hold of the Atomic Generation. Maybe some of them are even at the festival. They're young enough, at any rate. We should be so lucky. Get as much information as you can, but stay out of trouble. Where are you calling from?"

"The general store in Bethel."

"We'll meet you there. It'll be sometime between one and two hours. Okay?"

"Sure."

"Freeze, girlie!" A rough voice called from behind her. Faith glanced back to see an honest-to-God hick sheriff's deputy waving his pistol from behind aviator shades and an overgrown hedge of a mustache.

"Faith?" Athena's voice sounded worried.

"I have to go now." Faith hung up the phone.

"Put your hands on your head and turn around."

Faith turned around with exaggerated slowness. "Can't a girl make a phone call in peace, officer?"

"We don't want none of you freaks here. Now don't move. You're under arrest."

"For what? I haven't done anything wrong."

His eyes narrowed and he pulled back the hammer with his thumb. "Give me one reason, girl."

"Hey, man, she was just, like, making a phone call. You're violating her civil rights, you pig," the bearded man grumbled.

The deputy turned his head to glare at the hippie. "I'll run you in too, Nancy-boy, you don't watch yourself."

"Bummer, man."

The moment's distraction was all Faith needed. She exploded into motion. In a flash, she had crossed the distance between her and the deputy, snagging a box cutter lying on a stack of cans. One of the first things she'd learned from Athena was how to disarm someone holding a gun, and she could do it faster than anyone else in the world. One quick motion and she held the pistol by the barrel, having pried it neatly out of the man's hand. Her other hand flashed with the box cutter and neatly severed the man's Sam Browne belt. She yanked on the belt and it slipped free, speed-loaders, handcuffs, and all. She stepped clear of the store into the street just as the deputy realized he'd been snookered.

He spun around, cursing, and tripped as his pants fell around his ankles. Faith giggled and dropped his belt and pistol in the middle of the street. "I'd love to stay and chat, officer, but I gotta run." Cheers erupted from the kids in the store and on the street as she blazed away, heading back toward the main stage. She had no intention of following Athena's orders.

She would take down the Malice Group herself before any of the others arrived. There'd be no way they could say no to her joining Just Cause after that.

In a few moments she had returned to Bobby. "Hey, sugar. Just Cause is on their way. They want me to stall the bad guys until they get here. Any change?"

"No. They're just kind of hanging around, waiting to start. I'm not sure I understand what they're going to do. Something about a vote in Washington, but I don't understand what that has to do with Woodstock."

Intuition flashed through Faith's mind. "It's a bill that my dad is supporting. A parahuman rights bill."

"You mean like civil rights?"

"Yeah, but for parahumans. It's been illegal to use parahuman powers since the Fifties, and they're trying to change that. The Malice Group must be hoping to affect the outcome of the vote by some kind of big, public display."

"Yeah, but affect it which way? Is it better for them if the bill passes or not?"

"They do something at this festival, it's going to be big and loud. That'll turn popular opinion against parahumans. No way that parahuman rights passes after that. We'll still be against the law just by existing. I've got to stall them."

"How are you going to stall them? Do you have some kind of ray power or something?"

Faith paused for a moment. She hadn't considered how she was going to take them out. "Nope, just super speed. I'll think of something quick, though. It's my specialty. See you in a flash." She bussed him on the cheek.

"Be careful."

She tore across the edge of the woods. In a few seconds she'd made up her mind on her strategy. It involved significant bluffing, some psychology, and a whole lot of luck. She zipped into the midst of the Malice Group brazenly. "Just Cause! Nobody move!"

The group of six froze in mid-conversation. Close up, she recognized five of them from the files she'd read at Headquarters: Winternight, who looked like an older version of James Dean; Bean, the Mexican desperado; Mouse, the gigantic strongman; Suncore, the fire-blaster; Slipstream, the flier; and the sixth woman, whose pale translucent skin Faith didn't recognize.

They all broke into laughter.

"How old are you?" Winternight wiped his eyes in amusement.

"Oh, I'm so scared." Bean sounded like Speedy Gonzalez.

Faith raised her hands up, as if she were threatening to unleash devastating powers upon them all. "I'm warning you. One false move and you've all had it. I—I mean *we've* been watching your every move. Whatever mischief you've been planning is not going to happen today, Malice Group."

Winternight smiled at her with shiver-inducing cold in his eyes. "You know what I think? I think you're here all by yourself. I think you don't have the power to back up your threats. And I definitely think you haven't thought this through. Otherwise, you'd know you're outnumbered, outclassed, and outpowered."

"Shut up!" Faith was suddenly worried that her rash decision was going to get her killed. "I'm warning you . . ."

Winternight said, "Moonbeam."

Lights flared behind Faith's eyes and the last thing she thought was that *Moonbeam* was such a pretty name for a villain.

* * *

"Wake up."

A hand slapped across Faith's face. She came back from a muddled dream to a state of semi-consciousness. Her jaw hurt from the blow, and she tasted blood in her mouth. A painful throbbing filled her entire head, reminding her of the morning after she and Bobby had swiped a bottle of gin from his dad's liquor cabinet and polished it off at a drive-in movie. She tried to raise her hands to wipe her eyes and mouth, and realized her hands were bound behind her.

Taking a deep, shuddery breath, Faith raised her head a couple inches and opened her eyes. Her eyes showed her two of everything and she struggled to regain some focus.

A hand struck her across the face again.

"Ow, cut it out, man!" Her whole face ached and felt swollen, but the blow had an unintended side effect of clearing her vision enough to see her surroundings.

She was in a van with lime green shag carpeting on the floor and sides, and curtains over the windows, leaning against one wall. All the windows were up, making it terribly hot and stuffy. The collar of her costume was soaked with sweat. Winternight crouched across from her, dabbing a streak of blood from one of his gloves. An expression of distaste spread across his handsome face.

The woman called Moonbeam sat with her back against the driver's seat, her strange translucent skin almost glowing in the dim light. Next to her, Bean leered at her, his chin unshaven and a wicked glint in his eyes.

"Who are you?" Winternight sat back, keeping his attention upon Faith.

"P-Pony Girl."

"What are you doing here?"

"I could ask you that too."

Winternight's hand looped out but she managed to roll with the blow. It still hurt, but did more to wake her up than anything else. With her thought processes accelerated, she considered how to get out of her predicament. Her hands and feet were bound, but otherwise unfettered. She faced three opponents, two with known abilities and one unknown, probably psionic. Feeling around behind her, she discovered a spot where a bolt protruded from the carpeting. It wasn't much, but enough friction against it with the ropes should have her hands free in a couple of seconds of super-speed effort. From there she could get her feet free and get out of the van. All she needed was a moment's distraction.

Winternight's smile was as frosty as his name. "I'll tell you what I think. Stop me if I make a mistake. I don't think you're part of Just Cause at all, unless they started recruiting from junior high schools. I don't think you've got any backup here or on the way. I'm not sure how you recognized us, but I think you decided to be the hero of the day and bust us all on your own." He leaned close to her. Late morning sunlight reflecting off the van's shag carpeting turned his white mask a sickly green color. "So tell me, hero . . . how am I doing so far?"

Faith squirmed from fear and discomfort, but also to move her bonds directly over the nub of the bolt. "What . . ." She swallowed and licked dry lips, tasting blood on them. "What does the Malice Group want with Woodstock?" She cringed as Winternight raised his hand to strike again, but then lowered it.

"Come on, man, hit her again." Bean looked like he was practically salivating at the thought.

"Shut up, pervert." Moonbeam focused her pale eyes upon Faith.

"The question is how badly do you want to know?" Winternight said. "Because Moonbeam can pull anything she wants out of that pretty little head of yours. And she can tell when you lie to us. So maybe you answer my questions and I'll answer some of yours. Deal?"

"I'd shake on it, but my hands are tied." Faith glared at him.

"Are you really with Just Cause?"

"No."

Moonbeam nodded. "Truth."

"And you're doing this on your own."

"Yes."

"You sure you're on the right side?" Winternight dropped his voice to a conspiratorial whisper.

"I don't understand."

"Listen, kid. You've obviously been reading too many comic books and dime store novels. The world isn't black and white. It's all shades of gray. There's no such thing as absolute good or absolute evil. You've got something in common with all of us already. Know what that is?"

Faith sniffled and wished she had a drink of water. It was so hot inside the van that Suncore might have been toasting it for all she knew. "Our powers?"

"Bright girl. Powers set us apart, above the other men and women of this world. Why do you think you got powers and your neighbor didn't?"

"I don't know."

"Because you're destined for better things. You're a higher form of life than those cattle out there. And we are your brothers and sisters."

Faith managed a slight sneer in spite of her swollen lip. "Think I'd rather be an orphan, then."

Winternight started like he was going to hit her again, but stopped.

"Come on, boss, let me question her. I'll get some answers out of her," whispered Bean.

"You're a sick fucker, Jorge," said Moonbeam. "She's just a kid."

Winternight reached out and Faith flinched, but he just took her chin in his hand and lifted it so she was facing him. "Yes, she is a kid. So were we all, once. Filled with power . . . anger boiling off us because nobody understood us . . . needing a greater goal, a greater purpose in our lives." He lowered his hand, but Faith kept her head raised. "You don't have to be alone, you know. We welcome anyone with power. Anyone."

"You sound like Hitler." Faith could barely focus in the sweltering heat of the van.

Winternight snorted. "I've been told worse. The man had the right idea, but used the wrong people. There is a master race, but it sure as shit isn't the Germans or Aryans or whoever it was supposed to be. It's us." He raised his hand and a tiny, swirling ball of snowflakes coalesced above it, whipping around like a miniature blizzard. A refreshing cold breeze emanated from him, raising goosebumps on Faith's arms.

"If you're so damn noble, why are you one of the bad guys?" Faith snarled, starting to feel more feisty.

He shrugged and smiled. "Only to some." The snowball disappeared, leaving only a lingering chill in the air. "It's more rewarding than you could possibly know. Unless, of course, you were to join us."

He was so sincere, so serious in his belief, that for just a moment, she actually considered saying yes. Her thoughts were interrupted by a familiar voice outside the van. "Hey, you guys got any weed?" Faith forced herself not to gasp in surprise as she recognized Bobby's voice.

"*Nein.*" The German super-strong villain Mouse must have been on guard right outside. "Fuck off."

"No, man, I'm serious. Those dudes back there said some dudes in a van had some weed." He was playing up the stoner role. Overplaying it, Faith thought. He was going to get himself killed.

"Is not this van," said Mouse. "Fuck off again."

"You don't have any weed?"

"No."

"Oh. Okay, then. Do you, uh, want to buy some? I got a baggie here . . ."

Winternight turned to Bean. "See what's going on." The big Mexican nodded, leered at Faith once more, then opened the side door of the van.

Moonbeam's eyes widened as she caught Faith's desperate thought. She opened her mouth to warn Winternight.

Faith severed the rope binding her hands against the protruding bolt. She moved so fast the friction ignited the carpet. The instant her hands were free, she planted them firmly on the floor of the van and kicked her bound feet forward into Moonbeam's face, just as she started to feel a tickle in her brain of an impending psionic attack. The woman had barely started to crumple forward, blood running from a shattered nose, when Faith whipped her feet sideways in a blindingly fast double-footed kick, catching Winternight right on the side of his head.

Time shifted into the syrupy slowness of accelerated perceptions as Faith cut the tape holding her feet together against the door latch of the van. Behind her, the flames erupted across the carpeting. She leaped out into the sunlight, staggering from the aftereffects of whatever ability Moonbeam had tried to use on her. Bobby was right there, his face just starting to register surprise. Mouse and Suncore stood in front of him, making themselves into a threatening barrier, while Slipstream looked on with disinterest. Bean was halfway out of the van when Faith slipped past him. Six to one odds; four to one if she was lucky and had knocked out both Moonbeam and Winternight. Either way, she'd swallowed a large dose of reality over the last hour. She wasn't in any shape to take on four—or six—other parahumans, so she did the one thing she knew she could do.

She ran.

Behind her, a great geyser of frost erupted, forcing the van apart at the seams. Winternight stepped out of the twisted, super-cooled metal, clouds billowing off him in the humid air. "Get her and bring her back alive."

Faith made tracks across the valley, hoping to draw the Malice Group away from the crowds of people. She raced across a sea of blankets and sleeping bags. So many innocent bystanders! She had to get clear of the entire festival if she could, draw away the Malice Group before they started killing civilians. She knew she had backup coming from Just Cause, but she had no idea how far away they were.

A black-and-white blur flew past her head. She ducked, but too late. A great blast of wind picked her up and tossed her into a grove of trees along with a cloud of detritus. She glanced off a trunk and hit a mossy bank hard. A roaring sonic boom washed over her like thunder from a point-blank lightning strike. Slipstream had shot past her, traveling at supersonic speed, and caught Faith in her wake, one of the most destructive powers Just Cause had ever catalogued.

Faith sat up and shook her head to clear it. She heard a distant rumble as Slipstream banked around, coming in for another pass, holding her arms out straight in front of her like a diver, parting the air like a missile. A gout of flame shot into the trees from Suncore's fists as he took to the sky as well. Faith sprang to her feet, dodging another blast of flame that flash-boiled all the moisture in the surrounding flora. Suncore laughed as the woods caught fire.

Faith only made herself a target by sitting still. She flung herself into motion again just as Bean dropped from the sky to crash down where she'd stood a moment before, striking with the force of a wrecking ball. He could alter his mass, preferring the tactic of leaping into the air while light as a feather and then becoming as heavy as a car when he dropped. Faith sped across a field and onto a dirt road, which allowed her enough traction to approach her top speed. She kicked up a double rooster-tail of dirt plumes behind her, knowing it would mark her trail to her pursuers.

She just had to survive until Just Cause arrived, she thought as she flashed by parked cars in a blur of color. She glanced back and saw Slipstream closing fast on her, blowing car windows out in her wake and sending people flying. Although Faith was no slouch in the speed department, Slipstream was much faster, and had the advantage of being airborne.

Faith ripped a large Indian blanket off the hood of a car. It flapped madly behind her. Just before Slipstream caught up with her, Faith hefted the blanket into the air. It spread open like a parachute as it shed momentum. Slipstream yelped in surprise as she plowed into the flying blanket. It did nothing to slow her, but it did wrap around her for a brief second, causing her to lose her aerodynamic shape.

The blanket-wrapped villain whipped past her and Faith braced herself for the buffeting of Slipstream's namesake blast of wind and debris. She bounced hard off a car's quarter panel and skidded to a halt. She raised her head just in time to be treated to the sight of Slipstream plowing into a muddy ditch along the side of the road. Mud splattered up in a tremendous, wet explosion. Screams echoed in her ears and she realized there were lots of people around, many having been tumbled by Slipstream's wake. Her first instinct was to check to see if Slipstream was still a threat, or even still alive, but Suncore was approaching fast, and behind him came Winternight and Bean. Even Mouse was probably back there somewhere, trying in vain to keep up with the faster parahumans.

Something grated in Faith's side and she groaned as pain shot down one leg and up into her neck. She wondered if she'd broken her ribs when she hit the car. She'd heard they could puncture lungs and other icky things that she didn't want to think about. She got to her feet, wincing as she imagined the worst. A lick of flame washed across her and she took off running again, knowing the only way to stay alive was to keep moving.

Suncore cut loose with another blast, setting a car ablaze, laughing and reveling in the sheer power of his fire. Faith wove in and out of the parked cars, trying to keep him from getting a clear shot at her, but he plainly didn't care whether he hit her or not. Several cars burned from his indiscriminate blasts and one exploded.

Faith sacrificed dodging for sheer speed. She knew she could outdistance all of the rest of the Malice Group, but she had to keep them moving further away from the innocents, further away from Bobby. She tried to stay just on the outside of Suncore's range so he wouldn't lose interest in pursuing her.

Winternight froze the air under his feet into a solid sheet of ice and slid along it like an Olympic speed-skater, moving as fast as Suncore. He raised a hand up, and a great wave of cold emanated from it. The wave passed over Faith, traveling as fast as a thought. The shock of it was like being dunked in ice water and it took her breath away. Suddenly her whole world was frozen whiteness as frost appeared on trees, cars, people, and even the ground. She took a bad step and slipped on an icy patch, winding up on her back underneath a tree branch overhanging the road. She nearly fainted from the pain in her side. Tears rolled out of her eyes and froze onto her cheeks.

I'm going to die of frostbite in August, she thought. *Or something even worse.* A great white icicle appeared to grow from nothing on the branch overhead and snapped off, falling toward her face in slow motion. Faith couldn't move; she'd been frozen to the ground by Winternight's powers. Her perceptions accelerated to maximum, she had plenty of time to watch the icicle descend. It was the worst moment in her entire life. She could see a reflection of herself in the ice, all twisted up in a splash of red and yellow. A warm breeze tickled her cheek and she wondered if Suncore was going to torch her before Winternight could impale her.

With glacial slowness, the falling icicle began to melt. Faith watched as the outside edges of the ice sublimated right into steam before her eyes until nothing worse than a few droplets of water hit her face.

A bright light appeared all around Faith, as if she was in a spotlight onstage. A dark-haired man in a gaudy yellow costume smiled down at her. "Hiya, I'm Photon. You look like you could use some help." He applied some sort of radiant energy to her and she could move again, the ice and frost purged by his glow. She sat up and looked around quickly for Suncore and Winternight. What she saw brought tears to her eyes again, for her backup had finally arrived in the form of Photon and Air Force, from the Atomic Generation, and Lady Athena of Just Cause.

Lady Athena stood over Faith. Her bronze centurion helmet and shield gleamed in the sunlight and her crimson cape fluttered in the breeze. "Faith, are you all right?"

Faith nodded, and grimaced. "I'll live."

"You're in big, big trouble, young lady. We'll talk after this is done. Go get 'em, boys."

At Athena's command, Air Force and Photon exploded into action just as Suncore, Winternight, and Bean closed the intervening distance. Both Just Cause and the Atomic Generation had tangled with the Malice Group at separate times, and they all knew how best to combat the villains.

Faith's ears popped as Air Force created a sphere of high pressure around Suncore. The fiery villain tried to blast back at the veteran hero, but the super-oxygenated air around him ignited in a sudden burst of flame. Air Force swooped in on the dazed Suncore, catching him in a whirlwind. It spun him around, twisting and turning him until his eyes rolled up in his head. Air Force grinned and released him, letting him fall to the ground. Suncore hit hard and didn't move but for some vomit that leaked from the corner of his mouth.

Photon, who could turn into a beam of light, flashed all around Winternight, using his radiant glow to counter every usage of the leader's ice powers, but his flashing did no more than slow Winternight down.

Bean dropped down in front of Lady Athena and Faith, who felt faint from the pain of her ribs. The big Mexican growled at Athena. "Cute, but a little old for my tastes. Step aside, grandma."

Athena stood her ground. "You want her, you come through me."

Bean charged at her. A bright, humming blade flashed out from under Athena's robes. It passed through the front of Bean's heavy leather biker vest, trailing a thin line of blood in its wake. He howled in pain as the fabric fell away. Faith saw that the sword had bisected each of his nipples, and blood ran down his chest in twin rivulets.

Athena kept her strange, shimmering sword raised between them. "Next time I'll cut something else sticking out, asshole. Think it over."

Bean let out an inarticulate yell of rage and, flexing his legs, shot into the air and away from the combat scene.

Faith leaned back, exhausted. She saw Winternight look over at her, even while beset by Photon's attempts to melt him. The look on his face wasn't of anger, which she would have expected, but of deep satisfaction. Suddenly a great cube of ice appeared around him as he froze the very air solid. Photon smashed into the wall of ice and tumbled to the ground. Air Force caught a glancing blow from it and spun out of control.

Winternight appeared on the far side of the cube, surfing away on his wave of frozen air. Air Force started to pursue him but Athena called him back. "Let him go. We've got to help these people first, and Faith's hurt. Check on Photon."

Air Force dropped down next to the golden youth. "You all right?"

Photon sat up, looking down at himself in disgust as his own blood stained his costume. "I thigk I broke by dose."

Athena looked at the organ in question. "It's broken all right. I hope you don't have any dates this weekend. Hold his head, Air Force."

"Wait, what?" Photon started to move but Air Force grasped his head. Athena's hand darted up to his bruised and swollen face and snapped his nose back into place. Photon hollered, filling the air with foul language for a couple of minutes until he ran out of breath.

Athena smiled. "You'll thank me for that later. But right now, we need some of that radiant energy of yours. On your feet, kiddo."

Air Force helped Photon struggle back up into the air. Winternight had frozen much of the surrounding area. Everywhere, there were people rimed in frost. Photon spread his arms wide like a religious icon, and radiated. His heat wasn't couched in primitive fire, like Suncore's; his felt more like lying out in the sun on a beach. Faith closed her eyes and felt her skin prickling, like incipient sunburn.

The frost in the area quickly evaporated in his glow and people began to move, talk, ask questions, threaten, and cheer. The cheering was the most infectious of the reactions among the bystanders and soon a whole throng of kids not much older than Faith whooped and applauded.

Athena looked over at where Suncore had landed but a patch of smoldering grass marked the only sign he'd been there at all. Slipstream, too, had managed to sneak away in the confusion. "Just once I'd like to catch them with the entire team on hand. Then all we'd have to do is figure out how to keep them locked up."

Faith nodded, wincing at what the motion did to the pain in her body.

"Does it hurt?"

"I'll live."

"Not if your mother has anything to say about it."

PRIDE

October, 1972
Joliet, Illinois

The day Richard Lyons was born, the doctor said it would have been more of a kindness to let him die. His face was disfigured, with a bifurcated upper lip and a highly placed, squished nose that gave him a catlike appearance. Downy soft blonde hair covered him from head to toe, and he had no nails at the ends of his tiny fingers. It was 1953, and a difficult time for children with any sort of disabilities, but Richard's mother had a different philosophy.

Her husband, Richard's father, died in Korea, never getting to see his baby son. Jennifer Lyons was unwilling to part with the last vestige of her husband, and so despite the triple-threat hardship of being a single mother of a disfigured child, all while trying to support them both in the small military town of Mercury, Nevada, she rose to the occasion of motherhood like a prizefighter to a championship belt.

Growing up in Mercury made for a peculiar life for young Richard. Established to support the teams handling atomic weapons testing, the town was packed full of military and science families. To some, Richard's deformity was a curiosity, especially as his body hair never stopped growing, claws appeared at the ends of his fingers, and his teeth came in sharp, like a cat's. To most families, though, he was shunned and outcast, and that made for a hard life of bullying and beatings by older, bigger children. If they'd lived in a larger town, perhaps there might have been other options, like private school or tutors. But all of those things required money, and as a single working mother, Jennifer Lyons didn't have the luxury. She couldn't just keep Richard at home; the boy needed schooling, because she was determined that he would have better options in his life than she'd ever had in her own. "It's your education, Ricky," she would tell him when he balked at going back to the torment of school. "It's your future. Someday, you'll understand. Someday, you'll thank me."

Many were the days when a heartbroken Richard would run to the Post Office where his mother worked, to hide beneath her desk, sobbing at the latest round of brutality perpetrated against him. Some days it was physical, and he had bumps and bruises from being punched or kicked, or cuts from when rocks were thrown at him. Other days, the torment was far simpler and cut deeper, when he'd find himself in the middle of a pack of students who taunted him without mercy until often as not, he lost his temper, lashed out, and then wound up getting beaten anyway. He could tolerate the jabs at his appearance, when he was called *catface* or *pussy*, but when the kids discovered they could get to him by implying his mother had sex with a circus freak, or a lion in the zoo, that became the brunt of their attacks. No matter what she was doing, Jennifer would stop her work, gather him up in her arms, dry his tears, and tell him she loved him.

Sometimes, it would make him purr.

Jennifer suffered her own ostracization, as the mother of a disfigured child, but where Richard's bullying often came right at him head-on, hers was in the form of whispers just out of her hearing range, stares from other women who would quickly look away if they caught her looking back at them, and a constant exclusion from any and all social activities and circles.

Then one day, everything changed when Richard finally fought back against a group of bullies. He was eleven, and got cornered by four boys from the high school. They pushed him around, punched him, spat on him, until one of them said "I seen his momma's pussy, man, and you know what? It looks just like him. I heard that for twenty bucks, anyone in town can see her pussy."

Something in him snapped. He popped his claws—something his mother had absolutely forbidden him to do—and waded into them, snarling and hissing like a wild animal. He slashed and bit, tossing the boys around like they were little more than balsa wood models. All four wound up in the hospital, and Richard wound up in the police station while his mother desperately tried to talk the chief out of taking away her little boy and locking him up.

"He's a menace, your son. He's a monster. We don't want him in Mercury," said the Chief. "He belongs in a cage. Or a circus, the freak."

"Then I'll take him and we'll leave," said Jennifer.

The Chief nodded. "See that you're leaving by tonight, or I'll take him out and shoot him like the beast he is. Waste of a bullet, if you ask me."

The Lyonses left Mercury as the sun set behind the mountains, Jennifer at the wheel of her old beat-up Packard. They didn't know where to go, or what they would do when they got there, but at least they still had each other. The Packard's trunk held all their worldly belongings, which after years of struggling, didn't amount to much more than a couple of suitcases' worth of clothing.

Tired and hungry, they arrived in Las Vegas sometime later, and Jennifer checked them into a motel for the evening. The room had a color television, the first one Richard had ever seen. He spent all night staring at it, flipping channels until every single one showed a test pattern. The last thing he saw before one channel went off the air was a late-night news report about a group of costumed superheroes in New York City called Just Cause. They had battled The Mob and come up victorious. He especially felt inspired by the team leader, Lady Athena. She seemed so regal and powerful, so self-assured. He wondered if he could ever aspire to be like her.

Richard popped his claws out and studied them in the glow from the cathode ray tube. He was more cat than human, with his claws and needle sharp teeth and the fur that his mother shaved off him every week. He was also so much stronger and faster than the other boys, even those in high school. Maybe he was like the ones in Just Cause.

Jennifer dashed those hopes the next morning. "No, dear, you're not a superhero. You're just my son, but that's all the hero I could ever want. You stay here in the motel today while I go see about finding a job. Don't leave the room."

"I won't, Mama." Richard was an obedient boy and stayed in the motel room all morning, looking at the television and hoping to find something more about Just Cause. All he ever saw were soap operas and commercials, though.

Around lunchtime, Jennifer returned with a bag of sandwiches, a quart of bottled milk, and news that she'd obtained a job at the same diner where she'd bought them. "We'll be back on our feet soon, darling."

"Yes, Mama."

They stayed in Las Vegas for the next several years. The Sixties became the Seventies and as he entered high school, Richard stopped cutting his hair. It grew out into a magnificent mane of tawny gold and ruddy brown, and when he stopped shaving, his entire face became covered with fur. He was still bullied, but it only took some judicious use of his strength, carefully metered, to convince others that he was no easy prey.

He found a peer group of sorts in the gearheads and motorcycle gangs. They were surprisingly tolerant of his oddities, and for the first time in his life, Richard had friends. They wore motorcycle boots, leather jackets, and dirty t-shirts. They cut classes and smoked cigarettes and wrenched on their cars and bikes.

And then one day, they went looking for trouble and they found it in a group of Hell's Angels only too willing to bring knives, chains, and guns to bear. None of Richard's friends came away unbloodied, and two of them wound up in the hospital. For his own part, Richard got sliced up on one arm by a bearded man who outweighed him by a good hundred pounds.

He ripped the man's face to shreds.

Richard knew he couldn't go home again after that. People knew about the cat-man in Las Vegas, and he was afraid the Hell's Angels would come looking for him. He hit the road that night, hitching a ride with a cross-country trucker who took him as far as Phoenix. The trucker gave Richard a hat to help hide his features, and five dollars to help him on his way, wherever it was that he was going. It killed him to leave his life and his mother behind. She had been in his corner since the very day he was born, and without her, he was once again a frightened and lost little boy, except now he couldn't run to find her in the post office and hide beneath her counter. Sometimes, in the dark, when he was huddled up in the corner of a railroad car, or a five-dollar flophouse, where nobody could see or hear him, he would allow the tears to come.

Richard drifted east and north, working odd jobs where he could find them and being hungry where he couldn't. He didn't want to stoop to stealing or mugging people, even though with his abilities it would have been so easy. He sent his mom postcards when he had a few cents extra to spend on them, but other than that he stayed on his own on the road. Sometimes he'd stay in a town for only as long as it took to find a ride. Other times he stayed for a week, or even a month. There was work to be had, and he forced himself not to be too proud to do anything. He paved a highway in New Mexico, he harvested corn in Colorado, and he roughnecked in Oklahoma. By then, he'd made enough money to buy an old Indian motorcycle, and his spare money went into fixing it up.

When he had a chance, he stopped by newsstands and bought magazines or papers that had stories about Just Cause or the other parahumans in them. He knew he belonged with them, and after a couple of years wandering, he set New York as his destination goal.

One thing he learned in his travels was that for every decent, kind-hearted soul willing to help out a man down on his luck, there were ten more eager to kick him while he was down. More than once, Richard had to run from the law, or from angry friends or family members in pickup trucks and guns, who hated hippies, bikers, and freaks. More than once, he left them bleeding by the roadside.

And then one day in the fall of 1972, everything changed for him.

He was washing dishes in a small town an hour outside of Chicago. A cold rain was battering the glass of the diner, and fallen leaves blew against it like bomb shrapnel. He'd been working there for only a week, sleeping at the town's YMCA and saving up money for a new front wheel. He'd blown a tire and wiped out on the bike. He'd been fortunate enough to land in soft heather and ferns along the roadside, but the sliding bike plowed into a stone and bent the front wheel into a pretzel.

The bikers roared into town, oblivious to the elements, and parked their steeds in a row in front of the diner. The waitresses, cooks, and patrons looked out at them nervously as they swaggered across the sidewalk and pushed open the diner door with a bang.

They weren't Hell's Angels, Richard observed, but that didn't make them less dangerous. By the patches on their sopping jackets, they were a group called the Demon Lords, and their leader was more like Richard than like everyone else in the diner.

The gang leader was huge, near seven feet tall, with muscles that strained to burst through his denim vest and t-shirt. His skin was a burnished bronze color, knobbed with hard bumps that looked like alligator hide. The skin condition continued up his face, where several of the knobs sprouted short ivory horns. A heavy brow ridge hooded his eyes, which burned with sulfurous intent. Thick claws decorated his fingers, and overlong canine teeth poked out of his mouth above and below.

The other seven Demon Lords were normal humans, but they had a sense of casual violence about them that made Richard's hackles rise. They sauntered through the diner like they owned it, leering at women and children, casually picking mouthfuls of food off patrons plates, being generally rude and boisterous.

"You, uh, gentlemen need to leave," said the oldest waitress, who'd spoken up on Richard's behalf when he asked for a job. "I don't care if he's ugly," she'd said, "so long as he can sling a mop and a rag." Her name was Alice, and Richard was pretty sure the diner had been built around her.

"Whatever happened to *the customer's always right*?" sneered the scaly Demon Lord.

Richard set down his sponge and wiped his paws off on his apron.

"What you doin', man?" asked the black guy working the fryer. His name was Jimmy, and he made the best fried chicken Richard had ever tasted.

"I can't just let them push everyone around," growled Richard.

"Man, there's ten of them and one of you. I don't care what kind of teeth and claws you got. They'd skin you alive, kid. Hush up and maybe they'll leave after they get what they want."

"Hey, the lady asked you to leave," said a brusque man in a hat with earflaps and a quilted vest. "Why don't you clear on out? We don't want your kind in here."

"My *kind*? What kind is that?" The Demon Lord's voice grew sly and quiet.

"Scum. Lowlifes." The brusque man clenched his fists.

"Scum. Lowlifes," repeated the Demon Lord. "I had no idea. Boys, did you know that we're scum and lowlifes?" The other bikers snickered. The Demon Lord bowed to the brusque man. "Thank you, kind sir, for your kind words. Nobody has ever complimented us quite like you have."

"I s-said clear on out." The brusque man lost his bravery as he realized he had the full attention of all the Demon Lords.

The leader lashed out his hand quick as a flash and knocked the man's hat off his head. The others laughed as it sailed across the diner toward an Oriental man sitting at the end of the corner, eating a bowl of soup.

Without moving a muscle more than necessary—indeed, without even looking—the man caught the hat before it could upend his soup bowl and set it gently on the counter beside him. Then he sipped another spoonful of soup as if nothing had happened.

The Demon Lord, already bored with the formerly-brusque man, stalked across the diner toward the man and his soup. Richard tore off his apron and threw it aside.

"You gonna die, man," said the fry cook.

"He's an old man. He's not bothering anyone," said Richard. "They can bother me instead." He came out from behind the prep tables and around the corner of the counter.

The Demon Lord paid Richard no mind. He had a new interest in the old man and his soup. "Well," he said, drawing it out. "What do we got here? Some kinda kung fu guy? Kwai Chang Cocksucker?"

The other Demon Lords laughed like it was the best joke any of them had ever heard.

"Hey, ugly, leave him alone," called Richard. "You want to mess with someone, mess with me." His claws were out and he didn't even remember popping them.

The Demon Lord turned to see who was addressing him in such a tone. He caught sight of Richard and looked him up and down. "Ugly? Well if that ain't a case of the pot calling the kettle black, I don't know what is." His ugly face grew hard. "You think you can take the Demon Lord, pussycat?"

The other Demon Lords laughed and made miaowing noises.

"You want to step outside?" asked Richard, eliciting even harder laughter from the bikers. They mocked his words, flinging them back at him like flying daggers.

"You know? I don't. It's raining, and I don't want to mess up my hair." The Demon Lord ran a palm across his bumpy, hairless scalp. "I see it's already too late for yours, though. Pussums got all wet in the rainy-rain."

"Hey Joe," called one of the others. "Maybe it's time to put the cat out for the night."

"Don't bother," said Richard. "I'll leave." The look of condemnation on Alice's face cut Richard to the marrow. He could almost hear her yelling *coward* after him in that same time she used when the line cooks messed up an order.

"And that's that," said the Demon Lord, apparently whose real name was Joe. "Now, where were we? I believe we were about to do some kung fu fighting with Bruce Lee, here."

Richard stepped out into the rain. He hated how the cold water seeped through his mane, matting it down against his thin t-shirt and enhancing the musty smell he never could quite eradicate. He looked back at the Demon Lords in the diner, about to cause even more trouble, then over at their bikes, parked diagonally to the curb in a neat row.

As a fellow rider, it galled him to do so, but Richard reached for the first bike in the line and shoved it as hard as he could. It tipped and fell into its neighbor, dislodging that bike as well and pretty soon, all eight bikes lay on their sides in the gutter amid broken glass and leaking fluids. Richard turned to the diner windows and grinned a mouthful of sharp teeth.

The Demon Lords, predictably, came running out of the diner into the rain, shouting their anger on counterpoint to the growl of thunder. Richard lowered his head and popped his claws. "All right, who's first?"

A biker wielding a switchblade charged at him first. Richard ducked under a clumsy thrust and swept the biker's legs out from beneath him. As he fell, the biker lunged at Richard, catching him with the very tip of the switchblade. Richard's t-shirt split apart and blood welled out from a thin scratch, matting the tawny fur on his abdomen.

He roared like the King of the Jungle. The biker struggled to back away, but Richard grabbed hold of one of the man's flailing feet. He wrenched the biker's ankle, raking his claws through the man's filthy blue jeans, and then swung the man around like an Olympic hammer-thrower to hurl him against several of his companions.

The Demon Lords pulled out their knives and chains and went after Richard. He was outnumbered and outgunned, but so long as he kept the bikers busy outside, they might not hassle anyone else in the diner.

It was what superheroes were supposed to do.

He drove a fist into one biker's face, smashing his nose like a water balloon full of blood. Another biker lunged in with brass knuckles, but Richard turned to catch the blow on the meaty part of his shoulder instead of his jaw. His arm went numb almost instantly and he knew he was in trouble. A bicycle chain wrapped around his legs. His feet slipped on the wet cement and he crashed to the ground. Hard steel-toed boots drove into his sides, his legs, his head. He felt a rib go, and boot sole caught him between the eyes, lighting up his vision like a photographer's flash.

Still, he tried to fight back. Richard took a kick to the jaw in order to hamstring a biker, slicing through his Achilles tendon with his claws. The man went down screaming, which made most of the bikers pull back. The one who didn't had a bike chain, and he swung it down at Richard so hard that it whistled like a train. Richard rolled to one side and then the other to avoid the steel links, but with every motion, the ends of his broken ribs rubbed together and nearly made him faint.

"Stop it! You're killin' him!" screamed one of the waitresses from the diner doorway.

"Shut up, or you're next," yelled a biker.

"Hold it," said a voice that hissed like anger in the rain.

Blows stopped hammering down upon Richard. His eyes wouldn't focus, and the world tilted around him, an amusement park ride out of control. Strong, knobby hands lifted him by his mane, adding throbbing agony to the other injury pain flashing through his body. Richard dimly felt his feet dangling as Demon Lord himself held Richard above his head.

"You think you're a tough guy?" asked the man. He punched Richard across the jaw, making him see stars. The biker wasn't just big, he was strong—inhumanly so. "You gonna be a hero?" *Punch.* "Save the day, get the girl?" *Punch.* "Let me tell you something, hero. There ain't no such thing in this world. There's only the strong and the weak." *Punch*. "You weak, man."

Somehow, despite his senses reeling from the repeated blows, Richard found the strength to rake his claws across the Demon Lord's face. The biker screamed and dropped Richard, who collapsed into a bleeding heap upon the cement.

"Call the police!" screamed the waitress. "He's going to kill him."

"She's right," hissed the Demon Lord. Blood ran down his ugly, misshapen face from four deep parallel scratches. One of his eyes was already swelling shut, but that didn't stop him from lunging down to pick up Richard and drive a knee hard into Richard's guts.

The broken rib grated. The pain of it galvanized Richard and he fought back tooth and nail, understanding that he was no longer fighting for the safety of the diner, but for his own life. He roared with all the power of a lion ruling the African veldt, found a reserve of strength, and attacked the Demon Lord.

The ugly biker punched at Richard again, just missing Richard's solar plexus. Richard responded by clamping his teeth down upon the biker's misshapen knuckles. The man howled as bright, hot blood flooded into Richard's mouth. He spat out a chunk of flesh and a lump that could have been a knuckle. "Come on, you ugly bastard," he said through swollen and split lips. "I got plenty more."

The Demon Lord staggered back, clutching his ruined hand against his chest. "You ugly son of a bitch just made the last mistake of your life." He fumbled inside his jacket and withdrew a small pistol.

Richard had never been at the wrong end of a gun before. Every nerve screamed for him to duck, to flee, but he squashed down that cowardice. "You leave this town. You're not welcome here. Leave, or I'll tear out your throat."

The Demon Lord raised his pistol and Richard knew his death was at hand. He didn't close his eyes, didn't back down. He would face his end like a man, not a coward.

A sudden sound of blows striking flesh in the rain made the Demon Lord pause in his execution. An odd look came across his face and a trickle of blood ran from the corner of his mouth to mix with the rain coursing down his skin. He opened his mouth to speak, but seemed to have no air to do so. He collapsed onto the pavement.

The elderly Asian man who'd been eating soup in the diner stood behind the Demon Lord, his fingers pushed together like spear points. He stepped over the Demon Lord, who was either unconscious or dead, and retrieved the biker's pistol.

The other bikers decided discretion was the better part of valor and fled on foot, leaving their bikes where they'd fallen. A siren cried in the distance, perhaps in response to the street fight.

The Asian man tossed the pistol into a storm drain and then looked down at Richard. "You are a brave warrior," he said. "And you are a fool. You have much to learn." He nodded at Richard and turned away.

Richard felt sick to his stomach with the taste of the Demon Lord's blood still fresh in his mouth. One of his eyes was swollen completely shut and his entire face felt like it had gone through a meat grinder. His broken rib burned in his side, and his kidneys throbbed from repeated blows. He couldn't imagine ever hurting worse. He wondered if anyone had called an ambulance for him when they'd called the police. He wondered if any doctor would even treat a freak like him.

A dozen yards away, the Asian man stopped and turned his head slightly back to speak, his voice barely carrying over the hiss of the rain. "Are you coming or not?"

Richard had nowhere to go, no prospects. The Asian man had, for whatever reason, saved his life. Richard didn't know a lot about how the world worked, but he knew enough that if his life was saved, it was no longer his; it belonged to his savior. Whatever the man had in mind for Richard, he would suffer through it, because a debt was a debt to be paid in full.

He struggled through the pain to get back to his feet and limp after the man. "Yes."

THE STEEL SOLDIER'S GAMBIT

February, 1976
New York City, NY

It had snowed two nights ago and the temperatures had plunged below zero, which ensured the several inches of fallen snow would hang around until the city crews got the streets cleared, in between their lengthy and numerous union breaks. John Stone tramped into the lobby of Two World Trade Center, careful not to crack the tile—a real concern since he was seven hundred pounds, with a body made of granite. The cold didn't bother him through his impenetrable stony skin, but the tenacious snow still clung to his feet and he had to shake it from his shoulders. As usual, he wore very little clothing; his stone body tended to wear out all but the toughest fabrics in days, if not hours. Tonight, however, he'd slipped into a gargantuan mohair overcoat and scarf along with his trademark fedora for the sake of decorum.

The elevator boy gave him a wide grin. "Evenin', John. Cold one tonight."

"Sure is, Wally."

"Got a late meeting tonight up at the H.Q.?"

John smiled and showed his teeth of quartz. "It's Wednesday, Wally."

The boy shot back a knowing grin. "O-o-o-h yeah. *Poker* night!"

Wednesday Night Poker had started back in '74, right after the team relocated their headquarters to the World Trade Center. It had been a slow day in early autumn, with no alarms or cries for help or even cats stuck up in trees in Central Park. The citizens of the City that Never Sleeps had been so quiet that Javelin had joked that somebody must have put downers in the water. But no unusual crimes meant no need for superheroes, so Lionheart and Tornado had broken out a deck of cards and started a game. John had joined in and soon Wednesday Night Poker became a tradition for the heroes of Just Cause. Most Wednesdays, at least five heroes gambled, smoked, and drank around the table.

John stepped off the elevator into the lobby of Just Cause headquarters, still as shiny and new as the day they'd moved in. Team leader Lionheart, in spite of his wild appearance, was a neat freak and paid a husband-and-wife team of Russian immigrants top dollar to make the facility sparkle. John reflected on how little of a life he really had outside of the superhero business. Here on his night off—when he could have been sitting in a bar, walking through Central Park, or even catching the Rangers in a late game—he'd chosen to hang out with his crime-fighting colleagues instead.

"Hi, John." Tornado's long flowing blond curls belonged on a rock singer instead of a red-blooded American superhero. John often teased the man about his locks. Tornado called it jealousy, since John could grow no hair of his own. The two were best friends.

"*Buenas noches,* John." Javelin's armor and energy dart projectors were piled in the corner of the room and instead he wore a burgundy velour leisure suit, looking more like a Puerto Rican pimp than a superhero.

The robotic Steel Soldier inclined his head in a stiff bow and spoke in a synthesized monotone. "GOOD EVENING, JOHN." A hundred years ahead of its time, the android had been discovered in '72 in the midst of a destroyed building, the victim of unexplainable circumstances. His memory had been erased and his armored body had showed signs of combat. Javelin had theorized the Soldier was an involuntary time traveler, for the android's construction was advanced far beyond the capabilities of present-day technology. The Soldier had proved its mettle against the villain called Tyrant, and been accepted into the ranks of Just Cause. After years of legal wrangling, with Just Cause members speaking on his behalf, the Soldier had been declared sentient and an American citizen by the U.S. Supreme Court.

"Anyone else planning to join us tonight?" John shrugged out of his coat.

Tornado shook his head. "Audio and Pony Girl decided to stay home and cuddle in front of the fireplace. Haven't heard from Sundancer. And no word from Lionheart either."

"Maybe he's sticking out the blizzard at home." Javelin popped the cap off a beer and tossed it across the room.

Tornado snorted in amusement. "Are you kidding? I don't think he even has a home. I thought he lived here."

"I'm here, boys . . . break out the chips." Lionheart stepped out of the shadows, a feral grin plastered across his face. His hair and beard grew together into a thick, tawny mane which framed his sharp features and piercing eyes. A fine layer of fur like suede coated his skin, which accentuated the contours of his powerful musculature. He popped one of his claws out from a fingertip and neatly sliced open the shrink wrap around a new deck of cards. "Who feels like some five card draw?"

"Hell, yes." Javelin lit up his first cigar of the night— illegal Cubans smuggled into the country by one of his distant cousins.

And so they began in earnest. In the old days, they'd just played for fun. Last year, they started to bring real money to the table and nowadays they played all hands for portions—or occasionally *all*—of a weekly paycheck. Since Just Cause was a private organization, the sponsoring Devereaux Foundation saw to it all members received a salary so they wouldn't have to work mundane jobs and risk compromising their secret identities. The funny thing about it, thought John as he dealt, was since the Foundation picked up the expenses for the actual team operations, the salaried heroes didn't have much use for those paychecks. Costumes, food, lodging, and transportation were all provided by the Foundation. It wasn't unusual for several thousand dollars to change hands on Wednesday night.

This particular evening, the money seemed to be flowing in two directions: either toward Lionheart or toward the Steel Soldier. The Soldier's central processor was capable of millions of calculations per second, making him an accomplished card counter and odds assessor. The others' parahuman abilities didn't help them when it came to gambling. Tornado could send cards blowing around the room, but had a lousy poker face and couldn't bluff with any effectiveness. John's face was as immobile as the Soldier's, but he didn't have a knack for knowing when to fold his cards. Javelin smoked a lot of cigars—permitted when Pony Girl and Sundancer weren't at the table— drank a lot of Mexican beer, but seemed to be having a run of bad luck. Lionheart, on the other hand, was playing some of the best poker any of them had ever seen.

John threw down his cards in disgust. "Did you develop some new mind-reading powers that we don't know about?"

"Just in the groove tonight. Ante up." Lionheart's voice was terse, as if he were preoccupied.

John looked at his shrinking pile of chips and sighed as he pushed five into the pot. "I may not last another hand. Especially if Tornado deals me junk like he did last time."

"Hey, it's not my fault you're losing. We're *all* losing." Tornado sounded sullen.

Javelin stabbed out his cigar and looked at his own miniscule stack of chips. "Maybe we should just let you two fight it out, since it looks like it's down to you two *vatos* anyways."

"One more hand, then." Lionheart's expression was smug as he regarded the large stack of chips in front of him. Then his face darkened to displeasure as he compared his pile to the similar stack in front of the Soldier. He reached into his belt. "Perhaps we might make this one a little more . . . *interesting*." He tossed a pair of Polaroids onto the table.

"What're those, bootleg pictures of Sundancer? Not much we haven't seen after she was Miss March." Javelin laughed.

Tornado reached out and picked up the pictures and then stared at Lionheart in confusion. "What is this?" He passed the pictures to John.

The images showed Lionheart, bound into a chair by tight ropes and chains, with a blindfold over his eyes and a gag in his mouth.

Servomotors whined inside the Soldier's torso as the robot stood up. "SENSORS INDICATE THIS IS NOT LIONHEART. MY APOLOGIES. I HAD NO REASON TO SUSPECT OTHERWISE UNTIL NOW."

The others gasped in astonishment as the impostor's appearance flowed like water and finally resolved into a thin man wearing a spiral-patterned black and white costume.

"Mento!" John crushed the edge of the table between his cumbersome fingers by accident. "I wish I could whistle so that I could do so cheerfully while I was tying you into knots."

Mento the Threatmaker was a notorious bottom-feeding villain whose grandiose schemes often went awry when his ego got in the way of his common sense.

Where any sensible villain would cut his losses and run away when his plans fell apart, Mento would get huffy and argumentative until somebody got tired of his monologues and knocked him over the head. He had proven himself a real irritant to the heroes of Just Cause with his antics and petty offenses, but had so far failed to cause any significant harm. Every time they caught him, though, he'd use his powers and escape. With his ability to read minds and generate illusions, he could make himself appear to be whomever he wished. Just Cause had never managed to keep him locked up for more than a couple days.

"Not so fast, heroes." Mento leaped to his feet and tried to look imperious and powerful but failed due to his slight frame and laughable costume, which looked like the demented scribblings of a color-blind toddler. "I hold your leader prisoner. If I fail to return, my henchmen will execute him."

"Where in the world would you find henchmen?" John growled with a sound like boulders rolling downhill.

"Why, I found them in the—*Aha*! You're trying to *trick* me. Well, it won't work, cretins. I'm holding all the cards now."

"Actually, *I'm* holding all the cards now." Tornado held up the deck for evidence. "What do you want, Mento? You've already got our money. Well, you and the Soldier, anyway."

"Just one hand. Winner take all. If you win, you keep your money and I release your leader."

"And if you win, *pendejo*?" Javelin looked with longing toward the energy dart projectors in the corner of the room with the rest of his armor.

Mento rubbed his hands together and cackled like a cliché villain in a bad movie. "If I win, I'll release Lionheart . . . after I get the control codes for the Steel Soldier."

John's, Tornado's, and Javelin's jaws all dropped like they were a school of guppies.

"We don't have the control codes." John spoke as if to a toddler. "And even if we did, we wouldn't give them to you."

"Why not? It's just a machine."

"Not according to the Supreme Court," said Tornado.

"JOHN, YOU ARE NOT ENTIRELY CORRECT; ONE PERSON DOES HAVE THE CODES."

"Who?"

The Soldier cocked its head to one side in a very human expression. "I DO, OF COURSE."

"What are you doing, Steel?" Tornado sounded aghast.

"THAT SHOULD BE OBVIOUS, TORNADO. I'M ENSURING THAT LIONHEART WILL BE SAVED. ASSUMING THAT MENTO WILL ABIDE BY HIS DEAL, THAT IS."

"Hey, I may be a crook, but I'm no welsher. Either way, you guys get Lionheart back. It's what you call a win-win situation."

"DEAL THE CARDS, TORNADO. ONE HAND, WINNER TAKES ALL."

"Yeah," said Mento, "because, uh, that's what I said."

"Are you sure about this, Soldier? You'd be a hell of a weapon in somebody else's hands." John flexed his fingers. It sounded like rocks breaking.

"I'M POSITIVE, JOHN. RETRIEVING LIONHEART SAFELY IS THE PRIORITY HERE. AND MENTO KNOWS VERY WELL THAT YOU'LL TURN HIM INTO PASTE IF HE FAILS TO FOLLOW THROUGH WITH HIS OFFER."

"Long as you know what you're doing." John turned to Tornado. "Deal the cards, Tommy."

"Don't bother dealing yourselves in." Mento's tone had turned nasty. "I can read your minds easily. I've known all night what you were holding."

"No wonder you've been playing so well." Javelin patted himself down for one more cigar, failed to find one, and crossed his arms in disgust.

"You can't read the Soldier's mind, can you?" asked Tornado.

"No. Of course not. It's a machine." A sheen of sweat appeared on Mento's upper lip. "Should we, uh, ante?"

"IF IT WILL MAKE YOU FEEL BETTER. AS YOU SAID BEFORE, THIS IS A WINNER-TAKE-ALL POT. THE ANTE DOESN'T REALLY MATTER, DOES IT?"

Tornado dealt out five cards each to Mento and the Soldier. They each picked up their hands and examined the cards, Mento with intense interest and the Soldier with the same dispassionate regard the android had used all night.

"No point in really betting, is there?" Javelin grumbled.

John counted his bills. "What the hell. I've got thirty-eight dollars that says Steel wins the hand. Anybody want to take that bet?"

Javelin chuckled. "Sure, why not? And I'll put up . . . thirty dollars even that says we follow Mento back to his HQ and round up his whole gang."

"I'll have some of that. I bet Lionheart himself gets the knockout shot on Mento." John grinned.

"Got you covered, Johnny." Tornado turned to Mento. "How many cards you want?"

More sweat formed on Mento's face, and a single bead of it threatened to drip the tip of his nose. He wiped it away with the back of his hand. "Uh, two." He laid them down on the table.

Tornado dealt two back to Mento. "Steel?"

The Soldier didn't immediately reply. They could hear the switches in his processors flipping back and forth like excitable fleas tap-dancing. With one smooth motion, the Soldier closed his hand and held it against his chest plastron. "I'LL STAND WITH THESE."

Mento leaped to his feet. "What? Not even one card? What do you have, flush or a straight? Full house? You think that's going to be good enough to beat me? I've been playing you all for fools tonight!" He broke into maniacal laughter.

The Soldier sat in silence and waited for Mento to wind down his tirade.

"Maybe you better quit, Mento. The Soldier doesn't bluff," said Tornado.

"He isn't programmed to," said Javelin.

"After all, he is just a machine, as you said. Machines don't lie; they can only calculate." John dug a small furrow in the tabletop with his index finger.

"Quiet," said Mento. "I'm thinking."

Javelin smiled. "Don't hurt yourself."

"NOW COMES THE TIME WHEN TRADITIONALLY A SECOND ROUND OF BETS ARE MADE BETWEEN THE PLAYERS. AS YOU LED THE LAST ROUND, SO WILL YOU LEAD THIS ROUND, MENTO. DO YOU WISH TO CHECK OR CALL?"

Mento blinked. "A second round? But I don't . . . I mean, I'm not . . ."

"Take your time," said Tornado. "Formulate your words. Think about what you're going to say before you open your mouth."

"Check. I check."

"VERY WELL. HERE IS MY BET; YOU MAY CALL, RAISE, OR FOLD UPON HEARING IT. IF YOU WIN, I WILL NOT ONLY GIVE TO YOU THE MONEY YOU WIN TONIGHT AS WELL AS MY CONTROL CODES, I WILL GIVE YOU THE COMPLETE TECHNICAL SPECIFICATIONS OF MY CONSTRUCTION. THIS WILL ALLOW YOU TO BUILD MULTIPLE COPIES OF ME. IF YOU LOSE, YOU WILL CALL YOUR HENCHMEN AND ORDER THE RELEASE OF LIONHEART, AND YOU WILL STAY HERE AT OUR MERCY. NOW THAT I HAVE ATTUNED MY SENSORS PROPERLY TO YOUR BODY, I CANNOT BE FOOLED BY FURTHER ILLUSIONS. YOUR DAYS OF LAWBREAKING WILL BE AT AN END."

"Holy crap." Mento's voice didn't rise above a whisper. "That's how I call?"

The Soldier raised its gleaming, brushed-steel hand. "I AM NOT FINISHED. IF YOU CHOOSE INSTEAD TO FOLD, WE WILL PERMIT YOU TO LEAVE UNHARMED AND

UNFOLLOWED, BUT YOU MUST STILL RELEASE LIONHEART FIRST BY TELEPHONE."

Mento looked very nervous and sweaty as he examined his hand again. "Ha. My henchmen are under strict orders not to release Lionheart except if I order it in person."

"Or you give them the code phrase," added Tornado.

Mento laughed. "C-code phrase? What makes you think there's a code phrase? Would I be that transparent?"

"Yes," chorused the others.

"I BELIEVE THAT IT IS NOW UP TO YOU TO DECIDE HOW WE PROCEED."

Mento drummed his fingers like a John Bonham solo on the table and his eyes flicked back and forth between his own cards and those held by the Soldier. "I win, I get your codes and your specifications?"

"YES."

"I lose, you lock me up here forever?"

"YES."

"I fold, I get away without any hassle at all?"

"YES, PROVIDING LIONHEART IS SAFELY RELEASED."

"Tough choice," muttered Mento.

Javelin blew out a cloud of stinking tobacco smoke. "I'd say fold. Sounds like your best option to me."

"Absolutely." Tornado failed to hide a grin.

"He who gambles with superheroes and runs away, lives to fight another day. Or some bullshit like that." John shifted in his seat, gauging how quickly he could smash the table into Mento.

Mento shifted in his seat like his underwear was riding up his butt. Beads of sweat dotted across his forehead. Finally he gave a deep sigh and threw down his cards. "I fold. I can't risk that."

"Fine. Tornado, get the man his phone." John almost pounded his fist on the table but remembered just in time that he'd knock it to splinters it if he did.

"With pleasure. But first, I gotta know what each of you guys had."

Mento shrugged. "That's fair, I suppose. I'm sure you are all honorable men here and aren't going to go back on your word."

"We don't welsh either, *pendejo.*"

Mento flipped his cards over. "Three of a kind. Eights. Nothing to gossip about. Pretty crappy hand, actually. What does the robot have?"

The Steel Soldier laid down its hand, face up, in a neat arc of cards: jack high only. Not even a pair. Javelin and Tornado burst out in laughter and John cracked a smile as Mento's face grew dark and thunderous.

"You said he didn't bluff!" shrieked Mento.

"He doesn't. Or I should say, he hasn't before tonight." John chuckled at the unfortunate villain's plight.

Mento spluttered, "What . . . how . . ."

"I WROTE A NEW SUBROUTINE THIS MONTH THAT ALLOWS ME TO PERFORM THE DISHONESTY YOU CALL BLUFFING. TONIGHT SEEMED AN OPPORTUNE MOMENT TO TRY IT OUT."

"You sly, metallic son of a bitch!" Javelin wiped his eyes in amusement.

Tornado handed Mento the phone. The thoroughly-cowed villain made a quick, whispered phone call. A few minutes later, they received a call from Lionheart, who had been released unharmed and was heading back to headquarters.

"I can just walk away?" Mento looked toward the exit door and licked his lips.

"That was the deal," said John. "You better go before we change our minds."

"You should change that costume," said Tornado. "It looks like an optometrist's office threw up on you."

Whatever pithy parting shot Javelin had prepared was lost as he fell out of his chair and collapsed in a fit of giggles.

"You . . . you haven't seen the last of me. Mento the Threatmaker will rise triumphant someday, and then you'll all be very . . . very . . ."

John pushed his seat back from the table. Mento turned as white as a sheet and fled the room.

"Think we've seen the last of him?" Tornado twirled a finger through his hair.

"I hope so," said John.

Javelin sat up from where he'd fallen on the floor. "Man, I'm starving. Anybody feel like a pizza?"

Tornado shrugged. "I'm flat busted."

"Me too," added John.

The Soldier looked at them, and somehow John sensed if he could have smiled, he would have when he said, "MY TREAT, GENTLEMEN."

COMPONENTS

December, 1984
New York City, NY

Some men might have returned to their hometown to great fanfare, like a victorious warrior celebrating an overthrown tyrant. There would be ticker tape falling from the high rises, brass bands, and soldiers kissing nurses in the streets. When Harlan Washington returned to New York City from Philadelphia, he did so under the cover of darkness, with his collar turned up and his hat pulled down low, and that was good enough for him. In his mind, he was the victorious warrior, but the tyrants hadn't yet been overthrown. They were still there in the World Trade Center, looking down upon all the little people supposedly under their protection.

Harlan knew better. Just Cause was full of assholes, like Javelin and Pony Girl. Even Harlan's older sister Irlene was part of that team who thought they were so much better than everyone else. She had played just as much a role as the others in taking him down, ruining his Destroyer suit, and sending him off to juvie hall because of all the damage he'd caused and the lives he'd taken.

It wasn't like Harlem hadn't been about to burn down anyway from all the firetrap tenements. He'd just helped them with a little urban renewal. And as for all the jerks who'd been in the wrong place at the wrong time? *You can't make an omelet without breaking a few eggs*, as Harlan was wont to say, and there had been plenty of bad eggs in his neighborhood that he hadn't minded breaking; not even the bitch who'd once called herself his mother.

The next suit was going to be incredible. Much stronger. Much faster. And it would be able to fly. The machinery sang to Harlan in his sleep, telling him its secrets, and when he awoke it was with plans and schematics dancing in his eyes.

"Yo, man, we're here," said Bay, the giant man with a baritone voice that could frighten Darth Vader. Harlan looked up from where he was doodling a circuit design for the Destroyer Mark II suit. The U-Haul's headlights made two bright spots up against the rolling vertical door of a Manhattan warehouse. Bay was Harlan's go-to guy, who solved problems and dealt with people so Harlan didn't have to.

Bay had been a guest of the New York Juvenile Corrections System, like Harlan, who had been almost fourteen when he was remanded into custody of the state. Bay was three years older and serving time for burglary and arson, and based upon his behavior in the clink, wouldn't be an adult long before graduating to assault and murder. Harlan had shared a cell with Bay. At first, Bay had been disinterested in the slight, smelly thirteen-year-old, but then Harlan had put together an electric shock stick out of some parts he scrounged up and used it to stop the heart of a much larger boy who'd been amusing himself by fucking younger boys in their asses in the middle of the night. He'd come for Harlan and left in a body bag, and after that Bay showed him great respect, even stepping up to protect Harlan when someone started hassling him. Harlan learned a very important lesson during his time in juvie: respect wasn't only about who had the biggest muscles. Intelligence was a clenched fist or a shiv in the dark, and Harlan had brains to spare.

When he made his escape on the eve of his fifteenth birthday, he brought Bay with him. The two boys lugged Harlan's steam-knife, built from parts he cannibalized from laundry and kitchen machinery, through the sublevels of the juvenile facility, cutting through wall after wall until they found freedom. A few carefully-timed gas grenades in their wake prevented any pursuit from the hapless assholes tasked with guarding children, and the boys had a few moments to savor their freedom.

"We go to Philadelphia," said Harlan. "Just Cause is still here. They're going to be looking for me."

"But I don't know nobody in Philly," said Bay.

"All the better. Gives us a place to start fresh."

"What we gonna do?"

Harlan smiled at the bigger boy. "Whatever we want."

What they had done, in fact, was to get connected with an up-and-coming organization in Philadelphia known as the Black Mafia. They were looking for good street soldiers, people who could follow orders, like Bay, and people who could give them, like Harlan. The two of them took charge first of a block, then a street, and eventually an entire neighborhood. Between the drugs and skin trade, the protection racket and the smuggling, Harlan and his group were taking in the money hand over fist.

But then the nightmares started. Bullies and rapists who looked like the superheroes of Just Cause ran rampant through them, chasing him through darkened alleys where he had no escape, no suit to protect him from their fists and worse. He found only tinkering could alleviate them, so he left Bay to run the business and Harlan became the threat in the background, the person in the shadows no one wanted to piss off.

The sound of another engine shook Harlan from his own thoughts back to the present. He looked out the window to see the one-eyed monster of a Pontiac that belonged to Barry, one of the young toughs Bay had recruited to Harlan's New York crew. The other three dark heads in the car's interior would be Darrell, James, and Troy. His time in the Black Mafia had taught him the usefulness of having local talent handy when one needed to hit the ground running, and he was determined to get his big project underway.

Just Cause had peeled him out of his first suit like someone picking a scab off his knee. They would find that a lot more difficult in the Mark II, and someday he would use it to get back at them for the humiliation he suffered the night of the Blackout, the night he'd cut his whore of a mother's throat as she slept in her chair and escaped into the riotous darkness with only his little sister Reggie to keep him company. If there was one person in the world Harlan could say he cared about, it would be Reggie. She had always respected him when they were growing up together in that roach-infested rathole of a Harlem apartment. She gave him space when he needed it, she kept secrets for him, and she had a sense about when he truly needed help.

Being being a fugitive meant he couldn't risk getting caught for a few minutes of face time with Reggie, so instead he had to monitor her from afar. Coming back to New York made him feel strangely moody about her. She was thirteen now, in middle school, and living with Irlene and Irlene's boyfriend, that Puerto Rican scumbag Javelin. In a moment of weakness, Harlan had picked out a postcard from a service station at the edge of Pennsylvania. It was an African veldt, with a herd of gray elephants basking in the bright sunlight. Harlan's strongest memory of Reggie was her dragging around that stupid, filthy stuffed elephant. He didn't even remember what she'd named it, but she'd loved that toy. He mailed the postcard to her blank, unsigned, nothing to show it had come from him. Maybe she would know he was thinking of her, and that made him almost feel something, although he didn't have the vocabulary to put it into words.

He stepped out of the truck and looked up at the building. It was a run-down, nondescript warehouse like so many in New York. The windows were caked over with dust, the paint peeling from the wood after years of coastal weather and neglect. It wasn't nearly as nice as the place he and Bay had left behind in Philly, but appearances weren't everything. Like Yoda had said, "Judge me by my size, do you?" Harlan wasn't imposing to look at, but people feared him just the same, and that was exactly how he liked it. "Pay the boys," he told Bay.

Bay handed each of the young men a bundle of singles. It was only a hundred dollars for each of them, and they knew that was all they were getting, but a stack of dollars felt like a lot of money, and it was easy to spend, unlike trying to unload a c-note at the nearest bodega. "Get the truck unloaded," said Bay. "We'll get settled in and then you can help us with the setup."

Over the next few hours, Harlan's workspace took shape once more. He and Bay set up the security system while the other four fellows unloaded crates full of tools, equipment, and components for the next Destroyer suit. They didn't ask about what they were moving; they'd been paid not to ask questions. When Harlan snapped at them because they weren't being careful enough in his eyes, or were putting things down in the wrong spot, they shined him off and let Bay smooth things over.

The Eggbreaker railguns Harlan set up to guard the warehouse entrances were his fifth iteration. They used motion sensors calibrated for human-sized targets and fired machined steel needles. His speakers and warning lights were less lethal, but had proven their effectiveness time and time again when vagrants and other undesirables found their way in, usually looking for something they could steal and sell. And if the warnings didn't drive them away, well, that was what the Eggbreakers were for, and Harlan's incinerator had seen plenty of use in eliminating bodies.

At last, the lab was set up the way he wanted it. The half-completed Destroyer Mark II suit hung from its frame, lurking like the skeleton of some monster from an engineer's nightmare. The basic design was smaller than the first Destroyer suit, and unlike that one, this was being built with all new, state-of-the-art technology.

Harlan could barely wait for the first time he could try it on.

He looked around the workshop, fingers itching to hold tools, to weld and solder, to wrench and create. "Bay, pay them the bonus."

Bay handed each of the young men another bundle of fifty singles. "Thanks for your help tonight, guys."

The young man named Barry tucked away his money. "Hey man, you gonna need any help again tomorrow?"

"Yeah, we ain't doin' nothin'," said Troy.

"'Cept shakin' down old ladies in the subway for their Social Security checks," said Darrell, and the others laughed.

"Yes," said Harlan. "I've got some work for you. Guy who knows electrical components named Goetz. He should be taking a train into Manhattan to get some items I need. If he won't do it . . ." Harlan managed a smile. "Convince him." He turned away from them to start rummaging through his tools. He had an idea screaming in the back of his mind and it wouldn't let him sleep until he acted upon it. "Torque converter," he mumbled.

"You gonna need anything else tonight?" asked Bay. "There's an all-night diner a mile up the road. Bring back some coffee and a sammich?"

Harlan didn't answer. He was already deeply engrossed in his tinkering. Bay knew to leave well enough alone, and he departed after the other young men.

Harlan worked.

* * *

It must have been many hours later when Bay burst into the workshop, his face pale and his eyes bulging with fear. Harlan jumped at the sudden intrusion, hands automatically reaching for the nearest lethal device before he recognized Bay. "What is it?"

"They got shot up. All of them," said Bay, sounding like he was holding down his gorge. "Cops everywhere. I was gonna meet them before they talked to Goetz. Kinda smooth things over. But somebody done shot 'em all up and he run. I saw them on the stretchers."

"Who got shot, Bay? What are you talking about?"

"The boys, man. Barry, Darrell, James and Troy. They been shot up. All of them by some dude in the subway."

"Did they get the components from Goetz?" Harlan felt irritated. He didn't need this kind of delay.

"Did they . . . Man, are you even hearin' me? Naw, they didn't get no components. They got shot!" Bay stomped his foot in frustration.

"Who shot them?" Harlan had been trying to work on redirecting his exasperation at Bay's suggestion, so he got up from his work and went over to investigate the sandwich and coffee that had been fresh hours ago.

"I dunno," said Bay. "I been askin' around. Don't nobody know. They said the dude ran into the subway tunnel."

"So they didn't get him." Harlan bit through the stale bread to the congealed filling beneath, not really tasting it. He didn't much care about eating, found it a waste of effort, and rarely bothered to taste anything. Food was fuel, like the electricity that powered his Mark II. "Anyone see him?"

Bay nodded. "A couple of passengers. The conductor even talked to him before he ran. Asked if he was a cop. Dude said no, of course. Just a white man with a piece, lookin' to shoot hisself some niggers. We seen plenty of those types in Philly."

Harlan drank the coffee. "What did he look like?"

"Skinny ass cracker. Goofy hair. Big square glasses."

Harlan looked up. "Square?" He went to the mishmash stack of papers that served as his files and dug through it until he found a ragged-edge newsprint clipping. "Like this guy?"

Bay looked at the picture Harlan was waving at him. "Mebbe. I didn't see him. I'm just sayin' what I heard."

Harlan looked at the paper himself. It was an advertisement for a store that dealt in custom electrical components. The picture was of the owner, Bernie Goetz. "It was you, wasn't it? You son of a bitch," whispered Harlan. "I'm gonna find you."

Bay stepped up beside him, always the faithful soldier. "What you need me to do, Harlan?"

"Charge up the suit batteries," said Harlan. "Then we're gonna go find Goetz ourselves."

"Doin' the cops' jobs for 'em?" asked Bay.

"No. I don't care about cops. But he threw off my whole schedule. I was going to use those components in the new targeting array and missile lock system. Now I'm going to have to go get them from him myself. And he's going to be sorry he messed with me and mine." He paused, and then lowered his voice to a dangerous growl. "I'm Destroyer, and this is my town now."

* * *

The suit wasn't ready to fly yet. It wasn't even armored, and not quite weatherproof, as evidenced by the persistent leak of icy air that played across the back of his neck as he stepped out of the truck. He and Bay had driven past Goetz's house and seen the car with plainclothes officers parked out front. Harlan needed to get into the house where he could run a full sensor sweep with the advanced equipment he'd installed right before they left Philly. If Goetz had left any evidence behind of where he might have gone, Harlan would find it.

"Okay, give me a five minute head start to draw 'em off and then go," said Bay out the truck's window, revving the engine as if it were a high-performance racing car.

"I could just chew them into kibble," said Harlan over the hiss of the suit's hydraulics. He hadn't put in the voice modulator yet so he had to shout to be heard. "Guns are full up."

"There's a time and a place for shootin' cops," said Bay. "This ain't it. Go find what you need and then we'll hunt down the man."

"You gonna need someone to peel you out of a squad car?"

"Maybe. You don't see me come back around the block in ten, come get me." Bay hammered down the accelerator and popped the clutch. The truck lurched into motion, swaying as Bay pulled away from the alley onto the street.

Harlan stood in his suit, patient and monitoring his systems as he counted down the seconds. Five minutes later, Destroyer burst from the alley, running up the road as fast as a car in the evening darkness. He knew people saw him. Some folks were coming home from their Christmas shopping, or from work, and they stared in disbelief at the eight-foot monstrosity that was the Mark II as it charged down the road like some monster from a summer tentpole movie.

His cameras enhanced building numbers until he spotted the apartment where Bernard Goetz lived. He switched the Mark II into its stealthy mode, making it quiet enough not to wake a sleeping dog. It couldn't stay stealthy for long because of overheating, but it would be fine for the few minutes Harlan would need in Goetz's apartment. He stood the suit in a shadow, shutting down all nonessential systems, and slipped out of the canopy. "Door," he whispered into the mic at his throat.

The onboard processor identified the target and fired a single round from the starboard cannon. The supersonic steel needle cracked into the doorknob of Goetz's back door, shattering it into pieces. "Protect," said Harlan, and he slipped into the building, knowing that Destroyer would keep him safe from prying eyes while he worked.

There was no sign of Goetz in the tiny apartment. A quick search told Harlan that the man had come back and packed in a rush, leaving dresser drawers gaping open and the closet light still on. Harlan helped himself to some components he figured would be useful in his projects and then turned his consideration to where Goetz might be. The man didn't have a car, and would most likely be avoiding public transportation. Harlan doubted the man would be much of a car thief. He'd probably rent a car.

The Mark II had a projection screen that stored computerized maps with details pulled from the phonebook. A little research turned up a likely car rental place. Harlan grinned as he sealed himself back into Destroyer's living embrace once more. He'd find Goetz soon enough, and the man would pay for his temerity.

* * *

The Hertz car rental company closest to Goetz's apartment was closed by the time Harlan and Bay—who had managed to avoid getting arrested by the cops purporting to watch over Goetz's place—rolled up to the lot. The gate was padlocked shut and Harlan spotted a couple of rangy dogs wandering through the lot in search of something edible. "Whatchoo wanna do?" asked Bay. "Them dogs look like trouble. What if there's a guard listening for them to bark?"

Harlan hopped out of the cab. "They won't bark with holes through their heads."

Bay looked dismayed. "Aw, come on, man. They's dogs. I can't watch you kill a dog. I love dogs."

"Then don't watch me." Harlan rolled up the back door of the truck and climbed back into the Mark II once again. The servos played their sweet music for him as he stepped down from the truck. Bay grimaced and turned away as Harlan locked in on the dogs and fired. The second one might have whimpered a little before the second needle silenced it permanently.

"Goddamn," muttered Bay.

Harlan ignored him and lowered the pincers on the left medial arm to cut the lock. He grasped the gate and pulled it aside, mechanical muscles flexing as the steel bent. "Go into the office. Check records. Even if he paid cash, there has to be some record of him renting."

Bay spat onto the ground, his face twisted up as he tried not to look at the dead dogs. "What if he didn't use his real name? I wouldn't."

"Then I'll think of something." Harlan wasn't given to extraneous motion, especially when cramped inside Destroyer. Where someone else might have paced back and forth outside the rental office, Harlan was content to stand quietly and think about how he would track a rented car that could have been driven in any direction.

His motionless silence probably saved Bay's life, for a security guard with a pistol came around the side of the building and hollered at Bay to freeze. Bay raised his hands and the guard grinned. "Boy, you in the wrong place at the wrong time. I can shoot you right now and the law's on my side."

Harlan turned on his exterior speakers. "Not if I shoot you first." He pulled the trigger on an Eggbreaker and watched dispassionately as the guard fell, twitching out his final throes on the cement. "Bay, hurry up."

Bay hurried inside the office, saying "Good shot, man," over his shoulder.

Harlan knew there was no way he could track a rental car short of putting a beacon on it, and if he could put a beacon or some other kind of marker in it, he wouldn't need to. There needed to be some kind of audio and video surveillance system, covering everywhere that he could access. He used cameras in his own security. Perhaps he might use some of his ill-gotten gains to develop surveillance devices that governments and private companies might be attracted to, devices which he could access at any time. With that kind of unfettered data within his reach, he would be able to find anyone or anything he needed to help with his projects. He could already see how computers could assist in such a task, and ideas were already firing off fast and furious in his mind as Bay came back out of the office again. "I got it," he said, waving a piece of paper. "Blue '81 Dodge, rented by a Bernard Hugo. Paid in cash. That's gotta be him, right?"

"Yes," said Harlan. "We're not going to find him ourselves. He's been gone for hours. He could be anywhere by now." He marched the Mark II back to the truck.

"So what we gonna do?"

"Get the word out on the street. Description of the car and of Goetz. Tell them I will personally pay a reward for good information."

"And what are you gonna do?"

Harlan raised the canopy and smiled down from the darkness in the back of the truck. "I'm going to make Destroyer fly."

* * *

Harlan retreated to his lab in a fever of creation and fabrication. While the word spread up and down the East Coast about the search for Bernard Goetz and his rented car, Harlan cut sheet metal, bent piping, mixed fuel, and wired igniters. Bay brought him food and drink regularly, and hours later, when it had gone cold and flies were crawling over it, threw it away. By the third consecutive day, Harlan's skin was covered with grease and metal dust, solder residue, welding burns, and he was hallucinating images of his dead mother.

Dehydration sores covered his mouth and he stank of days-old sweat and burned materials. When Bay found him screaming in frothy-mouthed laughter while staring at nothing in particular, he busted Harlan across the jaw.

When Harlan awoke, a day and a half later, he was hungry and thirsty for the first time in days, and somehow during his brief coma, he'd solved a fuel-mix ratio problem that had confounded him for some time. Bay looked at him with apprehension as he set a tray of silky grits and crispy bacon on Harlan's lap. "Hey, man, you all right?"

Harlan wiggled his jaw. It was definitely sore. He couldn't quite remember what had happened while he was in his fugue state of creation. Whatever it was, though, Bay had looked after him, like he always did, and Harlan respected that if nothing else. "Yes, I think so." He took a piece of bacon and dipped it into the grits. It was rare for him to have an appetite and he figured he'd make the most of it. "Any word on our missing quarry?"

"Not yet, but we got eyes all over the region. He sticks his head up anywhere, somebody's gonna spot it." Bay snagged a piece of bacon for himself. "How 'bout you?"

Harlan opened the paper carton of milk that sat on the corner of the tray and drained it. "I need six hours and sixty gallons of kerosene, and then we're ready to be airborne." He burped and Bay grinned.

"I'll go find your kerosene. Get that sumbitch up in the air."

Harlan smiled. "Oh yes."

* * *

The boot jets worked, of course. Harlan's inventions always did. He just had the juju for technology. All the same, though, he was already considering improvements during his maiden voyage into the skies. He'd designed the jets after he had the opportunity to dig through the guts of the robotic superhero Steel Soldier during his first outing as Destroyer. He could already tell he needed better and more control surfaces for stabilization, better vibration and cavitation control, better armament, and of course, better soundproofing, as his ears were ringing within seconds.

Still, flying was amazing, and Harlan figured once he perfected the technology, he might never walk anywhere ever again. He buzzed the George Washington Bridge once, amusing himself by targeting the cars crawling over it, and thought seriously about pulling a helicopter out of the sky, but he knew that despite the power of his jets, he wasn't faster than a police radio, and as an early-morning unidentified flying object, it would be better initially for him to be more discreet.

There would be time enough in the future for further destruction.

The same afternoon after Harlan's test flight, Bay informed him that they got a hit on Goetz. "He's in Jersey," said Bay. "A brother seen his car and followed him. He gone from one motel to another."

"He's hiding," said Harlan.

"Looks like it," said Bay. "Brother's waitin' by a pay phone for orders. You want him to take out Goetz?"

"No, I want to talk to him," said Harlan. He looked around. "There's no phone in here, is there?"

"Naw, but that deli has a pay phone."

Harlan set down his welding gun and pulled his goggles off. "Got any dimes?"

"Yeah, man, but you need to wipe off your face. You look like you done fell into a trash heap. Kind of smell like it, too."

Harlan sniffed at himself, but all he caught was welding smoke and rocket fuel, neither of which he found unpleasant. "I'm all right. Let's go make that call."

A few minutes later, Bay stood by the corner of the deli, his collar turned up against the cold, getting the motel address from the guy who'd found Goetz. Harlan paced back and forth. He had no patience for the telephone and left that unpleasant task to Bay. At last, Bay hung up and checked the coin slot just in case the quarter hadn't yet dropped. "Got it," he said with a triumphant grin. "You want to take the truck?"

"You can," said Harlan. "I've got a faster way to get there."

* * *

The Mark II dropped out of the sky like a missile coming down. Harlan was half-frozen from the cockpit leak, had a developing migraine from the combination of noise and fumes, and was happier than he could ever remember being. He felt powerful, like a force of nature. Massive shock absorbers in the suit's legs softened the landing, even though Harlan's teeth clacked together so hard he thought he might have bitten off the tip of his tongue.

His sensors had spotted Goetz's car turning out of the lot of a seedy motel and Harlan wasn't going to lose him again. He grabbed hold of the car's bumper with the Mark II's primary arms and lifted it right off the ground. The memory of the look of sheer terror on Goetz's face as he looked behind him would keep Harlan warm for many cold nights in the future. The car's engine howled as the rear wheels spun in midair to no avail. "Goetz," said Harlan through the external speakers. "Don't move."

Goetz tumbled out of the door, slipped on the ice, and wound up face down in gray Jersey snow. Harlan threw the car aside and smiled as it crashed into a parked truck and caught flame. Destruction was singing that familiar old refrain, a song Harlan knew by heart. He lunged down with a pincer claw and grabbed Goetz by the shoulder, hauling the frightened man to his feet.

"I'm sorry! I didn't do anything! I'm sorry! P-please ..."

Listening to Goetz grovel and blubber was sorely tempting Harlan to say to hell with the components and pinch the man's head from his shoulders. Instead, he lifted Goetz off the ground altogether. "Shut up," said Harlan. "You're Bernard Goetz. You shot my employees, and you inconvenienced me."

"I ... I ..."

"I'm going to give you the chance to make it up to me." Harlan pulled Goetz in close to the Mark II's head unit. "I'm going to give you five thousand dollars, and you're going to give me the following items from your inventory." Harlan ran down a list of high-tech electrical components using the newest microprocessors that Harlan had yet to take the time to understand.

"How . . . How do you know about th-that?" Goetz stammered like a pathetic cartoon character.

"It doesn't matter." Harlan smiled beneath the layers of metal and plastic separating him from his prey. He didn't enjoy dealing with people for the most part, which was why he had Bay. Scaring them, though, that felt powerful. The truth was he'd seen some of Goetz's work elsewhere and was able to derive some of the man's other developments using his sense of technology. "You can agree to the deal and walk away, or you can refuse, and then I keep my five thousand and take your components . . . and your head."

Goetz took the money, and Harlan got what he came for.

He dropped Goetz, who stumbled and fell as he tried to run away. Harlan looked down at the components in Destroyer's medial claw. They were so small, and yet they would unlock the secrets to his targeting systems and make him powerful enough to take on a fighter jet, or a military helicopter, or a Just Cause asshole. And yet, now that he had them in his possession, he could see how they worked. He could extrapolate new, better designs from them. It wouldn't be hard.

It wouldn't be hard at all.

He chinned on his external speakers again. "Goetz," he hissed.

Goetz shrieked, like a scared little girl. Harlan wanted to laugh at him, but kept himself sounding scary and mean.

"Here I've been thinking these would be difficult designs. Something I'd need someone who had your specialized knowledge to acquire, design, and repair. But you know what? They're not, and I don't need you."

Goetz let out one final terrified scream, urine staining the front of his trousers just before a dozen finely-machined steel needles turned his chest cavity into ground meat, making it look like someone had splattered an industrial-sized can of chili across the snow.

"Guess you'll miss your trial date." Harlan had found his components, salvaged his wasted time, and wrought destruction.

It had been a good day.

Harlan fired up his boot jets. The Mark II shot into the darkening sky like a missile. Harlan swung around in a semicircle, orienting himself toward Manhattan. "New York, what a town," he whispered to himself with glee. "Destroyer is back."

DUST TO DUST

Thou turnest man to destruction; again thou sayest, Come again, ye children of men.
-The Order for The Burial of the Dead, The Book of Common Prayer, 1928

September, 1985
Kansas City, Kansas

"Ashes to ashes, dust to dust," said the preacher. "Go in peace, and God bless you all."

In turn, they each took a handful of dirt and dropped it on the grave containing Thomas Whitman, also known as Stormcloud, but Faith would only ever think of him as Tornado, the soft-spoken boy with the rock star golden hair and serene smile. It wasn't until after the Blackout of '77 that he'd left behind his sky-blue and white costume for one that was hooded and dark, that matched the moodiness of his new identity and the swirling black clouds in his heart.

AIDS might have waited until 1985 to take his body, but his soul had died years earlier.

Faith Thompson was uncomfortable thanks to the unusually hot day for September. She was six months pregnant and nine months retired from Just Cause. Bobby, her husband, stood with her, gently stroking her back. He had retired from active superhero duties years earlier, but had taken on the job of Team Administrator, and divided his time between following Faith's pregnancy and keeping Just Cause operating smoothly.

All living Just Cause members and alumni had come to the funeral. From the original American Justice team of the late '40s came Adrian and Judy Crowley, Faith's parents, still fit even into their sixties. Lady Athena, who had grown even more elegant over time, stood with the Crowleys, her luscious black curls having long since gone gray underneath the burgundy of her hood. The only other living founder of Just Cause, known more by his heroic guise of Kid Crash than his birth name of Elliott Hines, was no longer the happy-go-lucky underage hero who'd charmed his way into America's hearts. He'd had double bypass surgery, and the whispers among the parahuman community was that his prognosis for long-term survival was, at best, poor. The White Knight had died in a car crash in '64, and Isaiah Mohammed, who'd never felt like he truly belonged among all the white parahumans of American Justice and Just Cause, had died just two years ago, angry at society all the way to the end when a stroke felled him in front of his typewriter.

All members from the Just Cause of the Sixties and Seventies had come as well. John Stone had forsworn his normal fedora for a pair of oversized dark glasses and a jacket bigger than anyone could buy from a Big and Tall men's clothing store. Lionheart, still looking heroic despite several years of retirement, filled out a dark suit and tie. He was starting to develop a paunch but his mane was as full as ever, framing his face like a tawny halo. He wouldn't meet Faith's gaze; there was too much history between the two of them. Beside her, Bobby glared at the lionish man and said nothing. Likewise, too much history.

The active members of Just Cause wore their costumes out of respect for the dead. They had known

Tornado the longest, and his death had hit them the hardest of anyone. The Steel Soldier stood along with Imp, Javelin, and Sundancer, looking as somber as possible for a robot.

Three generations of the Devereaux family had crossed the Atlantic to be there. Although Georges, the man with whom it had all began, had died thirty years ago, his son Lane, granddaughter Grace, and great-grandson Jean-Michel had all arrived only that morning. Lane had taken his father's fortune, amassed an even greater fortune, and used it to become the benefactor to the team. Grace was one of the world's foremost experts on parahuman physiology, and her Institute of Parahuman Medicine in Paris was at the forefront of all research. Jean-Michel was ten, and looked like he'd rather be anywhere but at a funeral.

The current Just Cause team stood together across the grave. Sundancer's younger sister, Estella, was a tactical genius and the leader of the team. Ten years younger than her sister, she'd taken the name Sunstorm as a tribute. Beside her were Foxfire, the Timekeeper, Danger, and Fast Break. The newest, youngest members of the team were Juice and Crackerjack. They were still in college, and were strictly part-timers.

It was the largest collection of parahumans the world had ever seen, all there to pay their final respects to the quiet, friendly man they had all known as Tornado. He had died from advanced pneumonia, although they all knew that it was the compromising of his immune system that had allowed him to contract the deadly illness in the first place. AIDS was the watchword of the day, and despite Thomas Whitman's sexual proclivities, it was still a terrible shock to all who knew him when he was forced to retire as diseases began wearing him down.

Nobody knew how long he'd had AIDS, or even from whom he'd contracted it. In his final weeks, he'd worked to try and track down those men with whom he'd had relations, to warn them lest they might continue to spread the infection. In the end, not one of them had come forward to see him, or even contacted him. Thomas had died surrounded by only his teammates, who certainly loved him far more than any of his lovers had.

The group began to break up, somber and quiet, each hero lost in his or her own thoughts at the graveside.

Lady Athena hugged Faith carefully as Adrian and Judy looked on with a mixture of sadness and pride. "It's wonderful to see you again, Faith. You too, Bobby."

Faith wiped her eyes. "I just wish it could have been under better circumstances."

Lady Athena's own eyes were bright under her hood. "Your daughter will be a beautiful baby, and will be a great hero in her lifetime. This I know."

"Thank you," Faith whispered.

"Take care of yourself, Bobby." Lady Athena's gaze strayed to Bobby and seemed to grow troubled.

He nodded and put his arm around his wife. "I will. Can you join us for dinner tonight?"

"Of course."

Faith's parents walked away with Athena, quiet and introspective. It was an unwritten rule that superheroes died doing their duty, like Flicker and Strongman. Dying young was a privilege of the parahuman condition, and they had somehow avoided feeling death's sting. It was like living on borrowed time, her mother had told her, so they cherished every minute knowing it might be their last.

"Would you bring the car around please, love?" Faith asked Bobby. "I need to sit down for a minute." He walked away and she found a bench and eased herself down onto it, wishing she had a pillow to sit upon.

"How are you feeling?" Estella Echevarria walked up with her older sister a pace behind. Her costume sparkled with warm colors in the bright sunshine of the early afternoon.

"Like a blimp with legs," said Faith, absently stroking her belly and feeling her daughter kick. Her superspeed powers had vanished literally the moment she conceived. She had been in a panic, for they had never forsaken her before. She flew to Paris on the first available flight to visit Grace at her clinic, sick the entire way. Grace had come to the clinic at three in the morning and run a battery of tests. She hadn't been able to explain why Faith's powers had suddenly stopped working, but when Faith described the symptoms of her *illness*, Grace ran one more test. The discovery that she was pregnant was so startling to Faith that she'd fainted and spent three days in bed under Grace's watchful eyes. She asked Grace if her powers would come back. Grace couldn't say. Perhaps it was her body's way of protecting the unborn baby. All they could do is wait and see. Grace prescribed a strict diet and exercise regimen which Faith had given up her fifth day home and replaced with walks in Central Park and lots of tin roof sundae ice cream.

"I envy you so much," said Sundancer. "Bringing a new life into the world."

"You could have a baby if you wanted one, stupid," said Estella.

"Shut up already, pest."

Faith sighed, wishing she could take a really deep breath. "I've missed you guys. I miss Headquarters. I even miss your staff meetings," she said to Estella.

"Hey, they aren't that bad. Are they?"

"Oh yeah, they suck," said Sundancer.

"How are the new guys working out?"

"Well, James is pure business. No fun in that boy at all. Jack's his complete opposite. And, oh, is he a fox!" Sundancer shivered. "Too bad I'm old enough to be his, uh, stepmother."

"It beats me why they're such good friends. It's like the *Odd Couple* or something," Estella laughed.

Bobby pulled up in the Skylark and put it into Park, letting it idle while he got out and opened Faith's door for her. "Ooo, how gallant," Sundancer said. Bobby's brow furrowed suddenly in an expression that Faith recognized meant he'd heard something.

"Bobby?" She asked, worried. He swung his head slightly from side to side, zeroing in on the source of whatever he was hearing. He turned around suddenly and looked up. Faith followed his gaze, as did Sundancer and Estella.

A plane was falling on them.

It was some kind of private jet. Its engines were off and the only sound was the air whipping past its hull as it fell in a corkscrewing tumble. Faith would later replay the scene over and over in her mind, torturing herself and wondering if she could have done anything. It seemed like everything was happening in slow motion, but even her advanced perception abilities had vanished with the pregnancy. Several people were running in their direction, but they, too, seemed to be hardly moving at all.

Faith's instincts were to run to Bobby, but she struggled to even get up off the bench. Estella wrapped her arms around Faith and pulled, flying as hard as she could to get clear. Sundancer and Fast Break both lunged for Bobby as the plane came down, hitting the ground hard only a few feet from the Buick.

A puff of warm air blew past Faith. Estella's powers protected her from heat and she was able to extend the envelope to cover Faith as well. Pieces of the jet and the demolished car whirled outward in every direction, jagged razors of scorched metal. Faith saw a chunk of wing neatly decapitate Danger as he ran. His body took several more staggering steps before falling to the ground. Something long and sharp hit Lionheart in his abdomen and knocked him flying back into a gravestone, which shattered.

Estella set Faith down about thirty yards away from the crash site. "I can't carry you any further," she said, panting with the exertion, "but you should be safe enough here. Are you all right?"

Faith nodded. She felt a sharp twinge in her abdomen that might have been a contraction. *Where was Bobby?*

Estella's body became consumed in flames as she activated all her powers and truly became Sunstorm. She flew off like a phoenix, heading for the burning wreckage with a vengeance. She drew the flames away from the plane, pulling them through the air into her own fire.

Faith gasped as another contraction rocked her. *No, it's too soon!* In a few seconds it was over, and then Grace Devereaux was kneeling down next to her, holding her hand and calming her. Faith could see Lane towering above, standing protectively over them. Unwilling to leave his daughter, he dug in his pocket, considering, then handed his keys to Jean-Michel.

"*Apportez l'auto,*" he said.

"*Mais, Grand-père . . .*" the boy began nervously.

Lane smiled at the boy, sadness in his eyes from the events that had transpired. "*Je vous fais confiance.*" *I trust you.* Jean-Michel gulped and ran toward the distant car, keys held in front of him like a holy talisman.

The other heroes tore apart the plane with frantic intensity as they searched for the missing. Danger was in two pieces, obviously dead. "I can't find a pulse!" Crackerjack shouted. He was hunched over Lionheart. Imp was shrinking pieces of the plane while Juice tossed them aside.

Faith suffered through another contraction, squeezing Grace's hand, seeking strength. She tried to remember her breathing techniques, but she and

Bobby weren't due to go to Lamaze classes until next month. *Where was Bobby?*

Sunstorm gave a roar of dismay, the sound of a plasma jet slicing through sheet metal, as she found her sister amid the wreckage. She gathered up the body in arms aflame and lifted her as easily as if she were a child. Sundancer's arms and legs dangled in a way that would be impossible if she were still living.

"There!" Imp cried, and pointed at a piece of wreckage, shrinking it to the size of a postage stamp. Juice pushed another piece aside and came upon the remains of poor Fast Break, who had tried to knock Bobby clear of the plane only to be crushed by one of the engines. Somehow, though, he was still alive. He gasped in agony through the shattered remains of his crash helmet.

Juice shouted, "Timekeeper, get him into stasis!"

The Timekeeper stepped up and created a bubble of frozen time around Fast Break.

Where was Bobby?

They found him underneath the tail. Fast Break had nearly succeeded in saving Faith's husband. He was alive, but only barely with a critical head wound.

"Bag him up, Timekeeper," said Juice.

"Already on it." Another bubble of frozen time formed around Bobby. There was still hope.

Faith heard sirens faintly, and her next contraction wasn't so severe. "Help's on its way," said Grace, as the Timekeeper put another stasis bubble around Bobby.

"Where the hell is the pilot?" Juice shouted. He'd torn open the remains of the canopy. "There's nobody in here!"

A high-pitched whistling sound rose over the confusion. Foxfire was the first to get it. "It's a trap! Incoming!" An object was diving from on high, and it was moving fast, a pair of contrails streaking in its wake.

Steel Soldier's eye lenses whirred as it focused on the intruder. "BATTLESUIT. UNKNOWN CONFIGURATION.

HOSTILE INTENT ASSUMED. INTERCEPTING." The Soldier snapped on its wings and blue alcohol flames shot out, incinerating a hedge. The robotic hero blasted into the sky like a missile. Half a second later, Sunstorm and Javelin followed suit.

Imp shrank Bobby and Fast Break down to doll size within their stasis bubbles, then she and the Timekeeper hurried to get them to safety inside a nearby mausoleum.

Foxfire had no obvious powers. Like the original Dr. Danger, she depended largely on athletic prowess and technological assistance to battle for Just Cause. Instead of arrows, her specialty was explosives and demolition. She followed the others into the mausoleum, pulling her first aid kit out.

Another contraction hit Faith, and she winced with the pain. *Not yet*, she told her unborn daughter. *You're not finished*. She faintly heard the sound of an engine and a car braked uncertainly behind her. She craned her head around to see Jean-Michel peeking over the rim of the steering wheel of a Cadillac. Lane ordered him to help Grace with Faith, then slid behind the wheel.

Between the wiry ten-year-old and his mother, they managed to get the ungainly Faith into the passenger seat of the Caddy. Grace and her son climbed into the back and Lane put the car in gear.

"No," said Faith, choking on her own tears. "We can't leave. The others might need us."

"We've got to get you to a hospital," said Grace. "I don't have anything with me to get your contractions stopped, and it's too soon for the baby to be born."

"Absolutely not!" Faith clenched her teeth, willing her body to obey her. "I won't leave without Bobby."

"All right," Grace said. "But I'm timing your contractions. If they get any closer together, I don't care what you want, we're leaving."

The armored figure dropping from the sky fired braking rockets and slowed. Sunstorm, Javelin, and the Steel Soldier surrounded it. The angular armor was a uniform dark blue and looked like something out of an imported Japanese cartoon show. The head turned slightly, examining the Just Cause heroes surrounding it.

"DO NOT MOVE," the Steel Soldier said. "WE HAVE YOU SURROUNDED. STATE YOUR BUSINESS." The fifteen-foot-high battlesuit raised a hand and spat a bright globule of energy at the Soldier. The Soldier attempted to dodge but the globule expanded and enveloped the robot in a nimbus of sparks. "SKZZRRT . . ." The Steel Soldier's voice failed as the halo of energy condensed into an actinic point in its torso.

Then the Soldier exploded. Pieces of arms and legs flew in all directions. Irreplaceable components burned and shattered.

"Stupid machine," said a digitized voice from the battlesuit. "I never should have fixed it in the first place."

It was Harlan Washington, the Destroyer.

"Oh, no!" Faith groaned.

Javelin shouted, "Cook him!" He and Sunstorm cut loose with full power. A curved shield unfolded from each of Destroyer's arms. Sunstorm's flame splashed across one, harmlessly deflected into the sky. The other shield blocked Javelin's energy bolts, simply trapping them in whatever material from which it was made.

There was a flash of smoke and flame from a unit mounted on Destroyer's shoulder. Twelve miniature missiles, each no longer than a foot, arced out, zeroing in on Javelin. He yelped in surprise and dove for the ground as the missiles turned to follow like a horde of angry bees. He bounced off a heavy gravestone, sparks flying from his burnished armor. The missiles struck the gravestone and exploded, sending granite splinters flying in all directions.

Destroyer trained his hand-cannon on Sunstorm. "I've got nothing against you. This is personal between me and them. Leave now."

Sunstorm growled and sent a bright stream of plasma hotter than the sun at Destroyer's weapon hand. "Personal? I'll show you personal!" Metal bubbled and ran like melting butter. "You killed my sister, you son of a bitch!"

"Your problem, hero. Here's another." Something sharp and shining lanced out from Destroyer's damaged arm, struck Sunstorm in her chest, and poked out of her back. It was a wickedly barbed spear.

Sunstorm looked down at it in surprise. She raised her head slowly, red flames flashing in her eyes. "You stupid asshole. You might as well try to spear a campfire." To illustrate her point, she simply moved aside, letting the spear slide out of her flaming side.

It gave Destroyer pause, and he dropped out of the sky like a stone before she could light him up with another plasma stream. Powerful shock absorbers took the impact of the heavy battlesuit striking the ground. The suit's feet sank a few inches into the dirt.

Juice crouched down by one of the lampposts along the path, tore open the electrical access plate, and grabbed hold of the wiring. The lights flashed and then burned out in a tinkling of broken glass as he drained electricity from the surrounding grid to fuel his own abilities.

Javelin picked himself up from amid a pile of granite pieces. He stood gingerly, bleeding from several deep gouges. His left arm hung useless and broken.

Imp flew in front of Destroyer, scolding him like an angry hummingbird. "Harlan, just what do you think you're doing?"

Destroyer batted a hand at her that would have turned her into paste if it had connected. "Just a little payback, dear sister. I spent two years in hell because of you people."

"Juvie hall," called Javelin. "And you earned it, you little bastard. They shoulda locked you up for good."

A multi-barreled gun lifted out of Destroyer's undamaged arm and fired, barrels spinning in a blur. Jack leaped in front of Javelin, who was caught unawares. The stream of bullets drove him back and both men went tumbling over the rubble. Javelin hollered as his broken arm twisted.

Juice came crashing in, wrenching the gun loose in a shriek of overstressed metal. "I'm going to tear your ass right out of there," he shouted. "And when I'm done with you, you'll wish you were back in juvie!" He sank his fingers into the armor plating and tore a piece free.

"Watch it, Juice, he's clever," Imp warned, but not in time. A puff of white gas shot out of a hidden nozzle into Juice's face. The dark-skinned man coughed once, then his eyes rolled up and he dropped heavily to the ground.

"Get clear, Irlene!" Sunstorm opened up, raining flames down on Destroyer as if she had opened the very gates of Hell.

Destroyer staggered under the onslaught, trying to hold the shield up. With his other hand, he yanked a gravestone out of the ground and hurled it at Sunstorm. The heavy missile splashed right through her and melted into slag. Her body reformed once again. "I'm coming after you next time, you bitch!"

"There won't be any next time. You'll burn before I'm done with you." Sunstorm's flame was so bright it was actually painful to look at, casting new shadows in the daylight. Jack dragged Juice clear, clothes smoking from the nearness to the inferno Sunstorm had unleashed.

Something exploded in the battlesuit, causing everyone to look away. Faith saw something rising very fast out of the torso, riding a pillar of flame that paled in comparison to Sunstorm's. As she watched, stubby wings snapped out of it and it accelerated at an unbelievable pace. Sunstorm made a half-hearted attempt to pursue, but it was much faster than her and she was exhausted from the amount of energy she'd expended. She sank to the grass, shaking and spent.

In the distance, Faith heard all the sirens in the world approaching. She felt faint and realized she'd been holding her breath. Unable to take a deep breath because of her daughter pressing against her diaphragm, she panted a little and spots appeared in her vision. It occurred to her faintly that she hadn't had any more contractions. Grace was massaging her wrists.

Bobby.

"It'll be all right," Grace kept saying, like a soothing litany. "Bobby's in stasis."

"Eight years," Faith murmured, watching numbly as emergency vehicles began pouring into the cemetery.

Grace asked, "What did you say?"

"Eight years," said Faith. "He's been nursing that grudge against us for eight years. We can't fight that kind of hatred. We can only hope to survive it."

FALLING

September, 2011
New York City, New York

The image is impossible.
  A plane, hurtling toward the glass.
                    * * *

"Hi there," called a cheerful voice from above. Juice looked up to see a young woman clad in a black and white costume with yellow lightning trim floating over him. She couldn't have been more than eighteen.

"Hello yourself." He gave her his most dazzling smile. "I'm Juice."

"Doublecharge," she said. "You're in Just Cause, right?"

"Yes. I'm new."

Juice wasn't exactly *new*. He'd been part of the superhero team for over a year, having started in '85 only a month before Destroyer attacked Tornado's funeral, but only on a part time basis as he worked to get through law school. The handsome young black man had always planned to become an attorney, but had discovered a parahuman power by sheer accident when a power line had fallen on his car. His body absorbed electricity and converted it into superhuman strength and resistance to harm. But as quickly as he gained that strength and toughness, it drained away in minutes, leaving him once more as weak and frail as anyone else.

"I'm new too, but not on the team." Doublecharge pirouetted in the air and touched down gently onto the ground next to him. "I just finished high school and I was thinking maybe I ought to join Just Cause."

"Well, you can fly . . . What else can you do?" Now that she was close enough, Juice appraised her, using all the skills he'd acquired from four years in Alpha Phi Alpha. Slender, blonde, seemed cute underneath her mask. He certainly wouldn't kick her out of bed for eating crackers.

Electricity crackled between her fingers. "This."

Juice smiled. "Call me James, and I think this is the start of a beautiful friendship."

* * *

In a split second, she blasts electricity at him, not to injure, but to aid.

The window shatters inward as metal and flame rend the air to fling him and her and the others away like leaves in a gale.

His body, crackling with power, shields her from the force of the explosion as it hurtles them across the office. Cubicle walls flip end over end like a collapsing house of cards.

The screams of the dying are overpowered by the rush of heat and light, shattering hundreds of windows in a cacophony of destruction.

* * *

It was in 1989, four years after Doublecharge joined Just Cause, that the team had fought a particularly tough battle against the Malice Group and were celebrating at Shapiro's Bar and Grill, their favorite hangout near their headquarters in the World Trade Center. Most of the time, Shapiro's was a yuppie bar, but when Just Cause descended upon it, the yuppies generally left in search of facilities better-suited to their power ties, expensive cellular telephones, and wine coolers.

That night also happened to coincide with Doublecharge's twenty-first birthday, and she was doing shot after shot to celebrate. The Malice Group had given them all a run for their money, and many of them were nursing minor injuries from Javelin's sprained arm to Sunstorm's cracked ribs to the burns decorating the Timekeeper's skin. The Main Event of the battle had been Juice versus the Malice Group's Mr. Macho, and it would have gone very badly had it not been for Doublecharge keeping his electrical charge topped off even as she'd avoided Slipstream's headlong rushes.

Suffice it to say, they were all having a good time. Foxfire and the new Air Force made no secret of their carnal intentions toward each other. Sunstorm flirted with a tourist from Texas, stealing his cowboy hat and perching it jauntily atop her auburn perm. Javelin and the Timekeeper played round after round of darts, their injuries handicapping the one's accuracy and the other's time-altering abilities until shouts of laughter echoed throughout the bar. Crackerjack and Imp sat with Juice and Doublecharge, going over the best parts of the battle again and again and drinking more and more until all four sat in a happy haze.

"Last call," announced the bartender, a little earlier than he might have otherwise; he'd hosted post-combat celebration parties with Just Cause before and it was almost inevitable that somebody would break something like a chair, a window, or one time an entire pool table.

"You want anything else, Birthday Girl?" Crackerjack seemed none the worse for the wear after the half dozen beers he'd consumed.

"Thass . . . thass your new suh—superhero name," Juice struggled to form coherent words.

Doublecharge broke into helpless giggles at the thought. "God, no. I'm soooo wasted. I dunno if I c'n fly." She demonstrated, lifting shakily into the air and nearly braining herself on a ceiling fan.

The party broke up. Some of the heroes headed back toward the headquarters since it was closer than their various residences. Others, like Airforce, with Foxfire clutched firmly in his arms, simply flew off into the night. Doublecharge and Juice watched the others leave. She thought she could probably make it back to her apartment on her own, and said as much to Juice, then rushed frantically into the alley behind Shapiro's where she vomited up everything she'd drank that night and quite possibly everything she'd eaten for the past week.

"All finished?" asked Juice, and she realized he was holding her hair back for her.

She wiped her mouth and moaned. "Drank too much."

"Ever'body does on their twenny-firs' birthday," he said. "Better get you home."

He ended up towing her back to her apartment as she hovered a few inches off the ground, her head lolling to the side. They had to stop twice more for her to throw up, garnering odd looks from late-night passers-by.

Once in her apartment, he took off her boots and gloves and laid her on her bed. She asked him not to leave. He said he would stay. She asked him something else. He said she was drunk.

But in the end, they did anyway.

* * *

She picks herself up, blood streaming from everywhere, and sees only broken glass and smoky sky beyond where he'd been.

She flings herself outward, away from the stench of burning flesh and carpeting and fuel and sees him falling, arms and legs flailing as if he'd battle the very air to keep him aloft.

But he can't fly. And she can.

* * *

Five years later Juice got married.

He and Doublecharge agreed that their one drunken fling hadn't been a mistake, but they'd never repeated it.

They were both afraid of their friendship suffering with the additional complications of sex. Their relationship was both deeper and more intimate than one of lovers. They were best friends, confidants, like an older brother and younger sister sharing secrets and stories.

Juice finished law school, took and passed the bar exam with honors, and became the leader of Just Cause. The woman who would eventually become his wife was a paralegal in the firm that represented the superhero team.

Doublecharge felt very protective of her friend, but this woman was a good person, and she would be a good match for him, and she told him so in no uncertain terms.

"You have to marry her," she said one afternoon after a training session.

"Are you sure?" Juice rubbed his recently-shaved scalp.

"Definitely," said Doublecharge. "She's smart, beautiful, and isn't afraid of parahumans. She'd be good for you."

"You know, I was thinking about asking her."

Tradition didn't permit him to ask her to be his Best Man, but he would have, and they both knew it. She cried at the wedding, not because she was losing a friend, but because she was so happy for him.

Two years later, when she found love of her own, Juice was the one to tell her marriage would be a good choice.

Later, the two couples got together for dinner once a week, which would often end with the four of them sitting out on the large porch of Juice's house in Rhode Island, talking late into the evening. Many of these discussions became strategic planning sessions between Juice and Doublecharge, who was his second-in-command at Just Cause. His wife and her husband would often look at each other knowingly as the two heroes talked through their problems like the old friends they'd become.

* * *

She accelerates, faster than gravity, faster than debris, faster than him, glass slivers and shivering steel blurring beside her.

He sees her plummet after him and meets her gaze.

He shakes his head silently, an unspoken "no"; he knows he weighs more than double what she does and all she'll do is get them both killed.

Stubborn, she grabs his thick wrists in her small hands, refusing to let him go.

She pulls; pulls with all her might, straining to slow their plunge, feeling every muscle in her arms and back strain and tear.

And still, she doesn't let go, even though she could simply release him and save herself, fly away to go lick her wounds and heal.

The cement plaza rushes toward them, still too fast.

She pours every last erg of electricity into him, overloading his body with it, knowing he will instantly metabolize it into strength and toughness, and at last lets him go, hoping she's done enough.

He cracks the cement where he hits, creating a crater the size of a car.

Spent, she tumbles down next to him, exhausted and fainting.

He pulls himself free of the rubble and sees her.

He lifts her as carefully as a mother with her baby, and carries her out of the range of the constant rain of debris from above.

"Are you all right?" His voice is hoarse from the gathering smoke and dust.

"Yes. Are you?"

In spite of the pain, the scars which will never fully heal, he finds a ghost of a smile. "Yes."

She can't meet his smile.

GIDEON'S HORN

September, 2011
New York City, New York

The first plane struck exactly where it had been aimed, and half of the team died right then.

The Timekeeper could have created one of his stasis fields, halting time itself around the others to protect them if he'd had any warning at all. Fortune was not with him that morning.

Javelin could have flown to safety, if he'd had his armor on. But by then, he had retired from active superhero duties to be the team administrator. He prided himself on his ability to be organized and professional, but neither of those skills saved his life in the end.

Airforce was already dying, cancer slowly eating away at his insides. He hadn't yet told his teammates. He would never get the chance to do so.

Like so many others that day, Foxfire never came home to her family. Like so many others, her body was never found.

Javelin's wife and longtime teammate Imp was only days away from her own retirement party.

The impact of the plane knocked Juice right out of the building. He would have had several seconds to think of his wife and daughters before being liquefied on impact, had Doublecharge not intervened. First she had grabbed his hands and refused to let go, risking her own life to slow his fall. Then she blasted him with as much electricity as he could safely absorb, and then some, making his body tougher with every volt. She was not a strong flier, but her actions saved his life.

Crackerjack and Desert Eagle were off duty at the time and having breakfast on her rooftop terrace which she affectionately called her *aerie*. She had a healthy glow from the previous night's loving, and she winked at him over her coffee cup and then wondered why his own cup suddenly slipped from nerveless fingers to shatter on the tile roof. She turned to follow his gaze and saw the column of smoke rising in the distance.

They left their breakfast unfinished.

Glimmer wasn't on duty that day either. Half an hour before the first plane hit, he went into a *grand mal* seizure in the diner where he was eating. He was in an emergency room under heavy sedation that morning when the news announced the first impact.

Forcestar was fortunate, despite being in headquarters at the moment the plane struck. He had the presence of mind to erect a force field to protect some of the others on the floor from the burning jet fuel. Instead of trying to help individuals, which he knew would leave far more dead than alive, he set about the monumental task of trying to brace a skyscraper up with only the force of his will.

Just Cause's Second Team, rushing up from their headquarters in Virginia, abruptly turned back when the Pentagon was hit. The team commander, MetalBlade, dispatched half his team on to New York where they would arrive only in time to help dig through the rubble.

The Lucky Seven stopped at the impact site in Pennsylvania instead of continuing on the New York.

The other private teams around the country couldn't physically get there to help. Divine Right was stranded in Atlanta, unable to secure permission to take off. The West Coast teams were too far away to do any good anyway. The Secretary of Defense personally contacted the New Guard in Los Angeles and asked them to be on high alert status in case further attacks were pending in their area.

The staff of the Hero Academy canceled all classes and required all students to return to their dorms. Naturally, most of them wound up in the study lounges, watching the images from across the country on CNN and SkyNews.

Fifteen-year-old Salena Thompson placed a long-distance call to her mother in Phoenix, asking if she should do something to help. She could have run all the way to the East Coast in a few hours if needed. Her mother said no, in a voice choking back tears. "Stay there," Faith Thompson said. "I'm coming to you." Although she had been retired since Sally's conception, Faith kept herself in good shape despite the pain in her knees and hips that no amount of exercise could abate, and she could still push three hundred miles per hour for sprints and two-hundred fifty regularly.

From the observation deck on the Empire State Building, Harlan Washington watched each plane impact without any emotion. This had been part of his and Heinrich Kaiser's plan. It hadn't been hard to find a group of Islamic terrorists willing to perpetrate the scheme. Eight years previously they had tried to destroy the World Trade Center using car bombs and failed. It only took an infusion of some funds and a single session of treatments by Kaiser's pet psi Bertram to turn the terrorists into a weapon that would strike into the heart of the great superhero organization. Those who would pilot the planes would know exactly what point to strike the buildings to do the most damage to Just

Cause. And the rest of the world would only see a terrorist attack. It was a dangerous, yet brilliant move by Kaiser. Harlan had learned the ex-Nazi soldier was a skilled strategist with strange political bedfellows and allies around the world.

Kaiser's plan was to do significant damage to the venerable hero organization, something which would demoralize some and strengthen other survivors. "Why risk having any survivors at all?" Harlan asked.

"There will always be some," Kaiser said. "The key is that they will know they are vulnerable. Just Cause has been unchallenged for so long now that they merely go through the motions. Think of it as culling the herd, leaving the remainder stronger as a whole."

"I still think it's a mistake. You might never convert any of them to your cause, and then all you've done is strengthen those who oppose you. That which doesn't kill you makes you stronger and all that crap," said Harlan.

"And should they best me and my army, then perhaps it is they who have evolved fastest and should inherit the earth. I'm prepared to accept that possibility."

"Kind of hard luck on your people if that's the eventual result of your plan," said Harlan. "You won't mind if I plan for my own contingencies."

"Of course," said Kaiser. "I would expect nothing less of you. I, too, have my own plans-within-plans. I believe it is my destiny to rule this world with those who choose to accompany me, and I won't forgo that because of a setback."

Watching the towers shiver as fire tore through their interiors was sobering to Harlan. He wondered if they hadn't perhaps gone too far. How this could play into his grandiose plan was beyond even Harlan's considerable intellect. Still, though, it certainly sent a message, but Harlan thought perhaps the intent would be mistaken. This was a planned attack on Just Cause, a culling of the herd, as Kaiser had called it. Harlan believed it would have long-reaching political implications. This was the sort of catalyst that could touch off a world war, like the assassination of Archduke Ferdinand.

"Sir, you're going to have to get off the deck now." Harlan turned to regard a hollow-eyed security guard. "We're closing the deck for safety."

"Of course," said Harlan. "For safety." He walked calmly to the interior of the building. He wouldn't miss anything new; the media would see to that.

Juice kept Doublecharge by him as he worked to help get people out of the stairwells. She had strained all the muscles in her arms and back trying to slow his fall from the ninety-fifth floor, so all she could manage was to keep his electrical charge topped off, maximizing his strength. And he needed it, too, for he put all his effort into moving debris to keep stairwells clear. Her energy flagged slowly as she tried to keep funneling electricity to her partner.

When the second plane hit, Forcestar was caught by surprise. The blast of flame from exploding jet fuel would have burned him alive in midair, had his personal force field not taken the brunt of it. Even so, he lost control of his flight and crashed to the roof of one of the shorter buildings nearby, breaking both legs and fracturing his pelvis. It would be more than a year before he would walk again instead of flying. Without his help, many people fell to their deaths.

One of those who fell crashed down upon Crackerjack and a New York fireman, who were rushing in to assist. Crackerjack, who had not yet found anything in the world which could hurt him, was knocked sprawling by the grisly impact; the fireman was killed instantly.

Desert Eagle saved four of those who fell, clutching them one at a time. Of those four, one died of heart failure before she could be safely lowered to the ground anyway.

When the first tower collapsed, Juice barely managed to get an exhausted Doublecharge clear. The rain of girders and glass made a sound like the end of the world. Beyond caring, he wrenched the door off a parked car and laid her across the back seat, admonishing her not to move. Paper fragments drifted down like snow. Coughing, Juice tore off his uniform shirt and wrapped it around his face to keep from breathing all the dust and ash billowing through the air. Somewhere, there were people who needed his help, and he was going to search for them until he couldn't stand up.

Crackerjack was buried in the rubble of the first tower. Pinned down by a six-ton girder, all he could do was to lie quietly and wonder if he might finally die from suffocation or dehydration. Five days later he was uncovered, the only one alive in a tomb of hundreds.

Dr. Grace Devereaux arrived on the first plane allowed back into the country from Paris, armed with an open line of credit secured by her research facility. She took over Just Cause Second Team's medical clinic and upgraded it with the latest and greatest equipment so she could personally treat the surviving team members.

Juice worked himself to exhaustion, digging through rubble for days on end without rest, pausing only long enough to drink cups of muddy coffee or to eat stale, tasteless sandwiches. When he finally collapsed, Dr. Devereaux had to install a temporary pacemaker to keep his heart beating.

Forcestar required careful monitoring because of the severity of his lower-body injuries. His physical hurt was nothing compared to his emotional pain. He had to be regularly sedated or he would awaken screaming in fear, reliving the explosion over and over again.

Doublecharge was the emotional pillar that Dr. Devereaux leaned on time and again. Then one afternoon while helping in the clinic, she dropped a water glass. The explosion of shards brought Dr. Devereaux into the lab at a dead run, where she found Doublecharge standing forlorn, holding her face in her hands, inconsolable tears dampening her collar. The two women embraced, trying to find solace in one another.

Jack disappeared. Sondra was very worried about him and spent hours circling over New York, looking for any sign of him. He finally turned up, three weeks later, knocking at her door. He wouldn't say where he'd been, and she didn't ask. They held each other for hours, not speaking.

Glimmer volunteered to help find survivors. With his psionic abilities, he could sense the nodes of pain and suffering deep under the tons of debris. Many times, they would wink out long before rescuers could reach them. He felt the loss of each mind on a deeply personal level. If it wasn't for the survivors that he did get to, the sense of personal failure might have overwhelmed him.

In the aftermath of the attacks, things happened very quickly for Just Cause. The Second Team, under the competent command of MetalBlade, assisted federal agents in rounding up potential terrorists around the country. The Office of Homeland Security was created, and the President signed an Executive Order bringing Just Cause under the aegis of the federal government. Almost fifty years after American Justice had been blacklisted, there was once again a government-sponsored superhero team in America.

The coffers of the government opened wide for Just Cause. As it had always done in the past, Washington solved problems by throwing money at them until they went away. In the case of Just Cause, this entailed building a new, state-of-the-art headquarters on a stretch of federally owned land in Colorado.

Numerous arguments ran rampant in the Senate and the House about the place of parahumans in the country. Some argued they should be wholly inducted into the military and shipped overseas with the troops. Others believed all parahumans should become federal agents within the U.S., and those who didn't accept should be considered traitors. In the end, offers were extended to the other teams to become part of Homeland Security

None of them accepted.

They all had very good reasons for declining the offers, much to the chagrin of Just Cause leadership. Divine Right felt it would be too much of a conflict of interest to serve the federal government and the Catholic Church. The New Guard and the Lucky Seven were privately owned teams, preferring the inherent benefits of working in the free market.

As months passed, the Just Cause survivors became able to sleep through the nights without awakening in fear once again. The new headquarters opened and the six heroes and their families left the East Coast for the sunny skies of Colorado.

They spent many of the early days in the new facility trying to prove the attack on the World Trade Center had been directed specifically at Just Cause, in spite of evidence to the contrary. Jack believed it no coincidence the first plane struck right in the spot it would do the most damage to the team. He argued Destroyer was the most likely suspect; the man hated Just Cause and had the technical know-how to rig up a plane to act like a missile. He'd used a plane as a weapon before, in 1985, hurling it onto Tornado's funeral. Homeland Security discounted his theory, considering Destroyer had been mostly quiet since '85. He had only surfaced twice in the last fifteen years, staging complex robberies of high-tech equipment in the late '90s.

The investigation mostly went for naught. Eventually even Jack was forced to admit it looked just like an unfortunate coincidence that the first plane struck right at the level of Just Cause headquarters. It was time to move on.

But if ever he ran into Destroyer sometime in the future, Jack was going to ask him a few questions.

BULLETPROOF

My name is Harry Blaine, and I have a secret. It's the sort of secret that could keep some people from having a real job, or a life, or a marriage. I've managed to keep it hidden for many years, even learning to live with it. Some days, though, it eats away at me like a cancer.

I am a parahuman, and I wish to God that I wasn't.

At puberty, my strength began to increase. Every month, I could lift twice as much as I had the previous one. I knew right away I'd have to hide it, so all through high school I avoided anything athletic. I joined the choir, the AV Club. I hit the books so I wouldn't accidentally hit something—or *someone*—more fragile. Anything to keep people from thinking I was *different*. I told everyone that I had mono, or chickenpox, or anything that would explain my extended absences from school. I eventually had to drop out and get a GED through the mail. Along with my increasing strength, my muscular tissue was growing denser as well. It made my growing pains far beyond anything normal teens experienced. Every month, it seemed, I had to learn and relearn basic motor skills like walking and feeding myself because of my uncontrollable strength, and I developed a reputation for being ham-handed and clumsy.

Even now, my strength increases by a factor of about three every year. Here I am, forty years old with a second mortgage, a fifteen-year-old daughter, and the ability to knock a skyscraper off its foundation. By the time my daughter Dannan was born I was fortunate to have more or less mastered control over my musculature, but it still terrifies me when I think of how easily I might have crushed her fragile bones in my overpowered hands. My super-dense muscles have resulted in virtual invulnerability for me from physical damage. My skin can still be broken, and it's conceivable that I could die from blood loss, asphyxiation, or any number of invasive agents, but I have yet to find anything that can penetrate the musculature under my skin.

You'd think that I would have become a superhero, dressing up in brightly-colored Spandex and beating the heck out of this week's bad guy. Or maybe I would be some superhero's recurring villain, always popping up with some far-fetched plan to rule the world. Or maybe even a vigilante, leaving unconscious criminals at the doorsteps of local police departments or dead ones in back alleys. The fact is that I never wanted these powers. Like the song said, I wished I were just an average man with an average life, working from nine to five.

So I hid my powers. My parents knew about them, of course, but they agreed that telling anyone else was nobody's business but mine. When they died in the car crash that I walked away from unhurt, my secret died with them as far as I was concerned. I had just turned eighteen, so I didn't have to explain myself to anyone. People said I'd been fortunate to survive the accident. Nobody ever suspected the truth. By that time, I had settled upon a career choice, and worked my butt off to get it.

Maybe my powers had manipulated my subconscious desires, for I chose to be a cop. For twenty years I have worked for the Bay City 7th Precinct. I have seen more young idealists come and go through the department than I can count. After five years as a cop, I married a beautiful woman who then bore my daughter. My wife Alisa knows my secret, but Dannan does not. Every night I go to bed praying that she will never develop the curse of these powers.

I still have to manage my strength, and the only way to do that is to apply them to lifting weights. There is a special gymnasium here in Bay City called Powerman's. Membership is free but only to a select, exclusive clientele. Powerman's caters to those paranormals with strength like mine. There are no fancy machines there, nothing with the word *Flex* attached to them. Only free weights are available in differing denominations. The lightest one-handed barbells weigh in at an even ton, and they go up from there. Exactly how strong am I? It's not really important. I'm not the strongest person at Powerman's, not by a long shot, but there are plenty of others who can't even spot me. I am, though, one of the only people there who wears a mask.

They all call me Hood, because of the full-face mask I always wear. They respect my privacy and only once has anyone had the temerity to try and take it off me. I broke his jaw for trying. I don't want to be known to these people; I don't want them to call on me. Let them go out and fly around and save the world. That's not what I want. I just want to make a difference in my little section of Bay City. And I want to make that difference the same way all my friends do: from behind a badge, not behind a mask.

It's a cliché to say so, but it really was just another day in Bay City. My partner, Fred Grimes, and I had just hit the Giant Burrito stand off Renfro Drive. Fred had been riding with me for two years. He was ten years younger than me and hadn't yet got that cynical streak that most cops develop over time. He was a talker. He talked incessantly about anything and everything. He talked about his girlfriend. He talked about sports. He talked about last night's bust by the narcotics division and wondered when we might get some of that action. "Shut up and eat, rookie." I took a careful bite but still managed to spill some habañero sauce down my front. I always called him *rookie* to get a rise out of him, because he only had five years on the force to my twenty.

Grimes took it in stride, like he did everything, and flapped his lips some more. "Whatever you say, old geezer." The two of us sat and ate. Except for his noisy chewing, Grimes had stopped talking for the time being, allowing me to hear the sounds of the city. I've always loved to sit and listen to the bustle of people going about their business every day. That's one of the reasons I became a cop—so I could be nearer to all those wonderful, lovely, normal people. It was kind of like when the nerd goes to all the popular parties in the eternal hope that he may eventually be popular as well.

The constant radio buzz was interrupted by the two-note attention signal used by BCPD. "All units stand by . . ."

Grimes sat down his drink and I started the car.

The attention signal repeated. "All units in vicinity respond to East Bay High School Code Three. We have multiple reports of shots being fired and at least three casualties. Switch to channel 8 for further information."

East Bay High was less than a mile from our current location, and *Code Three* meant lights and sirens. I yanked the shifter into Drive and spun the tires as the car launched like a scared rabbit.

"One Mary Thirteen responding," I said into the radio.

"Jesus!" Grimes shouted as I whipped through an intersection against the light. Behind me, tires squealed and a surprised horn blared. "Killing us won't get us there any faster, Harry!" He cursed as we hit a bump and the top of his soda came off, drenching his lap with cold Sprite. I didn't hear him. All I heard was the rushing in my ears.

East Bay was Dannan's school.

Then we screeched to a stop in front of the school. Unlike most Bay City schools, East Bay didn't have a large acreage of open lawn surrounding it. Except for the parking lot on the north side, it sat right up against the street. Grimes grabbed the shotgun between us and we spilled out of the car. We could see kids huddled behind parked cars and in doorways across the street. In the distance we could hear other units approaching, sirens screaming. And below the sirens, we heard a single popping sound that could only have been a gun discharging. Grimes dove over the hood of the car to put it between the school and us.

"How many of them are there?" I called out, hoping that somebody had seen something. I got a chorus of "I don't know" from a few of the kids. One boy, dragging on a cigarette with shaking hands, said there were two of them, and they shot his friend Rob. "Okay, short answers, son. Are they carrying pistols? Rifles? What are they wearing?" I snapped the questions out with all the authority vested in me by being the father of a teenage daughter. They had rifles, he said, they were wearing fatigues, and he thought they were sophomores. Two more pops sounded, from either the second or third floor. Some muffled screams echoed through the windows that had been opened to let in the pleasant spring air.

I looked at Grimes, who had bitten his lip and had a streak of blood on his cheek from it. "We can't wait, or this will turn into Columbine all over again." He nodded his head. "The door, on three. One . . . two . . . three!" We jumped from our cover and sprinted for the main door, guns drawn. It couldn't have been more than thirty feet, but it felt like it took hours to cover that distance. A startled exclamation followed by a hail of bullets came down upon us. Grimes cursed and flopped forward, blood leaking from under his shirt. I grabbed and carried him until we were under the canopy over the front doors. I heard maniacal laughing from above.

I took a minute to assess the damage to Grimes. The bullet, fired from high above us, had come down at a sharp angle and struck the top of his shoulder along the straps between the front and back pads of his vest. I didn't see an exit wound and his arm was hanging. His face was pale but he looked furious. "He shot me, that little bastard!" He coughed and wheezed as some blood flecks came out of his mouth.

"Grimes, don't move. You'll be safe here until backup arrives." I could see the flashing lights approaching from both directions. "I'll go get them." I grabbed the shotgun from him. He made an attempt to get back to his feet but I gently pressed him back down. I grabbed the radio clipped to my shoulder. "One Mary Thirteen. Shots fired, officer down!"

Grimes coughed again and wheezed with a sound like someone trying to suck the last bit of milkshake out of a cup with a straw. "Okay, geezer . . . Just hurry. You owe me . . . another soda." He gave me a weak smile. I smiled back, put a hand on his other shoulder, and then ran into the school.

Normally what I was doing would be considered foolhardy. I had no backup, unknown perpetrators, and was likely outgunned.

But I was bulletproof.

Ever since Columbine we've had dozens of people lead workshops in the best way to deal with school shootings. Nobody ever says the same thing, because there is no right way to do it, no sure-fire method of bringing a quick resolution to the situation. I figured that my method would be as good as anybody's. I was going to come in loud and fast, and I hoped that they would shoot at me instead of at anyone else.

I glanced around the entry hall, looking for a stairway. I fumed at myself for never having had the time to come and visit the school that my own daughter was attending. That would change, I promised, even if it means leaving the Force. I found a stairwell with two gunshot victims at the bottom of it. One was clearly dead; the other was wounded but in shock. I gently lifted the head of a pretty young brunette my daughter's age and asked her if they were upstairs. She nodded, shivering. I told her to stay there, help was on the way.

I whispered into my radio, "One Mary Thirteen, Officer Blaine on scene. I've got civilian casualties here inside the school. I'm going silent. Will report in five minutes." I shut off the radio.

As I reached the top of the stairs another shot rang out, followed by several screams. A rough, adolescent voice commanded them to "shut up, or I'll do all of you." I flattened myself against the wall, holding the shotgun tightly across my chest. They were in the classroom right around the corner from the stairwell from the sound of it. My heart was pounding like I'd been doing an hour of twelve-ton curls. The roaring of blood in my ears was almost as loud as the sounds of children crying in the next room. I took a deep breath and counted silently down from five. I wasn't afraid that I would die, but I didn't want any more kids to come to harm because of my actions. I lowered the shotgun and leaped out of the stairwell, taking the corner tight and low.

The door to the classroom was closed, but that wasn't a factor for someone like me. In the split second as I rounded the corner I saw an acne-ridden youth holding a hunting rifle at high point beyond the door. His body was turned toward me but he was watching something in the classroom. He started to turn just as I hit the door full on. The glass in the window of the door shattered as I knocked it from its hinges. It cartwheeled across the classroom, striking the skinny boy with the rifle and felling him like a bowling pin. I rushed in like a freight train without brakes, the shotgun tracking around, looking for the other gunman.

He was standing aghast across the room. His assault rifle drooped in impotence as he realized his escapade was coming to an end. Several kids were huddled against the wall in a tight knot of fear. Two others and an older woman, probably a teacher, were sprawled in awkward positions on the floor and across desks, their lives leaking out onto the tile floor. The boy's jaw tightened and he raised the gun, firming up his resolve for his final stand. In spite of my years of training, I fumbled like a first-year rookie. My palms were sweating and I gripped the shotgun so tightly that I heard the stock splinter.

Nobody should ever have to see a gun barrel pointing right at them. It feels like you are tied onto train tracks in front of a tunnel with an express approaching at high speed. In the movies, these things always happen in slow motion, with the camera lingering on every nuance of the action. In reality, they move so quickly you never even have a chance to react. I had been beaten to the trigger by this child, this punk with his Army Surplus fatigues and a military weapon from God-knows-where. I could only trust to my unnatural toughness to survive. Without warning, I heard a voice scream in denial and a body lurched from within the huddle of students in the corner right into the path of the bullets. My heart stopped as I saw it was my own beautiful daughter.

The boy had his weapon on full automatic and he emptied his clip into the both of us. The funny thing about being shot at close range is you can't hear the shots with any kind of clarity. It sounds like thunder. Each shot felt like I was being pulled backward instead of pushed. I hit the wall and fell with my daughter in my lap, her blood mingling with mine. The pain from my wounds hit all at once, like I'd been hit by a thousand ball-peen hammers. It paled in comparison to the fear I felt for Dannan. The bullets had nearly ripped her blouse off and I could see crater-shaped wounds where they had struck her.

My shotgun was bent beyond use. No matter. I threw it away. My rage built to a feverish intensity and I went for the boy, not like a man but like a wild animal, scrabbling at the floor and the desks for purchase as I hurled myself at him. His eyes grew wide and I heard the click of an empty chamber. I hit him hard with my fist. He flew backward and hit the opposite wall so hard that it cracked and plaster rained down like snow. I stood over him, my head spinning, dizzy with blood loss. I wanted to crush him, to rend him into nothing. I grabbed the first thing that came into my hand—a desk —and raised it high to beat him into tiny pieces, when I froze at the sound of my daughter's voice.

"Daddy, don't!"

I turned and saw Dannan getting to her feet. "I'm . . . okay, I think." She took a small step toward me and I dropped the desk I was holding like a club. I could see a tiny black dot in the middle of each of her wounds; bullets, flattened against the super-dense musculature that she must have inherited from me. Fifteen years and I never noticed. The thought struck me as funny, and I began to chuckle, then to laugh, whooping like a madman and gasping for breath as I took my beautiful, alive daughter in my arms. More people came into the room, storming around the two of us, collecting the guns, doctoring our wounds, taking out the victims.

Dannan and I, we just held each other and laughed at the joy of being alive together.

YOUNG GUNS

Sometimes a car chase is just like in the movies. This one was more like the ones you see on *Police Camera Action* specials. In other words, there wasn't a lot of tight cornering and screeching skids. Mostly we were just barreling along the road in a straight line, occasionally swerving onto the shoulder to avoid slower traffic. Only the hills made it slightly less than routine, if there is such a thing.

I was driving, because Grimes' shoulder was still bothering him. We had been enjoying a quiet morning patrol through East Bay when the call came over the radio about the carjacking. Of all things, it was a dairy truck. The mysteries of modern criminal minds once again made me wonder what had happened to our society, but only for the moment it took me to toss my coffee out the window and flip on the lights and siren. We had the good fortune to be only a few minutes away and spotted the milk truck right away. Of course, it was hard to miss when it was tearing down Santa Ana Boulevard at seventy miles per hour. It was Sunday morning, and traffic wasn't much of a factor this early, so we had clear sailing and were able to move in behind the van. Fred winced as an exceptional pothole jarred his shoulder the wrong way. "Hey, Harry, I'd like to avoid the hospital today. Spent enough time there last month."

I chuckled and guided the patrol car past an early-morning bus. "Don't worry, rookie. You're in expert, veteran hands today." I always called Fred Grimes *rookie* because he had the misfortune to be ten years younger than me. He returned the favor in kind, referring to me as *geezer*. My name is Harry Blaine, and I'm a twenty-year veteran of the Bay City Police Department. I'm also strong enough to yank a building off its foundation and bulletproof, but that hasn't stopped me from pursuing my chosen avocation of law enforcement. I didn't ask for my powers, and I didn't once consider using them in any way to fight crime as a vigilante or superhero. I preferred my justice by the book, thank you very much. The first—and only—time I ever used my abilities anywhere but at Powerman's Gymnasium was last month when I'd stopped a couple of teenage killers on a shooting spree in my daughter's high school. That was where Grimes had been shot. My daughter Dannan, who I learned had inherited my powers, was a survivor of that bloody massacre. Neither of us had known about the others' abilities before that day. Since then it has caused . . . problems.

There were two young men in the milk truck. Both were howling and laughing like madmen as they swerved from lane to lane. I guessed they were just joyriding, the sort of *boys-will-be-boys* stuff that people used to laugh off back in the days when I was the rookie. Times had changed, and so had people, and they took stuff like high-speed chases seriously when it came to Internal Affairs investigations. It was important Grimes and I did everything By The Book, just in case anything unexpected happened.

The stolen truck whipped through a busy intersection. Cars screeched to a halt, horns blaring. Grimes cursed and grabbed the Jesus bar on the dash. Without really thinking the maneuver through, I tromped on the emergency brake and spun the wheel to the left. The rear end of the patrol cruiser fishtailed to the right. As we pointed towards a clear section, I released the brake and hit the accelerator. Wheels squealing, we leaped over the curb and bounced back onto the road again.

Okay, maybe it was a *little* like in the movies.

Grimes let go of the Jesus bar and leaned back in his seat. His face had gone white and I couldn't blame him in the least. I couldn't have repeated that maneuver with a month of practice. "So . . . uh, how about them Bulldogs, geezer?" The Bulldogs had squandered their strong season start with a fourteen-game losing streak and were going nowhere fast.

"Next topic, rookie," I grumbled. Grimes grinned, knowing I was a card-carrying fan. He had perfected the annoying habit of never shutting up. It was pointless to try to silence him, a fact I had learned after my first year with him. The best I could hope for was to pick a neutral subject when my concentration was required and just nod and agree when he paused for breath.

"How's Dannan doing with her new team?"

I clenched my fingers and the rim of the steering wheel cracked from force it was never designed to withstand. Shortly after I discovered she had inherited my unnatural strength and muscular density, Dannan announced to my wife Alisa and myself over dinner one night that she was going to join the Young Guns. The Young Guns were a trio of parapowered kids who wandered the Bay City area looking for crimes and super-powered villains. Sometimes they found them. They weren't old enough to attend the Hero Academy in Denver yet, and I often hoped Dannan would change her mind about the whole being-a-superhero thing.

They went out looking for trouble. More often than not they wound up finding it.

"Absolutely not!" I had told her. The discussion degenerated from there into a typical family squabble that ended with doors being slammed—in her case, cracking the door down the middle—and lots of yelling. The gist of her argument had been that just because I never used my powers didn't mean that she wasn't going to use hers. My argument had been that I was her father and while she lived in my house it would be by my rules.

My lovely wife Alisa, peacemaker that she is, managed to bring Dannan and me to . . . well, it wasn't exactly an *agreement*. More like a treaty. It was understood by Dannan that if her grades slipped, or we got a call from anyone about vandalism or property damage or we ever had to pick her up at a police station, she would be grounded until she was thirty. It was understood by me that she would parade around in a skimpy, colorful outfit and I would grit my teeth and bite my tongue, which wouldn't do any good because it was as tough as the rest of me.

She called herself Bombshell. Oh, the humanity!

Just then one of the rear doors of the van swung open. I could see one of the young men bouncing around inside. In a second he kicked the swinging door open all the way and he held a half-gallon of milk in a glass bottle in each hand. "Watch out!" yelled Grimes as the punk let fly with them. I swerved to avoid the homogenized grenades. One impacted on the grill of the cruiser and smoke billowed from the engine as milk congealed on the hot block. Soon all manner of dairy products were being flung from the escaping van and our car was beginning to look like it came out second-best in an elementary-school cafeteria food fight.

A pint of thick cream impacted on the windshield and the wipers only smeared it instead of clearing it completely. I hit the washers and turned it into a sticky mess. Grimes grabbed the radio. "One Mary Thirteen," he yelled, announcing our call sign so everyone would know it was me and Grimes in the milk-mobile when we got back to the station. "We're under attack . . . sort of . . . where's our backup?"

The radio crackled with giggles. "One Mary Thirteen, this is Air Three, we have the suspect vehicle in visual range." Bud Jenkins was Air Three's pilot and a terrible practical joker. I just knew that by tomorrow this chase would be national news and going viral on YouTube. I groaned aloud, wondering if it could get any worse. "Uh . . . One Mary Thirteen, be advised there are four Code Twenty-Sixes approaching from the South up Santa Ana."

I muttered a word that I usually save for sporting events. *Code Twenty-Six* was the department's code for parahumans. That could only mean—

"Hi dad!" Dannan's voice rang out. She was riding on Surfboy's back as he flew past. Alongside of them was Toxic, cute as a button if you discounted the cloud of accumulated pollution on which she rode. Johnny Go ran beneath them, electricity crackling between his arms and legs. Eighty miles an hour was only a brisk stroll to him—he could do over two hundred easy. Together, they were the Young Guns, and that meant trouble with a ten-story-tall "T."

Toxic. Surfboy. Johnny Go. And of course, Bombshell. None of them sounded like the superheroes I remembered when I was a kid, and certainly none of them dressed like the heroes of my youth. Surfboy wore wraparound sunglasses, a pair of Army surplus jump boots, and an off-the-rack wetsuit with the logo of whatever company was sponsoring them this week—I think it was a skateboard manufacturer. Toxic dressed like a Goth, with a pierced lip, nose, and eyebrow, with short spiky greenish hair that looked like it hadn't been clean in awhile. Johnny Go favored Nikes, goggles, and the low-friction suits worn by Olympic speed skaters. Dannan preferred to fight her battles in hip-hugging blue jeans with flared legs and a matching denim top that was barely bigger than a sports bra, because, she'd explained to me, denim was a more durable fabric than most in combat situations.

The four youths overtook us in a matter of seconds and surrounded the speeding truck. As they approached, the boy in the back of the van spooked and stopped hurling dairy products at us. He hurried back into the front seat. The driver began to weave the van, trying to keep the young heroes from catching up, but to no avail.

Once Johnny Go reached the side of the van, he climbed onto it using his adhesive abilities, and stuck there like a spider on a wall. Toxic levitated her cloud in front of the truck and began to fill the cabin with smog that she called out of the air molecule by molecule. Surfboy flew over the top of the truck, Dannan riding him like his namesake. She looked like she was getting ready to jump onto the roof. I resisted the temptation to shut my eyes.

The truck swerved towards some parked cars as the driver gave in to panic and started to lose control. Johnny Go bailed off a second later, and Toxic drifted clear. The van sideswiped three cars in a row, rocking from side to side as it hurtled past. The driver over-corrected and nearly turned it sideways. Somehow he managed to regain control but at a price. The quick changes in direction catapulted his friend out of the step-door like a human missile. Johnny Go caught him in mid-air. He wasn't strong enough to stop the young man's flight, deflected his impact enough so that it wouldn't be fatal. In the process, he delivered a shock of about forty-six thousand volts that he produced as a side effect of his speedy metabolism.

As we tore past in our stained and dented cruiser, the man slumped to the ground, where Toxic wrapped the man up in a gummy substance that she drew out of the ground. Dannan yelled something to Surfboy, who nodded and sped up passing the truck altogether. I didn't understand her plan until I saw her leap lightly to the ground, rolling and turning to face the onrushing van.

"No!" I cried out as the van hit her, expecting to see her body flung away by the impact.

Grimes grabbed the radio.

"Air Three, One Mary Thirteen. What happened?"

"Bombshell's hanging off the front of the van, Thirteen. She's got her hands through the hood . . . Oh my God!"

There was a terrific sound of metal tearing and machinery breaking. The truck's rear wheels smoked as the driver stood on the brakes. In an instant, I knew what Dannan had done, as the entire engine of the delivery van bounced onto the ground, digging a long furrow in the pavement and skidding to a smoking halt.

"The engine," yelled Jenkins over the radio. "She ripped out the entire motherloving engine!"

Within an hour, it was pretty well cleaned up. The suspects were both shaken up and had been taken to a local hospital. The Young Guns had given their statements, as had Grimes and myself. My supervisor cleared the Young Guns of any wrong-doing, since they had brought the chase to a halt without endangering any innocents and apprehended both suspects into the bargain.

It all felt to me like dental surgery without anesthesia. I couldn't believe that they were just going to walk away without any consequences. Dannan could probably see the steam rising off my head and gave me a wide berth, saying she'd see me later. She and the rest of the 'Guns left without fanfare, television cameras tracking them until they were out of sight.

Grimes looked me up and down, and then suggested we go get a fresh cup of coffee and fill out our reports somewhere quiet. The rest of the shift passed without incident, except for occasional involuntary growls from somewhere deep in my throat.

* * *

Dinner was a tense affair. I managed to avoid blowing my top at my daughter, and she managed to avoid mouthing off. Alisa sat between us, working hard at keeping topics neutral. Later that night, I was sure, I would appreciate her efforts. For the time being, though, it wasn't helping my mood any. Finally, I pushed my plate away, folded my hands, and leaned my elbows on the table. I had been debating for hours the best way to approach this subject with Dannan.

"Dannan, do you know why I never used my powers? Why I never became a superhero?"

Her eyes narrowed and she set down her fork, folding her arms as she went on the defensive. "No."

"In a nutshell, because there aren't any clear rules governing it." I was ready to elaborate, but held off, banking on her curiosity. I wasn't disappointed.

"What's that supposed to mean?" She leaned back, tipping her chair on its rear legs and started to crack her knuckles—something I hated. Alisa gently reminded her that the privilege of sitting at her table included the keeping of all four legs of a chair on the ground at all times. Dannan mumbled that she was sorry and tipped forward again. I always admired the way Alisa handled Dannan, especially when she was being a difficult teenager.

"How does a superhero know what laws to enforce? What punishment is appropriate? And what about due process? When you choose to put on a costume and 'fight crime', as you call it, you are ignoring the laws of this country."

"Oh, please spare me," Dannan pushed her chair back to stand up.

"Please, hear me out, Dannan. This is not a chew-out session. I just want you to understand why I made the decision I did, and maybe it will give you something to think about. Ten minutes, then you can go anywhere you want. Fair?" All things considered, I wanted to scream at her and shake her until she saw the light. In that respect, I felt I was doing fairly well when she sat down, closed off and unreceptive. "Those two guys today, they will probably walk. Sure, we can charge them with some minor things, but when they were stopped by parahumans, that opened up a whole can of legal worms. We don't have laws in this country—yet— about parahumans using their powers on normal humans, but every time there is a case like this one, new precedents are set. You could make your acts of heroism illegal without even intending to. Do you want to do that to your friends? Your community?"

I saw the little line appear between her eyebrows that showed she was actually thinking about what I was saying. Her body language still conveyed extreme disinterest, but her ears were open.

"Nobody can really oppose a para but another para. When that happens, things tend to degenerate into slugfests where property damage and injured bystanders are almost common. The only recourse normals have is to try and sue the combatants, and so far only the largest organizations have even offered any settlements. If somebody sues you for a half million dollars, what are you going to do? If you go to court, you'll lose because the court system in this country is unsympathetic to vigilantism. If you skip out, you can become a fugitive, and suddenly you are running from those who you wanted to ally with." I stared across the table, unclasping my hands. "Dannan, I don't ever want to have to be called to take you down."

For the first time since I started talking, she looked at me, a spark of comprehension somewhere in her blue eyes.

"I avoided the path you are setting out upon, because I saw these things I've tried to explain to you. I didn't want to make the one mistake that could hurt everyone I know and love. Even those heroes who are doing such good work around the country could be seriously hampered simply by some clever legislation. Right now it's illegal to be a drug addict. The law actually penalizes someone for what they are. What if they pass a law making it illegal to be a parahuman? What recourse would we have? Dannan, that's what the Nazis did to the Jews before World War II."

She pouted. "So what are you saying, Dad? You want me to quit?"

Yes! I screamed . . . on the inside. "No, I'm just asking you to really think about all the factors involved in your lifestyle and what it could mean for you, for our family, and for the entire country. It's a lot of weight to place on your shoulders, even as strong as you are. It's a lot of weight for me. And I didn't want to chance letting that weight come crashing down. I chose to make a difference in peoples' lives; I became a cop. You don't have to be a cop, but you don't have to be a superhero either. Think about it, okay, hon?"

Dannan stood up, still pouting but more subdued than defensive. "Okay, Dad. Can I go now?"

"Anywhere you want. That was the agreement. And, Danni?" She stopped, halfway down the hallway.

"Yeah?"

"You might think about a mask. I don't want to have to take apart a bunch of disgruntled perps here at the house who got beat up by my little girl."

TUESDAY NIGHT AT POWERMAN'S

Some days it doesn't pay to get out of bed. Others it seems like everything is going your way. I was having the latter. My name's Harry Blaine. I'm a cop in the East Bay Police Department. I also happen to be a paranormal, but that's my little secret. I'm strong enough to toss cars like shotputs and tough enough to laugh off bullets. Most days those abilities don't make a difference in my job. A day like today and I didn't even think about them.

Grimes and I had been on the run all day from one call to the next, but none of them were really anything serious. We changed a tire for an old lady on Santa Ana Boulevard. We broke up a potential bar fight. We directed traffic around a family of ducks that decided to cross Haxtun Street. We even pulled over a teenage speeder who was so nervous and polite that we gave him a warning and sent him on his way. People thanked us. People smiled at us. These things are uncommon in my line of work and they make a day memorable and enjoyable. Needless to say, I was insufferably cheerful when I got home.

I rushed into the kitchen where Alisa was cooking spaghetti and Italian sausage—my favorite—and swept her up in my arms. She squealed and beat me with her spoon, splattering sauce everywhere. Leering, I lowered her to kiss her, sauce dribbling off my nose. "Don't you dare!" she giggled, pushing futilely at me. I chuckled and rubbed noses with here, smearing the sauce onto her face. I felt like I was twenty years younger instead of forty-one. I set her down and grabbed some paper towels and began wiping up the splashes. "What happened to you? Did you get promoted or something?" Alisa took a towel from me and wiped her own face.

"No, I just had a good day; the kind of day that I really don't mind being a cop." I opened the fridge and removed a pair of beers. Alisa gladly accepted one from me after I stuck my thumb under the edge of the cap and popped the top for her.

"Good. Then you can make the salad, handsome." She pointed to a pile of vegetables sitting in the sink. I started chopping dutifully, filling a large bowl with lettuce, carrots, peppers, and so on. In a few minutes my daughter Dannan wandered into the kitchen, opened the refrigerator and removed a soda. Dannan inherited her strength and toughness from me, her strong will from her mother, and missed out on either of our good sense. She had opted to join a superhero group called the Young Guns. It was more of a club for super-teens and they seemed to spend more time causing trouble than stopping it, in my opinion. I didn't like her to be a part of that lifestyle, but we had an agreement that as long as she lived up to her scholarly obligations that she could continue running around in her denim costume.

"Hey kiddo, what's the good word?" I asked, brushing the last bit of salad debris into the trash.

"Nothing," she mumbled. Typical teenager, I thought, never answers with a sentence when a single word will do.

"You have a lot of homework tonight?" I finished cleaning up my mess and took a sip of my beer.

"No," she replied.

"Any plans?"

"Uh-uh." I could see she wasn't much interested in talking to someone as uncool as her father, but I was determined that my good day was going to continue and I was going to have a conversation with my daughter.

"Listen," I said, a thought occurring to me. "I've been thinking. How would you like to come to the gym with me tonight?" Alisa stopped stirring her sauce and glanced sidelong at me. I could tell she wasn't sure this was such a good idea.

"And do what, watch?" Dannan sat on one of our stools and kicked her legs indolently. She knew full well that there wasn't a gym in town that could even make her break a sweat. Or so she thought.

"There's a place near the docks. It's called Powerman's. Ever hear of it?" She shook her head. "It's a special gym. They cater to . . .people like you and me." I could tell she was getting interested in spite of herself and continued. "They don't have machines - only free weights, but I promise you'll get a workout. What do you say?"

She finished her soda and squeezed the can into an aluminum chunk the size of a golf ball. "Sure, I guess. Whatever," she replied carelessly, which was as close to an affirmative answer I ever got from her these days.

An hour after dinner, we headed out. For the most part, the drive was quiet. Dannan resisted most of my attempts to engage her in any meaningful communication, but I was used to that. It was about a thirty-minute drive to Powerman's from our house. When I pulled into the lot and parked, Dannan stared suspiciously at the run-down warehouse with a single oversized door. There were maybe a half dozen other cars parked in the lot.

"This is it? You've got to be kidding," Dannan grumbled, getting out of the car and looking down the street with distaste at the rows of warehouses and factories. I reached into the glove compartment and removed the full-face hood I always wore when I came to Powerman's. I had decided long ago that I'd prefer to remain anonymous, even with the fairly exclusive group that frequented Powerman's. I knew for a fact that some of the men and women that I worked out with were on the wrong side of the law, but they respected my privacy and I in turn respected theirs. If I ever came across one while I was working, well, that was different.

"Touch the ground," I suggested to her, pulling the mask over my head. Obediently, she placed a hand on the pavement and her eyes widened as she felt the uneven vibrations of ten-ton weights being dropped. She looked back at me and her mouth fell open as she saw the hood over my face.

"What's that for?" She asked. I told her.

"Call me Hood when we're inside. You're a friend of mine. The rules are simple. No fighting, even if you recognize someone inside. Put the weights up when you're done. Always use a spotter, and write an emergency contact number on the clipboard. Keep the location a secret, unless it's for another super-strong type. Any questions?" We walked to the entrance. Dannan shook her head, a mystified expression on her face. I motioned to her to open the door. She turned the knob and pushed on it.

"It's stuck . . . uh, Hood," she shrugged.

"You'll have to push a little harder, that's all." I smiled. Powerman didn't have a security system. In fact, he didn't even have a lock for the door. What he did have was a 750-pound block of concrete right behind it. Dannan pushed and the sound of concrete grating on concrete echoed across the lot. The two of us entered the building and slid the concrete piece back into place. The warehouse itself was empty. We walked over to a freight elevator. We boarded it, I shut the grate, and we descended into the gym.

It was fairly deep underground, deeper than any of the sub-basements of any of the other buildings around it. From a safety standpoint, it was best if Powerman's had nothing else near it. The elevator ground to a halt. I swung open the gate and let Dannan take in the scene.

Powerman's was built by two paranormals almost twenty years ago. The Architect and Fusionne had been part of Company A, one of the premier superhero organizations of the late Seventies and early Eighties. When Powerman retired from Company A, he recruited the other two heroes to help him set up his gym. The Architect was gifted in shaping materials with his thoughts, whereas Fusionne could use her gravitational abilities to compress matter almost infinitely. She had provided the raw material for the gym by compressing the mass of a small island in the Aleutian chain that nobody would have missed. The floor, walls, and weights of Powerman's were hundreds of times as dense as the heaviest man-made radioactives. The foundation ran over three miles into the bedrock, spreading out the thousands of tons of mass over nine square miles. Once a paranormal named Anchor had lost her footing and dropped a weight and it registered on seismic detectors halfway across the continent.

Dannan's eyes bugged out as she recognized three of the six people currently working out. I knew all six of them, and the list read like a Who's Who guide to paranormals. Powerhouse was benching a few thousand pounds with Clydesdale spotting him. ManMountain and The Amazon were taking turns doing flies with the ten-ton dumbbells in spite of the fact that they fought against each other in the field. They were glaring mightily but each respected the other's space. Captain Lunar, who like me worked out in a full-face mask, was just finishing loading up a straight barbell with six of the eight-ton weights. He called out to us in greeting. "Hey, Hood, just in time. I was waiting for a spotter." Off in one corner of the room stood a man doing shoulder presses by himself. His muscles bunched like knotted rags as he balanced the most weight anybody had ever lifted across his shoulders. His bald head was glistening with sweat and his goatee was soaked with it. Everybody in the world knew this man, or at least his alter ego.

"Is that . . .Giant?" She whispered in my ear.

"Yes, but here he prefers Steven. He's exempt from the spotters rule," I mentioned briefly. Giant was unquestionably the strongest man in the world. "Come on, let me introduce you around." I took her elbow and led her into the room.

The next hour was one of the most enjoyable I had ever spent at Powerman's. Everyone took to Dannan immediately. Powerhouse helped show her the right way to perform different lifts. ManMountain spotted her while we found her maximum bench press - something on the order of twenty-eight tons. The Amazon offered to teach her some useful dirty fighting tricks. Captain Lunar made a bad joke and everybody laughed. Even Giant came over and solemnly shook her hand, saying he was pleased to meet her.

Later, I took a short break with the Captain while we watched Dannan flirt with Clydesdale. I must have reacted unfavorably because Lunar put his hand on my arm. "Don't worry, Hood, nothing will come of it. Clyde's a straightforward fellow. As much as a mercenary thug like him can be, at any rate," he amended. He handed me a water bottle, which I accepted gratefully. "She moves very much like you. You and your wife must be very proud."

I started at that, coughing as water ran down the wrong pipe. "How did you-?" I spluttered.

"Relax, Hood, I'm not going to tell everyone your secrets. You forgot to take off your wedding ring once, so I surmised you were married. You move like a married man and a father instead of a bachelor, and I ought to know." I had forgotten that one of Captain Lunar's powers was his ability to gain information through observation of motion. He could identify the pilot of a plane by how it flew, or what a man was thinking by how he jingled his keys. "I've seen your daughter fight with the rest of the Young Guns. She's undisciplined, but she always wants to do the right thing. You've been a good father and role model to her, in spite of what she tells you."

I grinned wryly at that. The man really could read people like open books. "Man, cut that out. It's creepy!" Under his mask, he smiled.

Dannan and I finished our workouts and said our goodbyes. Everyone invited us to come back. Clydesdale told her to come by on a Saturday so she could meet Powerman himself. The Amazon gave Dannan her phone number and told her to call so they could go shopping sometime. As we waited for the elevator to return to the gym level, Giant stepped up to us. The man had the presence of an earthbound god, a strength and power so tangible that you could feel it when he spoke to you.

"Bombshell," he said quietly, speaking to Dannan. The silver cross around his neck glinted in the overhead fluorescents. "You're doing good work. Never let that change." With that, he took a deep breath, turned his eyes toward the ceiling, and vanished.

Dannan let a word slip from her mouth that I had forbidden her ever to say. I couldn't blame her; I'd said the same thing the first time he did it in front of me. "Don't say that," I commanded, but without much in the way of parental force. Having Giant speak to you was a lot like it must have been for Moses on Mount Sinai. We stepped onto the elevator and rode back up to the surface. "How do you feel?" I asked her.

She flexed her shoulders and arched her back. "A little sore, I guess. It was fun. Can we come back again?"

"As often as you want," I replied. I felt a bit stiff in the arms myself, and decided that a hot shower with my wife would be just the thing to wind down the evening.

"Dad?" Dannan asked me as she buckled her seatbelt. I pulled the car out of the lot and headed for home.

"Hmm?"

"Some of those guys, those people, were super-villains, right?"

I nodded absent-mindedly. I knew that Clydesdale and ManMountain both had warrants out and were wanted for everything from petty larceny to assault. Captain Lunar was wanted for questioning in connection with a couple of dead gangsters we'd found in rather unusual circumstances that would have been tough for anyone else to arrange.

"I couldn't tell who was and who wasn't. Is that wrong? I mean, does it make me a bad hero?" Dannan twisted her hair around one of her fingers.

"Of course not, sweetheart," I replied. "Sorry," I quickly said when she winced at the word. "It just means that under the right circumstances, even the most diverse people can get along with one another."

She looked wistfully out at the city lights passing by. "It's too bad that can't happen all the time," she said.

I looked over at her and saw simultaneously a great superhero, self-assured and powerful, and the little girl who had tumbled into bed begging for a story from me. Face it Harry, I said to myself, she's growing up faster than you like. "Maybe someday, kiddo. Maybe someday it will."

TEETH OF THE NIGHT

Sometimes when you're a cop you have to go looking for trouble.

Sometimes it finds you.

My name's Harry Blaine, and I'm a pretty good cop. I don't mean to imply that I'm a superstar or hotshot or anything. Hell, I've been up for Detective twice and failed the test both times. It's okay, though. I'm happy being a simple beat cop, and I like to think I'm decent at that part of the job. It helps that I've got a good partner in Fred Grimes, who keeps me on my toes. He's ten years my junior and doesn't hesitate to remind me of that fact every time we have to chase down a runner.

Of course, it also helps that I'm bulletproof, something *I* make sure to remind him of every time we're in a situation requiring our weapons. If that wasn't enough, I'm also strong enough to tip over a fully-loaded semi truck. Being a parahuman has its privileges, but I've tried to keep it a secret. I don't know if I'd lose my job if it became public knowledge, but I suspect it wouldn't reflect well on the department, having a super-powered cop busting run-of-the-mill perps.

Grimes and I had been on nights for several months. It was a welcome change during the hot spring and summer months in Bay City, and there was still plenty of nighttime activity to keep our shifts interesting. My wife Alisa had adjusted her own hours to match mine and the only thing that changed was that we ate dinner at eight in the morning. Our daughter Dannan, who had parahuman powers like mine, tended to stay out all night anyway with her own superhero team, so if anything we remained pretty close as a family.

This particular evening, we were on a patrol on the east side of town, where the hills rise up from the bay into ritzy neighborhoods full of paranoid executives and their private security contractors. The security contractors didn't like us cops much because in their eyes, we interfered with their jobs, and we didn't like them much because their jobs seemed to smack pretty highly of vigilantism and petty vendettas.

Grimes and I had just eaten lunch from an all-night Korean deli at the bottom of the neighborhood when we got the call.

"*Three Mary Thirteen, proceed to one eight nine one Hawthorne Place to investigate an Eleven Forty-Four.*"

Grimes, driving, reached out for the radio. "Ten-Four. Three Mary Thirteen on route . . ."

"Eleven Forty-Four," I said. "That's a dead body."

"Geezer Geezer, should I turn left or right at the next intersection?" asked Grimes.

"I don't know, rookie. That's why we have GPS." I looked out at the darkness. "Bad lighting up here in the hills. All these streets look the same."

"You know I don't trust that damn machine. I'd rather keep a map in my head."

"I can't do that."

"They say the mind is the second thing to go."

"Ha ha. No, I really can't keep a map up here." I tapped my skull.

"Why's that, geezer?"

"Because, rookie, my head doesn't have enough empty space in it. Unlike, say, yours."

"Touché." Keeping one eye on the directions from the GPS and one on the road ahead, Grimes navigated our cruiser deeper into the hills. Trees rose up on either side of the road like huge, misshapen giants casting their dark shadows against the high clouds.

We passed a large house with a lot of cars parked in front of it. Echoes of merriment and mayhem ensued from within. It sounded like someone was throwing one hell of a party. "Looks like a good time," I said. "Maybe we should stop by on our way back."

"Rich kids!" scoffed Grimes. "For God's sake, it's after three. Want to go bust it up?"

"Tempting. Ask again later."

"Want to go bust it up?"

"Shut up, we're here already."

Eighteen ninety-one turned out to be the next *mansion* up the road. I say *mansion* because it was one of the richest houses I'd ever seen. A high, wrought-iron fence lined the street. The house itself was bathed by spotlights and floods, announcing to all who happened by that *this* was the house that you could *never own* unless you were making eight figures, stock options not included.

A security contractor's jeep was parked by the gate. The two rent-a-cops waiting by it sucked in their guts and puffed out their chests as we pulled alongside.

"Security contractors," grumbled Grimes with the same venomous tone he usually reserved for child abusers.

"Easy, sunshine. These are the bright lads who probably clued us in about the body."

We got out of the car. I made note of the name of the contractors' company, *Dayton Security Associates*, and the names on their badges: *Ortiz* and *Klostermeier*. "Evening, fellows," I said. "Somebody find a body?"

Ortiz nodded. "That's right, officer. Mr. Drury's dogs happened upon it tonight while taking their evening constitutionals."

"Evening constitutionals," repeated Grimes as if he hadn't quite heard clearly. "And Mr. Drury would be . . ."

"William C. Drury, Esquire, the owner of this property."

"I see. And would Mr. Drury be here this evening?" I asked.

"No, he's in Puerto Rico," said Klostermeier.

"I thought it was Porto Vallarta," said Ortiz.

"Some kind of port," continued Klostermeier. "Anyway, it was the maid who took the dogs out and found the body. She's in the house having a lie-down. It was a pretty shocking sight for her."

"Is someone with her?" asked Grimes.

"No. We thought it would be better for us to wait out here to meet you." Ortiz grinned a mouthful of gold teeth at us.

Grimes glanced at me. He didn't have to roll his eyes; I could practically read his mind. *Rent-a-cops.*

"All right," I said, "Grimes, you go talk to the witness and I'll take a look at the body."

"I'll show you where it is," said Ortiz.

"Dude," said Klostermeier, betraying a surfer's heritage, "She doesn't speak a word of English. You gotta translate!"

Ortiz grumbled something under his breath. "Okay, but remember I saw it first."

"Lead the way, Mr. Klostermeier," I said before Grimes could suggest that I'd be better-suited for questioning the maid.

"Jerk," muttered Grimes at me.

"Privileges of seniority, rookie."

Klostermeier escorted me along the long driveway coated with bright white rocks so clean they must have been washed regularly. We went around the side of the house, sticking to established paths so as not to tread along the pristine, country-club-quality grass.

"The dogs were pretty upset by the whole thing," said Klostermeier. "Mr. Drury shows them competitively, and they're high-strung."

"What kind of dogs?" I asked, more because Klostermeier seemed less dangerous when he was talking than quiet and thinking.

"Beagles. Purebreds." Klostermeier clicked on his flashlight and led me deeper into the woods to one side of the house. "Listen, uh . . . This body, it's kind of . . . messed up."

"Messed up?" I turned on my own light and swept it back and forth.

"Yeah. There." Klostermeier's light illuminated a pair of boots. He swept the light up the body.

I felt the spicy beef rolls I'd eaten earlier rumble around as I saw a body that looked like it had been savaged by some kind of wild animal. I gulped and tried to recreate a clinical image of the victim. Male, age indeterminate but in pretty decent physical condition. He was wearing practical, outdoorsy clothes: hiking boots, jeans, a cotton shirt and a fishing vest. At least, that was the best recreation I could manage given the shredded nature of his clothing.

I found his gear much more interesting than his dress. A set of military-grade night-vision goggles laid near his head, the lenses shattered. He possessed a large, shiny knife I thought was most likely a Bowie. It would be easier to be sure once it was removed from his abdominal cavity—something I was neither willing nor qualified to do. He had a quiver of arrows slung across his back, which made me wonder if he might be a hunter, although I didn't see a bow.

If not for the knife sticking out of his guts, I'd suspect he'd been attacked by coyotes or wild dogs. That knife was bothersome, though. Unless he'd stabbed *himself*, which was possible but unlikely, he'd been killed by something with thumbs, which cut the number of suspect species down to roughly one.

"You didn't touch this body, did you, Klostermeier?"

"No sir." The big blonde idiot stood a bit taller and puffed out his chest. "I know what to do when a body is found."

237

And that, of course, was to call the *real* cops. However, as a representative of the boys in blue, I didn't have a clue how to proceed from here. The important thing, though, was to maintain appearances for the security contractors.

I clicked on my radio to fill Grimes in on what I'd found. He acknowledged me and then called me a dirty name for sticking him in the house with Ortiz and the Chilean housekeeper.

I called into dispatch and requested a coroner and a forensic investigator, and then turned my attention back to the body, pulling on a pair of latex gloves so as not to contaminate any evidence.

One of the arrows had fallen on the ground near the body and I picked it up, looking more closely. It was heavier than it looked. I'd never shot a bow in my life but I imagined this arrow wouldn't fly very far because of its weight. It seemed to be made of solid metal from tip to fletching. Although a bit tarnished, it had the same sparkle as Alisa's good tableware that we got out for holidays. *Silver?* I wondered.

Looking more closely at the body, I realized the dead guy was clutching something tightly in one hand. I glanced up at Klostermeier, who was grinning like a beatific saint at me, basking in the glow of *real* law enforcement. My curiosity got the better of me and I removed the object. It was a small parcel, about the size of a cell phone, wrapped in plain brown paper and taped shut. One corner was slightly torn open.

"Klostermeier, why don't you head back down to the gate?" I suggested. "The evidence tech and coroner will need directions up here."

Klostermeier gave me a smart salute. "Yes sir!" He ran off. I didn't tell him that he might have to wait a few hours.

I returned my attention to the parcel. "Don't do it, Harry," I said aloud. "That's evidence." Thus having warned myself away, I felt I had done my job and could fairly feed my curiosity.

I tore the parcel a bit more. Inside was a flip box covered with fine black velvet, like a box that holds a gift watch. I snapped it open. Instead of a piece of jewelry, which is what I'd expected, I found a syringe full of thick dark red liquid. Surely it had to be blood, right? Who would carry around a syringe of karo syrup with red food coloring in it?

"Curiouser and curiouser," I muttered, holding up the syringe and shining my flashlight on it.

And there, standing behind a bush, was a man watching me.

I don't startle easily, but I was in a dark forest in the middle of the night with a *very* dead body in front of me and my imagination was running a little crazy. My hand found the handle of my nine-millimeter and I yanked it free from the holster in a credible fast pull.

"Freeze!" I cried, barely keeping my finger from crushing the trigger back into the grip with my superhuman strength.

The man grinned, showing a mouthful of pointed teeth that must have been filed, winked at me, and ran.

I froze, unable to fire a shot.

His eyes had been sulfurous yellow and inhuman.

"Shit!" I jammed my gun back into its holster, knowing that I'd inadvertently squish it if I held it while running, and took off after the man.

He must have been some kind of parahuman, I thought. Some of them didn't look like normal people. He sprinted through the dark forest, moving with a peculiar loping gait. I went crashing through the underbrush after him, making up for my lack of foot speed with utter disregard for dodging obstacles since my strength and bulletproof skin were sufficient to bull straight through almost anything in my way.

"Grimes!" I puffed into my radio. "In pursuit of suspect, heading . . . heading . . ." I had no idea what direction I was running. "Away from the house," I finished.

"Roger, Harry. I'm on my way," he called back.

The man bounded over a six foot fence with no effort at all. "Double shit," I grunted, panting for air. As he leaped, I saw he was buck-naked with a wild mane of hair stretching halfway down his back. The reason I could see that detail so clearly is the fence he jumped led into the yard of the house further down the hill where the party was still going on.

Screams erupted from the partiers as the man pulled up short from his headlong rush and I crashed right through the fence. He turned to face me. No wonder the kids were screaming.

His face was lengthening, nose and jaw pushed outward. His mane of hair was spreading across his skin with the speed of time-lapse photography as his back arched forward. Every second his appearance became less that of a man and more that of a . . .

"Hold it . . . right there . . ." I wheezed, refusing to believe that I was confronting an actual werewolf. Surely this was some new parahuman. I wasn't really up on all of them, but I'd picked up bits and pieces from Dannan's animated conversations at the dinner table about her exploits with the Young Guns. I didn't recall her ever mentioning a shapeshifter in her tales.

The man, if he could still be called that, growled at me. The menacing sound chilled my bones.

Kids not any older than my daughter ran screaming for their BMWs and sport utilities parked in the front drive while others hid in the house and peeked out windows.

I reached for my gun and discovered that my entire holster was gone. It must have been ripped away at some point during my pursuit. Ditto for my radio.

"Wonderful," was all I had time to sigh before the wolf-man sprang at me, clawed hands lunging for my throat and slavering jaws seeking to tear and rend.

I wasn't having any of it. I put my fist right into that furred face. The shock of impact flipped the wolf-man backward, sending him ass-over-teakettle into some lovely rose bushes.

He bounded back onto his feet right away, lupine face contorted into a wrinkled snarl. I was impressed. I'd never traded blows with any other parahumans before and had never brought more than a fraction of my strength to bear against a normal human, but this guy had taken a solid hit from me and looked hungry for more.

He approached me, caution and uncertainty evident in the way he kept shifting from side to side, growling curse words at me in a mouth unsuited for human speech. He circled me and I turned, keeping my face toward him and my arms raised, ready to defend against him when he next attacked.

It happened faster than I believed possible. One moment he was circling, the next he was in my face, bowling me over. Not only was he of comparable strength to me, he was *much* faster. I was going to have my hands full. And a moment later, I did as I locked my fingers around his throat to keep him from getting his jaws on my face. Deep down, I knew I was bulletproof and probably had nothing to fear from his teeth, but didn't want to take the chance that my toughness didn't cover werewolf bites.

We rolled around, breaking things that sounded expensive. I winced more in sympathy than in pain as we crushed a dual-tank, triple-level gas grill. It was all I could do to keep those gnashing teeth a few inches from the tip of my nose. The creature's breath reeked of stale blood and fresh fury.

Finally I caught a break. We smashed into a garden shed and a cross member caught him hard enough that his grip weakened and I was able to throw him off of me. Quick as a flash, he rebounded off the wall of the house and was back in my face, but this time I was ready for him.

My fingers, questing for some kind of weapon, closed around a reinforced handle and I clocked him hard across the jaw with what I had grabbed—a chainsaw with a dull, rusty blade. The tool shattered from the force of the blow, sending the chain whistling away. The next implement I found within easy reach was a square-headed shovel. I swung it upward like a home run hitter and lifted the wolf-man off his feet. He flew through the air to splash into the deep end of the large pool.

I was at the side of the swimming pool a moment later, brandishing my shovel as if it were Excalibur itself. "Come on!" I yelled at him as he floundered in the water. "Plenty more where this came from!" I twirled the shovel through my fingers until it whistled.

I watched him thrash around in the pool. His motions took on a frantic cadence. He didn't seem to be making any progress toward the edge. Then he dropped under the surface, still flailing away. A moment later his head broke the surface and I saw a look of pure panic on his face, stuck halfway between wolf and man.

"Crap!" Of all the stupid things, he couldn't swim!

And thus the dilemma: save the werewolf and probably get torn to shreds in the process or else let him drown and spend the next shift filling out paperwork. No choice at all once I looked at it that way.

I jumped into the pool. I'm not much of a swimmer, but I get by well enough, and I managed to drag the sodden and subdued wolf man to the edge of the pool.

"Freeze!" yelled Grimes from the hole in the fence where I'd crashed through earlier. He had his gun out and was standing braced in a firing stance.

I felt the wolf man tense up, as if he was considering leaping from the pool. I forestalled those thoughts by firmly rapping his head against the tiled edge hard enough to crack one of them. "Bad dog, Fido," I said. "Stay."

"Harry, you all right?" asked Grimes.

"Good enough." I blew some water and matted werewolf fur out of my nose.

"What you got there?"

I grinned at him. "Good question." I looked at the wolf man, who was wearily raising one hand while holding onto the pool edge with the other. "What are you, anyway?"

He snarled, tired and barely intelligible. "I don't have to answer. I know my rights."

"You do? Good. Then we can all say them together. It'll be like a sing-along." I smiled. "You have the right to remain silent . . ."

DOMESTIC DISTURBANCE

"Honestly, I don't know who she is. I got home from work, threw my coat on the chair and went to the kitchen to fix myself a sandwich when I spotted her under the table." Mr. Arnold F. Gernsbeck brushed a nervous hand back through his thinning hair.

"And you have no idea how she got into your house?" asked my partner, Grimes, who stared curiously at the strange girl huddled underneath the table. We've seen a lot of strange things over our six years patrolling together on the force, but a naked, hairless woman with green skin crouched under a table in middle-class suburbia, eating peanut butter by the fistful . . . well, that probably ranked in the top two or three.

Gernsbeck shook his head. "My alarm was still armed when I came home. I haven't gone through the house yet, though. I was afraid to go where I couldn't see her."

I hunkered down beside the table. My knees popped, reminding me that forty was only a fond memory and fifty not too far away. "Miss? I'm Officer Harry Blaine. Would you mind coming out from under the table?"

She petulantly flicked a bit of peanut butter at me.

Grimes knelt down beside me.

"Easy, rookie. You don't want to spook her." I called him *rookie* out of habit—he was ten years younger than me and only had ten years on the force to my twenty-five.

"Stuff it, geezer." Grimes always gave as good as he got. "Miss? Are you hurt? Are you lost?"

No response except for a baleful glare from yellow-tinged eyes. Fingers dipped into the peanut butter, then into her mouth over and over.

"You think she's a parahuman?" whispered Grimes.

"How should I know?"

"Well, I just figured . . ."

"Look, it's not like we all have a secret handshake or something." I happened to be a parahuman myself. I never had any grand designs on wearing colorful spandex and beating up A-List bad guys like they do in Just Cause or the Lucky Seven. All I ever wanted to be was a cop. I'd managed to keep my own powers secret for fifteen years. Nobody had known that I was strong enough to bench press a city bus or tough enough to shrug off bullets at point blank range, and that had been good enough for me.

But then I'd been put into a situation where I'd had no choice but to use those powers publicly to protect a classroom full of schoolchildren from a gunman. I figured I'd be expelled from the force after that, but when the captain had called me into his office, I was given an award for bravery in the line of duty instead of my walking papers. I'd asked the captain about it and he'd told me that he didn't care about parahuman powers. He was glad I was a good cop and as such, thrilled to have me stay on the force.

There'd been a bit of a flap about it in the papers and the ACLU made some threatening noises about parahumans, namely me, using their powers against normal humans, i.e. criminals, being an infringement of their rights. Ultimately, a sympathetic judge declared it legal for me to continue to work in my capacity as a police officer, and that's why five years later I found myself crouched under Arnold F. Gernsbeck's kitchen table having peanut butter thrown at me.

"I think I can get her out," said Grimes, and reached for her.

Her eyes flashed like golden coins and Grimes flew backward across the kitchen to fetch up against the dishwasher with a crash and a groan. Gernsbeck yelped in surprise, tripped over a chair, and fell backwards to end up sitting on his rump facing the girl under the table.

"Fred!" I yelled, unmindful of any risk to the homeowner when my partner might have been hurt, and slid across the floor next to him. "You all right? Don't try to move."

Of course, he moved right away; Grimes was no parahuman, but he certainly was a tough old bird. He sat up, pieces of the shattered plastic facing of the dishwasher door spilling down his uniform, and groaned. "Oh-h-h . . . I think she's a parahuman all right."

"Figured that out all by yourself, rookie?" Now that I could see he wasn't seriously injured, I could tease him once more. "She never touched you. Some kind of whatchamacallit. Tele-something."

"Telekinesis," said Gernsbeck behind me, an odd timbre in his voice.

I turned around to see him floating six inches above the floor, rotating around his belly button like somebody strapped to a wheel.

"Crap," I muttered. I hadn't dealt with many parahumans in my time on the force. That was more my daughter's style. She'd inherited all of my strength and toughness and none of my common sense. She ran around with a group of like-minded incredibly young twentysomethings and fought what she liked to call The Good Fight. They called themselves the Young Guns and were loved by the young, fresh, hip kids of the Bay Area and only tolerated by the rest of us. If I'd have been a weaker man, I might have pushed off this problem on them. Let the superheroes deal with the weird green telekinetic girl. Grimes and I could go on to answer a noise complaint that had come in half an hour ago and, as usual, got kicked aside in favor of higher priority calls.

In this case, criminal trespassing.

"Mr. Gernsbeck, do you have a robe or blanket or something you could loan to this young lady?" I asked in as quiet and non-threatening a voice as possible.

"Bathroom," he grunted, at the moment upside-down with his tie hanging across his chin. He continued to spin around.

"Grimes, go get it, would you?"

"And leave you alone with this freak? No way."

"Grimes," I said. "It's a parahuman problem. I'll handle it." I hated pulling out that card, but desperate times call for desperate measures, and we needed to get this girl out of the house and away from civilians before somebody got hurt. I heard him grumbling as he left the kitchen in search of Gernsbeck's bathroom.

I hunkered down as much as I could—I'm not exactly a small fellow and nowhere near as fit as I was twenty years ago—and smiled at the girl while studying her features.

Her skin really was green, I marveled. It wasn't body paint or even a tattoo. Most of her smooth, hairless skin was the color of new grass, but it lightened on her palms and soles of her feet to a faded celery color. Looking closer, I realized her skin was covered with tiny scales, like those on a gecko. Her fingers and toes had no nails, but sported dark spots at the tips where claws might extend. Her eyes were human, although the brown irises swam in a sea of gold instead of white, and they were just a bit too large for her head. High cheekbones, a slender aquiline nose, and dark lips added an exotic flavor to her mostly-Caucasian features. The upper tips of her ears came to points.

"Miss," I said carefully. "Can you understand me?"

Her hand stopped partway to her mouth, fingers coated with peanut butter. Was that a brief nod? I decided it had been.

"My name's Harry. What's yours?"

"Tigi." Her voice was smooth as silk and sweet as honey and every other lame metaphor I could think of.

"Tigi," I repeated, hoping more might be forthcoming, but to no avail. "It's nice to meet you, Miss Tigi. Would you mind setting Mr. Gernsbeck down gently? This is his house and you gave him quite a scare."

"Sorry."

Gernsbeck grunted as he settled to the floor next to me. "Back away slowly," I whispered at him. "Make no threatening moves." He scooted away, never taking his eyes off Tigi.

"Harry, robe," said Grimes from somewhere behind me. I glanced back to see him holding up a large fluffy white robe with the *Hilton* logo emblazoned on the breast.

"I didn't steal it," Gernsbeck said as he followed my gaze.

"I don't care if you did. Toss it here, rookie."

Tigi hissed as the robe fluttered through the air to me. I caught a sparkle of ivory teeth, sharp like a cat's.

"It's all right," I said, trying to soothe her. "It's just a robe. See?" I opened it up and held it out to her. "It's pretty chilly out today. Damp, too. You can't be very warm. Why don't you put it on and come out where we can talk?"

The robe tore out of my grasp to flutter across the floor to her. She grabbed it, unmindful of the peanut butter smears she left on the snowy fabric. After examining it, she shrugged into it. Did I watch? You better believe it. I'm happily married, but no way was I going to take my eyes off this girl while I tried to gain her trust.

"Thanks," she said in that lovely low voice of hers.

"Miss Tigi, I'm a police officer. I'm not going to hurt you, but you're someplace you're not supposed to be. Would you please come out from there so Mr. Gernsbeck can make himself some dinner?"

"Okay," she said without hesitation, and unfolded her lithe form to stand beside the table. She was a full foot shorter than me, and slender enough she seemed lost in the oversized fluffy robe.

"There. Isn't that better?" I asked, as bright and cheery as I could be. Behind me, I could hear Grimes requesting a female officer.

"Mr. Gernsbeck, may we borrow your robe until we can get some clothes for Miss, uh, Tigi?"

"Yes. Yes, of course." Gernsbeck's eyes were so wide as he stared at the strange girl in his kitchen, I thought they might fall right out of his skull.

I asked Tigi the usual litany of information-seeking questions, but was either met with stony silence or one-word answers that were mostly unhelpful. In the end, all I could get out of her was the name *Tigi*, which didn't match as a first or last name in the law enforcement database. Grimes thought her name sounded like an alias or nickname, and I agreed, but she wasn't forthcoming with anything else.

She did give us one more impromptu demonstration of her telekinetic powers by floating the empty peanut butter jar in a lazy circle around the kitchen before letting it drop into the trash.

An unmarked car pulled up behind Grimes' and my black-and-white. The quiet, authoritative voice of Detective Susan Lukascz announced her arrival on scene amid the mishmash of radio traffic from the unit clipped to my shoulder. I smiled at Tigi in the hope it would keep her relaxed. "Miss Tigi, would you mind coming outside with me? I'd like you to meet a friend of mine."

For several seconds, the only sound in the kitchen I could hear was the ticking of the clock on the wall.

Then Tigi said "yes" and Grimes blew out the lungful of air he must have been holding.

"Lead the way, rookie."

"Why me? What if she goes off again?"

"I'll stop her," I said with a confidence I certainly didn't feel. Besides, we needed to handle her with kid gloves. She may not have trusted either of us, but at least I'd built some rapport with her and that might make her comfortable enough for me to follow behind her.

Despite his complaints, Grimes headed for the front door of Gernsbeck's town home. Tigi followed, her lean limbs unfolding with serpentine grace. I brought up the rear, murmuring "stand down, Lukascz," into my radio.

Lukascz waited for us outside, her hands in the pockets of her overcoat to ward off the chill of the rain. "Well there's something you don't see every day," she said. "Are you arresting her?"

Grimes turned to Gernsbeck, who'd followed us and now stood in his door, blinking at the cold rain. "How about it, Mr. Gernsbeck? Do you want to press charges?"

"N-no," said the man, shivering. "I mean, she didn't really do anything except eat all my peanut butter. I think she'd be better off if you could find someone to help her."

"We'll do our best, Mr. Gernsbeck," I said, and then turned to face Tigi. "Miss Tigi, we're not arresting you, but we'd like you to accompany us to the station. We're concerned about your well-being.

I talked her into getting into the back of Lukascz's car. Then Lukascz, Grimes and I huddled together and discussed what to do with our mysterious parahuman. The most important thing was for us to get a positive identification so we could determine if she was wanted or listed as missing or something like that. Grimes suggested I call my daughter to see if she could put out the word through the costumed hero community about our unidentified telekinetic.

That's when Lukascz noticed Tigi was gone from the back seat of her car.

"How'd she get out?" she asked. Her car had a secure back seat, with no handles inside the doors. Gernsbeck's robe lay crumpled on the seat.

We spread out, searching up and down the street in the rain, even going so far as to ask some of the neighbors who'd been peeking out their windows and wondering about the police car in front of Gernsbeck's place. Nobody saw anything. Tigi had simply . . . vanished.

I lost to Grimes two out of three in *rock-scissors-paper* so I had to write the report. At least there wasn't much to write: unknown parahuman perpetrator, unknown method of entry into the residence in question, unknown method of escape. Far more questions than answers.

On my way home, I called Dannan. Just when I thought her phone would go to voice mail, she answered.

"Hi, Daddy!"

"Hi there, sugarbear. How'd you like to come have dinner with your uncool parents tonight?"

"Oh, that sounds great, except we're out of town. We got a lead on Mr. Macho and we're following up on it. We're in San Diego—drove down last night."

I had no idea who Mr. Macho was. "Sorry to hear that. Alisa would have loved you to stop by. She's making spaghetti tonight." Spaghetti was Dannan's favorite. If she could have come by, she would have.

"I'm really sorry, Daddy."

"That's all right. Listen, Danni, have you ever heard of a weird telekinetic girl with green scaly skin?"

"Doesn't ring a bell. Why? Did you run across her?"

"Yes. Could you maybe . . . I don't know, ask around?"

"Sure. Oh! I have to go . . . it's going to drop in the pot. Love to you and Mom. Bye!"

Drop in the pot meant she and the rest of the Young Guns were about to get into a fight, presumably with this Mr. Macho character. I was sure I'd hear all about it in the morning—if not on the news, then from the other officers at morning roll call who liked to follow Dannan's exploits.

* * *

The next day, Gernsbeck called to report Tigi had returned to his house. He'd found a brand new jar of peanut butter on his table and the green girl sitting in his study, wearing his robe, and slowly paging through a *Calvin and Hobbes* collection. Guess who got dispatched to respond?

"This is just plain weird," Grimes complained as we stared at Tigi in Gernsbeck's study. "It's like she thinks she lives here."

"Or she's stalking him," I said.

"Stalking me? That's crazy talk," cried Gernsbeck. "Why would she stalk me? I'm nobody, just an account manager for an insurance company."

"I don't know," I said. "The reason we call them crazy is that they don't operate rationally like normal people."

"Well that's just great. How do I stop her?"

Neither Grimes nor I had an immediate answer for him. Tigi was a fairly strong telekinetic and apparently could either teleport or use some other method to pass through walls. I wasn't sure how we could even hold her if we arrested her. But we'd have to try, because the civilian had a valid complaint against her and it was our job.

"Tigi," I said.

She ignored me.

"Tigi, you're going to have to come with us. You can't be here. You're trespassing, and you're disturbing Mr. Gernsbeck. Please put down the book and come with us."

"No." She didn't even look up from her book. Any rapport I might have had with her the day before was clearly gone.

"So much for Plan A," grimaced Grimes. "Now what?"

"Tigi, if you won't come voluntarily, I'm going to have to physically remove you from the premises." I tried to sound authoritative.

She didn't reply, but shot me a look that may as well have said *you and what army?*

"Fred, get Gernsbeck out of here for his own safety. And for yours. And Mr. Gernsbeck, you might want to get your homeowner's insurance policy just in case she doesn't come quietly."

"Christ in a sidecar," said Grimes under his breath.

"Oh God, please be careful. My book's in here," said Gernsbeck as Grimes escorted him out.

"I'll do my best to avoid damaging your property, sir." I focused on Tigi as they left the room. "Last warning, Tigi."

She made no move to comply, so I took a step toward her and, as Dannan would have said, it dropped in the pot. Her eyes flashed golden and suddenly I felt the unique sensation of pitting all of my strength against an unseen force. Her telekinetic wall wasn't solid like a brick wall. It felt more like I was trying to force my way through a barrier of strong but flexible rubber. It gave in some places while pushing back harder in others. It was like trying to divert a river of mud with a shovel.

Gernsbeck's telephone rang, and in that moment, Tigi vanished. With nothing to push against, I over-balanced and staggered into the desk, sending a stack of handwritten pages flying.

I groaned, knowing yet another report awaited me. Two appearances by this odd parahuman, and twice now she'd made Grimes and me look like fools.

Somehow, I suspected we'd see a lot more of Tigi before we solved the quandary of who she was and what she wanted.

I spent that evening sprawled in front of my laptop on the bed, surfing various parahuman forums and trying different search parameters to see if I could find any mention of Tigi online. Alisa, good sport that she is, sat on my hips and rubbed my shoulders while search after search turned up nothing.

"Maybe Dannan has had some luck," Alisa said as she dug an elbow into a stubborn knot in my lower back. "She brought down that Macho guy last night."

Dannan and the rest of the Young Guns had fought Mr. Macho and some of his henchmen on a stretch of beach north of San Diego the night before in a struggle which ended with her pounding him into unconsciousness. Then she sat on him until the authorities arrived to take him into custody. The morning news had reported he was wanted for a string of smash-and-grabs on Oakland. I still feared for Dannan's safety every time she fought other parahumans, but I was awfully proud of her nevertheless.

Unfortunately, my call to her proved fruitless as well. She'd called a friend in Just Cause, the country's premiere team of heroes, who had in turn called a contact at the Parahuman Resources Agency, which maintained the world's most thorough database of information on parahumans. No luck. "It really sounds like you've run across a brand new parahuman, Daddy," said Dannan. "I wish I could be more help."

"It's all right, sugarbear. Thanks for asking."

She promised to come by for dinner on the weekend.

I closed the laptop. Alisa slid off my hips to stretch out next to me. "I don't know what to do next," I said to her. "I'm worried that she's going to keep coming back to that guy and sooner or later he's going to get hurt. And I don't know how to stop her."

Alisa kissed me on the forehead. "Well, who's this guy? Maybe if you could figure out why she's targeting him, you could get to her that way."

And just like that, an idea occurred to me.

I smiled at my wife. "You're brilliant, you know."

"I know." She smiled back. "You thought of something?"

"Yeah." It was crazy, but I figured I'd run with it.

Tomorrow, I decided, as Alisa rolled into my arms.

* * *

"You look like the cat that swallowed the canary," said Grimes the next morning. "Geezer get laid last night?"

"Quiet, rookie. Respect your elders."

"If you were any elder, I'd be stealing your social security check and hiding your false teeth." Grimes looked out the cruiser's window at the nondescript office building as I parked. "What're we doing here?"

"Following up on a hunch. Watch and learn."

The receptionist stiffened when we walked into the lobby. "Can I help you?" she asked. Most people get nervous when uniformed officers approach them. Some guys love the power it conveys. You can see it in their swagger. Not me, though. I'd much rather people would see me before they see the badge, but habits are habits.

I'd called Dannan back late the night before and she'd given me a name. "May we speak to Dr. Wyler please?"

The receptionist stabbed at a button on her phone. "Dr. Wyler? There are some co—some *police officers* here to see you."

A few minutes later a bespectacled young man with fine features and an earring came from the back offices. He wore a white lab coat over a T-shirt emblazoned with the logo of some band I faintly remembered hearing about a couple years ago. "I'm Dr. Carson Wyler. What can I do for you guys?"

"Harry Blaine, and this is Fred Grimes. Bombshell of the Young Guns gave us your name." *Bombshell* was Dannan's superhero name, bestowed upon her by the Chronicle when they first reported upon the *Blonde Bombshell of the Bay Area.*

"Of course." He stared me up and down and although he tried to hide it, I knew he'd seen the family resemblance between Dannan and me.

"We've encountered what I believe to be a new parahuman here in the Bay Area and, er, *Bombshell* said you had a gizmo that could do a rapid MK test." The Musashi-Kitaro test identified the genetic markers common to all parahumans.

Grimes raised an eyebrow but didn't say anything. I was rather enjoying keeping him in the dark. It made me feel just a bit superior, something that happened far too infrequently these days.

"Oh, are you the officers who've discovered the new teke? I was hoping to get a chance to meet her." Wyler's face lit up at the notion.

"I think we might be able to arrange that. Would you mind packing up your little black bag and taking a trip with us?"

"I'd be thrilled. Give me fifteen minutes to collect my gear and clear my schedule." Wyler ran back into the rear of the building.

Grimes turned to me. "You're onto something. Care to share?"

"I'm running on a hunch here," I said. "I did a little background research into Mr. Gernsbeck. Did you know he's a published writer?"

"Nope."

"He writes speculative fiction. Aliens and magic and stuff like that."

"I see."

"His last book was about magical lizard people."

"Magical lizard people," said Grimes. "Sounds fascinating."

"It sounds a lot like Tigi," I said.

His eyes widened. "Oh, so you think she's obsessing over his book and that's why she keeps coming back to him?"

"Something like that."

Wyler returned with an honest-to-God black bag and a leather jacket instead of a lab coat. "Okay, I'm all geared up."

"If you'll follow us, please."

Wyler went to his car and soon we were leading him across town. "Go to Gernsbeck's place," I told Grimes.

"You going to let me in on this or what, Perry Mason?" He checked the rear view mirror to make sure Wyler hadn't dropped behind.

"Soon." I dialed Gernsbeck's work number. When he answered, I identified myself and asked if he could meet us at his house.

Less than an hour later, the four of us met at the townhouse. Gernsbeck looked nervous and Wyler looked interested as he pulled a football-sized device from his bag. He introduced himself to Gernsbeck, who blinked in confusion. "But you already know she's a parahuman, right? So why is he here?"

"Just open the house and go in, please. We'll be right behind you," I said in as soothing a tone as I could manage.

Gernsbeck opened the door. He glanced around cautiously and then stepped inside. I followed behind him along with Grimes and Wyler bringing up the rear. We could all hear the sound of water running. Steam drifted out of a hallway. Gernsbeck's white robe lay in a crumpled pile on the floor. "Somebody in the shower," whispered Grimes.

"Go check who it is," I said to Gernsbeck. "Don't worry, we're right here. You'll be perfectly safe."

He padded down the hall and peeked into the bathroom. "It's her," he said. "She's in the shower. Why is she in my shower?"

"Ask her to come out, and emphasize that we're not here to harm her or to take her away." I turned to Wyler. "Got your thing ready?"

He nodded. "I'll need a blood sample."

"We'll get you one."

A moment later, a dripping Tigi wrapped in a towel followed Gernsbeck out of his bathroom. She glared at us but made no move to harm us or escape.

I said, "Tigi, this is Dr. Wyler. He helps people like you. May he take a sample of your blood to help answer some questions?"

"Yes," she said.

Wyler slipped a band around her arm, swabbed the inside of her elbow with an iodine pad, and carefully stuck the syringe into a vein. We all saw greenish blood fill the tube. He bandaged the needle hole and plugged the syringe into his machine. It beeped at him. He frowned and adjusted the controls. It continued to beep.

"What's the matter?" I asked, pretty sure I knew the answer ahead of time.

"Something's wrong. The machine isn't registering her blood at all. It says it needs a sample before it can run the tests."

"Maybe it's broken," Grimes said.

"Try taking another sample," I said. Wyler unwrapped another syringe and moved toward Tigi. I stopped him. "Not her. Him." I pointed to Gernsbeck.

"Me?" Gernsbeck's mouth dropped open. Tigi vanished instantly, which made Grimes jump and curse. The towel fell to the floor, as did the unwrapped bandage Wyler had used on her arm.

"Will you humor us, Mr. Gernsbeck?" I asked.

He shrugged. "I guess so, but I don't see what's the point." Nevertheless, he stood still and quiet while Wyler carefully withdrew a vial of his blood and fed it into the analysis machine.

The scanning process only took a few minutes to complete, and the results didn't surprise me in the least. "Congratulations, Mr. Gernsbeck," said Wyler. "It's a positive match. You are a parahuman."

"I'm . . . wait, what?" Gernsbeck sounded aghast.

"A parahuman," repeated the doctor. "And from what I've seen just now, I suspect you're capable of creating extremely convincing illusions as well as some telekinetic ability. If you'd like to come down to my offices, we can run a full battery of tests to help you positively identify your abilities."

Grimes punched me in the shoulder and then rubbed his knuckles where he'd bruised them. "You knew all this time, you jerk."

"No, but I suspected. He's a writer and he made one of his characters come alive. I'm surprised he never made the connection."

"I . . . I did make the connection," said Gernsbeck. "But I thought she was an obsessed fan or something. I never thought I could be the cause of this."

"Try to bring her back," said Wyler. "See if you can consciously utilize your ability."

The air before us shimmered and Tigi winked into existence. She bent down to retrieve the towel from where it had fallen and held it modestly over her front. She smiled at us, winked, and strolled up the stairs.

"Amazing . . . amazing . . ." whispered Gernsbeck.

I looked at Grimes and he looked at me. "Well, gentlemen, it appears our job here is done," I said.

We retreated back to our black-and-white.

"Thai?" asked Grimes.

"Sure, why not?"

"It isn't every day you get to meet a new parahuman." He pulled the cruiser out into traffic.

"I guess not."

Grimes snickered. "I'll bet you lunch he turns up in three months in some ridiculous costume committing pathetic crimes."

I shrugged. "If he does, we'll do what any cops should do when faced with a dangerous parahuman opponent. Call the Young Guns."

We laughed all the way to the Thai place.

SILENT ALARM

My partner, Ed Grimes, and I were back on the night shift. I always liked working nights. Apart from the cool breeze blowing in from the bay, you never knew what you were going to get. It could either be all peace and quiet, or a freak show marathon without even a minute to take a breath between calls. Also, summer was approaching in East Bay and we were happy to escape the hot, muggy days. My wife Alisa didn't mind so much, being almost as much of a night owl as I was. She was more than happy to stay up half the night, quietly watching shows she'd DVRed during the day while she attended the various chores of being a full-time mom.

Dannan, being a teenager, only seemed to sleep during the daytime anyway. It was almost like nothing changed except the light outside when I was on third shift. She was only a month away from graduation and I was damn proud of her. In spite of her parahuman powers, she'd buckled down and hit the books hard enough her last semester to not only make the honor roll, but she received a scholarship to attend the Hero Academy in Denver as a post-high-school graduate.

The Hero Academy was a unique institution sponsored by Just Cause. They took super-powered youngsters and taught them how to be superheroes. The classes not only taught them tactics and strategy in the use of their abilities, but ethics, law, and communication as well. In short, it was like a Police Academy for parahumans.

Within hours of receiving her scholarship, it seemed like the entire world knew that she was going and it didn't take long for people to put two and two together and realize that maybe, just maybe, someone else in her family had the same powers she did.

Captain Youngfield called me into his office that same week and asked me if I was a parahuman. What could I say? The events of the past year had certainly raised some suspicions. I acknowledged that I was. In fact, I thought I was extremely cool about it for breaking a secret I'd held for more than twenty years. He asked me a few more questions, about my capabilities and if I wanted to stay with the department. I told him I did and that seemed to be the end of it. A few of the guys seemed standoffish, but most of them treated me exactly the same as they had before, which made me feel bad for keeping my secret from them for so long. I got asked to help a couple of them move, but got beer and pizza for my trouble. Life went on in East Bay like it always does.

Grimes, on the other hand, always wanted to talk about my powers. It seemed that my junior partner had quite a thing for superheroes and couldn't quite get over the fact that he worked with one. "I'm not a superhero," I was constantly reminding him. "I'm just a cop. That's all."

It never made any difference to him. He was like a kid at a damn amusement park. However, enough hero worship can make anyone start to believe his own press, and I was secretly basking in it.

Earlier that day, a line of squalls had come in from the ocean and now it was raining steadily. It wasn't a downpour, but enough of a drencher that nobody wanted to be out. Lightning flashed occasionally and thunder grumbled across the Bay.

Grimes pulled the car around a corner, splashing through a puddle, and headed down Santa Ana, which was practically deserted. Even the hookers knew when to come in out of the rain. It seemed to be a quiet night all over town, judging by the lack of anything important coming over the radio. Grimes and I were discussing baseball, which was his other passion besides superheroes. The Bulldogs had actually started the season off with a bang and were already four games ahead of the other National League West teams. I cracked my knuckles and looked at my watch. 3:30 on the nose.

"You want to eat, rookie?" I always called him that because he only had six years on the force to my twenty-one.

"Meh," he said. "Nothing that's open this time of night sounds good. It's all gut bombs." He glanced over as I rummaged through my lunchbox at my feet. "Why, what have you got?"

"Half a baked lasagna," I said.

I swear I heard his stomach rumble over the engine. "Alisa's recipe?"

"Of course." I began to silently count down.

Right as I reached one, Grimes said, "Hey, uh, how much is there?"

I smiled. I knew he couldn't cook to save his life, and he'd sampled a fair share of my wife's cooking. I'd packed extra. "Enough. Want some?"

His stomach growled again but he only said, "Sure, if you don't mind sharing."

"Not at all. Let's go find a microwave." I reached for the radio to call us in for lunch, but as I did, the dispatcher called us first.

"Seven Mary Three."

"Never fails," said Grimes. "I'm going to waste away."

"Seven Mary Three here, go ahead, Dispatch."

"Investigate a silent alarm at—" She read off an address. It popped up on our in-car computer as well.

"Ten-four," I said. "Seven Mary Three on route now."

"I hate those damn silent alarms," said Grimes. "Never know what we're walking into."

"Same here."

"Yeah, well, not all of us are bulletproof."

"That doesn't mean I like being shot."

"That makes two of us. You can go first tonight, geezer."

"Thoughtful of you to volunteer me like that, rookie."

"I've got everyone's best interests at heart."

We kept up our snappy patter all the way to the address in question, our voices playing counterpoint to the staccato tapping of raindrops on the roof and the rhythmic slap of the wipers. Grimes shut off the headlights and pulled the cruiser into one of the new industrial parks built along the waterfront. Most of the glass-paned building fronts had For Lease signs in them, but our destination had a sign: *Cupric Wire and Cable Company.*

"Cupric? What's that, somebody's name?" asked Grimes.

"It means copper. This is a copper warehouse. That means that for once, it's actually stuff worth stealing. This might be more than just a cat."

"Great," said Grimes. "You go first. Seriously. I've been shot enough for this decade." He zipped up his jacket and pulled his hat down tight against his ears.

Likewise, I bundled up. Being bulletproof had plenty of perks, but I was just as vulnerable to the cold and wet as anyone. And if I came down with a cold and passed it along to Alisa, I'd never hear the end of it.

We didn't see any cars parked in the lot, which was a good sign. Anyone planning to steal a decent amount of copper would need something to haul it. "You think they might be around back?" asked Grimes, echoing my thoughts.

"Maybe," I said. "But just the same, we'll check here in front first." We plunged into the rain. Despite my hat riding low and jacket zipped all the way up to the collar, cold water still found its way to my neck and leached downward to soak my uniform blues. Grimes undid the flap of his pistol. "Really?" I asked, shooting a pointed glanced at the flashlight I held.

"Just in case," he whispered. "In case there's shooting."

"If there's any shooting, you best duck down and leave the shooting part to me." I looked around for an alleyway or something to lead to the building rear. No such luck, of course. We'd have to walk all the way around the outside of the building.

We checked the front door first. It was locked tight and didn't budge even when Grimes leaned his shoulder into it. He didn't bother asking me to check it. I hadn't yet found a lock that could stand up to my strength. I looked at the building. We were essentially in the middle, with equal distance to each corner, so we'd get just as wet no matter which way we went. "Meet you around back?" I said.

"May as well," said Grimes. "Don't get shot."

"You neither. And don't shoot anybody."

Grimes waved me off and disappeared into the curtain of rain. It had picked up quite a bit in the past couple minutes and I could feel the water squelching in my boots. Keeping an eye out for any movement in the shadows, I trotted around the outside edge of the building. As far as I could tell, none of the windows had been broken in either. I'd already decided by the time I rounded the back corner that unless we saw obvious signs of a break-in, we were going to report it as a false alarm and go find someplace to warm up and dry out. At that point, I'd even have gladly gone back to the station to do paperwork, because I had a change of clothes in my locker.

Of course, no such luck. I found Grimes standing beside a bicycle, playing his flashlight on something leaning against the wall. "What have you got?" I asked as I splashed through the puddles towards him.

"Hell if I know," he said. "You're the superhero, you tell me."

I looked at what his flashlight had illuminated and understood his confusion. At first, it looked like someone had leaned a mannikin's leg against the wall. Then it looked more like the leg had been fastened to the wall at a peculiar, natural angle.

Then I touched it, and it twitched. Both Grimes and I jumped back and cursed in surprise. "It's real! I mean, it's alive," I said.

"That's what I was afraid of," said Grimes. "It's some damn parahuman burglar. You better just call your little girl and we can split."

I pulled out my cell phone, ready to call Dannan so her team could come and deal with it. Then I stopped.

"Come on, Harry. I'm freezing out here." Grimes shuffled from foot to foot.

"Something just isn't right," I said, and put my phone away.

"Yeah? What clued you in, Sherlock? The damn leg sticking through the wall?"

"Okay, forget for a moment *that* it's there, and *why* it's there, rookie. It's a real leg, which implies . . ."

Grimes' eyes widened. "There's someone on the other side of the wall!"

I smiled in spite of the rain dripping off my hat brim. "Thank you, Captain Obvious." I cupped my ear with one hand and pressed it against the wall. Then I tapped the wall several times, hard enough to dent the aluminum siding. Oops. "Hello?" I bellowed. "Is there anybody in there?"

"Just nod if you can hear me," muttered Grimes.

I ignored him, shut my eyes, and listened. Faintly through the wall, I heard a replying tap and what might have been somebody yelling for help. Well, that settled it. "Whoever it is, they're in trouble."

"So what do we do, call for help? It's a parahuman. Call the Young Guns already. Hey, what are you doing?"

Grimes' jaw dropped as I took hold of the door handle of the rear entrance and yanked. The steel handle tore loose from the metal door, which I had expected. I set it down and forced my fingers deep into the holes left behind in the hollow metal door. I braced my feet against the building, careful not to slip on the wet cement, and pulled. For a moment, nothing happened. Then the deadbolt snapped and the door flew open in my hands. "Easier to ask for forgiveness than permission," I said.

"Holy crap," said Grimes, all shaky-voiced as if he'd just seen a ghost. I realized it was the first time he'd ever seen me really bring strength to bear on something.

"Snap out of it, rookie. Time to protect and serve." I entered the building, flashlight shining into the darkness of a warehouse. "Hello?" I called. "This is the police. Do you need help?"

"Y-yes," said the broken voice of a teenage boy somewhere in the darkness to my left. I swung the light around, illuminating pallet racks laden with cable spools and stacked copper ingots. Then the light caught the tearstained face of a peach-fuzzed youngster. He was smallish and slight of build, with the artful-bedhead look that was all the rage with the young, hip crowd. He wore jeans and an oversized dark blue hoodie. His eyes were shadowed with exhaustion and dismay. On the floor beside him was a backpack in which I could see a box of copper welding wire. He was pressed up against the wall with his right thigh sticking right into it.

"Are you hurt?" I asked.

"I . . . I don't know. I'm stuck."

"Kid," I said. "I know you're probably terrified right now, and the truth is, you're in quite a bit of trouble. But I've got a daughter about your age, so I guess you could say I'm a little sympathetic to the teen mindset."

For a moment, the kid forgot to be scared and instead said, "Huh?" He squinted into the flashlight, trying to see me.

"Grimes, put your light on me." Grimes stepped to one side and did as I asked. I lowered my own light so it wouldn't keep blinding the kid. "I'm Officer Blaine, and this is Officer Grimes, and we're going to help you get unstuck. This will go much smoother if you're honest with us. What's your name, so I don't have to keep calling you *kid*?"

"Shadowfax."

Grimes cleared his throat beside me and I knew he was struggling to keep a straight face.

"Your *real* name, kid."

"Shane."

"Shane what?"

He was silent.

"Shane, look, I know you're scared, but we need to know who you are."

"My mom doesn't know I'm here."

I smiled. "I would hope not."

"No, she thinks I'm at a friend's house tonight. She's probably got her stupid boyfriend over again." He dropped his voice to a whisper. "He hates me."

I filed that away for future reference. I'd seen my share of kids from broken homes, and the symptoms were disturbing in their similarity. If this kid didn't get a good intervention early on, his criminal career would grow, and maybe one day I'd have to arrest him for assault, or armed robbery, or murder. "Your mother . . . does she know you're a parahuman?"

He bowed his head. "No. She thinks they're stupid."

"But you don't, do you, Shane? How old are you?"

"Four, uh, thirteen."

"Let me show you something." While I'd shined my light around earlier, I'd spotted what looked like a scrap pile of bent copper tubes and cut sheets. I went over and picked up a thick pipe. "See this?" I bent it across my chest. If it had been a longer piece, I might even have tried to tie it in a knot to show off.

Shane's eyes grew to the size of saucers. "You're one? That's so cool!" His own situation was momentarily forgotten in his astonishment of learning the world was a little bigger place than he'd thought.

"Yes. And I understand about keeping it a secret, because I have since I was your age. So can you trust me?"

"I guess so."

"What were you doing in here in the first place?" I bent down to examine the spot where his leg merged with the wall. It was blurry and wavered like heat off the pavement.

"It was just a stupid dare. I was trying to be cool."

"You don't look very cool right now. Probably not the best decision, Shane."

"Yeah, well, duh."

I smiled. Dannan and this kid would hit it off famously with their matching attitudes. I just hoped I could turn this aspiring young supervillain away from a life of crime. "Fair enough. How did you get stuck?"

"I don't know. I just started to walk through like I always do, and then my power just stopped working."

"It hasn't stopped completely," I said. "Otherwise your leg might have fused with the wall. But you can't move it? Not forward or back, side to side, or up and down?"

Shane sniffled and I feared he'd break down but to his credit he wiped his nose and looked at me. "No. I already tried all that. I'm getting real tired, though. I've been standing here for hours."

"Grimes, go see if you can find something for the kid to sit on while we figure this out." I looked at him. "We really ought to call your mom and let her know what's going on with you."

"No, please! She'll kill me. Especially if Eric is there."

I took a deep breath, drawing upon the reserves of patience I'd developed from parenting a teenager of my own. "Shane," I said. "You're a juvenile, you were caught in the act of attempted burglary, and you know the law looks poorly upon parahumans who use their abilities to commit crimes. I can help you out here, but you're going to have to give me something to work with. Just like on TV. How big do you want this to blow up?"

He shook his head. "I don't. My last name is Gleason. Please don't call her, though. I've never been in any trouble like this."

"Ever been in any other trouble?"

"No. I mean, yeah, but just, you know, the usual stuff."

I didn't ask him what he meant by *the usual stuff*. I wasn't so old that I didn't remember being a teenager myself. Grimes returned with a chair from one of the offices. "Gleason," I said. He nodded and I knew he'd call in, make sure we didn't have a young criminal mastermind already on our hands. Shane sank into the chair gratefully, twisting his body so his leg stayed at the same angle.

"That doesn't hurt having your leg in the wall like that?" Grimes asked. I could tell he was both curious and a little freaked out at the idea of intersecting solid matter.

"No, it just feels like it's stuck. Like in glue or something." Shane yawned and I wondered how long he'd been there. It was well past the hour when any kid should have been in bed. "You got any energy drinks or anything?"

"No. That stuff will kill you."

"I'm kind of crashing, dude."

"Maybe that's affecting your power. You should cut back."

Shane considered that for a moment. "Maybe it's enabling it. Maybe you should get me a Red Bull right now and then I can fly away from here." His smile was tentative and turned genuine when I grinned back at him.

"Don't press your luck."

Grimes bent down to look at the joining of wall and leg. "So if the wall is what's holding you, what if we cut it out around your leg? Would it just fall through and you'd be fine?"

It was an innocent suggestion, but it started me thinking. "That's not actually a bad idea, rookie. Maybe we should call it in before we start knocking holes in walls." I reached for my radio.

"Hang on, geezer. We're already here. We've got the best tools for the job available at the ends of your arms, and the building owner's insurance will cover the damages."

"That was good. You been practicing that?"

"Not all of us want to stay beat cops forever," he said. "Look, we might have to tell a bit of a story to get past all the bureaucracy, but you and I both know it wouldn't be the first time and won't be the last."

"So you want me to tear the wall out around him?" I didn't doubt that I could do it. The building was steel framework and outer sheath, with insulation and cinder blocks on the inside. Nothing I couldn't tear through like cardboard. I was more concerned about the potential fallout. As in, from the lieutenant and higher-ups.

Shane looked like his resolve was crumbling. "I just want to go back to Troy's house and pretend none of this ever happened. They can call me a loser and a pussy and I don't care. Can't you get me out? I won't tell anyone it was you."

I imagined the destruction I could wreak upon the warehouse if I accidentally tore through a load-bearing structure. "Kid, I think they'll know."

"Harry? A word?" Grimes tugged gently at my elbow.

Shane stiffened. I tried to offer him some comfort by handing him my flashlight. "Don't worry, we're not leaving. We're just going to step over by those racks. You can shine the flashlight on us the whole time, okay? Just a quick conversation and we'll be right back here."

"Okay," said Shane. He shone the light right on us.

I looked back at him and winked. "Don't go anywhere."

With the light in my eyes, I couldn't tell if he smiled. But I hoped he did.

Once we were out of earshot, I turned to Grimes. "What's on your mind?"

"Do you get the sense that this is a bad kid?" he asked.

"No. He was trying to impress his friends and got in over his head. I've seen that happen with Dannan I don't know how many times. What about it?"

Grimes kicked a sullen foot at the edge of the pallet rack. "It's just that . . . We're going to mess up his life by arresting him. Criminal trespass, burglary. A kid doesn't need that hanging over him. I called in to check on him. No priors, not even prior contacts."

"So are you saying we get him out of here and let him go?"

Grimes wouldn't look me in the eyes. "Yeah, that's what I'm saying."

"Ed . . ." I rarely called him by his name, and he gaped at me. "I agree. But I can't see a way to get him out of here without cutting a hole in the wall, and I'm no structural engineer. We should really call in some help on this."

"And if we do that, he's screwed."

I sighed. I knew he was right. "Okay, here's what we'll do. Call in that we've found damage to the building and are questioning a possible witness. I'll dig him out of the wall and we'll figure out what to do about him after that. Fair enough?"

Grimes shook my hand. "Deal. I'll handle it. You get the kid free."

I went back to Shane. "See? Told you I'd be right back."

"Are you going to call the fire department to get me out?" Shane looked nervous and excited at the prospect of the F.D. with their huge power tools operating around him.

"No," I said. "I think we'll just do this real quietly by ourselves. But first I need you to make me a promise.

Two promises, in fact. The first is that you won't ever get yourself in trouble like this again. I don't want to see your name on a report anywhere unless it's because you were commended for doing a good deed."

"I promise." Shane shivered, and I was pretty sure he was serious about wanting to stay clean. Two decades on the force had made me pretty good at reading people, and I didn't get any kind of habitual offender vibe from the kid. If anything, he needed some positive role models in his life, like a parahuman cop who came to rescue him.

"The other thing is that I'm going to bend the law a little here to get you out, and I want you to promise you won't ever say what really happened."

"I can do that. I'm embarrassed enough as it is."

"All right." I dumped the wire out of his backpack and handed it back to him. "Keep this up over your face. I don't want any loose chips flying out and cutting you. I'd hate to have to explain you losing an eye to your mother."

He held up the bag. "Me neither. She'd ground me until I was thirty."

I tapped the wall a few times, trying to get a sense of how solid it really was, but like I said, I was no structural engineer. The cinder blocks would be easy to shatter. I popped a fist against the one right above where his leg was trapped. My plan was to take out as few blocks as possible, hoping that the wall wouldn't settle or anything. The block broke apart and I swept the loose pieces down onto the floor. I glanced back at Shane, who had lowered his backpack enough to watch me. When he saw me look at him, he raised it back up again, but I knew that he'd lower it again as soon as I turned back to the wall. Ah, to be young and invulnerable again, instead of middle-aged and invulnerable. I popped another block, and then a third. I paused after each one, feeling the wall for any vibrations that might indicate it shifting. So far so good.

The last block came apart and I pulled the fiberglass insulation away from around his leg. Some of the fibers passed *through* it as I worked, which was a good sign in my eyes. It meant that the material wasn't trapped in his leg so much as it was the other way around.

"Can you move your leg a little?" I asked.

Shane strained to pull it free of the wall, but it remained stuck through the aluminum wall exterior. I'd hoped I wouldn't have to tear through it. As he wiggled, a chunk of cinder block fell *out* of his leg. Relief immediately passed over his face. "Hey, I actually felt that drop out," he said. "It feels better."

"Okay," I said. "I'll keep working." I bent to the hole in the wall I was creating, thinking to myself that this could very well be my last day in a patrolman's uniform. "It's a rescue operation," I muttered out loud. I opened my fist into a flat palm and stiffened my fingers. The aluminum siding looked much more solid than I knew it would be. Nevertheless, it was a little nerve-wracking as I shot my open hand forward and drove my fingers right through the metal sheeting with a noise like a gunshot. I could feel rainwater on my hand as I flexed my fingers down to grasp the aluminum.

"Whoa," said Shane. "That's bad-ass!"

"Punching through the cinder blocks wasn't?" I repeated the stiffened-fingers punch with my other hand.

"I guess. But breaking through metal's a lot cooler."

I glanced at him over my shoulder. "Then you're going to love this."

I took a deep breath and strained at the aluminum sheet, trying to tear it asunder. For several long seconds, I didn't move. My uniform grew damp with sweat and droplets beaded up on my forehead to run down my nose and cheeks. I heard a seam burst in my shirt as my back muscles bunched up.

"Yeah, I love it," said Shane, getting some of his teenage cockiness back.

"Don't . . . be . . . a smartass . . ." I said through gritted teeth.

Then the aluminum parted in one sudden rending, like I was drawing aside curtains. The tear went right through Shane's leg. I froze, terrified that I'd just severed the poor kid's leg. But he tumbled out of the office chair as his leg came free. He immediately felt himself up and down, checking to make sure he was all there.

"You okay?" I gasped for breath, my heart pounding from the exertion and the adrenalin flooding my system.

Shane gave me a thumbs-up. "It's all there. I'm solid again."

Grimes hurried over from where he'd just finished making his radio call. "Harry?" he asked.

"We're good. Let's get back to the car. I need some water," I said.

"You don't think my power is gone for good, do you?" Shane asked me, like I was some kind of expert on the subject.

"I don't know," I said. "But I'd prefer that you don't try it again tonight. I don't think I have it in me to tear anything else apart on your behalf."

We went back to the cruiser. We sat Shane down in the back, promising him that he wasn't arrested, just that it was the only place he could sit out of the rain while we sorted out our story with the sergeant on duty. The long and short of it was that they believed the story Grimes and I told them, which I'll admit may have stretched the truth a bit. Apparently, a couple of guys with a truck and some tools had knocked a hole in the wall. They must have heard us coming, because they cleared out just before we arrived. The kid had been riding past and saw the truck, but hadn't gotten a license number or good description. As far as we could tell, they hadn't had time to steal anything. The sergeant nodded at our report and told us to write it up and not leave anything out. Shortly after that, the building owner arrived and was very grateful to us for scaring off the burglars. It took another hour before Grimes and I were cleared to be on our way. By that time, Shane had fallen asleep in the back of the car and I decided we'd just go ahead and take him home. The building owner said he'd keep Shane's bike locked in his office so nobody would try to steal it, since we didn't have room in the cruiser's trunk for it.

I opened the back door of the car and gently shook Shane awake. "Hey, kid," I said. "We're going to take you home. That all right with you?"

He wiped his eyes and looked around at the gray pre-dawn light. "Yeah."

I handed him one of my business cards. "Listen, you find yourself in any kind of trouble again, you call me. But it better not be the kind of trouble that comes from breaking the law. You get me?"

"Yeah." He took the card.

"And if you have any other kind of problems . . ." I had to be careful here. I didn't want to tread where I wasn't welcome. "Like with your mom, or her boyfriend, or bullies at school, drop me a line. Maybe I can help."

A muscle twitched in his jaw. I hoped what I was saying was helping him.

"Also, if you don't want to tell your mom about your power right away, I can write a letter of recommendation if you want to enter the Hero Academy in a couple years. I can even go talk to her about it, because she'll still have to give her permission for you to attend. I hear they teach you a lot about how to use your powers the right way. And my daughter will be there too. She can look after you. Bombshell. Heard of her?"

His eyes widened. "Yeah!"

Shane didn't live very far away from the building he'd attempted to burgle. As we turned onto his street in the quiet suburb in the hills up above the bay, he said, "Hey, I just wanted to say thanks to you guys. You rock."

Grimes glanced sidelong at me. "Well, I'm pretty sure *I* rock, but the geezer here thinks it's just noise and people screaming."

I turned to say something back to Shane, but just as I cranked my head around, he vanished straight back into the seat. "Whoa!"

Grimes looked in the rear view mirror, realized that our passenger was gone, and stood on the brakes. The cruiser came to a sudden halt. "Where is he? What happened? Is he stuck in the trunk or something?"

I spotted a figure walking up the sidewalk. I recognized the hoodie and backpack even in the fading darkness. He must not have wanted to be seen leaving the cruiser. Couldn't say I blamed him. "It's okay, Grimes. He's clear." I smiled. "That kid's going to be something special someday."

"You think we did the right thing tonight?"

"Yeah," I said. "I do."

"There any of that lasagna left?"

"Always thinking with your stomach, eh, rookie?"

"It's not hard when I'm dying of starvation over here . . ."

GRACEFUL BLUR

September, 2008
Bonneville, UT

It's just before dawn. Salena stands by the entrance to the Flats and breathes in the scent of the salt on the early morning air. The sky is pink in the east behind the mountains and soon the salt will be crawling with men and machines. A few of them are already here, tuning up engines, adjusting fuel and air mixtures, jarring the morning peace with caustic rumbles.

She's been here for hours already, though. She couldn't sleep with the nervousness and anticipation of today's run. By four in the morning she gave it up as a lost cause, kissed Jason on his cheek—he murmured something unintelligible and went back to snoring—and stole out of the room with her shoes in her hands.

Even as early as it had been, racers had already begun to stir, and she wasn't the only one in the parking lot. "Mornin'," a cheerful fellow called as he tightened lug nuts on a carbon-fiber-bodied pickup truck.

"Good morning," she replied while she slipped on her shoes.

"Out for an early-mornin' run, huh?"

"Yep."

"You're gonna be runnin' the Flats later, ain'tcha?"

"That's my plan."

"Good luck."

"Thanks. Same to you."

He saluted her with his tire iron. She smiled back and then left the lot at an easy jog.

She didn't mean to run out to the Flats; but her feet led her there anyway. And when the pavement gave way to compacted salt, she knew there was no turning back.

The course is plain, beyond minimalist—a single black stripe painted down the snow-white salt by the Utah State Highway Department. At mile intervals are the timers and recording equipment. She knows, because she's been here before.

It still gives her shivers to know her name is already in the record books, that people out here discuss her along with those who came before her: Breedlove, Gabelich, Nobel, Green. In a sport dominated by men and machines, she's the anomaly.

But she's the fastest anomaly ever.

She ran a few wind sprints, back and forth, nothing too fast, to shake the cobwebs loose, and they helped to refresh her somewhat, but she's not scheduled to make her official run for four more hours.

A familiar horn beeps behind her and she turns to see Jason's Bronco crunching across the salt toward her. She smiles and a moment later is by the car, stands on the running board, and leans in to kiss him.

"Hi, baby," he says. "I figured you'd be out here already."

She looks behind the Bronco and sees nothing. "Is it just you?"

"So far," he says, and pushes his chin-length blond hair back from his face in a signature move that always makes her want to jump on him. "I brought some coffee and donuts if you want any."

"Neither just yet." She opens his door and climbs in across his lap to sit next to him, which she can do because she's just a couple inches over five feet and slender like a figure skater. Compared to her, or even to most people, he's a giant of a man; seven feet and three hundred pounds of rock hard muscle.

He grins. "More for me, then. You know you're never going to grow up big and strong if you don't eat, Mrs. Tibbets."

She punches him in the shoulder, not hard enough to bruise herself, but hard enough to amuse him. "And you're getting love handles, Mr. Tibbets."

He stops, a half-eaten donut in his hand. "I'm not! Am I?" He lifts up his shirt and examines his belly.

She kisses him again. "I think they're adorable."

He snorts. "A fat superhero."

"Shush."

It's their honeymoon, and she loves him dearly for it. Only two weeks ago, she answered the preacher with the words I do when he asked if she, Salena, would take Jason to be her lawfully-wedded husband. The marriage proceeded, as so many things in her life, with blinding speed and it seemed like only a blink of her eye and she was married to this wonderful man, their five-year engagement only a distant memory.

They didn't make specific plans for the first part of the honeymoon, partly because their jobs as full-time superheroes wouldn't allow them to stray too far from home, partly because they always tended toward spontaneity in their relationship. The first week, they went to Moab, rented a jeep and tried it out on the easier trails. She let Jason do all the driving since she never had gotten the hang of operating a car. When they got stuck—and she'd known they would sooner or later with the way he drove—at least he was strong enough to lift the jeep free of whatever obstructions they encountered.

After a week of playing in the hills, camping under the stars, and once sneaking into a truck stop shower together, they headed here to Bonneville for Speed Week, where she will try for yet one more land speed record.

This time, it's The Big One. The only one that still matters.

Andy Green did it over a decade ago in Nevada in a car called ThrustSSC, and shook the entire desert with an unmistakable sonic boom. Nobody else has repeated the feat since. Salena intends to be the first to do it . . .

. . . on foot.

She awakens with a start. She must have fallen asleep after all. Jason isn't in the Bronco, but he's rolled down all the windows so she won't cook in the morning sunshine. The two RVs for her team are parked on either side of the Bronco to give her some privacy and shade. She rubs her eyes and climbs out of the truck.

"Good morning, sleepyhead!" Her best friend, Sondra, stands to one side with a cup of coffee and a smile. "I was about to wake you, anyway. Your run's in ninety minutes." Sondra is a parahuman too, like Salena. The beautiful Amerind woman has magnificent brown feathered wings folded neatly against her broad back and shoulders. "Time to start getting ready."

"It's kind of silly, isn't it? All this hype and hubbub?" Salena stretches her arms over her head and does some knee bends. "I wish I could just throw on my regular costume and go. It's what I do every other time I run."

"Your sponsor might see it otherwise. Coffee?"

Salena wrinkles her nose at the sharp, tarry blend Sondra prefers. "No thanks, I'll find my own. Too much caffeine makes me jittery."

With a throaty rumble, a brand new convertible Ford Mustang pulls up in front of the Blazer. It is bright red with yellow pinstriping, the same colors she uses in her costume. A man wearing a Ford polo shirt, shorts, and a visor steps out of it, all smiles and handshakes.

"Good morning, good morning! How's our little racer today? Feeling fast?"

Salena tries not to roll her eyes. "Hi, Chad." Chad Forrester is the representative from Ford Motor

Company, who is sponsoring her run today in return for her endorsement of the Mustang. It makes sense, seeing as how she calls herself Mustang Sally. She feels kind of weird, selling out like a Hollywood celebrity doing ads in Japan, but her ultra-high-speed suit is ridiculously expensive and she can't wear her regular costume for this run because it's not rated past five hundred miles per hour.

"Sally, I can't tell you how thrilled we are that you'll be running for us today."

"I'm not running for you, Chad."

"Sure, sure. Of course. Listen, would you mind autographing the quarter panel of the car, here? I brought a Sharpie." He presses a thick permanent marker into her hand.

She looks at Sondra, who shrugs back. So Salena lopes over to the Mustang, a beautiful car that she feels bad about defacing, and writes Salena Tibbets "Mustang Sally" over the fender. Chad grabs a can from the back seat, and proceeds to spray it across her signature. "Spray fixative," he crows. "The factory guys tell me it's permanent. Thanks so much, Sally! I've got to set up the satellite feed. I'll see you at the starting line." He jumps back into the car, revs the motor unnecessarily, and drives off.

"I loathe that man," says Salena.

Sondra bursts out laughing. "He's not so bad. He's just a yes-man. I think he's a real fan, and not just because they're paying him to be one."

"I guess I should get ready."

A track official awaits her in the RV, along with a paramedic and a representative from the World Motor Sport Council. The paramedic checks her vital signs, draws blood which will be tested for any performance enhancing drugs, and asks her questions about her health and habits. No, she isn't taking any medications at this time. No, she doesn't smoke or drink alcohol. Yes, she does drink coffee, but only a little.

The WMSC official informs her they will once again record her speed in their books, even though she is doing so on foot. He is gracious but a bit stand-offish, and Salena knows it's because he's rationally offended at the idea of a human being running faster than the speed of sound.

She doesn't know if she can do it. The fastest she's officially gone, a number she committed to memory years ago, is 697.045 miles per hour over one mile. She set that record when she was eighteen, six years after Andy Green broke the speed of sound, which made her officially the second fastest person in the world, the fastest woman, and the fastest ever on foot. She knows she's faster now, because she's trained long and hard to become so.

The Bonneville Speedway official is nervous. There are so many things that can go wrong with this run. He wants to know about her safety equipment and finally takes off his hat, runs his hand through his thinning hair, and says he just doesn't know how to deal with parahumans. He knows engines, frames, tires, and fireproof suits. Jason and Sondra do their best to settle the man down while Salena changes into her racing suit.

The high-speed suit is heavier than her normal costume, but with good reason. Nobody is sure what will happen to her if she breaks the sonic barrier, so the engineers decided to risk additional weight in favor of some specially-designed airbags. Sensors in the suit will deploy them if they detect her falling, surrounding her and turning her into a big, red beach ball.

The suit clings to her like a cool second skin. The innermost layer is cotton, followed by an insulating gel to protect her skin from friction heat and to keep her body cool, and finally the outermost layer is the low-friction fabric used by Olympic speed-skaters. The airbags are located strategically around her body to help redirect airflow more efficiently around the non-aerodynamic human form. Normally she eschews a helmet in favor of goggles and a breather mask so she doesn't accidentally rupture a lung when inhaling at high speed. For this run she's wearing a lightweight helmet shaped like a teardrop, with her horse-head emblem on either side and the Ford logo across the top of the visor.

Her boots are a marvel of engineering, created by an unlikely team of an Italian footwear designer and an aerospace engineer. Lightweight and comfortable, they fit her legs to exact tolerances. The soles are thick and layered with ceramic wear plating and tungsten carbide cleats.

Salena finishes dressing and looks herself over critically in the mirror. The suit designers tried to follow the basic look of her costume: red with yellow trim and the yellow horse-head logo across her chest. But she doesn't really look like herself. It doesn't help that she has patches for all her sponsors across her shoulders.

"I look like a race car," she says out loud.

"Honey, you look wonderful," says a voice and she turns to see her mother and grandmother in the doorway. The three generations of speedsters embrace. Each of them was the fastest in her time. Her grandmother, called Colt by her teammates, is a veteran of World War II and a founder of the superhero team Just Cause. Her mother, known publicly as Pony Girl, was a member of the same team in the '70s and '80s.

And now there's just Salena, Mustang Sally, the youngest member of Just Cause, about to set a world land speed record.

"I'm so happy to see you, Mom," says Salena, and she means it. The two had been at each other's throats all through Salena's school years, but have since buried the hatchet and decided it's much more fun to get along as mother and daughter than otherwise.

"You do look like a race car," her grandmother says.

Her helmet under one arm, Salena steps out of the RV. All her friends wait for her; the whole Just Cause team has flown in for the event, but she only has eyes for the man with the goofy grin and the unshaven chin whom she's loved for years. She accepts some apple slices and a small cup of coffee from Jason. The combination will give her a quick burst of energy when she hits the starting line.

"Fifteen minutes, Ms., uh, Mustang Sally," warns the track official.

Most of her retinue will watch the satellite feed provided by Chad and his people. A few will be with her at the starting line; she has asked for Jason, Sondra, and her mother to accompany her.

As the small group walks down the line of parked cars, trucks, and bikes, where mechanics work feverishly to get their machines ready to run the speed course, people pause to watch her pass by. Applause begins somewhere and soon she is blushing as it seems everyone at Speed Week is cheering and whistling for her, chanting *Sal-LEE Sal-LEE Sal-LEE.*

"All right, honey, we've talked about this." Her mother pauses in her final instructions as a motorbike under a fiberglass shell roars away from the starting line. "Use the first mile to warm up and check your boots. No faster than four hundred, four hundred fifty miles per hour."

"I know, Mom." Salena can accelerate very quickly, reaching her "cruising" speed within a few steps.

"Once you pass that first mile marker, use the second mile to accelerate, and work up to your top speed."

"I know, Mom."

"Run the next two or three miles as quick as you can at top speed. If you break the sound barrier, that's where it'll happen."

"*I know,* Mom." She turns to Sondra. "What's my target speed?" There is a digital speedometer inset into her helmet visor.

Sondra pulls a Blackberry from her pocket and punches some numbers. "Temperature is about twenty-nine Celsius . . . looks like you'll need to hit just over 780 miles per hour."

"That's a lot," says Jason. "Do you think you can do it?"

Salena knows she can. She jumps into his arms and kisses him hard. "Yes."

"Be careful, baby."

"Three minutes," says the track official. "Better get to the line, Miss."

"Do you have my starting blocks?" Salena asks Jason. He holds up them up proudly.

She smiles at him. "Set me up, then, big guy?" She coils her long blonde hair into a bun at the back of her head so it will fit underneath her helmet. She's used to keeping it in braids that flap behind her but at these speeds, she's afraid of it tearing or burning away.

Jason takes each aluminum starting block and presses it into the salt at the starting line. The long spikes underneath them anchor them firmly in the ground.

"One minute," announces the official. Over the loudspeakers, Salena can barely hear her name being read over the roar of the onlookers. She looks around at the faces of her friends and loved ones and smiles at them. Then she pulls the helmet over her head and switches it on.

A readout to the left of her visor shows her the current temperature, wind speed and direction. To the right is her speedometer, which constantly changes as she moves to the starting line. "Radio check," she says.

"Read you loud and clear," says Chad's voice in her ears. "Are you receiving me, Sally?"

"Affirmative." She hunches over into a sprinter's stance and places her feet against the blocks. "Got my iPod ready?"

"That I do."

The track official waves at her. "Whenever you're ready, Miss."

"Push play," she says.

Jason's band is named Velma's Glasses. On their first date, he took her to a show they put on in a local bar. Since then, she's enjoyed supporting them as much as possible, given that both she and he are in Just Cause. He and his bandmates recorded a hard-rocking cover of Mack Rice's *Mustang Sally* for her, and this is what she's going to listen to on her journey across the salt flats.

The first notes sound in her ears, and she leaves the starting line behind in a graceful blur. Her feet pump like pistons across the sparkling salt. The speedometer numbers jump almost randomly until settling into the low 400s. At that speed, it takes her less than ten seconds to cover the first mile. The air whistles past her, the shape of her helmet forcing her head to stay pointed straight forward.

"You're looking good, Sally. How are you feeling?" asks Chad.

"Fast." She passes the first mile marker almost before she realizes she's come upon it. She leans into her stride, and accelerates.

She covers the second mile in six and a half seconds at a speed of six hundred forty miles per hour.

Not fast enough.

She pushes harder. The landscape around her narrows with tunnel vision until all she sees is a small space straight in front of her. Her entire world becomes that five-inch black line in the white salt.

The third mile marker comes and goes in a flash at seven hundred and thirty-five miles per hour.

Still not fast enough.

Patches on the front of her outfit tear away. It doesn't matter. She can go faster.

She only needs another sixty miles per hour. She can do that; she's a superhero for God's sake!

But she's pushing a column of air and it's tough to force her way through it. She leans down further to change how the air moves past her. And then she is going faster again. Seven hundred forty. Seven hundred fifty. Seven hundred sixty. Seven hundred seventy. She's beaten Green's top speed; she's now the fastest person in the world.

Still not fast enough.

Mile four passes in five seconds. So does mile five. Seven hundred seventy-two. She's already halfway down the course. Seven hundred seventy-three. She can barely see where she's going from her tunnel vision. But she can still see the black line. Seven hundred seventy-six. Mile six.

Still not fast enough.

Salt kicks up on either side of her at the edge of her vision, disturbed by the growing shock waves of compressed air as she approaches the magic Mach number. Seven hundred seventy-eight. Mile seven.

Mile eight.

Seven hundred seventy-nine.

Mile nine.

Her whole world condenses down to a pinpoint. Five seconds tick down. She finds that extra step she needs.

Seven hundred eighty-one miles per hour at the last mile marker.

BOOM.

She slows from sprint to jog to halt in a few hundred yards, listening to the echoes of her sonic boom echoing off distant mountain peaks, satisfied for the moment with yet another speed record.

Her satisfaction will be fleeting, though; because as fast as she is, it's never fast enough.

ARCHENEMY

January, 2009
New York City, NY

Once again, Mustang Sally wished she could run across water. She'd tried, of course. Dozens of times. She'd spoken to physicists about it and it wasn't a question of speed, especially for someone who was the sole member of the world's most exclusive club of people who had broken the speed of sound on foot. According to every scientist she'd ever spoken with, she should glide across the surface like a jet boat on hydrofoils. She'd tried running faster, slower, stomping, and tiptoeing. She'd tried shuffling her feet like a supersonic speed skater, all to no avail. No matter how fast she was going, if she hit water, she was going for a swim.

Jason always laughed at her, but not in an unkind way. "Babe, I've seen you jump across gaps at speed that would terrify me, and I'm a lot tougher to hurt than you are."

And it was true; she could do running long jumps that made some people think she could fly. But still, the water thing frustrated her to no end. "I should be able to."

"Maybe it's all in your head. Maybe you need a parahuman psychologist."

"Are you calling me crazy?"

"You'd have to be, to do what you're doing. Let me examine your head, though . . ." And then of course, things had been better.

With the change in presidents had come a dramatic reorganization of Just Cause, going from two teams to eight. Sally had expected she might get promoted to a leadership position somewhere in Just Cause, but she was completely floored when they asked her to take over the New York branch.

And so she and Jason, and a couple of her friends from the Denver team, packed up and moved to the City That Never Sleeps. It was hard leaving behind so many people she loved, but the adventure of a lifetime awaited her amid the towering skyscrapers of Manhattan.

The new headquarters, officially known as Just Cause New York but colloquially as Fort Justice, wasn't even within the confines of Manhattan. Instead, the government had purchased a floating oil drilling platform and refurbished it into a secure, mobile headquarters with nearly all the comforts of home.

There were lots of ways to get to the mainland. A regular ferry serviced the facility every four hours. Speedboats were available for faster response, and for full emergency deployments, the team had a brand new VTOL jet called the *Dorothy*, after Dorothy Dandridge.

But Sally wanted to run, and she was impatient, and she couldn't run across the water.

It was only her second day in New York. Every minute of hers and Jason's arrival had been filled with unpacking, getting to know the layout of Fort Justice, getting lost and then found again, greeting new team members as they arrived, meetings with everyone from the chief of staff to the legal and public relations directors to the chief cook and bottle washer. Oh, and paperwork. Reams and reams of it. Sally wondered how many forests had been leveled solely for the purpose of having triplicate copies of every single form and document that a government-run superhero team might require.

At last she couldn't take it anymore. She left Jason in charge of getting their apartment in order, since her husband was far more organized than she was, threw on her thermal costume (it was ridiculously cold in a miserable way that made Sally's bones ache for the warmth of her home state of Arizona), and hopped onto the departing ferry for Manhattan. She didn't get seasick—and thank goodness for that!—but she felt a nervous queasiness lapping around her edges like the cold gray waters of the Upper New York Bay at the hull of the ferry. She was barely twenty-four years old and the President of the United States had asked her to lead the most important branch of the most important superhero team in the world. That she wasn't running to the bathroom to throw up every few minutes was a small miracle.

The ferry bumped up against the Pier 11 slip and people filed across the gangplank onto the pier itself. Everything was shades of gray; gray clouds reflecting upon gray water, the gray walkway with gray railings. Sally found herself scanning up and down the pier, focusing upon any splash of color she could see. Although the passengers on the ferry from Fort Justice were Just Cause employees, inured to the brilliance of superhero costumes, many of the pedestrians on the pier were staring and snapping pictures. Even the lifelong New Yorkers, which Sally equated with a certain willingness to step on another human's face, lost some of their blasé, already-seen-it-all expressions as they took in the crimson and gold of her costume, from her traditional horse's-head logo to the horseshoes slung at her waist to the tremendously expensive running boots that had been created by an unlikely partnership of an Italian footwear designer and a NASA engineer. She made herself smile at the citizens; part of her job was to be a visible representative of the parahuman community and to do whatever she could to cast Just Cause in a positive light.

"Mustang Sally, checking in at Pier 11." The microphone button sewn against the collar of her bodysuit picked up her voice and relayed it across the water back to Fort Justice. "I'm going to patrol."

"Control, receiving you," said the disembodied voice in her ear. "We'll monitor you and inform you if you're needed."

"Copy that." Sally took her goggles off her forehead and shook out her hair. She was still getting used to her new short hairstyle after years of having long braids hanging down her back. She'd felt like she needed a look that was more grown-up given her new position, and had spent an entire weekend flipping through webpage after webpage of hairstyles until she'd found one she thought she could live with. Jason had given her his blessing, and she'd cried when almost two feet of her hair hit the floor. Once the stylist had finished giving her a layered cut that accentuated her natural waves, she had to admit that she looked pretty good. At least it was easier to manage and could all fit beneath her cowl so it didn't get windburned. She pulled the cowl up and over her head, tucking any flyaway locks beneath the edges. The goggles went back on over the cowl, connecting to tiny catches that would keep them from being ripped away due to wind friction. She wouldn't be running fast enough to need the breath mask to protect her lungs, but she wore it anyway because there was nothing worse than aspirating road grit at triple-digit speeds.

Her face fully protected from the wind, she waved at the onlookers, and then lit out. Her perceptions accelerated along with her speed, giving her plenty of time to avoid collisions. She zipped across the pier and turned right to follow FDR Drive along the East River. She'd checked the GPS map on her phone on the ferry, and she knew to count bridges. The fourth one would be the Queensboro, and taking a left there would bring her right to Central Park, which was where her mother had run when she was in Just Cause back in the Seventies. The Brooklyn and Manhattan Bridges flashed past, great titans sprawling across the icy waters. Sally kept well to the right of traffic, running along the breakdown lane as much as possible. It had been her experience that running too close to the speed of traffic tended to be a distraction for drivers as they actually had time to look at her. Going two or three times faster than the flow meant she was gone from most drivers' vision before they really registered what they'd seen. When there was no breakdown lane, she dipped down an exit ramp to run beneath the FDR viaduct, having to weave around ubiquitous construction sites.

The buildings in that part of Manhattan were much more reasonable, reminding her of Lower Downtown in Denver. She passed by a lovely park near the Williamsburg Bridge, which was a welcome relief from all the gray. It was too early in the season for any real greenery, but a few hardy crocuses were pushing their way up through the dirt. Horns honked and a police siren blared and she wondered if she should stop, but one of the things Juice had told her was that Just Cause wasn't supposed to respond to every minor infraction or incident. If local law enforcement needed parahuman assistance, there were avenues for them to request it, whether from local-level Champions or escalating to Just Cause if needed. "It's important that local police don't grow to resent you. We want them to be willing to call for help, and they can't do that if they feel like you're trying to replace them."

"But how will I know what to do to help, then?"

"You'll know in your gut. You always have, Sally. That's why we chose you."

The buildings went from brown stone to gray as Sally continued her trek northward. She skipped off of

FDR to run along a bike path right alongside the river. "Sally, Control," said the voice in her ear.

"Go ahead, Control."

"We've got some unusual activity on social network monitoring. Your name has popped up tied to Central Park and we don't show that you're anywhere near there yet."

Sally skidded to a halt, startling several joggers. "What do you mean, *my name has popped up*?"

"We're seeing images tagged with you. It looks like someone has burned letters spelling out your name into the grass on the southern end of Central Park. We're seeing multiple mentions of it as well as pictures."

"I'm heading there to investigate it now, Control. Is the fire out?"

"We have no information on it at this time."

"Copy that." Sally launched into motion once again, blowing well past a hundred fifty until even in her accelerated perceptions, the buildings and cars blurred past. She spotted an exit ramp and turned down it to head inland, towards Central Park. She had to be very careful on the narrow and congested road, and there were a lot more pedestrians milling about. She zigged and zagged around them, outrunning the confused and typical-New-Yorker angry shouts in her wake. She realized she'd turned the wrong way up a one-way street but it didn't matter; she was moving fast enough that the cars seemed like they were standing still.

She slipped between a bus and a panel truck and then she was crossing a plaza into Central Park. "Control, I'm at Central Park. Where's this fire?"

"Roughly a hundred yards from the southeast corner."

Sally slowed her headlong rush and lowered her rebreather. The chill air made her skin prickle and sting. The trees that would be so lush and green by the spring were still mostly bare black and gray trunks with branches like skeletal fingers. She sniffed at the air and there was indeed a tang of smoke present, which she recognized as the burning of dry grass, a common enough scent in Colorado during fire season. She raised her tinted goggles and tried to pick smoke out against the cloudy sky, but with no success.

"Hey, Mustang Sally!" She looked to see a young man waving at her. "Somebody wrote your name on the ground."

She moved beside him in a flash. "Where?"

He jumped at her sudden appearance. "Whoa!"

"Sir, please."

"Oh, sorry. Right over there, behind those trees." He licked his lips. "You, uh, you seeing anyone?"

She smiled at him. "I'm married."

"Yeah, but is it working out?"

She didn't dignify his query with a response. Instead, she zipped past him, through the trees, to confront whoever had called her out.

A woman in a tight-fitting turqoise and black bodysuit similar to Sally's in cut and design stood there, arms crossed, looking impatient. She was several inches taller than Sally—no real feat there, given Sally was barely over five feet tall herself—but with a much more muscular build. She wore a blue helmet with a gold-tinted visor and a rudder emerging from the back. Her boots were much more stylized in design than Sally's high-tech utilitarian clunkers. Instead of matching the blue-and-black color scheme, the other woman's boots were orange and red with a flame design upon them that reminded Sally of hot rod paint jobs. "About time you showed up. For a speedster, you're pretty slow upstairs."

Sally felt her ears burn. She'd faced down some of the world's most dangerous supervillains and not only lived to tell about it, but in many cases been triumphant. How could this unknown woman get to her with such a simple insult? She made herself shake it off. The snide statement demanded a response, and although Sally wasn't the wittiest conversationalist in the world, she could at least hold her own. "If you were in that much of a hurry, why didn't you just call? I had to wait for social media to catch up." She folded her own arms. "Who are you and what do you want?"

The woman smiled behind her visor. Sally didn't recognize her face. It occurred to her that she ought to have cameras built into her goggles so she didn't have to take time to use her phone to snap a picture. She could take a picture faster than anyone could move, but she invariably moved too fast and the camera would only ever show a blur. "I'm Afterburner, and I'm here to take you down, Mustang Sally."

Sally snorted. "Just like that? You show up out of the blue, set some grass on fire, and now you're going to . . . to fight me like some kind of stupid archenemy? Who writes your dialogue, George Lucas?"

"Who's that? I don't . . . oh." Sally got the distinct impression that the woman was speaking to someone else. And then in a flash of motion the woman was in front of her. Sally's accelerated perceptions kicked in a fraction of a second too late—a side effect of never dealing with anyone whose speed could approach her own—and the woman shoved her backwards. Sally stumbled and fell onto her ass, bruising her tailbone on the hard-packed dirt with its layer of dead grass. "I'm not afraid of you. You ain't jack shit. Get up, or are you gonna just let me kick your ass laying down?"

Sally sprang to her feet, her heart hammering behind her ribs. In her life she'd encountered only two other parahumans with what she'd categorize as extreme examples of enhanced speed. Carousel was an advanced android who'd been a member of the Lucky Seven team where Sally had trained before joining Just Cause. Johnny Go was a good friend who'd gone through the Hero Academy and now one of the trainers for Champions. Neither of them had even come close to approaching

Sally's level of speed; they were like thoroughbred racing horses trying to compete against a Formula I car.

This woman, Afterburner, was dangerously fast. Maybe even as fast as Sally. She was also bigger, stronger, and knew how to fight by the way she carried herself. Smoke leaked from beneath her feet and Sally realized she had another, even more sinister power. She could ignite the ground where she stood. Hence the name, Sally thought. Sally hadn't ever trained in physical combat very hard; with her speed, standing and fighting an opponent was a poor use of her abilities.

Afterburner leaped and spun, her right foot arcing around in a devastating roundhouse kick. Flames trailed off her heel, making a whooshing noise. Sally just barely ducked out of the way as Afterburner's foot flashed through the air where Sally's head had been a moment before. Sally tried to remember all her basic combat training, which she'd had in her very first year at the Hero Academy. She hadn't paid attention then, trusting her speed to get her out of a dangerous situation.

She hadn't ever planned for this. She threw a punch the way she'd seen Jason do it when he sparred with other bricks.

Afterburner laughed, slapped aside Sally's ineffectual blow, and smashed her helmet against Sally's face. Sally felt her nose break and her mouth filled with blood. She staggered back, tears of pain blinding her. Her foot caught against something and she fell. Afterburner leaped into a forward tuck. She extended her right foot as she came up and around, lashing downward with an axe kick that could have broken any bone it struck. Sally rolled aside to avoid the strike and kicked at Afterburner's ankle. Afterburner turned her foot enough that Sally's kick only glanced off the edge. "That's more like it. Ain't no fun when they don't have any spirit."

She stomped down on Sally's leg but Sally's heavy boot absorbed the worst of the blow. Sally tried to fight back by grabbing at the woman's foot, but it was like grabbing a pan out of the oven without a hot pad. Sally yelped as she burned her fingers through her gloves. Blood ran down the side of her face and dribbled onto her logo.

Afterburner lunged and grabbed Sally's neck. "There's a new sheriff in town, bitch."

Sally felt her lungs burning and she struggled against the woman's grip. Afterburner lifted her off the ground. Sally tried to kick but she had no strength left as the life was being choked out of her. As a last-ditch effort, she let go of Afterburner's wrists, grabbed the woman's helmet, and twisted it hard to one side. The helmet turned faster than Afterburner's head did and the edge of the visor opening cracked hard across Afterburner's nose, breaking it much like she'd broken Sally's. Afterburner dropped her and struggled with her helmet, cursing and spitting out blood.

Sally ran. She couldn't stand and trade punches with Afterburner; the woman fought like a martial artist, and Sally barely had basic brawling skills. Afterburner was after her in a flash and they raced across the park, a red streak pursued by a blue one. Sally's head cleared as she ran, but she had to keep spitting out blood so she wouldn't swallow it, and she couldn't breathe through her shattered nose so her breath mask was out of the question.

They raced through the trees, whipping up a storm of dry grass, dead leaves, and twigs in their wake. Sally realized that not only was Afterburner a much better fighter, but the blue-garbed woman was keeping pace with her. Sally put her head down and poured on the speed. She'd broken the speed of sound once; she could outrun Afterburner. Everywhere her pursuer set a foot down, the ground was left smoldering. Sally quickly discovered her best bet to get away, or at least to gain an advantage, was to turn and change directions much faster than Afterburner.

She doubled back twice, forcing Afterburner to skid to a stop, cursing each time. "I know, I know," she yelled at whoever was on the other end of her radio.

That gave Sally an idea. She headed across the gigantic meadow where she could really unleash the speed. With her attention no longer needed to keep her from smashing into a tree trunk, she called in to headquarters. "Control, Sally. I'm engaged with an unknown parahuman assailant. Enhanced speed at my level. Scramble backup."

"Roger that, Sally. The *Dorothy* will be airborne in five minutes. ETA to your location in thirteen minutes, plus or minus two minutes."

Sally wasn't sure she'd last five minutes against Afterburner. Her backup might arrive to find themselves claiming her body. "Sooner would be better, Control. Also, she's in radio communication with someone. Try to locate and track that signal."

"That may be difficult given your speed and altitude, but we'll work on it. You could shave five minutes off the response time if you came to the southern tip of the island."

"Negative. Central Park is the safest place for this. Sally out." Being late winter, the park wasn't nearly as crowded as it might have been had the weather been warmer. She dashed across a bridge and around a rocky outcropping, trying to outmaneuver her pursuer.

"You won't get away like that." Afterburner sounded winded to Sally, which suggested that perhaps she didn't have Sally's stamina for long sprints.

"I don't have to get away. I just have to outlast you." She grabbed hold of a sign pole and swung, letting her momentum carry her around it like a tether ball. Her feet flashed over a sliding Afterburner's head, just missing a double kick that might have decapitated her assailant, or broken every bone in Sally's legs, or both.

Afterburner rolled into a combat crouch to face Sally as Sally dropped down beside the sign pole, her sides heaving. Behind her visor, Afterburner's face was crimson and evaporating sweat rose off her body like steam in the chilly air. "That was dirty." Smoke curled upward from around her feet as the grass beneath them ignited.

"You want to call this off now, before one of us gets really hurt? Come on, I'll buy you a beer and you can tell me what I did to earn your wrath." She held out a hand. "What's your name?"

"Martina. What? I know, I know!"

"Who are you talking to? Sounds like they're being a real pain in your ass. Somebody putting you up to this?"

"Shut up, I got this."

Sally couldn't tell if Afterburner was talking to her or to whoever was on the other end of her radio. "Look, if you're in trouble, let me help you. You might have heard that me and my people are pretty good at this sort of thing."

"I know!" screamed Afterburner, and she charged at Sally.

"Shit." Sally found herself engaged before she had a chance to flee. She danced backward, ducking underneath Afterburner's punches and jumping to avoid her kicks. The flurry of limbs seemed to come at her from every direction. A hard roundhouse kick caught her hip and made her right leg go numb. Afterburner followed up with a hard punch straight to Sally's face. Blood splattered up Afterburner's hand from Sally's already-broken nose, and she yelped from the pain. Her hands found her horseshoes where they were still clamped to her belt. Over the years she'd used them as brass knuckles when she needed a little more heft to her super-speedy punches, and if there was ever a moment where that was required, this was it.

Afterburner punched at her again and Sally dropped her chin so Afterburner's fist smashed against her forehead, breaking her goggles. Sally responded by driving the twin forks of the horseshoe clutched in her right hand hard into Afterburner's visor. The yellow-tinted faceplate cracked and the sharp plastic ends lacerated Afterburner's face.

She staggered back, shrieking incoherently. Sally knew she should have pressed the advantage while she had it, but her entire face hurt, and her nose and lips were swelling like an allergic reaction. Her vision was growing blurry but she didn't know whether it was because of swelling around her eyes or something worse. She'd suffered concussions before and knew she was high risk for them.

She hooked the horseshoes back on her belt and ran again, hoping that she could outrun Afterburner. With her goggles destroyed, she couldn't get up much faster than two hundred or so before the stream of icy air against her tender face became too much to bear. She skirted the edge of the large lake. When she looked back over her shoulder, she didn't see any sign of Afterburner, and thought perhaps she'd escaped the mysterious speedster at last. But then she glanced back across the lake and got the shock of her life.

Afterburner was crossing straight over the surface of the water, racing toward Sally like a speed skater. Her feet kicked up steamy rooster tails of water vapor with every step.

Sally slid to a halt among the loose rocks along the lake shore as Afterburner tore towards her. "No. No way." That wasn't fair. Not only was Afterburner fast, setting fires with every step, and a superior hand-to-hand fighter, but she could run on water too? She gathered up a handful of suitably flat rocks and hurled them at Afterburner, using her speed to accelerate the stones like bullets.

Afterburner stepped around the first couple of skipping stones but then one caught her in the knee and another followed immediately after, striking the top of her foot. With her accelerated perceptions, Sally saw the blood splatter from each wound. Afterburner yelped and lost her balance. She fell sideways, kicking up a tremendous wave as she plowed into the water. At Sally's speed, the water seemed to move like molasses, and she saw Afterburner tumble into it in a jumble of twisting limbs. Sally didn't like the way Afterburner's head snapped back when it hit the water, and she slowed her racing senses to get a better feel for time passing. Seconds ticked away and still Afterburner didn't emerge from the water.

At some point, Sally realized that the other speedster wasn't going to come up. "Shit!" She raced to unlace her tall boots. "Control. ETA to my location." Speaking hurt her face, she discovered, and so did wincing at the pain.

"Less than four minutes."

Sally shook her head. "Not fast enough. Tell them to prepare for a water rescue, and get some paramedics out here stat!" She yanked off her thick socks, cringing at the cold on her bare feet, and charged into the water.

She still couldn't run across the water, but years of trying had necessitated her becoming a good swimmer, and she struck out toward the area where she'd seen Afterburner go under. The icy water seeped into her uniform and made her hands and feet go numb instantly. At least the cold would help with the swelling in her face, although the broken nose made it impossible for her to swim in any way but a dog paddle.

It was a speedy dog paddle, though, and she found Afterburner after only a few seconds. The waterlogged woman was a few feet below the surface, unmoving. Sally took a deep breath and dove down beneath Afterburner, moving her legs in a blur to push the woman back to the surface. Their heads broke water and Sally grabbed Afterburner beneath her arms and kicked backward, pushing for the shoreline.

She was so cold that she barely felt her feet brush against the soft bottom, and a moment later she was dragging Afterburner up onto the sand at the water's edge. Both women choked, coughing up lake water. Sally's shivers seemed to take over her entire body. As the water drained from her ears, she heard the distant roar of the approaching *Dorothy*, loud enough to drown out the much closer howls of emergency vehicles. "Y-you all r-right?" she managed through chattering teeth.

Afterburner gagged and spit up a lungful of water onto the sand, so weak that she couldn't even raise her head. Steam rose from her feet as the heat they produced evaporated the lake water. Sally could feel the radiance from them and wondered if it would be too weird to use them to warm herself back up. "W-why? I t-tried to . . . You still s-saved me."

"I'm a hero. That's what we d-do." Her chattering teeth made her broken nose throb.

"What? No. I'm not—" Afterburner paused and her eyes narrowed. "What do you m-mean *no longer required*?" She started to say something else but Sally's perceptions accelerated to their maximum and for a moment she didn't understand why, but then she saw Afterburner's face tearing apart as slow-motion flames forced their way through her skin. Sally was fast, but she was exhausted and injured and the shock wave of the explosion caught her as she turned to flee and sent her tumbling along the sand of the lake front. When she rolled over to look back at Afterburner, she saw the woman's helmet split in half and nothing but ruin above her neck and below her wrists.

Feeling like she'd failed, Sally lay back and cried silent, painful tears as the *Dorothy* circled overhead, spilling colorful heroes from its bomb bay doors.

* * *

Sally had been very fortunate not to suffer a concussion, said the base doctor, given her history of them and the amount of trauma her head and face had suffered in the brief time she'd shared Afterburner's company. "You're off duty for a week. That means no patrolling, no training, and no running." He glared over the top of his glasses at Sally. "And no *buts.*"

Sally would have pouted, but the bandage over her nose, her swollen lip, and two black eyes made any kind of facial expressions extremely uncomfortable. "All right. I heal fast, you know. I might be good to go in a couple of days."

"One week, and if I'm not satisfied, I won't clear you." The doctor looked at Jason, who sat beside Sally. "You have my permission to sit on her for a week if she won't listen to reason."

Given that Jason outweighed her by some two hundred pounds, Sally knew he'd take his job of ensuring her rest and relaxation seriously. "Fine."

"It's all right, babe. I got you some new DVD box sets. You can nerd out to your heart's content."

"Sounds great." Sally registered the same enthusiasm as she might for a root canal.

They left the doctor's office to return to their quarters, far more spacious than they'd shared in the Just Cause base back in Denver, and filled with chunky wood furniture that they'd picked out together after learning of their reassignment. "It's probably best that you spend a few days on downtime anyway. You know I'll always think you're beautiful, but you look, um, pretty rough."

"I know. Any word on the autopsy? Have they identified Afterburner yet?"

Jason shook his shaggy blond head. "The lab says that she had residue suggesting C-4 was wrapped around the base of her skull and wrists, along with some kind of advanced detonators. Whoever did it wanted to make sure she was very difficult to identify. No dental records, no fingerprints. They have DNA, but the only way that will help identify her is if her DNA's on file somewhere."

"She said her name was Martina. She was a good fighter. Like she was trained. And that combination of parapowers was really unusual. Super speed and flaming feet. There's nothing about her in the PRA files?"

"No." Jason looked troubled. "And there wouldn't be." He opened the fridge and got out a beer. "Want one?"

"Why wouldn't there be anything about her at the PRA? Yes, please."

Jason popped off the cap for her and handed her the bottle. Sally held it up against her face, letting the cool glass soothe the ache. "They ran the tests three times. Babe, she wasn't a parahuman. She didn't have any of the genetic markers. No nanotech anywhere anybody could find. No advanced technology of any kind in her suit or in her, um, her remains." He took a pull from his beer. "She shouldn't have been able to do any of the things she did."

Sally shivered. "What does that mean? How is that possible?" She set down her beer with out tasting it. "What if there are others?"

But Jason couldn't answer her.

Nobody could.

SUN-KISSED

Akamai was the Sun-God of Hawaii.

Not really a *god*, of course. But he was a superhero, and the only one in the islands, and that made him a celebrity. His name wasn't really Akamai either, it was Martin, but whoever heard of a superhero named *Martin*? That was a lame name, a name for a *haole*, a white person. Akamai was *kanaka*, a native Islander, and he was proud of that fact.

He was also proud of his power, which made him a human searchlight. He called himself the World's First Solar-Powered Superhero, even though he probably wasn't. He could absorb sunlight all day surfing or chilling on the beach, and he'd become suffused with a gentle, golden glow that could be seen even in broad daylight. If he concentrated, he could brighten and focus that power into a sunbeam that could illuminate, heat, or even ignite things.

At night, though, that's when he looked really spectacular. He was a walking lightshow, a beacon, a tourist draw. He'd help the Coast Guard go after lost boats, help find idiot nighttime swimmers, and drive off sharks by heating their tails until they left. It was a good life, one that didn't require him to hold down a job. He didn't live in luxury, just a trailer, but it was right on the beach. And the government paid for it because he was registered with the PRA. He was the only resource they had on the Islands.

Plus he was a damn fine looker, and there was no shortage of tourist *wahine* willing to give it up for a taste of his golden glow. Between his surfer's body, easy smile, smooth brown skin, and floppy hair, he was never short of offers.

He rode the last wave in and picked up his board. The sun was sitting low, which meant the *lu'aus* would begin soon and tourists were starting to think about dinner. That meant it was time for Akamai to start hunting up his night's entertainment. Sometimes that meant a cougar celebrating her recent divorce. Other times it meant a college girl on a trip with her friends or family. Once in awhile it event meant a local girl, although most of the *kama'aina* were immune to his charms.

"Hey, Mister," said a voice, and Akamai turned to see a chubby red-headed kid with curly hair and a lobster-red sunburn.

Akamai looked him over. Typical tourist kid. Mid to late teens. Overdid it the first day. "Howzit, *opu*? You looking for an autograph?"

"What? No, I'm—"

Akamai spotted a couple of ladies he hadn't yet met beyond the ginger kid. "*E kala mai*, brah. Catch you next time." He pushed past the sunburnt redhead. "Aloha, ladies. Federal bikini inspector. I'm afraid I'm going to have to see some identification . . ."

* * *

The first rays of sun peeked through the blinds in the bedroom of Akamai's trailer. His golden glow had diminished to a faint luminescence. It was enough to highlight the curvy behind of the blonde who'd come home with him. She'd been a tiger in the sack, to the point he suspected he had scratch marks on his back.

He'd spent a long time perfecting his morning-after technique. "Hey. Wake up, *wahine*."

She stirred and muttered something unintelligible.

"Girl, you been a real pleasure, but it's morning and I've got to get back to work."

She rolled over and sat up, unashamed of her nakedness. "Work?"

He grinned. "Yeah. I'm a superhero, you know. I have to, you know, patrol and stuff. Do you want to use my shower? It's not as good as the one in your hotel."

"Oh. No, that's okay."

"Breakfast, then? I don't have a lot. I usually eat at one of the carts. They got better food. So does your hotel."

She found her bikini at the side of the bed and pulled it on. "How do you know what hotel I'm in?"

"I don't, but I know all the hotels around here." One of the bartenders at his favorite beach booze hut had asked him why he only ever went after tourist girls, why he didn't have the slightest interest in forming any long-term relationships. At the time, he'd said it was because he didn't need the emotional baggage that came along with a deeper relationship. He could enjoy himself for a few hours and then it was over without any aftermath. Everyone knew what they were getting into with him, and if they weren't okay with that, they didn't come back to his trailer.

"Oh. No, I guess I'll leave. This was fun."

Akamai grinned. It was like she had a copy of his script. He loved it when the morning after was easy. The truth of it was he liked his solitude. He didn't have to answer to a lover, roommate, or partner. If he wanted to eat nothing but Captain Crunch for a solid week (and he had), nobody was going to judge him for it. "Yeah it was. When do you leave?"

"Tomorrow."

"'K den."

She slid her shorts up her long legs and then tied her hair into a quick knot at the back of her head. "See you around later, maybe."

"Roger dat. Aloha!" He smiled and watched her leave, enjoying the swing of her hips.

"Oh, hello," she said, and left the trailer.

Akamai blinked. Who had she greeted? He peeked his head out of his bedroom door.

The chubby ginger kid with the sunburn was sitting at his small kitchen table, spooning cornflakes into his mouth like he was being paid for it. He noticed Akamai and nodded a greeting. "You're out of milk."

"What you doing in my place, brah?" Akamai tried to draw more power into his glow, but he was pretty well tapped out.

"Waiting for you," said the boy between mouthfuls. "I didn't think you'd ever get up."

Akamai concentrated his power into his hands. The glow was plainly visible in the dim kitchen. "You better talk, *haole*. Or we gonna scrap. I am a duly authorized representative of . . . Hey, you ain't gonna cry, are you?"

The boy pushed his bowl aside with his head bowed. For a moment, Akamai really was afraid the boy was going to start bawling right there in his trailer, and he wasn't prepared for that.

"Sorry I snuck in here. I was hungry and tired and I wanted to talk to you." He raised his head and looked at Akamai. "My name's Warren. Warren Eccles. I'm from . . . Well, I guess it doesn't matter. I don't have any family anymore."

"Anymore? What happened?" Akamai was curious in spite of himself.

"My folks, they died. Car crash. Two months ago. I been in foster care since. It sucks."

"Sorry, brah. How old are you, anyway?"

"Fifteen."

"Not too far off from *hanabata* days."

"Hana-whata?"

"Hanabata. It means small kid time."

"Oh. I guess I need to learn more Hawaiian if I'm going to start living here."

Akamai blinked. "Living here? With me? Are you *lolo*?" He opened his blinds, letting the morning sunlight into the kitchen. "Look, kid, you got to make tracks outta here. I got a job."

"I can work with you. I can help. I have powers too."

"Kid . . . Uh, Warren. Where are you from? Across the island? One of the other islands? You need to get back home. People gonna be worried sick about you."

"I'm not from here, I'm from Milwaukee. They're not going to miss me. That family was going to send me back into the system."

"Why?"

"Because they don't like parahumans. They said it's my fault my folks d-died." Warren sniffled and Akamai felt on the verge of panic. He knew what to do when a girl cried around him, but this was something new.

"Hey, uh, don't do that, brah. What hotel they staying at?"

Warren wiped his eyes. "They're not at a hotel."

"Oh. Uh, time-share? Maybe they're in on of those rental houseboats?"

"No, they're not here. Not in Hawaii. I teleported here."

* * *

"Maybe you best start at the beginning, brah." Akamai and Warren sat at the bar in a beachside hut, Warren having a virgin coconut daiquiri and Akamai manning it up with two fingers of Kentucky bourbon on top of two more fingers of the same. The bartender hadn't even asked if it wasn't a little too early; she'd seen enough tourists to know.

"I can teleport to anywhere I know really well, or someplace I can see." Warren sipped at his drink. "I always wanted to come to Hawaii, but TV shows and movies aren't live images, and I can't go to a place if I can't see it live. Even most sports are on tape delay because of the time zone difference."

"So how are you here at all then?"

"I found a live beach feed online and went for it. Scariest thing I've ever done. It felt like it took forever, but next thing I knew I was on the beach instead of in a strange house in Milwaukee. I walked around for awhile, sat on the beach, watched the surf."

"And got your *'okole* burnt up. You're a ginger, brah, you're always gonna be shark bait. Can you go back home?"

"No. The only place I know good enough back in Milwaukee is my folks' graveside, and I don't want to go back there."

"So you're stuck here." Akamai knocked back some of his drink, relishing the burn in the back of his throat.

"Yeah. I heard about you and I thought maybe you could use a—"

"A what? A sidekick?"

Warren might have blushed, but Akamai couldn't see it beneath the boy's vicious sunburn. "A partner."

Akamai burst out laughing, so loud he even surprised himself. Tourists looked up, whispered to each other about the strange native rituals, and went back to their fizzy pink and blue frozen concoctions. "Brah, you *lolo*. First of all, I never needed no wingman. I get all the *wahine* I want on my charm and good looks. And this glow don't hurt either. Second, you're just a kid. I could be liable or something. And third, what kind of weird sidekick would you be? I got the glow of the sun-kissed in me, and you teleport. That's lame, *haole*."

For a moment, Warren looked like he was about to cry again, and Akamai thought maybe he'd pushed the kid too far. Then the kid vanished right into thin air with a loud popping sound, as if someone had cracked open a huge bottle of wine. A sudden wind gust flipped Akamai's hair. He glanced at the tourists in the bar. They were staring at him in open-mouthed astonishment. He put on a supreme effort to appear unfazed by the boy's sudden disappearance.

"'K den."
He finished his drink.

* * *

The rest of the day was as typically uneventful as most days in Hawaii. Akamai prowled the beaches, signed autographs (and also signed some really amazing breasts he was looking forward to encountering again by nightfall), took photos with tourists, and soaked up lots and lots of rays. By evening, he was glowing like an earthbound star, and had a couple of possible companions lined up for his evening's entertainment.

"I want to make love on the beach," said one of the girls. "It looks so romantic in the movies."

"No, you no wanna do dat," said Akamai, playing up his native accent as much as he could. Girls liked it when he seemed more exotic. "Get sand up in your *'okole*. Mo' better you come back to my place."

"Yeah, but which one? I saw you first," said the tall brunette with a pout.

"Yeah, but once you go black, you don't want no white girls after that." The girl with the chocolate skin and dreadlocks hiccuped and patted her belly. "Oof. I had a lot of daiquiris."

Akamai put his arms over both their shoulders—having to stretch to reach the black girl's, as she was a good eight or ten inches taller than him—and steered them toward his trailer. He realized he was about to cross a very specific item off his list of fantasies and his glow had grown a bit more pronounced because of it. "Ladies, ladies. No need to scrap over me. I got plenty to go 'round."

The girls tittered and Akamai walked a little faster.

But when his trailer drew into sight, he pulled up short. The lights were on. He never left the lights on. Most of the time, his personal glow was sufficient illumination and the rest of the time, he used candles, because girls loved that kind of thing. If the lights were on, it meant someone else was inside the trailer, and given recent events, he has a pretty fair idea who that might be.

He looked to his left, then to his right. He wondered if either—or both, to be fair—of the lovely creatures clutching at his forearms would be around the following evening. It wasn't that he didn't think he could find suitable companion, but finding two of them willing to play in a threesome? That might be a good long while yet.

"Ladies, I am super sorry, but I'm gonna have to say good night now. Aloha."

The girls both went "Awwww," in stereo and pouted so sexily that Akamai almost gave in anyway. But no, he had to man up and do some adulting.

Hand in hand, the girls walked back toward the hotel, looking so fine in the torchlight of the beach that he almost called them back over just so he could watch them walk away one more time. Instead, he turned back to his trailer. "Man, I'm gonna kill that *lolo haole*," he muttered.

He pushed open the door and there was Warren, sitting on Akamai's ratty couch, watching Akamai's TV, and eating a bag of popcorn from the stand at the end of the beach. He saw Akamai. "Oh, hey."

Akamai sighed. "Kid, what you doing here?"

"Watching Cinemax. They show boobies."

Akamai felt like punching himself in the face to put himself out of his misery. "Kid, I know they show boobies. I was gonna get hold of some real ones if you hadn't been here. Two pairs, *haole*. You know how rare that is?"

Warren scrunched up his face. "You met a girl with four boobs?"

"No, kid. You really are from Milwaukee, huh?"

"Not no more. I live here now."

"Not in my trailer, you don't."

"I don't have anywhere else to go."

"*Haole*, I really don't care."

"What's that mean? That name you keep calling me?"

"*Haole*? It just means white dude."

"Oh, I thought you were being mean."

"No, kid. It's just . . ." Akamai paused as a close-up of a truly spectacular pair of tits graced the TV screen.

"Da-a-a-amn," he and Warren said together. Then they looked at each other and matched smiles.

"Look, kid, I get it. You need a place to stay. You need *ohana*. That's family. You don't wanna get it here, 'kay? I'm just a glorified beach bum. I got a lame power and if I lived anywhere else but Hawaii, I wouldn't be nothing at all."

"One day. Just give me one day. Let me be a superhero with you. If it doesn't work out, I'll find somewhere else to go. If it does, though . . . If I make a good sidekick, you have to promise to keep me around."

Akamai had no intention to say any such thing, so it surprised him completely to hear himself say *Roger dat.*

* * *

For the first time in his recent memory, Akamai awakened the next morning without having had any female companionship the evening before. He stirred, trying to collect his sleep-jumbled thoughts. What had awakened him? There was an unfamiliar scent in the air of his trailer, like something was . . . *burning*!

He sprang out of bed, his glow casting odd shadows upon the walls, and raced down the short hall to his kitchen. He skidded to a halt as he saw what the *lolo haole* had wrought upon his kitchen.

Warren had bread in a frying pan, dripping with butter, and had just cracked an egg into a hole in the middle of it.

"What the . . ." Akamai couldn't even. Not yet. Not before . . .

"I made coffee," said Warren, grinning behind his sunburn. "I figured you probably wanted some. And eggs and toast. That's like the only thing I know how to make."

"But . . . I don't have any eggs. Or bread. Or butter."

"Yeah, I know. I got up early and went to the market up the beach. I, uh, said you'd be by later to pay for it. They were cool with that."

"Course they were. This is Hawaii, *haole*. Everyone is chill here. But you didn't need to do that."

Warren flipped over the piece of fried bread with the egg in it. Akamai had to admit it smelled really good. The extent of his cooking skills was limited to pushing the right buttons on the microwave. "I wanted to. I want you to keep me around."

"I promised you one day, kid. Nothing else."

"So let's make the most of it. Let's go patrol." Warren handed Akamai a plate of food.

Akamai grabbed a fork and shoveled it in, even though it was steaming hot. He was determined not to enjoy it, but the creamy, eggy center mixed with the perfectly-toasted bread and butter to make a tremendously satisfying meal. "Oh man, that just about broke da mouth."

Warren grinned. "Is that good?"

"Yeah, that's good."

"Can we go patrol now? I mean after you have your coffee?"

Akamai poured himself a cup. He couldn't remember the last time he'd had coffee at home instead of from the shop up the beach. "What exactly do you think patrolling is?"

"Uh . . . Walking around, looking for trouble to stop? People to save?"

Akamai shook his head. "No, it's more complicated than that. It's . . ."

"What?"

"Okay, so maybe that is what it is. But you got to know where to look in the first place."

"On the beach, right? Isn't that your beat?"

"My beat? You make me sound like a cop."

"Well, aren't you?"

Akamai was getting frustrated. "No! Well, kinda. Shoot. Maybe you're right."

Warren held up a plastic tube in one hand and one of the cheap fake straw hats from the tourist gift shop. "I got some sunscreen and a hat, so I won't burn so bad today. Can we go?" He nodded at Akamai's glow, noticeably fainter than normal. "You look like you need some sun."

Akamai sighed, wondering which of the Hawaiian gods he'd offended to get saddled with the kid from Milwaukee. Oh well, it was only for one day. He could tolerate anything for one day.

* * *

Two hours later, Akamai wasn't so sure.

Warren had an unending stream of questions for Akamai, most of which he had no idea how to begin to answer. What was it like to be a superhero? Pretty cool, mostly. Did he see a lot of action? Outside of his bedroom, not really. Why was that? Probably because no supervillain gonna come to Hawaii to beef when they can come to chill on the beach and soak up some sun.

It seemed like every time Akamai saw a girl smile at him with a twinkle in her eye, Warren stepped into his line of sight to ask another inane question about how did he choose where to patrol or did he have a special hotline for people to call if they needed his help.

At last, Akamai had enough. He stopped trudging along the shore, unmoved by the graceful sparkling waves, the sweeping arc of blue sky, the pristine white and gold sands, the breeze scented with sea salt and coconut lotion. "Kid," he said. "This ain't gonna work out. I think you better move on."

A flashing in his eyes distracted him. Exasperated, he turned back to look out at the ocean and see what was trying to blind him. The flash was coming from one of those overpriced tourist boats. Someone was reflecting sunlight toward him, which would normally do nothing but power him up except now it was irritating him. Then he saw someone standing on the deck waving a red flag back and forth, and realized it was an actual call for help.

"Hey, you see that? Someone needs our help!" Warren almost bounced up and down like an excitable puppy.

"And they're gonna get it, too, soon as I find me a jetski to borrow."

"You don't need a jetski," said Warren. "I can carry you." He seized Akamai's hand. A sudden icy breath washed over Akamai. His world became a swirl of dark and light, like cream diffusing through coffee. All the air rushed out of his lungs into the void beyond, leaving him nothing with which to scream.

Just as quickly, he returned to the warmth of sunlight and a hard, swaying deck had appeared beneath his feet. He realized he was standing beside Warren on the boat.

"Oh thank God," said the gorgeous blonde in the blue and green string bikini. Three other equally hot *wahine* clutched themselves in fear and excitement, all different shades of sun-darkened skin, bottle-bleached hair, and smelling of lotion.

Akamai slipped into his best working-it personality almost unconsciously. "Ladies, what seems to be the *hurrrk*—" A sudden upset stomach made him lean over the rail and puke without any warning. "Ugh."

"Sorry, dude," said Warren. "Sometimes that happens. What's the problem, ladies?"

"Ohmigawd, are you guys actually superheroes?" one of the girls gushed. "Our engine thingie stopped and won't start again. We're, like, totally adrift! You have to help us!"

Akamai wiped his mouth, feeling completely off his game. He started to reply but Warren beat him to it.

"Don't worry," said the chubby ginger. "We're here to help you. Come on, Akamai, let's go look at the engine."

"But I . . ." Akamai leaned in to Warren. "I don't know anything about engines."

"It's cool, bro," Warren said. "I got this." He half-led, half-pulled Akamai to the back of the boat. The *aft*, Akamai remembered. On boats it was called the aft.

"What are you even doing, *haole*?" Akamai watched as Warren undid some wing screws on the casing over the outboard motor.

The sunburnt kid pried it off. "Ha! Just as I suspected. You're missing a fuse wire." He held up a frayed piece of wire or cable.

"Hey, wait a minute." Something wasn't right, but Akamai couldn't figure it out.

"Don't worry, I'm on the case. You keep the sharks away from the boat and I'll go get a new amperwatt connector to fix this bad boy right up." Warren evaporated into thin air.

"Wait," whispered Akamai after him. "I don't think that's a thing."

"O.M.G. Are there sharks?" one of the girls shrieked. "Are we going to die?"

Akamai concentrated his light and made some seawater boil. "Not, uh, not while I'm here. Ladies." They cooed and squealed in approval and Akamai shot more heat rays into the water. "Take that! And *that*! No sharks here, brah. Paddle on."

Warren reappeared on the deck, holding a piece of wire. "Got it, bro. Everything golden here?"

"Uh, yeah. Shoots."

Warren connected the wire to two different places in the engine. "Try starting it now?"

The shortest of the blondes went to the wheel and touched the starter. The engine coughed and then started. "Yay, it works!" she cheered.

"Our heroes!" said one of the others, and she wrapped her arms around Warren and gave him a big kiss on the lips.

The third duplicated her friend's gratitude upon Akamai. She was a damn good kisser. "Girl, you just 'bout broke da mouth."

She lowered her eyelids in a sultry way. "That's not all I'm going to break, you gorgeous superhero."

Akamai glanced over at Warren. The kid was making out with the other blonde like she was starving and he was a buffet. The kid had set all this up, somehow. He'd played Akamai, played the girls just like a pro. "Hey, *haole*."

Warren disengaged himself from the girl's kisses. "Yeh?"

"Okay, you can stay."

ABOUT THE AUTHOR

Ian Thomas Healy dabbles in many different genres. He's a multiple participant and winner of National Novel Writing Month. He created the popular ongoing superhero series, the *Just Cause Universe*, and is also the creator of the *Writing Better Action Through Cinematic Techniques* workshop, which helps writers to improve their action scenes.

When not writing, which is rare, he enjoys watching hockey, reading comic books (and serious books, too), and living in the great state of Colorado, which he shares with his wife, children, house-pets, and approximately five million other people.

Visit *www.ianthealy.com* for more information.

www.ingramcontent.com/pod-product-compliance
Lightning Source LLC
Chambersburg PA
CBHW031542240626
47153CB00002B/349